Mirabai Bekowies was born in Melbourne, Australia.
She now lives in the San Francisco Bay area with her husband and two
children. *March Rains* is her debut novel.

To Samuel and Naomi, for being lights on the other side of the dark woods.

To Paul, for reminding me to stay the course and imagine beyond what I can see.

To all the healthcare workers who answered the call.

Mirabai Bekowies

# MARCH RAINS

AUSTIN MACAULEY PUBLISHERS™

LONDON ∗ CAMBRIDGE ∗ NEW YORK ∗ SHARJAH

A CIP catalogue record for this title is available from the British Library.

ISBN 9781035832323 (Paperback)
ISBN 9781035832330 (ePub e-book)

www.austinmacauley.com

First Published 2024
Austin Macauley Publishers Ltd®
1 Canada Square
Canary Wharf
London
E14 5AA

My deepest gratitude to Michelle, Kumara and Janice, who walked with me, as my readers, in the creation of this story. Your encouragement spoke volumes to me as I ventured, through fiction, to both process and bring to life a glimpse of the defining time in history we have lived through.

# Chapter 1
# Turning

**26 February 2020**

The hospital towers above began to bend, and nearby conversational laughter dulled. In this moment, a firm grasp of time and space had yielded to the pit in her stomach. She could feel her heart pounding in her ears. Her sense of control was quickly slipping away.

It was Jake, a travelling nurse from New Jersey, who had told Grace over lunch in the hospital's courtyard that Solano County had the nation's first case of Coronavirus from community transmission.

For the past weeks, Grace had scanned news outlets for confirmation of what she had been hearing from other hospital staff. *The Coronavirus was likely spreading all over the world.*

Grace had impulsively looked at her phone for the news alerts. She would momentarily lose focus on her tasks at hand to tune into snippets of newscasts streaming on the hospital room televisions. Seeking to catch key words alluding to the virus' progress and any measures that governments had put in place to control it. News on the Coronavirus' emergence in China brought with it gripping images of the sick and the toll it was taking on their healthcare system. She had watched footage of healthcare workers in China wearing full body hazmat suits tending to patients gasping under oxygen masks held over their faces, as they were wheeled from ambulances. Multitudes of people in blue masks in the streets of Wuhan and all throughout China signalled a collective public health concern. The Chinese central government-imposed lockdowns that followed to quarantine the epicentre of the outbreak indicated the gravity of the problem. What was happening in China appeared apocalyptic to Grace, and didn't require much of a stretch to imagine how such an outbreak would play out in the intensive care unit where she worked. She had watched with fearful interest as evacuees from Wuhan were flown out of China and brought to quarantine at Travis Air Force base, in the Bay Area.

The knowledge of the Coronavirus' global advances had woven a layer of uncertainty in their workplace for many weeks. Waiting to exhale, the healthcare workers in the hospital carried out their daily duties, praying and hoping that their newly admitted patient, coughing feverishly in their care, was not the United States' patient zero.

This situation had become more real by the day.

Grace leaned forward, hands encasing her chin, elbows either side of her plate pressed on the cold tabletop in the main courtyard at Harris Memorial hospital to steady herself. The day had come. The Coronavirus was now found to be spreading in a nearby county's community no less. Its impact on the local population would no doubt arrive at the hospital's doorstep in a matter of time, if it hadn't done so already.

"Do you think this Solano County case means there are like hundreds of people already out there infected with the Coronavirus?" Grace asked apprehensively, not truly welcoming Jake's honest reply.

"It's likely," Jake said.

She searched his face for a hint of assurance. "I mean, what's going to happen, do you think?" This question had been on most of her colleagues' lips, of late. Thrown into the mix of uneasy conversations that had bubbled up in hasty exchanges made between tasks during shifts, or walks to the employee parking garage. The uncertainty around an impending answer was an unwelcome feeling. The world was holding its breath. Grace panned news outlets daily for detail in the emerging story. Information felt limited, restricted even. The headlines appeared to be a carefully unravelling what was clearly a catastrophe at play in China. *What is this disease capable of? Is it contained?*

Now, it was clear that the story was closing in and grey clouds that had covered the horizon were drifting closer than ever before, threatening rain. Assurances that this virus was contained, and somehow a foreign problem changing the reality of Asia, had now in this first community acquired case, become solidified as an American problem.

Grace desperately wanted to be still as she processed the impact of what was happening. Her mind darted to home. She saw her two-year-old, Emma, sitting on a braided rug facing away from the window in the family room rocking her dolly in her arms. She was struck by how this image in her mind began to move her into a place of angst. Tears began to well in her eyes, breaking through her usually calm exterior. Not knowing what to do with this wave of emotions, she felt the need to move now. "I need to go clock back in," she blurted, quickly gathering her wallet and phone. Walking swiftly across the courtyard, she left Jake.

Grace's tears spilled uncontrollably down her cheeks, as she thought about her little one. Her perfect treasure in this broken world. Grace knew she loved nothing and no one as fiercely as she did Emma. Now, she wanted nothing more than to be with her. To hold her tight and protect her. A growing sense of helplessness in the present began to spiral within her. She strode quickly across the courtyard, feeling her intended pace a little ahead of her feet's ability to keep up. The scope of this feeling felt familiar, yet in the moments she sat with it, she could not place it. Despite walking terribly fast through the hospital doors, she could not outpace it. Grace usually had a knack for pausing her emotions as needed. It came with years of practice working as a nurse in the intensive care unit. She needed to do this now if she was going to be able to concentrate on her work. She closed her eyes as she stood in the elevator, catching her breath and centring her mind on the next task.

Grace returned to her unit and clocked in, dutifully she had returned to her work mindset. The relief nurse gave her an update on the patient asking for ice chips. Nothing much had happened in the past thirty minutes. Grace washed her hands, watching the hand hygiene timer counting down at a snail's pace to 20 seconds before drying off with a paper towel and heading into the ICU room to reposition her patient. Removing the patient's left side foam wedges and shifting lines for her patient half awake and half asleep in bed with another nurse to lean him to the other side with the wedges reinserted behind his back. The television newsreel hummed overhead. Grace heard 'patient' and turned to see the detail of the report. "The first case of community transmitted Coronavirus is being treated in Solano County, California. Health authorities are concerned that this may be one of many cases now spreading in the United States."

Grace bent down to adjust the side rails on the bed, emptied the catheter and then checked the intravenous line providing hydration to the patient. The patient's respiratory rate was a little high at 29. Oxygen saturation in the low 90s. Grace bumped up the oxygen from two to three litres per minute. Her patient coughed, the tanned secretions that lined his throat coming up as she suctioned the thick phlegm out of his mouth.

COVID testing in the hospital was taking time. Laboratories all over the country had begun to implement testing technology and were working hard to respond to the demand of a growing volume of COVID tests funnelling to them. "I wonder if this patient has COVID?" Grace wondered with a concerned curiosity. *We wouldn't know. All the symptoms they keep listing like cough, temperature and breathing difficulty are so common. Who's to say what we think is the flu, pneumonia or acute hypoxemia isn't Coronavirus?* She shook off that ominous feeling of uncertainty once more by making a move to the glass doors and back to the computer where she could keep an eye on her two patients while reading up on the latest orders placed and catching up on her charting.

Elle sat by Grace. They had worked together for the past three years and bonded over regaling one another with stories of their motherhood peaks and pitfalls—often comparing notes on the best way to deal with the logistics of motherhood. Now, Elle sat quietly at her workstation, panning through the medication administration record and checking for updates from speech therapy's diet recommendation for her new admit. "Are you free tomorrow after work to take the kids to the park?" Grace asked expectantly.

Grace and Elle often took their kids to the park on Wednesday afternoons for an hour or so, so the kids could play around while they chatted in the shade of a large maple tree with branches spanning the breadth of the playground. "Sure, I'll take the kids over after pick-up."

Grace nodded, "Great." She was glad to have a friend who was also a mother that she could have time to regularly confide in. She realised now that the stress she was feeling as a parent hearing this news of this spreading virus, was even more disquieting and she looked forward to the time she and Elle would have to talk about it.

The early afternoon pushed on. Soon it would be time to go home. Time to see Emma. Grace rounded on her patients, turning them, providing a call to one's husband to see if they could bring in the patient's hearing aids and dentures. Grace peered at the TV screens momentarily to try to catch any further updates on the Coronavirus news. At 3 PM, Sophie, the PM Shift nurse, found Grace to receive the shift-to-shift hand-off communication. Grace pulled out her day's patient note, a worn piece of paper with scribble notating—bowel movements, diet levels, medications, completed tests, scans, vitals and the pending tasks for the PM shift. The hand-off was efficient, and Grace was glad to be able to go grab her items from her locker by 3:20 PM today.

She stopped at the restroom on her way out and stood in front of the basin mirror. Looking down at her hands. She was struck by how she didn't recognise them so well these days. They had somehow aged and didn't really look to be her own. Her hands were dry and peeling. Working hands. Those that held emesis basins, assisted weak and frail bodies up out of bed, crushed medications in applesauce, connected oxygen tubing, and steadily inserted intravenous lines countless times. She washed and dried them peering in the mirror, eyes reddened from a long shift in the intensive care unit where she had worked full-time for the past four years. Pouring her efforts and attention to each patient placed in her care. Grace sighed, noticing the lines between her brows had deepened in recent months with the concentration and concern she carried through her days, attending to patients, and likely the additional responsibilities she had raising a toddler. Sleepless nights in the past two years attending to her baby followed by long days in the hospital must have been what had driven these inroads on her forehead, she thought. *Now this.*

"Time to go home," Grace said, walking down the long hall to the elevator, glancing with a tired smile at the transporter passing by with an empty gurney. She carried her half full coffee cup diluted by melted ice and her lunch pail now lighter than the day's beginning slung over her shoulder as she quickened pace through the closing elevator doors. Four other nurses stood facing forward, chatting about a potluck favourite and side-stepping to allow her in, checking their phones or staring intently at the stainless-steel doors, willing extrication from their day's duties.

The workers poured out of the elevator into Harris Memorial Hospital's atrium. Grace hung back as they crowded the breezeway. She checked her phone. A text from Lottie, her sister, wishing her a good day, received at 9:32 AM. Grace paused to reply but decided to wait. She didn't know if she had had a good day. She knew it was good to be on the other end of it. Through the breezeway, she was released back into the regular world filled with people and plans far removed from the hospital. The hospital filled with the raw realities of human life, suffering and death, bore stark contrast with the outside. The world outside its doors, bustled in a manner largely oblivious to the pains of the human experience contained within its walls. The weight of suffering was witnessed collectively by the patients, families, and healthcare workers who resided long hours and days in the corridors and rooms, day in and out.

Grace was often struck with how she could pass through both worlds as one person. She was undeniably changed from before becoming a nurse, but somehow moved between her two worlds with an ease that comes with practiced intent to not let one place affect the other.

Her sister had gone on to work as a project manager for the tech start-up, Delight, in Palo Alto after college. Grace had no idea really what Delight was. She vaguely recalled Lottie talking about it being a travel search engine company, but she couldn't be sure. All Grace knew was Lottie's life seemed to be filled with meetings, project deadlines and team building retreats in the Santa Cruz mountains or the Napa Valley.

Grace sometimes pictured herself dressed in slacks and a silk top with some accent jewellery, sitting in boardroom meetings, managing tasks and setting deadlines, as she suctioned, wiped and positioned her patients. It was hard work in the intensive care unit. The kind of work that required her to engage physically and mentally at all times. She had romanticised the idea of what a desk job would be like, but knew she was meant for her work.

Grace didn't blame her sister, but always noticed how Lottie would become quiet over the phone when Grace mentioned the tasks of her day. There wasn't much to say about the suffering of patients. It just was and it made those who lived separate from it uncomfortable to take the emotional plunge it would require to draw true sympathy much less understand its weight. Few could relate. Grace knew this and chose not to speak too much or too often about what she saw, had to do or felt in the day to day of her job.

The afternoon light illuminated the twisted oak branches, bare from winter's bite. Grace noticed the wind on her face, brisk and refreshing. Air didn't move in the hospital—the atmosphere and temperatures controlled all around. No windows to open. Gurgly suctioning, air being pushed into lungs dependent on machines to breathe or the swish of an abruptly closed curtain was all the air that moved. The breezes kicked up in the evenings over the bay. Dense fog rolling back in over the headlands. Dark nights ensued thereafter, near 5 PM, at this time of year. She would be arriving home by dark with a stop at the grocery store to pick up some bread, milk and cat food.

Grace paused to look up at the evening sky. Clouds gathered with plumes of faint pink and gold painted by the last of the sun's brushstrokes for the day. Kitchen lights were glowing from the street, with dinner cooking in the neighbourhood kitchens, the faint smell of a lit fireplace. She would check the mailbox and sort through mail holding it like a fan between her strained fingers, picking out the ads she could dispose of immediately from the bills that she would stack and schedule herself to go through in a few days' time. Life was a series of small check-lists. To Do's necessary to keep their family's life afloat. It had always come down to her to ensure the details of life were attended to. Grace enjoyed the sensation of completing task after task but begrudged the seemingly relentless train of conundrums that adulthood delivered. There was always something or someone to draw her focus and require her assistance.

Often, she felt alone in her marriage, steering the boat at the whim of its passengers. In truth, she had always felt alone with the sense of self-reliance she carried. Not willing to truly depend on another for happiness, for truth, for care. She looked up to the sky. Its breadth reminded her of how small her life was compared to the universe. She took a deep breath to inhale and exhale her memories. Like a trail of wind she exhaled memories of when she was young and unencumbered with the responsibilities of a family, a career, an obligation to uphold expectations of others. Her memories of freedom to do as she pleased were as fleeting as breath but she liked to conjure them like old friends that sustained her through hard times and even these mundane ones.

Every day after her shift, Grace would peel off her scrubs and toss them in the laundry basket she put by the door. She would hear Emma talking to Justin, her husband, in the kitchen area while her immediate attention and affections would be demanded by their cat, Jerome, at the door. Peskily meowing and coiling around her legs, an unrelenting encircling of her ankles as she attempted to climb the stairs without tripping. He just wanted something to eat. He must have known she had picked up his favourite dinner tins at the market. Not the food or water in his bowls. He wanted something prepared and served on the counter and maybe a scratch under his belly. He waited all day for Grace's return. She was his favourite person and had no reservations in communicating his utmost affections for Grace. After all, he feared Emma with her tromping boots disturbing his slumber on the chase lounge and her experimental curiosity involving a focused study on the stretching capacity of his tail. It was clear Jerome didn't care for Justin. He would hide and dart away from Justin's well-intentioned advances.

Jerome pursued Grace intently, meowing to beckon her to pause in her daily routine. Yet at the end of her long shift, Grace was set on making it to the shower to wash away the grime of the day. Promising Jerome that she would be back to get him his dinner, she pulled shut the curtains. The water heated slowly. Tepid for a time as she brushed her teeth awaiting the steam to fill the space. Her shower was the transition from her public to personal self. She did not feel clean enough to engage with her home life comfortably until the ritual of washing the day away had taken place.

She would sneak into the house to capture these quiet moments without Emma knowing she had arrived, which would inevitably result in the toddler clamouring down the hall and begging to 'stay with you Mummy!' This desperation strained Grace's nerves at the end of her long days caring for sick people and conflicted with her objective to have an uninterrupted and tranquil evening shower before launching into hands-on Mummy mode. For this reason, she snuck stealthily through the front door and up the stairway each time, even if it was with a little guilt.

The steam fogged the mirrors and hot water ran down her head, face and back shedding the fluorescent lights, the secretions, the blood, the vomit she had cleaned off her patient's hair, the imprint of another's weak and cold hand holding hers in his final hours.

Grace closed her eyes, unable to escape the image of one of her patient's family gathered around, praying and crying as they arrived in time to say their goodbyes to their mother, grandmother and wife of 62 years. She had left the door partially closed in case they called for her and retreated back to the nursing station to document with a watchful eye and sinking feeling. This would likely be the end of this person's life.

Jake was always saying, "we don't come into this life easy and we sure don't leave easy either." She pondered this often. The bookend of a life's story would often play out in front of her and her colleagues' eyes. Lives filled with relationships and people who loved them, were indifferent or at odds with them, aspirations and accomplishments, love lost, regrets, a few bad habits and poor choices. The summary appeared so stark, as a few would gather around or none at all present to witness their person's final breaths.

Grace turned off the water. She stepped out of the shower, a shiver coursing its way down to her toes as the cold night air that somehow permeated the house through the original thin glass windows had hit her. She wrapped herself into a nearby towel and coiled another into a turban balanced on her head to dry her long brown hair.

"When is that earthquake insurance due?" she thought out loud. Last week, a 3.8 jolt had taken her by surprise while she was in the kitchen washing dishes. A plate had slipped from the counter cracking into shards upon hitting her tile floor. Grace had hurried in panic to pick up the sharp pieces and, in an attempt to swiftly remove the dangers from Emma's path, had sustained a cut to her hand. She had let out a muffled scream, blocking the impact of her response with her good hand over her mouth so as not to scare Emma. Grace worked tirelessly to hide or downplay the scary or shocking things in life in front of her child, often substituting her anger or angst disingenuously with a sunny disposition and gentle redirecting words. It was her natural reaction to protect Emma.

Earthquake country delivered sometimes less than subtle reminders that humans were not authors of their fate, nor rulers of the natural world. She chuckled as she thought about this and the fact that for this reason, she was compelled to spend thousands a year on insuring her home and possessions.

"Are you coming down Grace?" Justin called up the stairs into the darkness of empty rooms, towards the dull light filling their bedroom.

Grace could hear the masked desperation in his tone with Emma in the background giddily yelling, "Giddy-up horsey. Go faster, Daddy!" She was always in full force at this time of day. The final sparks of energy on display as she would want to play intensely at an imaginary game requiring complete attention and participation on the part of any parent she could grasp in the moment.

"Yep, down in a minute." Grace relished in the quiet of the upstairs and the fact she was not plodding around the living room with an enthusiastic toddler riding her back and calling her Betsy, this very moment. Grace's mother sat at the edge of her bed with the day's brightness beckoning through the white linen curtains lining the large windows of Grace's bedroom. "Grace, if you won't let me brush your hair, we'll be late for church." Grace had loathed having her hair brushed. She preferred her wispy brown hair to fall freely around her face with no restricting ribbons or bows. Tangles did not concern her. Her mother had waited her out for some five excruciating minutes, while Grace facing away with a scowl and arms crossed. She contemplated the merits of her choice to be so obstinate, and how long she would in fact be able to see her position on the matter through.

At the age of five, Grace had in her a strong will, although, quietly it brewed as violet storm clouds gathering over parched earth. And when the rains released they fell as a cannonade, soaking all in its path. "I don't care!" She yelled and launched a nearby doll to the floor in protest. Screaming loudly Grace threw herself tearfully onto the bed, thoroughly catastrophising her situation. Her mother did not flinch. She had seen this theatre so often in recent weeks, over a seatbelt, a turtleneck sweater, or a head of broccoli.

"Well Grace, I will have to leave you with your father. He is on the porch, drinking brandy with the paper and most likely won't notice you're here. But, I will not miss another church morning." Grace knew this to be her mother's way of reminding Grace that her security was in fact truly only in her mother's care. With a sigh, Grace refrained from further fight.

Declaring truce, she reluctantly turned to her mother, crawled closer to the edge of the bed, "Sorry Mumma" and obliged to her mother's request. Grace was sure to moan and grumble with every knotted brushstroke and yanked gathering of her hair into two perfectly balanced pigtails.

"There, my dear. You are all ready for church. Let's hurry now."

Grace now stood in her closet, making out the shape of her shelves and hanging garments with the dim light streaming from the bathroom. She liked the quiet, the darkness, the reprieve she found in her closet. The air was cool and she felt at a safe distance from the ruckus downstairs. Here she could collect her thoughts about her day.

She thought about the early days, when Emma was first born. Grace would often retreat in the closet, leaving Emma strapped into her bouncer seat. Without any knowledge of what else to do, Grace would leave the infant for a time when she was screaming at the top of her lungs for hours starting at five o'clock every evening. As a young mother, with no real guidance or help, she did not know what to do with her colicky infant. Her heart would race in panic as she watched her baby cry inconsolably, turning bright red and crying so hard that breath and sound halted for a time before its ferocious return. No matter what Grace did to try to aid in Emma's resolve, she could not find a moment of peace or sustain the brief glimpses of peace they would encounter from time to time. Emma was unable to regulate her storms, and as her mother, Grace felt the pain of inadequacy in her inability to help.

It would not be for the lack of trying, as Grace would rock and sway and reposition Emma. She'd try to feed her extra milk pumped during the morning nap or the 2 AM feed. Yet Emma resisted. In truth, Grace had hated that daily assault on her senses and the generally stark contrast to her *pre-Emma* life that had been ushered in under the guise of what she expected to be blissful, life-affirming motherhood.

Justin would be no help and often nowhere to be found until around dinner time, Grace recalled. She was glad that he would prepare dinner, albeit silently moving through the kitchen, staying far away from the nursery. At the time, in sleep-deprived fury she would shout at him to hurry up and bring her some water or try to hold Emma, then retreat to the closet and cry into her hands that smelled of sour milk and spit up, regretting her temper.

It was now time to go downstairs. Grace knew her absence was felt and her time hiding in the upstairs would become noticeable a minute longer.

It brought her comfort to know that Justin had cooked dinner. The smell of Italian flavours and Bossa Nova music in the kitchen drew with a sense of a break from the mundane, as she made her way down to greet her family. "Mummy!" cried Emma, as she leaped off Justin's back and ran towards Grace.

"Oh my girl. My sweetheart. I've missed you!"

Emma pressed her face against Grace's knees and lifted her arms to be gathered up into a warm hug.

"How was your day, Miss Emma?" she whispered into her hair before inhaling an imprint of her smell. This was home. Emma didn't reply, in customary toddler fashion. Instead offered, "I got a boo-boo" pointing to a red spot on her finger. With the theatrical effects of grave concern, Grace asked, "Can I kiss it all better?"

"Yes Mummy, all better."

"I think Jerome scratched her when we got home from day care this afternoon," Justin offered. Grace nodded while maintaining full focus on Emma and took the traditional steps one must take in ameliorating a boo-boo.

"I opened the Cab. Would you like some?" said Justin, grabbing two stemless wine glasses from the cupboard and pouring the jewel-toned Cabernet in.

"How was your day, Mummy?" Justin asked in an easy manner, with a pleased smile on his face.

"Oh you know, it was a long shift."

"You look like something may have happened, are you okay?" He whispered away from Emma who was brushing her toy puppy's hair, lost in thought.

"Yeah, you know, just another day in the hospital," Grace said, with an uneasy pause, picturing that family bent down with the weight of pre-emptive grief. Gripping to the very last moments they had in the presence of a central figure in their world.

"Are you okay?" Justin was used to seeing Grace drift into a distant place from time to time when he would ask about her day at work.

Grace returned to the moment and stated unconvincingly, "Yes, I'm fine. I mean I will be fine. It's just been a long shift."

They sat at the table and dug into some gnocchi. Cream sauce made from scratch with her favourite chewy shiitake mushrooms. Emma sat in her highchair, pulling bread pieces apart with the crumbs scattering to the floor. "This is nice," Grace thought, looking into the faces of her husband and daughter. Her childhood evenings were rarely spent at the dinner table.

Grace grew up in Concord, California. A city below Mt Diablo. The city, spread out with long broad straight roads from its central square. Its reach, demarcated by grasslands in the foothills of the mountain. Working class families inhabited many of the ranch style houses that dotted the wide roads. Grace's was one of those houses lined up neatly along broad roads. In the evenings, she would eat her microwave TV dinners watching cartoons with Lottie while her mother sat on the porch smoking and her father was still away at work.

Her father, John, a mechanic and her mother had met in high school, married soon after, and began their lives down the road from their parents. Barbara, Grace's mother, had been the valedictorian of her high school. But when she married at 19 and was pregnant with Grace, she let go of her scholarship at UC Davis where she had begun majoring in Chemistry and moved back to Concord to set up a home life. John had grown up tinkering with tools in his grandfather's car shop under the premise of the generational obligation to carry on the family business someday upon his shoulders.

Grace often thought about how her mother must have felt giving up her academic pursuit and ultimately professional future for her. She saw it as a mistake in a course that her mother should have taken. Yet knew that her mum's sacrifice was perhaps the greatest gift she could have received. In her own life, Grace had been determined to overcome the diversions that arose in her early adulthood. She would purposefully avoid getting serious in relationships with men she knew wanted to take care of her for fear that she would let her guard down midway through her mission to become a nurse. It had made her nervous to place all bets on herself. However, she had known she could not settle to the pace of a life created for her. She had been pushing and running from the broken places in her past for a long time and couldn't and wouldn't stop until she achieved the stability she yearned for, on her own terms.

Grace cleared the plates. She wiped Emma's cheeks thoroughly, despite her protests, with a wet wipe and headed to lean over the large stainless-steel sink. The porch light cast a copper lining on the bent rose bushes in the foreground and outlined the overburdened lemon tree at the fence line. Grace peered past her reflection into the night, thinking about how simple and perfect the cycle of day and night, wake and sleep, sun and moon really was. And how in the silence of the night, she could dwell in her thoughts so much easier.

"Mummy!" Emma yelled up from the hem of Grace's pyjamas, seeking her mother's eyes before she told her, "Time for bath, Mummy." Grace held Emma's delicate fingers in hers and followed her lead down the dark hall away from the kitchen and up the stairway slightly bracing with every predictable creak of the steps underfoot. Her home was small, but cosy. Most of the walls having benefited from a fresh coat of paint within the past three years made the artwork pop. As she walked along the upstairs dark hallway towards Emma's bathroom, Grace made out the images she loved. Her mother's watercolour floral paintings, a charcoal sketch of the Berlin Dome from the Summer she backpacked through Europe on a shoestring. Grace had been careful to preserve these pieces of art that somehow encapsulated the important pieces of her own life. She liked to walk with Emma through the dark. She thought of it as a way to make Emma brave when faced with the uncertainty of shadows in the absence of light.

Emma flung open the bathroom door and soon the bright lights were on and the tepid bath water was running. Emma clambered to the tub as she shed her clothing with little assistance. "Bubbles, Mum!" She suggested intently. Grace knelt over the cold rim of the tub, tracing her fingers through frothy bubbles that had begun to gather in the warming water. Justin could be heard walking the upstairs hall behind the good water pressure that poured out of old pipes.

"Did you hear about that first US patient case on the news?" He inquired from the doorway.

"Yes, I did," Grace said, thinking about the news headlines in the patient's room with lowered volume. Grace pushed away the looming thoughts she had had earlier in the day. "Yeah, I think it's good they quarantined all those people at the Travis base. But, I wonder if some of it is leaking out into the community."

Justin noted, "It's hard to know what's really going on. We keep hearing everything is okay, it's contained but this sort of news begs to differ."

Grace looked over at Justin, with an attitude of denial. "I'm not worried about it. We dealt with Ebola and will do it with this." As the words left her lips, a sinking feeling consumed her. She knew she was speaking with a confidence she didn't fully possess but was choosing to assume to protect her mind.

"I don't think we should worry about anything."

Grace wanted to believe her words, for the sake of Emma, for their family, and for the illusion of security. In many ways at this point in her thirties, Grace felt entitled to a sense of stability, comfort and security. After all, she thought she had earned this stable and comfortable life.

Justin paused, contemplated and shrugged. "Yeah, I think you're right, I mean if this is really a problem we should worry about, I'm sure they will let us know."

Grace held Emma in their rocking chair beneath the window. She'd done this since Emma was an infant. Wrapped firmly in a blanket cocoon, Grace would hum the tune of *Amazing Grace* softly, as her mother had done in her nursery, to soothe Emma to sleep. The bright moon cast light through the shuttered window forming stripes on the hardwood floor. Grace shifted her slippers back and forth looking at how the light and shadows bent around her form. Grace kept a night light for Emma. A jolly looking giraffe sitting on his haunches kept aglow to comfort and guide anyone wandering around in the depths of night. She looked around the room at the angular shadowy figures of furniture in the room.

Emma's crib needed to be packed up soon and stored in the garage. Emma's small desk where she often sat and drew pictures of colourful flowers with oversized petals, sat cluttered and in disarray. *What's the point of even trying to reorganise that?* Grace thought callously. Grace knew that parenthood was largely about cleaning up after a party you weren't invited to and one that would take place over and over again even if you did clean up.

Above the chest of drawers sat a grey vase lamp that had belonged to her mother. Grace smiled, thinking of how her mother would sit under the glow of that lamp night after night in the sitting room and read the *Chronicles of Narnia* to her and Lottie. They would sit on the rug below looking up into their mother's face as she assumed the characters voices and undulating dramas of each adventure.

Grace also remembered when that light turned off, traipsing to her bedroom, a kiss on the forehead. The door left ajar. As darkness filled her room, Grace would listen through seemingly hollow walls to her parents arguing about money and the spending habits her father had down at the bar. The need to buy new clothes for Grace and her sister and the shame felt when Grace's mother had to ask for handouts from her parents that they could never repay. Some nights, doors would slam and off her dad would go trudging down the gravel path, out the gate to walk into town because he knew he would be too drunk to drive home. Her mother's quiet crying and pacing would be heard until she turned into bed, closing her door quietly, and fading into the austere silence of the night.

Wednesday came. The late afternoon was warm with a light breeze that occasionally swept through the park, rustling leaves on the big maple tree. Grace loved to look up into the branches as she spread out on a picnic blanket, leaning back on her elbows below. Early spring flooded the edges of the park with coloured flowers. Grace and Elle sat on a little slope overlooking the playground as Elle's kids, now school age, darted around in and out, over and under the play structure carrying out make believe games. Emma sat by Grace, leaning her back up against Grace's side, as she played with some toy animals that Grace always carried around in her diaper bag. Grace loved how Emma always seemed to enjoy sitting by her. She followed her around the house, asking to partner in all the household tasks. She was Grace's little helper.

"So how are things with you and Justin?" Elle asked casually but clearly as a follow up to their last conversation.

"I mean things are pretty good considering we are in a seemingly global pandemic. It's been a bit stressful with all that's going on, I guess." Grace knew Elle was pressing further to ask about their marriage but left it there.

Grace changed the subject, "I can't believe we are so short-staffed right now; they keep asking me to stay for a double shift. I just don't think I can do it, even if the money is good. It's just so depressing in the hospital, don't you think?"

"Yeah, I mean, I'm just overwhelmed by all these COVID changes. It's hard to know what's what from one day to the next," Elle replied. "I'm really hopeful that this whole thing blows over soon."

Elle looked over to Grace wondering what she was thinking. Wondering if she and Justin had resolved the argument, they had had the last time they spoke. The argument they had always had. She knew Justin wanted Grace to stop working, stay home, and take care of Emma. But Grace, practically outraged by the notion that she would give up her career, had fought his pressure. Grace thought Justin to be unrealistic, given he was an elementary school teacher, and she thought there would be no way they could live in the Bay Area on a teacher's salary alone.

Grace also loved her job. She had known being a nurse was clearly going to be one of her main life purposes from the moment she had stepped into the hospital, as a student. Elle decided to ask more directly, "Have you and Justin settled your argument about staying home yet?"

Grace gave a wry smile. "Oh, you know us, he just keeps pressing the issue which makes me want to push back more. I mean this is 2020, I have a career and a family. Am I expected to just give up one half of my life to be some sort of barefoot and pregnant shell of a woman cleaning and cooking in the house? Once you leave nursing, it's not like you can just rock up 10 years later and dive back in. I'd lose my skills." Grace felt her pent-up anger grow but chose to push it down. "He's just so traditional about things. Like just because he grew up with a mum that stayed home, he thinks it's the only proper thing to do now we have a kid."

"Is that what you see being a stay-at-home Mum as?" Asked Elle curiously.

"I mean no, not completely, but I think the more he guilts me about not being completely dedicated to my family, the more I imagine he'd only be happy if I was some sort of one-dimensional figure in our family, a housewife. My mum was just that also, a housewife. I saw what that did to her." Grace paused, remembering her mum leaning over the stove top stirring steaming pots or scrubbing floors. In their day-to-day life, Grace couldn't recall a day that went by where her mother wasn't cleaning, cooking or attending to the family. Her image of her mother was in their home always and seldom leaving the house. That is, other than Sundays when she would dress up in heels and pearls and exit the house with or without her family to attend church.

Her mother had loved to paint before they were born. She had so many complete and incomplete canvases filled with flowers and seascapes stored up in the attic. Left to gather dust when there were more pressing matters to attend to with her growing family. Grace's feelings about motherhood had been shaped by what she saw in her mother, and there was so much about her life that Grace did not want for herself. "I'd rather like to stay home all day with my kids," Elle offered. "Definitely now that this Coronavirus thing is hitting, I'd stay at home in a heartbeat."

Grace agreed that working in healthcare in the hospital was especially challenging and draining these days. It made life at home somewhat more appealing.

Elle yelled across the playground at her son Casper who had acquired a stick from a fallen branch and was wielding it around on the play equipment. "Casper! Put that stick down!" Casper responded after the third request, as Elle scowled with exasperation. "My children don't listen to me."

"So how are you and Joe doing?" Grace asked, serving back the same question that undoubtedly was tricky to answer for any married person, as it so often inspired contemplation of which part of one's life one wanted to share.

"Joe and I are doing great," Elle beamed. "We got a sitter last week and he took me out for a big seafood lunch in Sausalito. We just sat by the marina there with beers afterwards and watched the most amazing pink and gold sunset sky stretch over the bay. It was so nice just to be together, alone."

They both chuckled at the rarity and desirability of alone time. Grace knew that feeling of disconnection after kids. It had been shocking to her when Emma arrived as to how their life that was filled with romantic getaways and uninterrupted talks turned into a home bound existence filled with silent handoffs and exchanges of duties to care for Emma and maintain their routines. The routines made inroads into their lives so significantly. Such that their spontaneity dimmed and they no longer considered a break from routine with disregard for the responsibilities that bound them.

"That sounds amazing, Elle. I'm so glad you got the chance to reconnect. Justin and I need some alone time, but I'd feel guilty about leaving Emma, especially while she's so little." Grace thought about how her and her husband's relationship had become a shadowy backdrop to the bright and colourful life they were creating for Emma. She missed paying enough attention to him. Her understanding of who she was married to felt like it needed an update. Her references to what he liked and what he thought about things felt like they had been placed on pause once Emma came along.

What his current interests, thoughts and preferences were at present admittedly blurry in Grace's mind. She knew she hadn't had enough time or energy to pay attention to him in the ways she did when it was just them. Grace sat quietly watching the children play, reflectively admiring the bright green outlines of the illuminated leaves high above. She felt the warmth of the day's end sun on her back against the cold air. Winter's memory lingered but not for long in Northern California as the sunbeams pushed through the fog and revived blossoms early. She enjoyed lazy afternoons at the park with Elle. It was a time to put her feet in the grass, feeling the grounding sensation of earth as they would largely unpack the detailed mental load they carried, as mothers, constantly navigating a path forward.

As Grace went about her life, mothering as best she knew how, she often remembered the ways in which her own mother had faded away while at the task. It was hard to pinpoint when things changed, but what she recalled most was her mother's uncanny ability to make herself small in the face of imposing forces. And as forces in their world grew, she recalled her mother's presence in it shrinking. Her mother was able to deny her own comforts and wants in an instance if it was not aligned with what others in her life wanted.

Grace watched, even as a young child, how her mother would bend and contort her very being to accommodate her children and her husband's wishes. Grace would feel uneasy when she would watch her father overpower her mother, from the smallest thing like choosing what television programme to watch that night to telling her she didn't understand something. Grace saw her mother as meek and dependent, unable to ever stand up for herself. She lived with a passivity to her circumstances that then revealed growing melancholic detachment to her life and those in it as time went on.

Grace's mother would save change from the grocery store in a shoe box hidden on the top shelf of her pantry. Grace knew where it was hidden because she would tell Grace that it was their 'rainy day fund' as she would reach from the height of her tippy toes to dislodge the plain brown box with a burgundy emblem of a lion on its side. In it, she kept a postcard from Santa Monica Pier in Southern California that she had collected on a trip there as a child. The vintage style drawing of the Ferris wheel and rollercoaster perched out on a long pier jutting out over the ocean on a clear sunny day looked so splendid and inviting. It's like a day at a carnival and the beach all at once she had described.

Grace's mother would tell her girls that maybe one day they would have enough saved to take a trip. "Just the girls," she would add with a glimmer in her eyes. Those days were bright when Grace's mother would imagine out loud what their girls' trip to the Santa Monica Pier would be like. With her descriptions, she would paint the outrageous fun they would have when riding the Ferris wheel high up over the pier and leaning over the railing at the pier's end with ice-creams in hand at sunset, consuming the grandeur of the broad pastel horizon stretched out before them.

Grace knew then that this notion of their time away together was imbued with the sweetest sensation of a promised escape. This dream became more and more desired with every ounce of her daddy's fury Grace that she continued to witness towards her mother. In truth, they lived in constant anticipation of their daddy's loss of control. This tempest that he conjured, often rising out of seemingly nowhere, would most inevitably storm the temporary quiet of their home life and leave wreckage in its wake. After the shattered glass was picked up or the side table turned back on its four legs, it was wreckage that lay quietly and in secret within Grace, Lottie and their mother's hearts, as they silently moved through their lives accepting the destruction.

That trip never came. As money dwindled, Mumma would often need to dip into her shoebox savings to pay for groceries when her daddy drank the regular funds. He liked to frequent the Spotted Monkey bar a few blocks away in town. There he would spend hours after work leaning over a mahogany bar talking to the regulars, jeering at the local sports broadcast, and throwing back enough whiskey to tilt his vision. Grace believed so very much in that dream her mother had of taking her and Lottie to Santa Monica that as an adult it was almost a memory of something that did take place. Grace preferred to remember those things about her mother and her childhood. The brightness that was in her mother's eyes, as she would laugh at the thought of the adventures they would have, filled Grace, even though it had never amounted to anything.

These memories contrasted so greatly with what she watched take place over months and years when her mother's spirit faded. It was like a candle, deprived of oxygen, becoming snuffed out slowly. Grace could only remember how she stood by, unable to stop it.

Grace placed Emma's soundly sleeping body into the crib with a gentle drop as her arms didn't reach all the way. As Grace gazed down at her little girl, sleeping undisturbed. The world outside felt threatening. The ominous Coronavirus headlines had been accumulating—Gathering like rain clouds close to home. She closed those thoughts quickly as those uneasy feelings began to bubble up. Those feelings of being powerless in the presence of a brewing storm.

She countered her disturbed feelings with a redeeming notion—*This is just a fleeting public health complication that the government will eliminate quickly.*

She felt a little selfish to think that United States citizens, although watching with horror, would remain voyeurs peering out of portholes towards the open ocean of foreign calamity as they sailed away from it. Grace caught herself lost in thought, still gazing down at Emma. She would find herself losing track of time frequently, contemplating.

It was Friday night which meant she and Justin would be leaving the next morning on a long-awaited trip. They had arranged for Emma to stay with Auntie Lottie in her apartment in San Jose overnight. They would all head down the peninsula, drop Emma off, and keep going to stay in a bed and breakfast nestled in a Carmel-by-the-Sea side street. This was their first time taking a trip without Emma since she was born. Grace had cautiously agreed to go when Justin asked, grabbing her waist in the kitchen and whispering his plan for them to get away down the coast. She had a glimpse of her old self with excitement to get away with her husband. But just as soon as this set in, she began to feel uneasy at the thought of time away from Emma.

Justin felt taking a trip together was long overdue. There had been holes in their relationship—emerging in subtle constellations, not numerous or significant enough to weaken the fabric. Justin had sensed Grace's preoccupation with Emma shift their relationship over time. He quietly stood by, choosing to see the benefit of Grace's full investment in their child. But as he examined the progression of his standing over the months that turned to years, he had realised he had never fully regained his previous foothold in the hierarchy of Grace's attention and affections. Fatherhood had been a shock to him when Emma was born, although his heart swelled with love for this little child who had burst into their lives, he somehow felt just a little less relevant to Grace. He felt he stood on the outskirts of their bond, as though he was peering through a window into their warm and cosy home.

He admitted to himself in the between spaces, and quietly so, that he missed the old Grace. The Grace that had placed him at the centre of her world. It felt duplicitous to still be embracing the new purpose formed for them, as parents together, yet he had little time to stew at length on any misgivings he held, as life was on the move. It was beautiful, ever changing, and challenging him constantly.

Justin had dinner reservations at the Beach House restaurant, a swanky eatery that overlooked Lover's Point, and plans to take Grace to Cannery Row and walk along the beach. He was glad now that he had insisted it just be the two of them alone when Grace mentioned that Emma loved the beach and it might be fun to bring her along. Justin knew it was complicated for Grace to leave Emma behind. So he left the subject alone, and with unsaid intent pressed on with the plan.

They loaded the car with two small bags, far less than their typical packing routine. Usually an entourage of stuffed animals, and bags of extra snacks, diapers, and spare clothes crowded the back seat and trunk.

Emma sat in her seat kicking her legs up and down, excited to be going on the adventure, partial as it were. "Okay, have we got everything?" Justin asked as he turned his head to smile at Emma as he backed up through their driveway. The sky was a piercing blue today, with billowing cloud formations that moved momentarily to gain rims of gold in the sunlight. They drove down the narrow back streets of Berkeley, pausing at stop signs as they headed through the eclectic neighbourhood of colourful houses, towards the highway. They were met with six lanes of traffic, congestion all funnelling towards the maze that branched out from the foot of the Bay Bridge.

The Golden Gate Bridge spread between two portions of land in the distance. Its rust red looked dulled by the haze of the marine layer. The speckling of houses rising from the town of Sausalito to the right, and the gradient of San Francisco buildings and landmarks emerging from the foliage of the Presidio to the left. A bed of water with scattered sailboats rocking and gliding in the foreground. They drove quietly, Grace's nerves about her impending farewell to Emma gripped her stomach making it churn a little as they crossed the Bay Bridge. She gazed up at the taught cables and out through the window as they passed through the Treasure Island tunnel for an up-close view of the shiny and interesting architecture that made up the San Francisco skyline that they more often only enjoyed with the abstraction of distance from across the bay.

Justin knew better than to mention anything about the trip at this point, so not to tip the scales that were in his favour to proceed. The intercom boomed with Lottie's voice when they arrived at her apartment complex, "Hi! Emma you're here! Come on up!" Lottie's cheerful voice soothed Grace's frayed nerves a little.

Grace carried Emma who was now sensing impending separation, noting only her bags were being carried up the stairs. Lottie welcomed them at the door. "Emma! I am so excited to have you visit." Lottie proceeded to give a tour of her small apartment now staged with little items of interest for Emma. Playdough containers stacked on the coffee table, some puzzles and some board books sat on the sofa. "I made a special little bed for you!" Lottie said, opening the second bedroom door. She had placed a small teddy bear and a bright pink fleece blanket over the guest bed.

"Oh look Em, you have a special bed," exclaimed Justin with a tone drenched in positivity.

Emma buried her head further in Grace's shoulder. "Mummy stay," she replied sharply. The unease of this transition struck all three grown-ups in the room until Lottie motioned to offer Emma the opportunity to play with the playdough. Justin was relieved to see Emma leap from her mother's arms and independently walk back to the living room.

They all sat around the coffee table and chatted about the drive over, the view of San Francisco, and Lottie's latest projects at work for a time while Emma gained more comfortable footing in the new environment, cutting and pressing lime green playdough. She mixed it with blue and dropped little playdough crumbs all over the cream carpet. Grace and Justin didn't notice, but Lottie, masking her uneasiness with a bright engaging smile, began to pick up the small bits, pulling them from the carpet before they could be stepped on and pressed in further.

Lottie had lived alone since she was 23. She had gone on to work in the tech industry down in Palo Alto straight out of college. Her life was filled with meetings, project deadlines, and work retreats. No pets, some potted plants, succulents mainly, inhabited her apartment with her. She was used to an unencumbered lifestyle. She made good money, travelled when and where she wanted, had some good friends that she spent time often brunching with on the weekends. Lottie was quite content with her life. She saw little reason to change and enjoyed short stints with her niece, which helped fulfil that maternal side of her that loved to play and laugh with children without spilling over the brim.

Since having Emma, Grace marvelled at the simplicity of Lottie's life. She even wished at times that she could have one night in her shoes. To come home from a day of work and pick up some takeout at the nearby Indian Restaurant. Kick up her feet after a long day wearing heels and watch some TV while sipping chardonnay. No questions, no responsibilities. Once Grace passed through this recurring fantasy, she would then imagine a certain loneliness Lottie may feel being alone. Grace wondered often why Lottie was still single and had been for a long time to her knowledge. She had a charming personality and was quite attractive, accomplished in her project managerial career throughout her twenties.

Lottie had had a steady boyfriend in college, Sid. That seemed to have been the last stop on Lottie's romantic train. Grace remembered the explosive fights they would have and juxtaposing passionate make-ups that Lottie would report. Lottie wanted a family when they were growing up. She'd always talk about the names she wanted to give her kids and clearly had a way with children. *Perhaps this was all on hold for a reason* Grace thought but didn't dwell much further. Simultaneously, Grace smirked ironically when she realised, she was imposing societal expectations for settling down and having kids upon her sister in her mind when she knew in truth, how challenging parenthood and marriage could be.

"Okay then," Justin motioned with a head tilt to the door.

Grace braced herself for one last lingering hug and kiss. "I love you, sweet girl. Mummy will be back very soon, I promise," she whispered into her daughter's wispy hair, as Emma continued to cut and press the playdough, somewhat ignoring her mother's farewell. Grace held back the pang of angst that came over her yet some tears swelled in her eyes as she got up from the floor and headed to the door.

"She'll be well cared for. Don't worry, just have some fun." Lottie said in an unaffected yet assuring tone.

Grace was embarrassed that she was crying now in the parking lot, wiping her eyes and cheeks fiercely with her hands to try to make it stop. "It's just so hard, Justin. I love her so much and don't want anything bad to happen while I'm gone."

"Don't worry," Justin said, "this is good for her. This is good for us."

This angered Grace a little, inspiring more tears. She felt her fear grounding her in her tracks, unable to keep walking to the car to open the door. Justin took her in his arms, hugging her long and hard, steadying her trembling. Grace knew this wave of emotion was perhaps more than what she wanted, but it just was.

"It's okay, my hon," Justin whispered into her hair, as they lingered by the car for some time. "It'll be okay." Justin had a way of speaking into Grace's heart. He steadied her so often as she would rise and fall on the current of her emotions, constantly fuelled by her vivid thoughts.

As the wave of emotions began to subside, Grace was able to breathe more steadily. "I need to call her when we get there and we need to check in on her all weekend."

"Okay, that's fine we will do that," Justin assured.

An air of perspective and shallow optimism began to solidify within her after her fearful exterior had been released through tears. "I suppose you are right. We need to spend some time with just you and me."

*More than you know*, Justin thought.

# Chapter 2
# By the Sea

They drove down the freeway, watching the dense collection of buildings and houses in San Jose give way to pastures and roadside fruit stands. Garlic wafted briefly through the car as they sped through Gilroy, the nation's garlic capital. Grace had settled under her sunglasses looking out the window pensively as they went. Her feelings now resided in a place of resigned calm, the type that comes after a good cry. The weather was overcast, but the ground remained dry. Justin placed his hand on her leg as they drove, to comfort her, remarking occasionally at the gas prices he saw or what a particular song on the radio reminded him of. Rolling Stone's 'Satisfaction' came on as they sped along.

"Remember that night when we went skinny dipping at Kaui?" Justin looked over with a boyish smirk aiming to humour Grace. "I remember we had too many drinks on that beach with the bonfire those locals invited us to, and you had the bright idea that we should connect with the spirit of Hawaii by jumping into the surf in our birthday suits." Justin chuckled amused by the images in his mind. "Remember that moon? It was such a gorgeous full moon." Justin's fervour for life and appreciation for nature was one of the things that Grace loved about him.

"I do remember that…somewhat," Grace admitted. She looked out the window, as a corridor of eucalyptus trees flashed by.

She sat quietly looking still out of the window thinking about that night. "We really were probably moments away from being eaten by a shark, don't you think?" Grace added.

"Probably," Justin said with levity. She remembered the unadulterated sense of adventure that had once fuelled her. For a moment, remembering the trains of rising water rolling under them, as they floated on their backs holding hands, and gazing at the full moon with the rise of mountains and palms back on land. The hush of the waves breaking on the rocky shore behind them, the soothing silence in between. "That was a magical evening wasn't it?" Justin said, looking over at Grace, reaching for her hand. He squeezed it, letting his fingers linger in her palm before drawing away slowly to attend to the wheel.

As they both drove, they acknowledged silently that things were so very different now. Their lives had become more predictable, their paths solidified. They told themselves that things were better.

Grace felt the unsettling tug of memory rest upon her. As fog fills a valley. She had caught a glimpse of her old self while reminiscing and she felt a longing to be that person once again. Not so long ago, she had been only herself, not someone else's. She used to write poetry and journal entries along with sketches that filled leather-bound notebooks. Deep truths laid out plainly on the pages, now stored away. She thought to find her journals packed away in the garage someplace when she returned from the trip. For now, she acknowledged that her sense of creativity lay dormant beneath the curtain she had drawn to herself when she became a mother. Her focus, her efforts, her consuming thoughts revolved around her child and she was powerless to take back the pieces of herself that were in the process dismantled.

"I'm so glad we are doing this," Justin said as he recoiled from the amusement he had created by sharing this memory.

"If you think we are jumping in the Monterey bay naked tonight, you should think again." Grace smirked at the notion.

"You're right, it's too cold for that," Justin smiled.

They had met after college through friends at a party where they hit it off over bocce ball and red wine one night. Grace looked at him now, remembering that spark she had had for him early on and how, if she paid attention enough, and committed her mind enough to the present, she could recover fragments of those feelings. Love had to be more intentional now, as its place in day to day living had in many ways been diluted by her distraction.

Emma had become the centre of her world. She knew that the sense of excitement and adventure that had once been central to their relationship was now overrun by the press of responsibility and routine. Embracing the prosaic day-to-day had not come easy for Justin, she knew. She had acclimated to motherhood naturally and without much thought typically for what she was missing out on. She had watched Justin shrink his big ideas and aspirations down to fit the parental mould. At times, parenthood looked like an ill-fitting piece of clothing that Justin was determined to wear. She was grateful for his intent.

Grace began to make out the towering sand dunes on the outskirts nearing Monterey that formed near the highway's edge. Falling to the sea beyond. Carmel, some miles further, was a quaint escape. The main street, with boutiques, restaurants, eateries and souvenirs storefronts, was built along a long slope leading down to the beach. People walked along the sidewalks peering into beautifully laden storefronts. The beach was popular with people regularly spreading out along its broad white sand to take in the ocean with a picnic. Dolphins were often spotted leaping amidst the waves as well as migrating whale pods that could be seen releasing spray from beneath the water's surface. Grace stepped out of the car immediately once they arrived at their Bed and Breakfast. Her legs were tired from the inactivity during the drive, so she stretched. Breathing in the cold, clear, seaside air deeply. It felt good to have finally arrived.

Justin went to check them in and returned quickly with keys to their room. "Let's go, my love." He carried their bags up the stairway, where they found their small clean room with a view of the garden and a fireplace.

*This was delightful*, Grace thought. "I've made dinner reservations at an authentic Italian restaurant tonight that I think you'll really like," Justin noted. "We have some time this afternoon to walk downtown and perhaps to the beach if you like."

Grace agreed to the idea and in an hour's time they ventured out on foot. Grace loved how Justin took her hand in guiding them along the narrow sidewalks, pausing to marvel at ornately curated storefront windows, as they went. They picked up ice creams to take down to the beach. The distance to the beach wasn't as close as expected with a steep hill they would need to climb upon return. "Well, I guess we will get a good workout to earn our dinner," Justin said, looking back up the hillside towards town.

The cool breeze met them more fully once they arrived at the beach. Justin had carried a blanket which he wrapped around them as they huddled together looking out at the ocean, where sky and water meet. The evening began to grace the horizon, casting a misty veil of peach and lilac beneath the fog bank in the distance. It was moving towards them swiftly. "Grace, I am so happy to be here with you. I know it's been a long time since we spent quality time, just the two of us," Justin said, looking into Grace's eyes. He pushed away the strands of her hair as he leaned in to kiss her.

"Me too," Grace answered.

"I love you, darling," he whispered intently. They had barely any time to hold conversation in their day to day lives. The time to kiss and stare into each other's eyes was a distant memory.

The dinner and the wine were delicious. They sat at a window table admiring the glow of candlelight casting quivering reflections on the glass, and for once in a long time, each other. White linen and small glass vases holding single red roses and baby's breath marked each table with old world charm. He had the Shrimp Scampi, and she had the Salmon on a bed of mash potatoes with glasses of wine. Neither could recall tasting food so good. Their laughter floated across the restaurant as they re-enacted humorous memories.

Grace paused to take in Justin's storytelling. She remembered how much she loved listening to his stories. As the candle wax pooled, more serious conversation emerged. "I'm feeling concerned about what's going on in China and now here Justin," Grace confided. "I had a moment at work the other day where I kind of panicked while I was on my lunch break. All this news about this Coronavirus and now that new case in Solano County has really thrown me." She paused, looking for his eyes.

He met her with a solemn look. "It feels different now, now that we have Emma. It just feels like the world has been going to hell in a handbasket and we've landed a front row seat."

Justin looked at her, concerned. "I'm sorry it's been upsetting. I feel it too. Unfortunately, there's just not much we can do about what's going on. We just have to hope that the government has it under control."

Grace looked over her wine glass dubiously. "That's what Lottie said. She said they'll have it under control." She paused, "I've been hearing that there's going to be a lockdown too. Just…I just don't want anything bad to happen to us. I'd never forgive myself if I caught it at work and brought it home to you."

Justin paused, considering for the first time the increased risk his wife may have working in healthcare in a pandemic. "I know you will do your best there to stay safe."

Grace nodded, feeling that sinking feeling approaching but pushed it away to ask the passing waiter what was on the dessert menu. She wondered how Justin could be so calm. It annoyed her a little. They soon settled into some cannolis. Crunchy and delightful with the vanilla bean gelato. The restaurant began to clear as the evening wore on and Justin paid the check before they headed to Ocean Avenue, the main street. The night was dark. A marine layer had rolled in moistening the air. The faint rumble of the waves breaking at shore could be heard in the distance. Justin took Grace's hand as they walked silently together both admiring the simplicity of walking in the evening's quiet past the glow of storefronts in town. They arrived at their bed and breakfast.

"Thank you for this, Justin," Grace said sincerely, acknowledging he had been right to insist they come away alone. Justin leaned in to kiss her on the eyelids, then her neck, as they stood outside their door. Once he found his keys and fumbled at the lock, they began to unclothe each other and step backwards into the large bed. Their bodies intertwined there and all their cares evaporated into the night.

A soft drizzle came in the morning. Justin woke up early and stepped out to get some coffee at a nearby coffee shop he had spotted before Grace woke. He greeted her in the pale morning light. "Thank you," Grace said, pleased to have a warm coffee to warm her hands. She looked around, half expecting to see Emma or to be called to a task, but all she found was quiet. They spent time lingering in bed a little longer, reading the newspaper and Grace a book she had picked up at the drugstore. Grace's morning routine was to turn on the news, but she suppressed the urge to let the world into their perfect weekend.

"Do you want to go on a hike today?" said Justin. "Point Lobos is not far from here, and I'd love to see those beautiful coastal views it's famous for."

"Sure." Grace loved to hike. Her heart was at peace when her feet were taken to a trail. She loved Northern California for this. The opportunity to feel so very far away and immersed within dramatic landscapes. Point Lobos did not disappoint. They had arrived early and got a good parking spot within the park. Hand in hand they set out on a narrow forest lined trail out towards the beach. The trails linked through the park to Whaler's Cove where brittle whale bones lined the small cabins that whalers had inhabited long ago.

"The park has been dubbed the 'Crown Jewel' of the California parks," Justin said with confidence in the statement, although never having been to Point Lobos before. As they walked, the pristine coves appearing to be teeming with life and brilliant colours proved his statement true. Pallets of different coloured coastal rocks were seen layered and slouching above coves filled with boulders. Sea urchins and large lumpy bright orange starfish could be seen submerged by the tide when Grace peered into a nearby tidepool. Clamped shut muscles and a speckling of barnacles clung to ash-coloured rocks while sea lettuce rocked back and forth under the surf. A sea otter could be seen out far as it floated on its back seemingly oblivious to the rise and fall of calm water below or the dark kelp ropes that encircled him. The cry of gulls dampened by high winds. They flew pressing against the overcast sky.

The Sea Lion portion of the trail jutted out along a cliff with sheer drops and breath-taking views along the coastline. The wind blew back her hair as she faced south, admiring the system of rock formations, jagged and unapologetically breaking the trains of winter's waves rolling to the shore with large crashing spray. It was thrilling to see how land and water collided. Every wave, a new demonstration of nature's power. The draw was how unsettling it was to behold the forces of nature carry out their plans, unhindered by human will or design. They stood for a time, marvelling at the spray, a V-formation of pelicans flew low above them along the coastline. Wings spread, making brushstrokes in the air with ease. They moved in synchrony as they took flight up and down and around the bluffs. It was cold and overcast, but the world felt alive and Grace along with it.

They had packed some bread and cheese with a few apples and decided to rest a little along the trail on a bench. Some hikers passed by at a pace with pleasant smiles, their colourful water bottles dangling from their day packs. The view up and down the coastline was breath-taking. Grace and Justin marvelled at the ocean's majesty as they gazed out at the rugged outcrops to the south that took the brunt force of the waves. Gatekeepers to hidden inlets.

"Let's bring Emma here someday," Grace said.

"Yes, she would love it. We should come back in the summer. She'll think she's flying with those pelicans up here." *This is exactly what we needed.* Grace revelled in the freedom she felt, as they continued along the bluff. Time away from it all to have their senses refreshed, and a reminder that the world was much bigger than their problems, and even their worries. Nature's vibrancy hummed and flowed with an accepting ease. Everything played a fleeting role in the natural perfection all around. After a few hours walking and taking pictures, Grace and Justin headed back to Monterey to grab some clam chowder on the Wharf before they headed home. As they drove and listened to music, they both appeared to breathe a little easier.

"Mummy!" Emma burst through the door into the narrow hallway, as it opened, grabbing at Grace's legs, pressing her face into her knees. "Carry me, Mummy!" she exclaimed enthusiastically.

Grace swept her up, feeling the ache in her legs from the morning's hike, but felt so fulfilled to be now in this moment with her sweet little girl. "I missed you, Daddy," Emma said once ensconced in the angle of her mother's neck as they walked into Lottie's apartment. The clean and precisely placed apartment that had greeted them the day before had transformed overnight to bear the distinct and slightly unhinged mark of a toddler.

"You can definitely tell Emma was here," Justin said, looking around amused by Lottie's slightly unkempt appearance.

"We had a lot of fun." Lottie's tired yet genuinely cheery tone assured Emma. "I've packed her dirty clothes in this plastic bag, the rest is clean in her overnight bag," Lottie said, handing Justin the bags with a doll's foot sticking through the zipper. "How was your trip?" Lottie asked politely.

"It was great." Both Emma and Justin responded, laughing at their choral response immediately.

"Well, you two look rested."

"Thank you so much, Lottie, for helping make the trip happen," said Justin.

"Yes, it was my pleasure. Emma and I had a great time."

They walked back to the car and loaded Emma in. This time, Grace felt a fullness in her heart that she hadn't in a while. *This is what happiness is.* She thought to herself, looking over at Justin as he drove with Emma in the backseat looking out at the window with tired eyes. *Small portions of bliss doled out just when you needed it.*

Evening had set in as they pulled into their driveway. The porch light had been left on, and was a welcome sight, as they unloaded their sleeping toddler and bags from the car and trudged up the stairs to their Tudor home in the Berkeley hills. Justin carried Emma to bed. She was now fast asleep with limbs hanging limp. He left the nightlight on and staggered down to the kitchen to pour a glass of wine. "Want one Gray?" he offered.

"No thanks, I've got work early tomorrow. Will you be able to drop Emma at daycare?"

"Sure," Justin said, thinking about his own morning which would also be early.

Morning came and the smell of eggs and toast burning in the kitchen wafted through the house. Grace, standing in her scrubs leaned over the sink scraping off the burned egg. She had never truly loved cooking. She was good at it but felt it more of a chore. Something she made herself do out of necessity or service to others. Justin sat in the breakfast nook consuming juice, jam on heavily buttered toast, and scrambled eggs intently, with an eye on the clock.

As a 5$^{th}$ grade teacher, he'd need to be at work by 7:40 AM to prepare briefly for the day before opening his door to a loud group of students striding in. Grace's shift started at 7:00 AM She kissed Justin and Emma both on the forehead before she gathered her lunch bag and tumbler filled with a fresh batch of coffee. "I'll pick her up at 4:00 PM," Grace called from the front door, as she headed out.

After brushing teeth and putting on shoes, they followed suit out into the mild February morning. Everything looked a little different to Justin, a little more treasured and a little more interesting. They reached the home daycare down the road. Mrs Corrine would wear scrubs just like Grace, and greet the children with a cheery voice, as she welcomed them through her doors. The smell of apple sauce simmering on the stove mixed with the lingering odour of yesterday's spaghetti O lunch, and the faint yet pungent smell of diapers filled the air. Other parents strode in the gate from the sidewalk holding diaper bags, baby carriers or little sticky hands that clung tight with apprehension. Emma had been attending since she was six months old and strode in with confidence ready for her day of play.

"Thank Mrs Corrine," Justin said as he hugged and waved goodbye to his little girl.

Grace clocked in and put her belongings in her locker. The hospital felt different. The ICU felt different. There was less chatter or laughter amongst staff in the halls. A more serious tone overshadowed. There was something more formal about COVID now, acknowledged in the way that staff now wore scrub caps, surgical masks and face shields as they went about their work. Supply chains were slowing down in their ability to provision hospitals all around the country. Grace looped her mask over her ears. The loops felt tight and irritated the back of her ears. The face shields had foam and a band that pressed firmly against her head. The glare distorted her perception as she went about her nursing tasks.

It felt restricting to need to wear all the PPE. Headaches would come, especially if she forgot to drink enough water. It was harder to breathe and harder to see through the glaring film of her face shield, but she was thankful to have the protection. Every patient she had displayed at least one COVID symptom. A fever, a cough, an elevated D-Dimer, and ground glass opacities on the chest x-ray would prompt an order for a COVID nasal swabbing she would administer quickly to be sent to the lab. There were no visitors allowed in the hospital now which made for more room to work Grace supposed but less hands to assist with the patients or calm their nerves. The environment was charged with anxiety, as the team went about delivering care. Everything looked and felt different but needed to be the same care for the patients.

Grace took a break on the courtyard balcony overlooking the street. This was a place to pause and regroup from time to time. The intensity of the suffering within the ICU sometimes drained Grace more than other days. The work was hard, requiring Grace to constantly apply her clinical reasoning, as she monitored and assessed her patient's status and needs while moving through task after task. Her hands were the hands that kept the care moving for her patients, for whom many would likely die if she and her team did not execute properly. The pressure felt higher than ever before.

Outside on the balcony, Grace felt like she was drinking cool water as she inhaled deeply, after removing her mask and closing her eyes for a moment. She focused on her breath. In and out, in and out. Suddenly, she heard some laughter at the other end of the courtyard behind a pillar. *Not a lot of laughter happened out on this balcony* Grace thought. Grace could make out two people, in hospital issued scrubs seemingly pressed up against one another. She couldn't see their faces, just shoes and arms occasionally poking out from behind the brick. *Who has time to date round here?* Grace thought, amused.

She finished her granola bar and took a swig of water and breathed in deeply before masking up again. The annoying strap on her N95 gripped and pulled at little hairs, getting caught as she pulled the red loops, becoming worn with reuse, over her hair to secure the tightly sealed air filtering mask to her face. The air she inhaled now was trapped, thick and warm and smelled like her chocolate granola bar mixed with sour breath. She was getting used to living with it.

She thought it amusing to know there was a romance occurring amidst the crisis, as COVID-19 had truly permeated and coloured practically every element of life at work. The fact that some people were living out their desires and hopes in this place challenged Grace's sense that the work, the grind, the tedious replay of hardship was the only experience for everyone here in the trenches. As she walked away, she wondered who they could have been. She thought about her weekend with Justin and smiled. *Love needs to grow wherever it can.*

She drove with the windows down, to catch a breath on her way home. It was a mild Northern California late February day that had seen little rain. Yet the hills were turning back to emerald after a dry hot summer and fall. Grace liked to take some minutes between work and arriving at Emma's daycare to recollect herself. She truthfully preferred it when she had an errand to do after work, and Justin would pick up Emma. She could then spend some more time unwinding, staring at the road unfolding while listening to the classical music that she kept on a playlist. Her mind felt so wound up in a constantly vigilant and analytical state that required her to give her physical, mental, and emotional energy consistently while working most days in the ICU.

Listening to music as she drove soothed her often frayed nerves. The challenge and the responsibility made every shift feel purposeful and she truly loved to take care of her patients. But this Coronavirus knocking on the door seemed to make everything more tenuous, constantly working on edge. The situation felt surreal. Almost as though she was on the outside looking into it at times.

That night Grace lay awake thinking about how the whole world was changing, and seemingly in many ways closing in. Grace turned over, bulking up her pillow and watching Justin breathe heavily, almost snoring, in a deep sleep. She wished she could sleep with such ease. Ever since Emma was born, a creak in their house built in the 1950s, would send Grace leaping out of bed to investigate. Her senses had been heightened with a propensity to launch into fight or flight mode at the drop of a hat since becoming a mother. It would often take Justin, ambling out of bed to rub her shoulders as she stood in the doorway watching Emma sleeping, to urge her back to bed. Sleep did not come easy most nights until exhaustion took over and Grace would then get a full night's sleep. The cycle continued where sleep deprivation was the norm for her. She drank extra coffee and tried to ignore the dull headache and eye twitches.

The days passed; a new month came. The hillsides surrounding the bay flourished with bright wildflowers. Mustard seed, California poppies, and blue valley phacelia illuminated hillsides in golden yellow, orange and purple this time of year. Twisted oak trees lent along emerald hillsides, gilded with fresh sets of ultra-green leaves. Grace loved this time of year. When the dormant trees and bushes became reanimated with cheerful bright flowers. Breezes and rain showers punctuated generally mild and clear days.

Grace would spend her free afternoons and evenings pottering in the garden with Emma in tow, carrying a small trowel and digging her fingers into the earth. When inside, Emma liked to stand on a stool at the sink splashing in shallow soap suds washing and rewashing Tupperware. These quiet days felt more real than ever to Grace, as she appreciated any time to be away from the high pressure and busy intensive care unit.

Days passed and inside the hospital, the pace of policy and procedural changes had picked up. It stressed Grace to know each day a new workflow would emerge or a current one would be altered. Team huddles at the beginning of her shift brought new updates, proving new reminders that so much was emerging about how to deal with the virus. Transmission risk, community prevalence, and what clinical indicators could be used to identify individuals who were likely COVID patients in the absence of immediate test results were the topics of many discussions within the team before heading back out to attend to patients.

Grace felt a heightened need to make sure her infection prevention methods were infallible. She worried about bringing it home to Justin and Emma. As she went about her work, she paid attention to every surface she touched, never touching her face, unless she washed her hands when she had to take off her mask for a water break. She made sure to wash her hands with soap and warm water frequently, as she felt the residue of the hospital grade hand sanitiser build up, and coat her skin, like grease on a skillet. Grace would go for minutes, and even hours with an itch or an irritation on her face that she would not attend to so not to touch her PPE. She ate alone outside each day and missed taking a midday break with her colleagues.

The rigour of the daily drew her into herself mostly. She noticed her desire to talk to others and socialise at work faded. The job was very task driven—a maze to navigate until the end of her shift when she could get out and return home to rest and prepare to do it all over again the next day.

She imagined what soldiers may experience down in their trenches awaiting the arrival of an imminent threat, hoping their artillery and armour against this enemy would be adequate. She knew her family depended on her staying safe and so worked diligently day to day to ensure that. It was exhausting to operate with such vigilance all the time.

"So, they're cutting my contract short by two weeks here to head back on urgent assignment in New York because of what's going on over there," Jake began as he packed his backpack into his locker.

"Oh wow, okay. What have you heard on the ground over there about how bad it is?" Grace replied.

"My buddy at a hospital in New York said it's becoming really bad in the Emergency Department. I guess Governor Cuomo announced a state of emergency yesterday. It's not looking good."

Grace was bothered by how the spread of Coronavirus was accelerating in New York. She looked around at all the nurses crowding the breakroom, some wearing masks, some with the masks pulled down under their noses or chin, feeling the urge to quickly close her locker and head out to some more open space. She had never felt so paranoid and uncomfortable in these spaces that she had inhabited for hundreds of shifts. Never concerned about the close quarters she kept, the baby shower cake the team would pick at over the course of shifts, or the many high touch surfaces in the hospital. Now it all felt contaminated, *dangerous*.

"I'm really bummed you have to leave, Jake. Do you know where you will be assigned?" Jake wasn't sure what his assignment would be. He just knew that his agency's quick decision to break his contract for an urgent reassignment meant there was a lot of work ahead. "So, my last shift is Sunday," he added.

"Well, we should exchange numbers so you can keep in touch and text me about what's going on. I really hope you stay safe out there."

"I will do my best." He looked her in the eyes with a steadiness she knew she'd miss amidst all that was going on.

Grace walked away feeling a sense of loss. She felt anxious about the healthcare crisis that was emerging rapidly in New York and what he may be walking into, and nervous about what he may report back, as she acknowledged that it was just a matter of time before what was happening in New York would make its way to California.

The following week, Grace sat out on the back deck late at night after Emma had been put to bed. Early March brought some clear sky nights where the fog was held back, a band out over the pacific. Night's inky cloak drew across the sky and scattered stars had emerged. She contemplated the naivety of a conversation she had had with Lottie in late October last year over the phone. They were talking about how things were so tense politically in America but that their generation really hadn't encountered any full-blown catastrophic events like those before who lived through world wars.

They had remarked at how in America, disinformation could run rampant, be consumed indiscriminately, and erode the sensibilities of a population largely too consumed and concerned with creating an image of perfection on social media to look up and around at what was becoming unhinged. Where information and opinion travelled all over the world, to be consumed with a single click, before it could be verified, or even after it was proven false. She laughed a little to herself at the irony of how the catastrophe was now here. Gazing out into the dark night, she felt troubled, stuck on the ride.

Grace sipped her wine hoping to get a little drunk in order to numb her nerves, frayed from the day.

The following week, a text came through from Jake. "I'm here in NYC. This place is a hot COVID mess." Grace didn't feel she had it in her to reply immediately, she figured she couldn't handle any more bad news right now. She looked around at all the filled beds in the ICU. Starched sheets and blankets smoothed over human mounds. She felt a wave of anxiety pass over her. *It's just a matter of time.*

Grace returned to her shift and worked away at placing an IV requiring multiple attempts on her patient with small veins. She hung a saline drip, flushing the IV before she attached it. It made sense to her to just focus on her task. She knew that remaining task oriented, keeping her head down, and purpose-driven, was going to be the only way she would be able to hold it together.

Grace stopped in her tracks on her walk to the garage. She looked down at her phone. It was Jake again. "Patients are really sick and doctors and nurses have been getting sick. Short-staffed and we have one doctor who is now our patient. Not sure how long we can keep up. If we are even keeping up at all…"

Grace had seen images emerging out of New York over the news. Open bay emergency departments with healthcare workers in full PPE weaving between beds, adjusting vents, giving respiratory treatments, adjusting their patients' intravenous lines. It looked like a hospital in wartime—soldiers, men and women, now young, and old being wheeled in from the battle ground outside with oxygen masks placed over their faces. There was no blood or lacerations that marked the carnage to those looking on, rather, the insidious disease took form in various ways within its host.

Grace shuddered when she read the news about how some people who had COVID-19 were asymptomatic and likely spreading it unaware. For some, cold and flu-like symptoms were the greatest complication experienced, but for those people inundating the hospital rooms and halls, the Coronavirus was swift and relentless in its ability to ravage respiratory systems, and cause organs to shut down. It was shocking to see such a high volume of patients coming through.

"Do you have the PPE you need?" She knew that if he answered her question affirmatively, she would feel a little more at ease. "Yes. I'm living in my PPE for so many hours that it's creating permanent lines on my face. Will match my new grey hairs I guess." Grace texted a thumbs up and put her phone back in her pocket. She imagined the intensive care unit in New York, as she had seen glimpses of it on the news. Open bays with patients laying, struggling to breathe all around. Staff rushing from one critical situation to another.

Grace felt relieved that Jake was doing okay. She hadn't known him well, but there was something formative about their friendship beginning as the pandemic was unfolding. She thought of him as a comrade of sorts. He had been someone to confide in about the pressures of this job that seemed to be transformed overnight to a new level. She could share her fears about PPE malfunctioning, catching COVID or the pressure to help her very sick patients survive it. The things healthcare workers spoke about because they couldn't tell their families who wouldn't understand or would be sent into a tailspin of concern.

When Jake had left so quickly, Grace didn't have enough time to process what it would mean for her day to day. She was concerned for his safety walking into the fire but missed being shoulder to shoulder with him in the same trench, able to process what was happening together. As she watched the story evolve, she couldn't imagine how she would feel if she had to leave and go work in New York during the wave of Coronavirus cases it was seeing. Soon the subway would be closed, and makeshift morgues opened all over New York in order to manage.

Grace drove home, thinking about all of her workflows she had carried out during her shift. Playing back her steps taken to don and doff PPE sequentially and properly, not to cross contaminate anything. She made judgments for the times she recalled going in and out of a patient's room. Concerning herself with whether she did the correct steps for keeping her hands clean and putting on plastic gowns, N95s, face shields or the respirator helmets. She would perseverate on whether she had touched her face after pulling the mask away from her face.

These thoughts played and replayed in cycle many days and nights in which her mind fixated. She would think back on her day and would remember a missed step. She wasn't used to this heightened level of vigilance that had overcome her. The compulsion of her thoughts grew. When wiping a surface, rewashing her hands, and keeping track of everything she touched, she bore certainty that she was coming in regular contact with the Coronavirus, and therefore could not miss a beat in her safety precautions. All this added another layer to her cognitive load. She found herself having a heightened awareness and memory for all the things she had touched and cleaned as she went about her work as a nurse but would forget that she left her breakfast burrito in the microwave or where her to-do list was last placed when she was home.

Motherhood had brought upon a haze in her ability to remember things, but what she did remember was crystal clear. It would be the details of Emma's day and her basic needs, the grocery list, and the at-home to-do's that floated around in Grace's mind when she was not laser focused on her work.

\*\*\*

Grace hurried to pick up Emma. The stoplights lurched into action after lengthy pauses. Grace wondered if she had missed the green when contemplating her day while waiting so long. She knew she had a window of 15-minutes to get to Emma before turning around to head to Emma's doctor's appointment. Grace stood waving frantically through the screen door as Mrs Corrine and Emma approached. "Thank you, Mrs Corrine," Grace said with an unsteady smile, as she lifted Emma with her unicorn backpack into her arms.

Mrs Corrine was accustomed to the hurried habits of working parents coming to and from her door. She never seemed bothered by their frantic apologies. She bid them goodbye with a wide grin, waving to Emma now slouched over Grace's shoulder holding two partially dried pieces of artwork, bobbing up and down as Grace hurried back to the car. "I made a rainbow and a pony for you, Mumma," said Emma beaming with pride as she was strapped into her car seat. "A whale in the ocean is for Daddy."

Grace paused to take in the vivid painting, trying hard to discern where the said animals were. Equally excited, she exclaimed, "These are just so beautiful, my love. Thank you!"

Emma's eyes brightened, "I love you, Mumma."

"I love you too, bug." Grace lay the wet paintings on the dashboard as they drove, in hopes they would dry. She sped through the backstreets of Berkeley to make it to Emma's three-year-old wellness check-up, now aware of the five minutes she needed to make up in order to arrive on time. As they drove, a pedestrian darted out onto the street. With a screech of the brakes, Grace stopped abruptly. The pedestrian looked at her, pissed off, and raised his hands. It made Grace feel badly, she had not intended to be reckless. She felt like rolling down her window to explain her day, the causes for her distraction, and her complete apology. But she judged it would fall on deaf ears as the pedestrian had passed them by with an irritated expression. There wouldn't be enough time anyway.

"I'm so sorry, Emma, Mumma didn't see that man."

"Pay attention, Mumma, okay?"

"Yes, I know, sweetheart, Mumma's got a lot on her mind. I'll do better, okay?" Grace admitted. She realised how distracted her thoughts had made her. Her eyes took in her surroundings, but her mind processed elsewhere. The pressure to get to the next place was always pressing upon her, and she had missed what was right in front of her—a pedestrian in the street and her little girl in the back. She felt guilty for both.

Grace often felt like much of her guilt came about for reasons she couldn't quite get a grip of enough to control. She often felt like she was floating downstream in a current too swift to take in the detail of the things she passed, and too strong for her to stop moving past them. As a mother, she took deep breaths to inhale the perfection of small moments. Islands she could take in that popped up from time to time in the middle of the river. But the current pushed her along, propelling her forward, and causing her to have only single chances many times. She often thought when she turned her attention to one thing, another would invariably be neglected—the pace of life was always revealing of her inability to completely manage it all.

Grace remembered how her mother had always seemed so good at the task of 'mothering'. Although, somewhat stoically, her mother carried out daily tasks with a steady command of every detail, dutiful with artful precision. Laundry was washed and neatly folded, delivered to the end of beds every other day.

There was never a missed breakfast, packed lunch or dinner. She sewed beautiful clothing for Grace and her sister. The house was kept, and she baked delicious cakes and pies. Standing in the front room, Grace at the age of six, recalled how she stood painfully still as her mother tucked and pinned a pale-yellow cotton dress around her. "Now just stay still my June Bug" her mother would say, scaling the length of fabric down each seam with her eyes, looking for any imperfections. Grace wondered if her mother ever felt this sense of guilt that would creep up, *She must have*. But if she did, she never let on.

They arrived at the doctor's appointment 10-minutes late, but fortunately Dr Evans was running late also. Grace made a mental note of Dr Evans' pattern of being late every time. As she sat down, a little flustered from all her hurrying, she wondered why she hadn't calculated for this. Why had she forgotten and instead pushed herself so hard almost running over someone and endangering her and Emma? She felt stupid at that moment. Her calculations were always rapid, but not always accurate. In the waiting room, Emma twirled and played with the centre table's toy with the colourful beads on the wire tracks and pointed to the different tropical fish darting around a large fish tank. Grace tied her hair into a tight bun and read the signage throughout the waiting room about masks and hand hygiene.

The appointment was largely uneventful. Emma was growing well and meeting her milestones. The doctor lectured lightly on the need to cut down on juice and have more milk. Grace had read many books while she was pregnant to study up on how to be a parent. She even attended some classes with Justin. She realised how little she consulted those books now, and felt a little ashamed for her oversight with the juice. Nonetheless a good bill of health, and a happy child was good enough she thought as they made their way out the sliding doors into the fresh air. Emma peeled off her mask immediately, running for the pavement and dropping the flimsy mask into Grace's hand before she was ready to take it. They headed home, the evening was now setting in. "Home in 10," Grace had texted before they left the parking garage.

The front door was unlocked, and Jerome circled as they made their way out of the cold into the warm house. Justin had lit a fire, the crackling sound of a large fire consuming a log in the hearth met them. Justin was in his study—the blue glow of his screen outlined his silhouette as Grace peeked in the door. "Oh gotta go, bye, you too," he quickly ended his phone conversation. "There's my girl. Emma, how was your visit to the doctor?" Emma grinned from ear to ear, as she always did when Justin talked to her. "Doctor look my nose." She showed him her nose, tilting her chin so he could see in her nostrils. "See boogers, Daddy!" she laughed.

"That was Dr Evans encouraging her…" said Grace with a sly grin.

"Sounds like Dr Evans knows what he's doing," Justin grinned, taking in his little girl's big smile before heading to the kitchen to finish up cooking. Justin had a lasagna nearly boiling over in its glass dish in the oven, some sliced bread, and a Caesar salad on the table when Grace came downstairs from her shower. "Are you hungry, Grace?" He asked as he served up scoops of steaming lasagna.

"Yes, famished," Grace replied, thankful to have a warm meal to come home to. "Emma, did you tell Daddy about the book you got from the doctor today?" Grace asked.

"I Can Do It!"

Grace replied, "It's really a cute book. It shows little kids doing all sorts of things like riding a bike, putting on socks and shoes, and brushing teeth. Hopefully, she pays closer attention to that using the potty picture." After dinner, they sat for a bit leaning back in their chairs after taking a second helping and regretting the way it made them feel sluggish. Grace arranged the dishes on the counter but didn't have it in her to rinse and wash any. After dinner, they all headed upstairs to bed. It felt very late, even when it was early, during the dark wintery nights. Comforting to be warm and cosy.

Later that night, Grace woke to a whimpering cry coming from down the hall. At first, she thought it was the wind, but in her sleepy state made out her name being called, "Mumma." She heard coughing and whimpering clearly as she sprang out of bed.

"Something's wrong, Justin," she said loudly, as he turned over in protest to her turning the lamp on. She found Emma in her bed, sitting by a pool of vomit and heaving again to vomit. Watery chunks poured out, in a volume Grace did not think possible for her size. Grace, a trained ICU nurse who had dealt with many things, felt helpless at the sight of her little one sputtering and gasping, heaving and vomiting.

It happened a third time, as Grace lifted her out of her crib to the floor on a towel she had grabbed quickly from the bathroom. Vomit projected over her shoulder and down her back, making the flannel of her pyjamas wet and slimy. Grace didn't even notice; her concern was focused on Emma who couldn't seem to stop vomiting violently. It stopped for a few minutes, in which Emma curled up into the arch of her mother's torso laying across her crossed legs, sleeping soundly. The advice nurse had said let her sleep, and not to push fluids because it would make her keep vomiting.

Grace hung onto every word of advice she received. Her motherly angst overshadowed her ability to process the medical presentation. All she wanted was Emma to stop vomiting. So, they waited, although Grace felt unnerved by her daughter's panting and as an hour passed with a few bouts of vomiting, she became more concerned. She noticed Emma was becoming less lucid when she would talk, and her colour was pale, her pulse was very fast. Although a nurse, Grace felt somewhat paralysed in her ability to think critically as things progressed with Emma in her arms that night. She held her baby girl, laying listless in her arms, murmuring how much she loved her, rocking back and forth, not knowing what to do.

"We need to go to the hospital. She won't stop vomiting. Can you get a bucket for the car?" Grace said suddenly, in a decisive moment, as she launched to grab her coat, keys and purse. Her worst fear was that Emma could be harmed by the Coronavirus, and here they were rushing her into the car to take her to the emergency room. Did she have COVID-19? The adrenaline kicked in as they made their way to the hospital.

As they approached Harris Memorial hospital, Grace looked up at the towers that stood illuminated against the orange tinted cloud cover. When the city slept, the tireless cogs of the hospital's internal metropolis moved dutifully. Fatigued night shift healthcare workers moved through the dimmed lighting to dark rooms on the inpatient floors; flashlights were used so as not to wake their patients as they adjusted and monitored their sleeping bodies.

The darkness brought calm to most in the night. But for some, the night ushered in terror. Where hallucinations and disorientation took over as the sun went down. Some patients would yell out to hollow corridors, tormented by fear and paranoia they would climb the frames of their beds if given a chance or writhe in extreme agitation. Disrupting the slumber of the other patients with panic-stricken screams that pierced gaping holes in the dead of night. Echoing down the long hallways and dissolving into darkness. Nursing staff would enter patient rooms calmly, unaffected by near any display; there to console feverish panic with assuring melodic tones, treating each as though they were their own loved one. Calm and steady hands would work the room, adjusting suction canisters and hanging fresh saline, swiftly clamping and adjusting IV lines and equipment. Sliding patients up in bed and rolling them to allow for a reconfiguration of pillows and wedge placement so to alleviate pressures of lying in bed at length.

Ambulances arrived at varying intervals during the night. Flashing lights and sirens tempered as they entered the Emergency Department (ED) receiving bay. Gurneys transporting new patients jolted off the ambulance ramps and towards the welcoming ED doors attended by staff ready to jump into action. On occasion, these patients were quickly rushed through the corridors to the brightly lit operating room where teams assembled with streamlined coordination of roles and responsibilities to address the fresh case. The family members arriving in the ED bay minutes behind, weary, fatigued and exhausted from worry would run towards the ED reception desk, fumbling through their personal effects to get their driver's licence ready for check-in. Men and women wearily leaned and sat along a large glass window lining the waiting room.

Glancing intermittently at the clock that dependably ran 10 minutes late for the sake of tracking time spent in limbo and with no knowledge of when someone would come fetch them and bring them some news. Eternities were spent waiting in this place. Medicine took time and there was no hurrying the process of systematically ruling out the cause of what ailments brought patient upon patient through the hospital doors.

Now here in the waiting room, at 2 AM, Grace held Emma close, bundled in a pink polka dotted blanket. This was the hospital that Grace came to work at every day. In sharp contrast to the dark night that they had travelled through, it looked like a new place—not the place where she worked to help others. Rather, now as a patient, it was a place she desperately hoped would fix her baby. Now sitting in the sterile waiting room, everything looked different, less familiar and comforting. They waited under bright lights on squeaky blue vinyl chairs with grimy armrests.

A nurse called them through to an exam room to the side of the waiting room. Once in, the nurse vanished for a time to return with a portable vitals monitor. She listened to her heart and her lungs then attached a small blood pressure cuff to Emma's weak arm and told her she was going to feel a big hug. Emma, unable to maintain focus and too weak to protest, sat quietly on her mother's lap as the cuff squeezed her arm. "102/58. It looks okay."

Her temperature was 99.8 and her breathing was shallow. Emma began to whimper again. This is what she did before she vomited. Then dry heaving gave way to rust-coloured vomit. It was far less volume than her first eleven rounds, but this time the colour was alarming. It wasn't the bright yellow-green bile colour like before, it looked like blood. Grace's heart dropped. The nurse brought them back to another room. Emma protested when Grace attempted to lay her on the large gurney bed apart from them, so Justin climbed into the bed and held Emma on his chest.

The nurse came back with intravenous line tubing and prepped her small hands to place it. It took a nurse, Justin and Grace to hold her down as a second nurse passed the thick needle into her skin to secure a path for the saline to flow. "She's very dehydrated," said the nurse, concerned. We are going to give her a bag of fluid and see if she perks up. They taped her hand to secure the intravenous line and deter Emma from ripping it out. Grace thought that a good idea, given how greatly she protested when they placed it. She had had adult patients who weren't as strong as Emma tonight. They took blood samples to run to the lab. She looked stable, but she was clearly lethargic. They sat quietly. Justin fell asleep with Emma in the bed. Grace stayed awake, unable to close her eyes but to blink. She was exhausted, nervous and keenly attentive to every move Emma made. She was watching Emma breathe, watching the monitor, watching that Justin didn't let go of his grip as he held her, snoring.

An hour passed. Dr Ross, the emergency medicine doctor, came into the room and discussed his thought that this was a case of gastritis. The IV fluid moved through the tubing to reach Emma's little hand, placed over her chest as she slept. As she waited, Grace bit her lip to hold back tears that burned the rims of her tired eyes. She was glad she had brought her here, despite reservations about bringing her little one into the hospital during a pandemic. She knew though that if they stayed at home, Emma's condition would have likely worsened. This sense of duty to protect Emma above all things overcame her. It was instinctual, uncontrollable. She thought back over all the steps in the day and how she could have been more vigilant with Emma. *I should have washed her hands with hand sanitiser more often.* The sense of guilt dwelt in the dark spaces of her mind as she sat there, sleep deprived and unable to break her gaze from her sick little girl whose colour was now dashed from her usually rosy cheeks. She watched intently, scanning across every inch of Emma, resting there on her dad's chest, rising and falling upon his deep breaths. Grace braced herself as Emma would flinch or move, expecting to jump into action with an emesis basin and to sit her upright or on her side so the contents of her stomach wouldn't be inhaled into her windpipe. Grace in this moment wished that she could take this sickness from her child. Her thoughts darted to carefree moments in which they were blowing bubbles at the park and yearned for those simple perfect moments.

She also began to think about the moments she had ignored Emma's constant chatter or denied requests to play because she was too tired and felt the lurch of guilt for taking her daughter for granted. So there, with curtains drawn and her jaw clenched, Grace waited out the last of the night, still and stoic, willing her daughters return to good health. The doctor returned and offered Grace a cup of tea. "Yes. Thank you," she replied.

"Black tea or herbal? Sugar? Cream?"

"Black with one sugar and one cream please." In a pleasantly surprised tone, as she hadn't imagined a doctor would provide this kind of service. When he returned with the steaming paper cup, she held it tight with both hands. It was the warmest feeling to radiate out of this terrible night. "So, it looks like Zofran did its job and stopped Emma's vomiting cycle," Dr Evans said with positivity. "I think we can go ahead and plan to send you home once she's fully hydrated. There's about 15 minutes on this bag left. Your nurse will get your discharge instructions and we will have you on your way."

"Okay, thank you, doctor. Will there be any prescriptions we need?"

"I'll write for Zofran in case she begins to vomit again, but please bring her back in if she starts vomiting profusely again."

Grace's stomach sank at the memory and thought of her little one's whimpering as she heaved and vomited over and over. "Okay, thank you. Shall I pick it up from the discharge pharmacy?"

"Yes, it should be ready for you. Let us know if there is anything you need. Good job bringing her in. She should be right as rain with some rest and some Pedialyte," Dr Ross said with a reassuring smile, as he saw Grace's concerned and guilt-stricken face. Emma didn't vomit again that night. They were discharged from the hospital quietly a few hours later, walking through the corridors of the first floor, and out into a bright morning. The blossoms on the courtyard trees had been tricked into blooming in winter and were now transitioning with full affair. Grace breathed in the clear air and noticed the breeze brush past her. The air had been dry and still inside the hospital, and it comforted her to hear birds twittering way up high in the branches. *Emerging out of the hospital, with Emma fixed, felt like a second chance to take in the perfection of bright days,* Grace thought.

Justin carried Emma, while Grace carried their bags and an emesis basin for safe keeping, in case needed on the car ride home. Justin paused while driving as his phone buzzed. A text from his principal had come through. Justin, in haste grabbed his phone and read it while idling at a stoplight. "It looks like my school is closing. We are going to have the kids stay home starting next week on Tuesday, March 17th." Justin looked puzzled. "Something big must be happening now in California if they are closing down schools, don't you think?" He said, pushing through the intersection once the light went green.

That foreboding feeling Grace had felt the first day she learned of local cases of Coronavirus spreading, flooded in once more. She felt trapped by circumstance—her sick child, a risky job to have in a pandemic, and now schools were shutting down. "I don't know what's happening," Grace said, feeling her anxiety bubble up. "It's all too much to process right now. We just need to go home and rest."

# Chapter 3
# Lockdown

As Grace was walking down the long corridor, she noticed how her scrub cap was feeling too tight and her mask a little stifling. Realising her breaths had been shallow, she took some deep breaths feeling the filtered air fill her lungs. The dieticians were monitoring Mrs Edward's intake—deciding whether to do a calorie count based on the percentage of meals she ate over the past 24 hours. Mrs Edwards had come in for stroke symptoms, but she was very weak and not motivated to eat but a few bites of her meals. Grace charted the 10% breakfast and 0% lunch meal intake. It had been a struggle to coax Mrs Edwards to eat some bites of her cream of wheat and puréed pancakes with heavy syrup.

Her other patient had a respiratory therapist adjusting the ventilator settings. They were trying to wean him from ventilator support. Grace stood at the door watchfully. She felt protective of her patients, even though she trusted the respiratory therapist, as he worked to reduce the patient's dependence on the machine to push air in and out of his lungs. Moments later, an emergency huddle was called by the manager in the hallway between ICU wings. The nurses rushed to finish the tasks they were attending to. One nurse hung back to watch the main monitor. The nurses stood in the hall offering their partial attention to their manager's announcement and the rest to what was happening in their patient's rooms.

"Governor Newsom has announced a shelter in place in our county in response to the growing number of Coronavirus cases," the manager stated. "It's going to be effective tomorrow March 17th at midnight." The manager handed out Essential worker cards to attach to their badges, explaining that the police would be monitoring movement on the roads and if staff are stopped on their way to or from work, that they should show their essential worker card in order to pass.

The nurses looked around at each other. Soon many were raising their hands to ask questions about the impending lockdown's restrictions and if the manager thought they would see a lot more patients coming into the ICU soon. The manager stated that she did not have details beyond this announcement at this time but directed them to follow local news outlets for information on the terms of the shelter-in-place. They broke from their huddle and resumed work. A tension was building within the ICU, different from the day-to-day tension that comes with caring for people who are critically ill. There were rumblings the rest of the day about Martial Law and the deployment of the military to enforce this lockdown. That people would be arrested if they were out past curfew.

The fears people had been having about the Immigration and Customs Enforcement (ICE) raids that were happening all over the United States mixed with sober caution people felt about this impending lock-down. ICE had pulled undocumented immigrants from their homes in the middle of the night and transported them to detention centers to await deportation. This had been an unnerving, real and recent memory for some of the hospital workers who were now working extra shifts to pay for a good immigration lawyer or make ends meet in the wake of their loss. Now, the Coronavirus was coming to steal what was left. People worried that if they had illegal immigrant family members, that the lockdown and heavy police and military presence in their streets would surely expose them.

For the rest of the shift and the next day, healthcare workers went about their tasks quietly, as though afraid to speak their fears into existence. Fully clad in PPE, the nurses attended to their patients on the ICU floor with dutiful solemnity despite the fears that were eroding upon their motivation to continue working.

Grace didn't want to stay at work any longer. She felt like she wanted to rush home immediately after receiving the manager's announcement. With no one to relieve her, she kept working listening to the murmuring of passing conversations and checked the television screens throughout the unit for any information she could get. Local news reports on the patients' televisions began coming in to describe the terms of the shelter in place. "This Bay Area order restricting all residents to their homes for the next three weeks is the most drastic move announced to date in response to the Coronavirus," a news anchor stated. "The order allows residents to leave their home to go grocery shopping, go to the pharmacy, exercise and to provide caregiving to family members or other vulnerable people outside of their homes. Only essential workers will be allowed to go to and from their workplace. People are asked to consult their workplaces to find out if they are considered an essential worker."

Grace stood there, perplexed. She had never in her life imagined restrictions on where she could go and what she could do. Shelter in place was usually something reserved for natural disasters and shootings. *What would this mean for everyone? Stuck in our homes, together.* She texted Justin, "We need to stock up on food and water."

She passed other staff members huddled in enclaves throughout the unit to take calls or text and presumed it was for the same reasons with which she felt the urgency to plan out what to do next. "Can you stop on your way home? I'll go pick up Emma," Justin replied.

"Sure. Is Mrs Corinne going to keep running her daycare?" Justin didn't reply over the next hour until the change of shift. Grace hurried to provide her report to the oncoming PM shift nurse after finishing up her documentation. She clocked-out and moved swiftly past the groups of nurses exiting the hospital. She felt a small freedom in breaking out of the hospital today, leaving her shift behind.

Taking her mask off, she took deep breaths relishing in the quality of fresh air juicy enough to drink. She had never valued air as much as she did these days, working long hours under a mask and face shield. The daylight was shifting as she pulled up into the local store's parking lot. People were lining up outside in a line that wrapped around the corner of the building. *You must be kidding me.* Grace thought, annoyed that she couldn't go directly in. The line moved, as people maintaining their 6 feet distance carefully entered the large store.

Once in, Grace grabbed a shopping cart and headed through the aisles, chuckling to herself at the irony she was experiencing as she passed the swimsuit aisle, now displaying a bright summer collection of bikinis, at the thought of how remote a possibility it would be for her to need a bathing suit right now to swim in the public pool they usually spent many of their summer days at. She headed to the canned food aisle and grabbed numerous cans of soup, tinned fruit and vegetables and then made her way to get large jugs of water she thought to store in the garage.

Around a corner, she saw a gathering of customers quietly side-stepping and loading large cases of toilet paper and paper towels into their carts. Some had five to six 48 roll packs filling their carts. Grace watched for a moment, somewhat surprised by the interest shoppers were taking in these paper items.

She decided to jump in as the stock was beginning to dwindle on the shelves. She left her cart to the side, grabbing for a pack of 48 toilet paper rolls. The last on this shelf. She felt a yank, it was another customer who had also grabbed it and was silently yet aggressively pulling it from her. Grace had never experienced this type of desperation at the store, perhaps except for Black Fridays where people would trample you for the biggest deal.

As the lady kept pulling, clearly not willing to let go, she felt unnerved and yelled, "Fine. Go on, have it if you are going to take it," as she let go. Feeling the stress of the situation overcoming her intentions to remain polite. The lady with the toilet paper walked off, not acknowledging Grace or her comment, which infuriated her more. "Rude!" She said loudly.

People around her didn't even stop to look at her or for the source of the outraged remark that hung in the air. They seemed preoccupied, foregoing interest in their surroundings beyond meeting their objectives to gather as many resources as they could get their hands on. Grace remembered she had a pack of toilet paper in the garage which would be enough for now. She was uncertain that there would be toilet paper available the next time she returned to the store, if this is what things would be like now. She stood in line for the check stand, contemplating whether to do self-check-out but knowing it would cause her to have to pay attention to the scanning, weighing and bagging. Her mind was darting, her temper high, and she knew she couldn't take on another task reliably.

So, she stood and waited for the next 20 minutes to reach the check stand. "I've got Emma. Mrs Corinne is staying open (for now)," Justin texted back finally. Grace felt a little relief at this, but then began to think about how the increasing number of Coronavirus cases would mean greater risk for Emma at a daycare with the different families. She pushed the thought out of her mind as she approached the check stand. A rail-thin late teens boy with braces and a faux hawk checked her items through. "Couldn't get any toilet paper, hey?" He remarked, looking at her cart.

"I tried. Can you believe someone yanked it out of my hands?"

"Actually, yes," he replied with certainty, "We had to have security escort two people out today because they started fighting on that Aisle 16."

Grace believed it. "Wow." She stood there thinking about what it was that compelled humans to act so uncivilised when competing for resources. History was proof of this, and now human nature was playing out over toilet paper in Aisle 16.

She gathered her bags and made her way out. Relieved to now have at least two weeks' worth of canned food in her possession. She thought to fill the bathtub when she got home to keep extra water. The flashlight batteries would need to be checked. As Grace drove home on the freeway, she began thinking about what was going on. Preparing for this shelter in place brought a combination of priorities in view. And a confusion of sorts, as to whether they should be preparing for a natural disaster, militia in the streets, and civil unrest. This felt ominous when considered in addition to the prospect of extensive time at home, as a societal response to the Coronavirus. It was hard for her to keep it straight.

With the years of California wildfires, emerging realities of climate change, immigration reform, and polarised politics around the country and world, it seemed to Grace like this Coronavirus issue was just another threat to add into the landscape of this complicated and disheartening modern world. Grace's thoughts turned to Emma, as they often did. *What sort of world are we giving our children?* She thought contemplatively. Emma's welfare was central to Grace's sense of duty and purpose. Thinking about all that was beyond her own reach of control made her feel small and inconsequential to how time and circumstance would likely shape Emma's understanding of life and her future. Grace, at this point, was determined to focus on the here and now. Knowing that entertaining anything more than the details, challenges and thoughts of today would leave her feeling anxious and incapable.

***

Grace hid behind the bag of rice at the bottom of the pantry. Her small toes gripped spilled grains scattered on the floor. Her weight shifting, trying not to make the floorboards creak, or the glisten of her eye catch the light through the thin slit in the door. Mumma had shooed her and Lottie out of sight and into this familiar hiding place as Daddy's car pulled up. "Come girls, best be out of sight when Daddy returns," she had said hurriedly as she coaxed them into the small space.

Through the open kitchen window, Grace could hear her daddy's work boots crunching along the gravel pathway, uneven, and stumbling on his way. The door slammed, as her dad came in. Grace's heart sank and pulse quickened as she listened intently to his movement on the floorboards in the front of the house. Through the wall, she could hear Mumma meet Daddy with a polite tone, attempting to placate any sign of anger. She did this every time with hopes to avert his explosive advances, for her children's sake, as they hid in terror. Grace held Lottie's clammy hand tight as she heard a vase shatter and Daddy's voice raised. She didn't understand the colourful words that he launched with fury towards Mumma, but she understood his intent. He was angry with Mumma, like always.

Lottie began to cry when she heard their mother screaming out for help and motioned to run out of the pantry to her defence. Grace held Lottie back, for her own safety, for she had known first hand that Daddy became indiscriminate with who he would direct his blows towards if given the chance. Grace knew it was Daddy grabbing Mumma by the hair, as she pleaded for him to let go. Wherever he went all these nights, somehow what they gave him to drink stripped him of all decency. He was ruthless and clumsy as he hollered more at their mother about how she didn't keep the house clean enough or the flirtatious glances he claimed she made at George at the Christmas party four years back. He had a bag of grievances against Mumma and whenever he was drinking, he would pull out his complaints like an item to behold and then hurl at her.

One after another until she fell silent, and he got tired, and passed out on the couch, in an inebriated stupor. Mumma cried enough tears for them all, once he slept. She could be heard crying softly through the walls as she would clean up the shards of glass and move furniture back into place so Grace and Lottie's living room would be recognisable, normal even, when they came out from hiding. As much as Mumma cleaned up, the staining effect of what both Grace and Lottie witnessed on these terrible nights could not be erased from memory. They knew to stay hidden until Mumma, smoothing out her dress and wiping her eyes, came to retrieve them from the pantry.

"I know what you heard must have been scary, my loves. Your daddy just had too much to drink tonight. He didn't mean what he said or did. I'm so sorry you had to hear that." Lottie would cry into her mother's shoulder in the pantry doorway, unable to verbalise her feelings at the age of four. Grace, three years older, stood stoic and detached, imagining her body floating above, along the height of the ceiling, looking down at her family, unaffected.

***

The days wore on. Grace lost track of time easily. She missed a shift she had offered to cover for Elle one day. She thought it was one day when it was another time more times than she liked to admit.

Her home became a nest that was rarely left. Grace used online shopping services mostly to have packages and groceries dropped off at the doorstep. The outside world seemed changed and unsafe for her little family. She ventured out to work and retreated home again right after. This repeated day in and out with little variation.

Two weeks had passed since lockdown and Grace stood in the kitchen. She had been baking all sorts of delicious confectioneries and regretting the urge to eat them. Emma loved to stand at the counter in her ladybug apron. She leant over the large yellow mixing bowl and stirred away as Grace would add pinches, cups and teaspoons of all the ingredients. Many hours were spent researching and planning the next baking project and Grace wondered why she had taken so long, now nearly 37 years old to really enjoy and work at the art of baking.

She ordered some icing piping tools online to decorate her first cake. It was a chocolate cake that she covered in a dark red buttercream icing and applied small brown rosettes around the edge and on top. The cakes, bread, cupcakes and cookies didn't last long. With delight, Emma would sit cross legged beneath the double oven looking up through the slatted lights at the glowing bakeware for signs that it was ready. She would ask Grace over and over, "is it ready?" The smell of vanilla and cinnamon wafted through the house, as drifting comfort. All the social commitments that once filled her weekends had been suspended until further notice, with the lockdown expected only for three weeks. When she thought into the future, nothing took shape. Nothing planned. No exciting events punctuating the horizon. The future began to seem murky and monotonous. Predictable as the grey fog that rolled in over the San Francisco Bay midwinter, covering everything. Visibility felt only a short distance beyond her.

So much of life had changed so quickly and thrust her into a place of constant apprehension. In not knowing what to do or what might come next, Grace found herself in a state of uneasy pause.

The world outside her doorstep felt overly controlled by procedures designed to restrict the spread and yet the nature of the Coronavirus news reports that would flood Grace's screens, indicated it was anything but. COVID cases continued to increase at an alarming rate with numbers seemingly doubling weekly. People scrambled to understand it, were fearful of catching it, and exhausted by the uncertainty that dwelt indefinitely at the forefront of everyone's minds.

Grace came home after picking up some groceries. Emma sat in the driveway drawing with chalk while Justin sat on the porch texting. Grace wondered if Justin had made an effort to play with Emma while she was away, and felt perturbed by his grin, as he texted on his phone intently. "Hey Em, what are you drawing?" She said, kneeling to her eye level and taking interest in the big blue scribbles she had made. "Such pretty drawings!"

"Doggy, Mumma! Want to draw with me?"

"Sure." Grace could not turn down Emma's offer. She was glad to spend time doodling on the cool pavement. The grocery bags leaned onto one another, some tipped over entirely to the wayside, spilling some oranges that rolled a little. Grace enjoyed making pictures for Emma. They giggled as she drew a bee buzzing around flowers and monkeys swinging on vines.

"How about I pick up some takeout sushi?" Justin had finished whatever he was doing on the phone and had come to admire their work. "You're quite good at drawing, Grace. Isn't your mummy a good drawer?" Justin exclaimed.

Emma agreed passively as she went about the concentrated business of scribbles and wonky circles. They decided to walk to the neighbourhood park, once Justin returned from Shattuck Avenue with two big bags and sat at a picnic table. Emma, sitting on Grace's knee, played with chopsticks, as Grace shovelled bite-sized crab and rice mix into her mouth in between fiery protests. "How's Elle doing?" Justin asked casually, midway through their dinner.

Grace had told him about Joe's grand exit from their home and marriage. Justin had met this news with a shocked face and immediate sympathy for Elle days prior. "Oh you know. How you'd expect. She's been sad, angry, confused. She says she really feels powerless about this decision to get a divorce and fearful about the future. It's like he just made the decision for her, not with her you know? She's worried the kids will like his girlfriend more than her. She feels pretty mixed up right now."

"Where is she staying?" Justin asked with a concerned look.

"With her mum for now. But I'm not sure how long that's going to last since her mum is a bit overbearing, and Elle can't stand it. It's just a complicated and sad situation to have their family break up like that with all that's going on right now. It's like the stress broke them, yet the pandemic just makes everything harder. She's lucky she has a good job to fall back on at least." Grace searched Justin's face for the reassurance that he was committed to never doing something like what Joe had done to Elle.

Justin wiped his mouth with a napkin. "Well, I saw it coming when Joe got those promotions and had to travel more for work. Their dynamic changed," Justin added.

"How did you see it coming? I mean did he say something to you?" Grace asked directly.

"No Grace. It's just not a surprise to me that he left. He told me at that Labor Day barbeque that he and Elle were on the rocks and he wasn't sure how long it was going to last." Emma interjected to ask Justin to take her to the swing. Grace stayed back at the table pushing leftover wasabi and soy sauce around with her chopsticks. She was bothered that Justin had seen it coming and didn't say anything. She was bothered that she had missed what apparently was plainly obvious to him. Most of all, she felt discouraged by the fact that people would just give up on their marriage and seek a replacement life in one foul stroke, when the going got tough. Uncivilised relationship endings never sat well with Grace, and her heart broke for their kids. It was as though Joe had violated the decorum of marriage-ending decency with disregard. Grace's mood improved as she watched Justin and Emma laughing with glee, as her feet flew in the air. The sun began to set, and the damp coastal evening chill began to encroach upon their fun. "Five minutes and let's pack up, it's getting cold!" Justin and Grace walked along the uneven sidewalk taking in the evening air. Emma ran a little ahead. They held hands walking as the daylight faded, and as their sight ahead dimmed, the sound of twigs and stray pebbles crunching under their steps was all Grace could hear.

# Chapter 4
# Rocks and Sticks

The early mornings were always challenging for Grace to get up. She had to set her alarm for 5:30 AM to prepare lunches, the daycare bag and render herself presentable for the day. She was thankful to have scrubs simplify her wardrobe decisions. They were comfortable and easy to throw on. It was still dark when she left the house. Peering in at Emma still sleeping before she stole away before the sun came up. Justin would bring her to the daycare after waking up a little later. Grace felt like one of the few people leaving their homes these days to venture out into the still dark morning. It was pitch black when she had to leave the house and step out into what appeared to still be night.

The hum of frogs could be heard droning on from a nearby gully, and the night's fog was still set in. Although, a slight hint of sun could be made out from the yellow shining through thinned mist layers from time to time on the horizon. It was not enough to convince her it was morning. Traffic gathered on the freeway in clusters, slowing with distorting glare from the red taillights ahead. Grace had the heat running and listened intently to the radio news report. All news revolved around the Coronavirus, and the numbers that were climbing. Grace could have guessed they were climbing from the fact that each week the number of patients in her ICU increased. The patients would die quickly, or stay on the ventilator for a long time, their bodies debilitating by the day.

Grace donned her blue isolation gown and gloves, in addition to N95 and face shield, as she prepared to enter her patient's room. It felt so futile most days. A COVID patient's survival felt hard won in these conditions. The novelty of getting through her shift without some major complications began to be what she classified as success, as she went about the busy, messy work of keeping her patients alive. Most days it took everything in her to maintain motivation to keep going and showing up for her patients with laser sharp focus. There was yet, something entirely more evasive about the Coronavirus. The lack of efficacious clinical tools to tackle it meant it could move quickly, unabated, often leaving the medical team feeling flummoxed, and at times at the mercy of its whim, with the wide array of complications it inflicted upon the patients.

Managing patients with respiratory failure was a fragile task. The close clinical monitoring and the equipment all had to come together quickly to ensure a patient's lungs were supported at the level they needed, and those needs fluctuated. The fear of ventilators running in short supply cast an ominous feeling within the ICU, as each patient came in gasping. When a ventilator freed up because a patient expired or in some cases extubated successfully, then a slight relief was felt because there would be one more ventilator available. Grace worried that the generosity would leave them high and dry with ventilator supply soon. Dr Hendrickson, the chief pulmonologist, had led the morning's rounds and as he opened, he stated plainly and with little feeling that the Coronavirus was winning. The fact of the matter is that it had stumped the medical community, such that therapeutics and vaccinations were beginning to be trialled but were likely not going to be available for many months. He stood at the front of the team in the dictation room, without a hint of deception, as he posed the concept that the greatest and ultimately only line of defence the medical team had at hand to treat these Coronavirus patients was oxygen.

"We have nothing but oxygen to treat these critically ill patients. If cardiac arrest or organ failure comes up, then we treat that, but we are primarily in supportive care mode here with COVID. It's as though we are fighting a war against heavy artillery with rocks and sticks at this point," Dr Hendrickson went on. "So, we just have to do the best we can with that."

The team began to move around a little, some whispering to their neighbour, others chuckling at the irony of the seemingly insurmountable reality. Grace pictured herself throwing sticks and rocks as hard as she could. Oxygen ran through nasal cannulas, masks, BiPAPs, High Flow nasal cannulas, Ventilators and the like. Their indication would be monitored closely by respiratory therapists by whom the delivery of oxygen was provisioned primarily in the ICU setting. Grace's heart sank at the thought of many months until therapeutics and vaccinations would be part of the arsenal to fight this very terrible disease. She looked around the dictation room. Staff with trained gazes followed the attending physician intently and reported out their impressions succinctly. It felt routine and it felt surreal all at once. Grace felt like the ability to treat this novel disease had pushed the medical community back in time. *Rocks and sticks.* She had read a few reports ensuring scientists all over the world were scrambling to turn current technology, much of which had been decades in the making, or was to be repurposed, into tools for them to use in the trenches. But for now, their hands were essentially bare as they entered this fight. No vaccines and no therapeutic treatment proven to work.

Grace, who over the course of her relatively short career, had seen the medical community make strides in securing its advanced pharmaceutical technology as a means to answering most medical conundrums in one way or another. But to be in the year 2020 and to be told the best global healthcare strategy would be essentially supportive care such as oxygen delivery to address this virus until vaccines and pharmaceuticals could be invented was shocking to her, and ultimately humbling to think of how nature had once again one-upped humanity.

Grace shifted in her seat. She felt uneasy as she reflected on the task at hand. She looked around at her colleagues. Tired eyes behind colourful scrub caps, and pail blue isolation masks with flimsy face shields crowning their foreheads. Here for the long haul. *All of these people have loved one's at home too.* She had the sensation of being strapped into a rollercoaster, on a ride she didn't intend to be on, and desperately wanted to get off. *There's no way out but through it.* Grace paused at the enormity of what was supposed to be just another normal ICU Grand Rounds in the dictation room. This time, a global crisis was raining upon them, and they were incomprehensibly without umbrellas. They would be drenched and likely wading in this rain expected to bring forth flooding waters as this virus would peak. The key would be to tread water for as long as possible, until rescue came.

Grace's mother stood in the hallway. The light that was cast from the slim window panels surrounding the door, created her silhouette. She stood with her figure covered in a brown wool coat. Her dark blue dress peeked out from the bottom. "Come along, my dear," she said, with a haste that Grace knew well. They stepped out the front door into a frigid January morning. Living near Todos Santos Square, they enjoyed sidewalks, where much of Concord's unincorporated area did not. Lottie was in her stroller, holding tightly to a small stuffed rabbit, one of the church people had given her.

Mumma, Grace, and Lottie walked along the sidewalk. The crooked and bare branches of trees that lined the street appeared in stark contrast to the bright yet overcast sky behind. The wind possessed an icy punch as it blew her mumma's dress in bursts and reddened their cheeks thick. Grace looked down as she walked, measuring how many steps it took for her to reach the next crack in the cement, demarcating one section from another. Grace hopped and skipped when she reached a crack, so as not to step directly on it, as though the cement slabs were in fact lily pads.

"Stop Grace!" Mumma yelled, as she grabbed the back of Grace's coat, pulling her backwards and off balance. Grace had begun to hop out into the street with oncoming traffic without so much as looking up to notice the threat. Grace was shocked by the stern tone of her mother and began to cry, burying her face in her hands, and her head into her mother's skirt. "Grace, you need to pay attention. Always pay attention to what's going on around you."

They walked further along the way until they reached the square. Mumma reached inside her pocket and took out a lot of coins. "Why don't you take your sister into the ice-cream store and get a scoop each. I'm going to go to the bank and purchase some stamps." Grace was excited to have an ice cream treat, and eagerly walked hand in hand with her little sister into the store. The inside was filled with brightly wrapped candies, in jars, and on racks lining the entire store. The two, side-tracked from their mission immediately, spent time marvelling at the gummy candies shaped as pizza's and the crystal rock lollipops.

They debated whether Mumma would notice if they bought themselves some Gobstoppers instead of the ice creams. The rationale being that Gob stopper candies would outlast the pleasure of an ice cream. Grace decided against it ultimately, knowing they needed to use the money as was intended and agreed to. Grace could barely see over the counter, short for her age at eight years old, trying to peer into the brightly lit cases, large cylinders filled with brightly coloured sorbets and ice creams. "Strawberry please, Grace," Lottie said, brimming with excitement.

Grace gathered the coins that had spread in her pockets, digging her fingers into the corners to retrieve all of them. "May I have one vanilla and one strawberry scoop please?" The woman working behind the case, emoted little and seemed to care less that Grace was on an errand with her little sister all alone. She eyed Grace closely as she placed each coin up on the counter, counting out the grocery change coins down to three dollars and seventy cents owed. The lady gave an approving nod once all coins had been accounted for, reaching the price of the purchase, as she swept them away with her hands. Grace stood on her tippy toes to take the ice-cream from the holders they had been placed on until paid for in full.

"Thank you," she said cheerily, taking the vanilla ice cream cone in one hand, passing Lottie her strawberry cone. "Okay, let's go find Mumma."

They stepped out from the bright lights of Lunardi's ice creamery, and into the natural light of the gloomy day. The bank was across the square, they stood for a while, glancing across to the double doors as they ate their ice-creams. Nearly 15-minutes had passed on the old clock in the town's centre square. Mumma had not emerged as expected. Grace panned across the grassy square looking for her mother's brown coat and blue dress. People walked by glancing over at the two little girls with ice creams standing outside the storefront. No one stopped to inquire about where their mother was.

They stood there a while licking their ice creams slowly, as if to postpone admitting that their mother was absent. If they stood there eating the ice creams, as she had asked them to while waiting for her return, then she would be soon after, as planned. Once the ice creams were eaten, Grace took Lottie's sticky hand in hers and crossed the street to follow the path that dissected the square over to the bank. They entered the bank. The air was dense and smelled like heavy air conditioning and paper. Grace looked down the long line of the stainless-steel poles with thick dark red cord strung between, and attached with hooks, to cordon off walkways for customers. In numerous arched windows lining the large room, tellers peered from behind with bleak faces. They engaged purposefully with no rush in the tedium of counting money and stamping, shuffling, and handing off papers.

Mumma was nowhere in this place. Grace looked around and saw a security guard sitting by the door. He looked her up and down with an inquiring expression. "Have you seen our mother? She was wearing a brown coat and a blue dress." The security guard, who didn't appear to be the most observant fellow, shook his head. Grace, puzzled and now a little alarmed, thanked the security guard and stepped out of the thoroughly air-conditioned bank into the cold fresh air.

"Where's Mumma?" Lottie asked, becoming a little tearful.

"I'm not sure, Lottie, she's got to be around here somewhere." The joy of getting an ice cream all by themselves was quickly wearing away with the sobering thought that they had lost their mother. It had been 45 minutes now since they had seen her. Grace thought to look for a pay phone, and maybe call

Daddy's shop. She had memorised it from the business card stuck to the front of their refrigerator. Grace realised she had only a few pennies left over when she put her hand into her pocket, hoping to retrieve enough to make a call.

Grace brought Lottie to the square's centre to play on the playground, while she continued to scan the edges of the square, looking for that brown coat. Grace's heart was racing. She felt uneasy and worried more and more as the old clock hands knocked along the bright white face's contour. She wondered if she had forgotten about them. She had felt like this may be entirely possible lately, as their mother would move through the day with a distracted and strained look upon her face. Forgetting to smile when they showed her a drawing they had created or asked her to watch them perform a puppet show.

Grace put on a bright and cheery voice to encourage Lottie, as she took the plunge down the big slide, betraying her true feelings. She was terrified and at the age of eight had no idea what to do. An hour passed on the clock, as a virtuous reminder of what had gone wrong in the situation. *She left us.* Grace wanted to cry but knew this wasn't going to do anything but draw attention to her and Lottie, and they did not need some stranger coming up to them. Not until it was on their own terms.

Two hours passed, and the two sat under a tree in the middle of the square wiping their eyes with their wrists. Their sleeves became wet and darkened. "It's okay, Lottie. We will be okay. She is coming back," Grace tried to assure her sister, through her own tears. The confidence she showed her little sister betrayed the sinking feeling she felt all the way down to her toes.

Their neighbour, Mrs Dooley, from down the street had been walking her dog in the square and noticed the two forlorn looking children under the tree.

"Girls! Is that you, Grace? Lottie?" She called out. They looked up. Glad to see a familiar face, finally. "Where is your mother?"

"I don't know," Grace replied tearfully. "Where did you last see her, girls?" Her face was stern now, panning around the square in hopes she would spot her neighbour.

"She sent us to Lunardi's to get ice-cream and…and…she never came back from the bank." Grace pointed over to the bank with tears streaming down her cheeks. She wanted to believe that her mother's good intentions had been thwarted but a force out of her control. Yet, deep down she wondered if Mumma had just chosen to leave.

Mrs Dooley stood by them for a time looking all around the square. After a long pause, she decided to take action. "Come now, let's take you home. I'll ring your daddy's shop to let him know I've found you. Your mother might have gone home thinking you had headed back." Mrs Dooley entered quarters into the pay phone at the edge of the square to call the auto shop where her husband also worked.

Grace and Lottie stood nearby, watching cars pause at the stop signs and move through, occasionally waiting for a pedestrian to saunter across. Grace's heart sank at the thought of her daddy finding out Mumma had left them at the square. "Maybe she thought you girls had headed home," Mrs Dooley said with a shallow yet optimistic tone. It was the only proper explanation to be rendered. They walked along the sidewalks leading to their home, not far away. Grace was not inclined to hop and skip along as she did when coming to town.

The screen door was locked and Mumma came to the door, sure enough. The door creaked open before Grace and Lottie, standing nervously by. Mumma looked as though she was wiping some flour on her apron. A call to the door disrupting her baking. She peered through the screen first and then welcomed Mrs Dooley and the girls. It perplexed Grace, who stood silently as she noted her mother's expression was surprised but unaccountable, as Mrs Dooley explained she had found Lottie and Grace huddled under a tree.

"Oh, thank you, Mrs Dooley, these two must have run off and got lost. I'm so glad you found them." Mrs Dooley didn't press Mumma on the timeline but stated that the girls had said they were in town with her and couldn't find her after they had been left to get ice cream. Mumma appeared to ignore the details of this account. "Oh you know how it is, they know where the coin jar is and the next thing you know they are running off to buy some taffy. Too young to know how to get back again, I suppose."

"Yes. Yes, I guess that must have been the case." Mrs Dooley obliged, looking the girls over once more in case they would offer a differing testimony to the events of the day. Grace and Lottie stood still, now behind the screen silently, with their eyes to the floor. She felt misgivings course through her body as she stood silently, not daring to challenge this new narrative her mother had seemingly conjured.

"Now thank Mrs Dooley for helping you home," Mumma said, turning haste to the closure of the visit.

"Thank you, Mrs Dooley," they chimed with dull affect.

"And please promise, young ladies, that you will not run off to town again, will you?"

Grace knew very well that neither she nor her little sister had run off anywhere. Mumma turned around after cheerfully wishing Mrs Dooley a pleasant rest of her day and thanking her again for her trouble.

A dark look passed over Mumma as she sneered. "Now you listen to me. You were never left anywhere. I was right there waiting for you outside of Lunardi's and you sneaky children ran off." Grace detected the manipulation in her mother's words but didn't know what else to do but to try to believe this version of what happened. Her mother's logic had always been what she held to; it would be a betrayal to deny it now. "I don't want you to say another word about this to anyone, or you will wish you had never done so." Mumma brought her face close to Lottie's who stood there shaking in the face of this reprisal. "Do you understand?"

Both Grace and Lottie immediately nodded their heads and betrayed their own sense of justice to agree to these terms. For the rest of the day, the girls played quietly in their playroom, listening to Mumma in the kitchen baking some pies. Grace was bothered thinking about how her mother had not been truthful with Mrs Dooley and with them about what happened. It frightened her to see the callous side of her mother's nature in the aftermath. Grace felt even worse that she had stood by and let the lie take place, not voicing her account of what had happened for fear of reprisal, and the desire to protect the only parent she had to rely on.

Grace sat at the kitchen table doing her math homework while Lottie coloured in her Care Bears colouring book vigorously. Mumma lent over the stove stirring macaroni and cheese, while humming a lilting tune. Grace thought it misplaced that Mumma would be in a fine mood after what had occurred that day. Yet, she sat quietly focusing on her geometry, writing, and erasing over and over as her mind darted back to the square and the helplessness she felt being left there. The unsettling feeling of being forgotten lingered.

"Barbara, why in God's name did Mark Dooley receive a call from Jackie to say she had our kids at Todos Santos Square?" Daddy said, appearing from the doorway.

Mumma looked startled at first by his quiet arrival. A mortified look flashed across her face. "I-I don't know. It was a misunderstanding. The girls ran off with coins from the penny jar to the square and then they got too lost to find their way back, and Jackie rescued them and brought them back home." The girls by now had stopped writing and drawing. They stared down at the table, holding blank expressions with hopes that they could withstand the storm clouds passing over. Become invisible.

Daddy looked Mumma up and down with a distasteful expression then grabbed a nearby water glass, and with one strong pitcher's arm threw it at the kitchen table. "You little dishonest bitches!" He screamed as the cup hit the edge of the table with shards of glass scattered on the floor. Both girls jumped in their seats. Lottie screamed and cried hysterically while Mumma reached for her forbidding her to get off her chair, for fear she might step on glass.

"Daddy is scaring me!" She cried.

Daddy was not finished and ignored any cues to end his pursuit. Daddy wiped his now red face with his handkerchief and bent down four inches from Grace's face. She stared straight ahead, biting her tongue to defer the need to cry. His hot breath smelled like whiskey, now only 30 minutes after the shop closed. "Look at me, girl!" Daddy grabbed her chin and yanked it towards him. "Do you mean to tell me you took my hard-earned money from that penny jar and went and bought yourselves some candy without your mother knowing?"

Grace felt so conflicted. She knew that if she were to speak the truth much worse than a shattered glass would befall her mother. On the other hand, she knew Daddy's distaste for liars would send him deeper into his rage. Grace searched his eyes now dark with rage for a glimmer of empathy. She found none. At this crossroad, she didn't know what to do. Words failed her, as the intense feeling of fear paralysed her. He waited some drawn out seconds, breathing heavily near her face. Looking sternly at her. Ready to snap in whatever direction he was pointed next. He suddenly banged his fist by her right hand causing her to drop the pencil she was gripping to stop her trembling. "You are little good for nothing liar." Her silence was as good as a confession to him. "Get out of my sight. Barbara, put them to bed without dinner."

He stormed out of the kitchen and slammed the front door. Mumma sprang into action sweeping the shards of glass into a dustpan before quickly disposing of them and gathering the girls swiftly to head to the bathroom to brush teeth and go straight to bed. She said nothing, as they went about the night time routine, hours early and filled with nothing but the panging of empty stomachs. There was nothing more to say other than an apology and a retraction of falsified statements. Her mother was not, at this very moment, capable of summing up the fortitude for either.

Grace lay awake for most the night, trying to think through what was real and what was not. Why had Mumma said they ran off? Why hadn't she set the record straight when Daddy had come home, if not to keep up appearances with Mrs Dooley. Flashes of resent and even contempt swirled within her as she thought about how little the truth mattered to Mumma. How in fact Mumma had sought to cover up her negligence at the square even to the extent that she had let Daddy's rage be directed to her own children in her stead. Grace had never seen Mumma be so willing to save herself at her children's expense. This expansion of Mumma's character and capability to disown truth and the will to protect her children frightened Grace. Grace knew that she hated the lying but did not know what to do with the deep chasm of betrayal she now felt.

Justin lay on the couch, his head on a pillow against the armrest with his laptop leaning against his bent knees and his house slippers on the seat of the couch. Grace thoroughly disliked Justin's habit of putting his shoes on the light grey couch and somehow even more so today, seeing him still in his pyjamas working. The school district had sent students home and teachers now created some materials to send home and remained available for calls from parents and did some training and meetings online. Justin's schedule had become quiet and self-initiated.

Weeks into an extended lockdown now, and the days had begun to run into another. COVID numbers were growing in the hospital. Every day was similar and yet felt so surreal. The memory of normalcy—to smile at colleagues in the hall or hold staff potlucks was beginning to fade. The patients continued to arrive as their respiratory systems decompensated further and further in front of healthcare workers rushing to stabilise them. Long oxygen tubing with multiple extensions hooked up in emergency rooms at the outlets and reached out into the hall, when there were shortages in oxygen tanks for patients lining the halls, awaiting a bed. The entire half of the emergency department had become a COVID unit in which all patients were either being tested for or confirmed COVID positive. Staff wore their full PPE for hours without breathing fresh air as they attended to the human devastation at their doorstep, the best way they knew how.

On her break, Grace texted Jake: "How's it going?" She watched her screen for the texting dots to appear by his name. No reply. It unnerved Grace when she didn't get a speedy reply from him. She would start to think about the possibilities of him being stuck somewhere, or ill, or worse very quickly. The news showed New York at a standstill. Temporary morgues, as large freezers, were purchased and stationed outside of hospitals to house the overflow of bodies from the indoor hospital morgues, as people continued to die.

A text came through. "Hey Grace, I caught COVID, I think my mask stopped sealing properly after the fifth day wearing it. We are so short on PPE over here. I'm doing okay though. Just congestion, body aches and a sore throat. They sent me home to quarantine." Grace was relieved to a degree. Another text came through. "That doctor I told you about who got COVID, died last Thursday."

Her relief cut short; Grace stared at the screen. It was hard not to personalise this doctor's fate. A healthcare worker, working the crisis day in day out, likely with a family at home that loved him, depended on him. Just like her, but now dead. Tears began to form in the creases of her eyes, salty, mixing with the dried sweat that had made her skin feel tight while working hard for hours under layers of PPE. "I'm so sorry to hear this news. It looks like a war zone over there." She wanted to tell him something comforting, like that there were some signs of hope on the horizon beyond this crisis that she was certain of. She knew that if she said her thoughts and prayers were with him, that second part would be a lie. She hadn't prayed ever in her adult life. She didn't know what to say other than, "This sucks." The text exchange fell silent, and Grace returned to work.

***

Grace closed her eyes tight as she knelt at her bedside in their shared room reciting The Lord's Prayer in chorus with Lottie. The polyester comforter felt scratchy on her skin, a light draft at her knees. "Our Father who art in heaven, hallowed be thy name. Thy kingdom come thy will be done on earth as it is in heaven." Grace's mother stood by the door peering in. Daddy had gone outside with his pipe. The tobacco wafted through the screens into the house. Mumma waited until the prayer was over. She tucked the girls into their beds, kissing their foreheads each. Mumma smelt like vanilla and coffee beans. She looked radiant in the glow of their lamp. Her silhouette gracefully left the room, the light of their giraffe nightlight guiding her step between dolls, teddies, and plastic teacups.

Mumma sat in the living room, finishing up some needlework on the dress she was making for Grace. All was calm. All was quiet. It was on these nights that Grace would feel the presence of this God she had learned to pray to. Her mother had always said, "We must be still so we can hear God." As the most ardent church goer of their home, Grace's mother had always spoken with authority on matters concerning God, and what people should and should not do if they wanted to hear from him. She prayed with all her might that her daddy would stop hurting her Mumma and they could have quiet nights like this, *every* night. Grace believed the thing about stillness. She pondered the quieting of one's mind to let that little voice that whispered wisdom become heard.

She lay there focusing her mind on waiting to hear God. She could hear the rain hitting the metal drains and running off the house. "To sit still was to cease action. Action that busied hearts and minds and was often apart from God's intentions," Grace could hear her Mumma say. Grace often thought it was Mumma's way of getting her and Lottie to stop squirming in their seats during homework or dinner time, but as she lay there, looking through the windows distorted by bands of rain running down, she realised this advice could be more broadly applied.

She lay in silence some time longer until the quiet of night led her into a deep sleep.

# Chapter 5
# Montara

Justin grabbed his surfboard early in the morning and loaded it on top of his car. Heading to Montara State Beach, a few miles south of Pacifica, was one of his favourite things to do. He had not grown-up surfing, but during his twenties had learned to surf while backpacking in Portugal, and was immediately hooked. The Pacific water was frigid, but nothing a thick wetsuit could not compensate for. Justin left Grace and Emma, both sleeping in their large king bed with a note on the nightstand. *Headed to Montara. Be back around Noon.*

Justin liked the thought of waking up to notes left, instead of sending texts. He headed across the Bay Bridge, the fog was still covering San Francisco, and visibility was near a quarter mile ahead. These grey foggy days felt very fitting for the austerity of the pandemic. The California State Beaches had been closed or had limited availability for people to use for exercise only. He wasn't sure if surfing was what the state had in mind for exercise, but decided he would claim it all the same.

It was 7:30 AM when he reached the Montara State Beach parking lot. The fog was beginning to roll back over the ocean but kept its grip like wispy fingers gripping the cliff faces. Colourful wildflowers lined the top of the sandstone cliffs leading to the beach. An enthusiastic palette of colour and texture against the gloomy sky. A few surfers were already out catching the early morning swell and Justin felt eager to join them. He was glad to see they were there first, given all the lock-down restrictions. Only one other person in the distance could be seen walking along the sand.

Justin ambled through a narrow path at the bottom of the crevice between two large cliffs. Moisture leaked out of the sandstone at different points and had created a claggy floor to the path. It was slippery on the uneven trail, and he almost lost his balance and his surfboard, as he took a misstep on a slippery rise.

The coarse grains of sand were a welcome and relatively steadier surface, as he made it down to the beach. He ran towards the waves, taking a deep breath before he launched his body with his board over a rising wall of water about to break into a white furry. The cold water panged against his bare face, it stung like fire and ice at once. His wetsuit kept him at a sufficient temperature to carry on, but that first harsh bite of cold water that rushed past him lingered a while.

Four rows of waves were breaking today, and it took a little while and much effort to get past the first sets to find a steady patch of water past the breaks. The grey water shifted and murmured as it drew upwards and unravelled towards the broad band of sand that lay beneath the cliffs. The sun was pushing through thinning parts of the fog that was now moving quickly back out and rolling in, coming and going as it pleased. The other surfers nearby acknowledged him with a wave, but all were silent, determined to catch their perfect wave. Justin floated a while, focusing on his breath. His mind was truly free to roam in these moments, drifting between water and sky. He thought about home. He saw Emma in her highchair, laughing. He loved that little girl dearly.

As he floated over the swell, he felt gladness for the fact that Emma didn't know what was going on in the world. It was a gentle mercy he thought to be able to be oblivious to the unhinging of things. This pandemic had changed the lives of so many of his students and families. Many parents of the children at his school worked in service industries like restaurants that had had to close their doors and lay off workers. The stability of the community he served was being upended and destabilised. There had been years of smoke, as wildfires ravaged California, shutting down many Bay Area schools in the spring of the prior year. *This level of uncertainty and inconsistency had to have affected so many children.* He thought, as the faces of his students and what he knew about their lives through the weekend writing or stories they shared with the classes, drifted through his mind.

Now, this pandemic situation made wildfires seem only like an opening act to an even greater force of uncertainty carving out new stories of loss and change for children everywhere. This time though, he felt distant from the kids and saddened that he would not be able to hear how this whole thing was affecting them. And had no way to intervene in their lives in the way he had before. It saddened him to think of how some of his children may be fairing in their home lives, where food insecurity or even drugs and alcohol and poor role models would be potentially enhanced under the duress of new economic and relational pressures posed by the pandemic. He felt glad to know that Emma was so young, she might not remember the masked faces in public or the obsessive use of hand sanitiser, once she picked up some chalk left on the sidewalk, or his quick redirection away from other children she wandered towards smiling and greeting.

The blue sky was revealed, clear and steely as the swiftly moving fog now had made a bank far out to sea. It was hard for Justin to truly free his mind of the thought that he was in many ways trapped in his life. With COVID restrictions, he felt even further bound to the mundane. He had always been a thrill seeker, on the move, enticed by the exotic, the different, the new. It had been weeks now, since he had stepped foot into a restaurant, spent time with friends and family, or really done anything much outside of his house.

All the travel plans of the summer were going to fall apart on account of the pandemic. Countries around the world were restricting their borders. Everything felt like it was closing in. These few precious hours he spent out on the ocean in silence with complete strangers, was the closest he could get to feeling normal. Justin disliked how he could feel dissatisfied with what he knew to be on paper a wonderful life. He would feel his gratitude for his home, his job, his beautiful Emma being replaced with a desire to leave it all behind and break free into the wondrous wide-open world of his youth.

There, he fantasised that he would get a job as a travel writer, as he had initially aspired to be before he met Grace, and before she convinced him that a more practical and stable life would be attained if he got his teaching credential. The deepest secret he withheld was the resentment he felt towards his child for taking up so much of Grace's time, affection and attention. He sat with those raw truths, feeling both longing and shame for what he was contemplating, as the water swirled around him. He didn't want to sit with those uncomfortable realities for very long as they made him feel uneasy and ashamed, so he paddled as hard as he could to the ridge of a building wave. He caught it, and skilfully rode down its surface, skimming the dark water at a great speed. *If only the truth could be escaped with motion.* He slipped down off his board as the wave ran its course, unravelling into rushing white water just behind another wave. He held onto his board as the next wave battered him, pushing his head under water as he held his breath within the churning rush. The harshness of the water felt deserved, as he pondered how his thoughts had seemingly unravelled. *I must stay the course.* He told himself as his mind sought to think about the things that he did not have the courage to voice out loud, perhaps, as it would mean he would be admitting that they were his true feelings.

Within the hour, Justin had made his way back to the beach and up to the path along the moist gritty sand. He decidedly left the water thinking that those divergent thoughts he had had would be left there in the open water. He struggled to get out of his wetsuit behind the door of his car. The day trippers would be arriving soon normally, but fortunately no one was pulling in. Grace had texted, "Got your note. Have fun out there." Justin couldn't help but feel like turning back home now meant that the 'fun' that seemingly was mainly 'out there' would be sucked back, just like a wave that has broken and fanned out across the sand, then pulls back the water to reap its returns.

Justin could not help but entertain that feeling he had felt out on the water. He indulged the idea that he in fact would have chosen something different if he had a chance to do his life over. The question he now had was, what could he do about it. He stopped at a coffee shop further south in Half Moon Bay. With an Americano in hand, burning through the flimsy cardboard cup sleeve, he walked back to his car, sat it in the console to cool, and left for home.

"How was surfing?" Grace asked, looking up at Justin as he entered the room. She had cut up some boiled eggs and given Emma some buttered bread and chopped strawberries.

"It was great. I caught some waves. The fog came and went. Overall a nice time."

Grace appeared pleased with his response. "Well, I'm glad you got a chance to spend time out there." She appeared to acknowledge the fact that he had been cooped up at home for weeks and this surfing was a welcome outlet. "Maybe Emma and I can come with you some morning to watch. We can bundle up and pitch a beach tent." Grace seemed excited about the thought.

"Sure, but I don't think the state is allowing people to just sit at the beach right now. There was no one setting up on the beach today. Only walkers, joggers and surfers. It has to be used for exercise only. I'm going to hit the shower, then let's think about where we might like to go today." He smiled with an ironic smile that Grace caught, both knowing they couldn't go on an outing as they typically would have to San Francisco Zoo, Marin Headlands or Tilden Park.

"Sure, I thought we could maybe alphabetise the bookshelf." Justin and Grace both laughed. "Already done, my dear," Justin called back, as he strode down the hall.

They spent the day in the house and then planted some strawberries from an old packet of seeds Grace found in the garage in the raised planter boxes in the backyard. Emma wandered around in her rain boots with a plastic trowel, digging, and tossing dirt to new and often unwanted locations in the garden. Both Justin and Grace discussed the home improvements they thought they should make as they spent time in the yard. "A pergola with some ivy over the back patio would look great, and help with shade," Grace said, imagining it as she looked at the bare back of the house.

During the weeks of shelter in place, Grace and Justin had reconstructed their indoor and outdoor living spaces over and over. They wished for more space than their 1500 sq. foot house could offer, but landed on the idea that a transformation would be far more reasonable of a prospect than buying a completely different home. As the afternoon drew on, the family of three basked in the afternoon light that illuminated the petals and leaves of the giant sunflowers that lined their vegetable garden. Grace poured some lemonade and they enjoyed their little plot of paradise, ensconced and hidden from the world outside.

Grace loved these lazy afternoons at home with her family. There was nothing in life she enjoyed more than watching Emma feel happy spending time with Justin and herself. Grace looked over at Justin, appreciating his calm responses to Emma's countless questions and generally nonsensical tangents. She smiled and lay back in a deck chair closing her eyes to bask in the afternoon sunlight and absorb the sounds of her family in the garden.

The shadows grew long across the yard, and it was time to make dinner. Grace offered to cook something up and sauntered into the kitchen to pull some salad fixings out and chicken nuggets from the freezer. Her cooking repertoire was limited these days, and she knew Emma would not protest nuggets for dinner. Justin was busy amusing Emma by making shadow puppets with his hands against the shed wall. After dinner, Justin wiped down the table and kitchen, and loaded the dishwasher, while Grace put Emma down for bed after a quick bath. Afterwards, Grace and Justin sat in the living room on their deep-seated couch watching TV. It was their nightly ritual to share a blanket and binge a drama series for multiple episodes until one or both dozed off.

"You know, Grace, I'm really thankful for our day together," Justin said with sincerity, after pausing the show.

"Me too, Justin. It's so nice not to have anywhere to go and time to just be home."

"Yeah. I agree. Being with you two really makes me realise what's important in all of this. It's you, it's Emma, it's our family." His words hung in the air, as he recognised the duplicity of what he was saying and how he had been feeling about things out on the water earlier that day.

Grace turned to him with a smile and nodded. "Maybe something good coming out of all of this is that we are forced to slow down. Face ourselves a bit more, and spend time just being together." *Face ourselves,* griped Justin, as he pondered quietly how he really would rather not have to face himself. He felt conflicted about what he saw when he did. On one hand, he enjoyed indulging in the notion that the doors to a different future were still open and that he was being true to himself to admit how he felt about his life choices and wants. On the other hand, it felt like a betrayal to his current reality and what he was meant to value most if he spent time longing for something other than the path he was on. He would much rather live detached from the thoughts that drove him to face how he truly felt, and what that would mean, if he were to act upon it. In that unfeeling place, he could live with a passivity that ensured his tolerance of the status quo.

The next morning, Grace loaded Emma into the car to deliver her to daycare before she made her way into work. As Grace drove through the still dark morning, she felt fortunate to have a daycare that did 6:30 AM drop off, but at the same time knew it felt forced every time to leave the comfort of their warm home to brave the morning before the sun had properly risen. Emma sat in her car seat half asleep. Closing her eyes frequently to capture some more sleep as they drove the backstreets of Concord.

The ICU was buzzing at 7 AM. The day shift nurses were ready to spring into action with morning activities and medication administration. The night shift nurses, looking far less kempt than when they arrived the night before, fought back the urge to yawn as they gave reports to the oncoming nurses, and then mustered enough energy to make it home to sleep. Two new COVID-19 admits had been brought in from the Emergency Department during the night. One of those patients, Elsie Grady, was assigned to Grace. Grace came in to introduce herself to the 62-year-old retired elementary school teacher.

"Pleased to meet you," Elsie said to Grace. She put her hand out to touch Grace's gloved hand. Grace reached out to reciprocate her welcome. The night shift nurse told Elsie that she was in good hands with Grace and should let her know if she needed anything at all.

"'Grace'—that's such a beautiful name. My daughter's middle name is Grace. She's an accountant in Moraga and has three boys."

Grace could tell that Elsie enjoyed talking with people and was persistent in her intent to do so even though she was struggling to breathe. "Thank you, it's my mother's middle name," Grace said, hanging a new bag of saline.

"Well, to show grace and to show mercy are the best things one can do in this world," Elsie replied.

Grace appreciated that thought. She remembered how her mother would speak about the grace and mercy. As though they were two dear friends that should be invited to every situation, no matter how hard. "Would you mind bringing me some water?" Elsie requested. "My throat is so dry."

Grace knew that Elsie's oxygen requirement on high flow had caused the speech pathologist to recommend nothing by mouth for the time being. "I'm sorry, Elsie, right now your breathing makes it too dangerous to give you anything by mouth. That's why we had to put this nasogastric tube in your nose. That's how you have to eat right now."

Elsie sighed. "You don't realise how much you take eating and drinking whenever you want for granted until it's gone."

"I know. I'm sorry, this is hopefully only for a short while," Grace replied, taking Elsie's hand with her gloved hand. It felt cruel to disallow Elsie to have anything, especially when she was suffering so much. Grace made a split-second decision to bring Elsie a few ice-chips in a cup. She brushed her teeth and suctioned out the debris, then fed her four ice-chips. She watched Elsie savour each cold ice-chip in her mouth. Rocking it back and forth and around until it melted down and she swallowed it with increasing effort to coordinate the trigger of her swallow. "Thank you so much Grace." Elsie appeared truly grateful to be given even the little amount of satiation. "These ice-chips are perhaps the best thing I've ever tasted." They both smiled.

Grace checked on Elsie regularly to ask if she needed anything. Elsie appeared content. She was breathing easily and watching the afternoon news for multiple hours, dozing off under the beautiful dark purple and emerald green crocheted blanket her family dropped off for her. Grace had met them in the courtyard upon special request. "Elsie made this blanket for us, we want her to have it now," her daughter had said tearily.

When Grace went in to pass some medications, Elsie beckoned her to come closer. "You know, Grace. I'm not afraid of dying."

Grace looked at her, surprised by her comment. "Listen Elsie, we are taking good care of you and each day your breathing has been getting better and better. I don't think it's time to talk about such things. Dr Ranford says that you're getting closer to not needing so much oxygen support and we are going to try to wean you back onto a nasal cannula."

Elsie appeared pleased with that. "In that case, when I get out of here, I'm going to cook a huge Thanksgiving meal for my family. I don't care if it's May and I do it. That's my favourite meal of the year."

"Wow Elsie, you're a cook, hey?"

"Well, I enjoy cooking very much and my husband and children have always enjoyed eating, so it's worked out well," Elsie replied with a wry smile.

"So what dishes are you going to prepare?" Grace inquired, interested to hear what sort of dishes Elsie would make.

"Oh, I'll have turkey, cornbread stuffing, gravy, green bean casserole with those fried onions on it, chunky cranberry sauce, yams with marshmallows, and homemade bread rolls with butter." Elsie savoured the meal she imagined as served piping hot on a beautifully decorated table with all her dear ones gathered around.

"I can see it," Grace said, almost smelling those flavours and feeling the warmth of that imagined gathering. "I bet your spread is like a regular Norman Rockwell Turkey Feast."

Elsie knew the reference and laughed. "Yes, *Free from Want* is pretty much what I aim for." It was nice to think about something warm and comforting in this time, as they spent their day under fluorescent lighting, with alarms triggering at intervals within her enclosed room. Sealed off from the world.

With no ability to escape the present, they both took pleasure in running away with their imaginations. While charting, Grace searched the internet and printed off a picture of Norman Rockwell's Turkey Feast and brought it in the next time she returned to Elsie's room. "Here," she said, taping it to the bottom of the care board right near the end of Elsie's bed. "This is to remind you of what you are working to get back to while you're here. Okay? It's not time to give up."

Elsie was touched by Grace's thoughtful gesture. "Thank you, Grace. I suppose I can use the time I have now to think about the dessert menu."

They both chuckled. "Well, I do hope you have something in a Jell-O mould in mind."

"I sure do. I make an excellent orange cream Jell-O. I'll bring some for you someday." Grace liked the fact that Elsie was focusing on future events. Grace had seen the power of hope for the future carry many patients through the hardest of times in the intensive care unit.

*** 

Grace played in the backyard on the swing set with Lottie. The clear fall air brushed past her as she flew back and forth on the creaky swing. Lottie tried to keep up, bending her knees and leaning back and forth as forcefully as she could. "I'm flying!" Grace exclaimed, as she reached the furthest point she thought would be possible before her swing would wrap around the frame of the structure. This was always a fear she had, ever since her mother had warned her about this possibility so she wouldn't go so high.

"Help me, Grace!" Lottie had cried out, begging Grace to slow down.

"Just a few more, okay, Lottie?" She called back, turning her head to look down at Lottie slumped on her swing, having given up on trying. Grace dismounted the swing shortly and began to push Lottie so she too could fly. Lottie giggled with glee, gripping the chains on either side of her tightly. The fear and the freedom of swinging was what they both loved. Grace wasn't sure what she liked more. To push her little sister on the swing, and see her laughing with delight, or to be flinging herself back and forth into the clear sky. The maple trees in the backyard had turned amber and brown with leaves that occasionally drifted to the ground. "Catch it!" Grace urged Lottie, who would release one of her tightly gripping hands from the swing chain to try to reach for a leaf.

"I got it! I caught it!" They cheered this success and aimed to catch more leaves as they were released from the branches above with stirring breezes that kicked up from time to time.

"Girls!" Daddy was calling from the back door. He had cleaned up from his work overalls, having gone in early morning to work, and now stood at the doorway with his hair combed, in a burgundy plaid shirt and khaki trousers. Grace and Lottie like seeing Daddy get dressed up. It meant he would be well behaved and usually that was because Grandma and Grandpa were coming to dinner. Thanksgiving was either a raucous event with the cousins or a quiet one on the alternating years when Uncle Andy, Dad's brother would be spending Thanksgiving in Wisconsin with Aunt Patty's side of the family. This was that alternating year. The girls knew it was time to come inside and wash their hands before dinner.

Grandma was helping Mumma set the table and Grandpa was in the living room with Dad watching TV. "There they are," Grandma said, turning to the girls for a hug. She smelled like peppermint and always wore red lipstick which invariably ended up smeared on each of their cheeks. "Grace, you are getting so tall and oh my so are you!" She exclaimed, taking in how they had grown over the past five months since she had seen them last. "I'm so happy to see you both."

Grandma asked them about school and their piano lessons. She had never asked them about how Daddy came home smelling of alcohol or how it felt in their bones when he yelled and screamed and threw things. She never seemed interested in the dark things that surrounded. Just the cheery warm and bright parts of life. Grace stood there thinking how miraculous it would be to never have to face bad things.

The girls sat at their places and Daddy led the prayer. "Dear Lord, thank you for this beautiful day, this time together, and this meal for which we are so grateful. Thank you, God, for blessing us so richly and taking care of us. May we love our neighbours as ourselves. Amen." Grace opened her eyes during the prayer, looking at her daddy earnestly praying. He stood there, a picture-perfect father, leading a thoughtful prayer over a bountiful meal, with his family all around. *If only this would be who he chose to be every day.* He looked to believe every word that he said, and Grandma and Grandpa believed too. Mumma, however, shifted her weight uneasily and pursed her lips as she closed her eyes, enduring his words, silently, much as she endured his rage.

As Grandpa began to carve the turkey, his large knife pierced the taught brown skin, like stretched leather, and steam rose. A delicious savoury smell wafted through the room. Dishes filled with sweet potatoes, mashed potatoes, green beans, gravy, cranberry sauce, and a basket for warm bread rolls were clustered around the table. As the dishes were passed around the table and served, Grace sat there contemplating how different things were when Grandma and Grandpa were around. How predictably calm the evening would be, with them there. There was comfort in this and a sinking feeling would then emerge when she thought about how every other night would be thereafter. Unpredictable and wild.

Mrs Elsie was on high flow oxygen with visible work of breathing. The respiratory therapist was keeping a close eye on the patient, as she was expected to tire out and may need to be intubated if she didn't turn around soon. An Arterial Blood Gas result was pending and the live monitor of oxygen saturation indicated she was trending downwards into the mid-90s over the past hour despite increasing high flow oxygen and FiO2 support. The patient moaned as she started pulling at her lines in confusion. Additionally, the latest lab values were beginning to show troublesome inflammatory organ function, and cardiac distress markers. These markers were emerging amongst the medical community as indicators for elevated risk for increased severity of illness.

Grace attended rounds with her team. During rounds, the ICU chief pulmonologist began talking about hypercytokinaemia also known as 'Cytokine Storms' that the team should be on the watch for with patients as when they hit the data was showing a high mortality rate being associated with patients' immune systems triggering a flood of cytokine release throughout the body with the propensity to kill organ tissue, and cause acute respiratory distress syndrome. Grace sat through rounds, concerned about her patient's increased lab values and apparent onset of confusion. As she returned from rounds, she looked in at Elsie. Her colouring had changed, she appeared oedematous and more confused, mumbling incoherently to herself. Through the glass, she could see her oxygen was now skirting at 90 to 89. Grace quickly donned her PPE. Gloves, gown, gloves, her N95 mask.

Grace kept calm as she called a rapid response. Her patient was clearly decompensating, as she appeared to be really struggling to breathe now. She wrapped the blood pressure cuff around her patient's upper right arm. It came in low at 87/52. Her temperature was 102.3. In a calm voice, she turned to her patient, while attempting to rearrange the tangled and taught lines around her bed. "Elsie my dear, your numbers are reading a little abnormally, we are going to have the team come in here very soon to help you."

As Grace looked up from what she was doing when she noticed, there was now no movement out of the corner of her eye. Elsie's eyes had dulled, her breath had stopped. Grace yelled, "Elsie! Wake up, Elsie." Tapping her shoulders forcefully and rubbing hard on her sternum. Grace felt for a pulse briefly but knew it was time to initiate a code, as Elsie was clearly unresponsive and the monitor caught up after a few moments' delay to show her heartbeat was declining into a flatline.

"Shit," Grace said under her breath. The Code Blue button was on the wall and behind the middle of the bed, beyond her reach. The various lines that led to the wall or other monitors were tangled and taught, making it hard to reach across or move the bed over without stretching cords or dislodging them. Not being able to reach the Code Blue button, and in the absence of seeing a better option in the moment, Grace ran to the front of the room and banged on the glass doors, "Call a Code Blue!" She yelled.

Fortunately, she caught the attention of the unit assistant, who was printing labels, and heard her muffled cry through the thick glass, and knew to call the code. Soon the overhead speaker announced, "Code Blue, ICU Room 320. Code Blue, ICU Room 320." Grace immediately adjusted the bed into cardiopulmonary resuscitation (CPR) position to begin delivering compressions and grabbed an Ambu bag nearby for the delivery of two breaths intermittently between chest compressions. Grace realised just moments before she launched into compressions that she didn't have the proper PPE on to perform CPR. Grace needed a Continuous Air Pressure Respiratory, as no goggles that she had tried fit over her glasses, to start with cardiopulmonary resuscitation, to avoid transmission of Coronavirus aerosols that could waft up out of the patient below and into her eyes.

Grace felt extremely conflicted about leaving her patient who was flatlining to go put on the PPE, as this in all her years of practice before had never needed to be a workflow step. She remembered her nurse educator emphasising, "Put your oxygen mask on first before you help someone else." In the split second while she teetered between the choice of going and staying, she saw Emma. The choice became clear. *I need to be safe.* As she quickly left the room and doffed her current PPE except her N95, she pictured the analogy of the flight attendant instructing all passengers to secure their own oxygen mask before they helped another person. The same timeline would apply here, as much as it felt counterintuitive to essentially abandon a coding patient to do so. Minutes were now being wasted in which oxygenation could not be delivered to this patient. The prognosis for a positive outcome becoming grimmer with each second delayed.

Grace ran through the unit to gather a new CAPR helmet from PPE storage and assemble it with a new lens and check the battery was working. The flimsy shield seal was hard to remove and the snaps hard to place as her clammy hands moved as fast as they could to put the CAPR on. She slipped it over her head, pulling the bottom of the lens down below her chin for a tight seal. She cranked the headband that tightened like a clamp around her head. It needed to be tight enough not to fall off during vigorous movement while leaning forward. She was relieved when the battery connected and showed a row of three bright green lights. Fully charged and ready to go in. As she was entering the room, other team members were assembling outside performing the very same, and contextually tedious PPE workflow before they could wheel the crash cart inside in order to be able to assist.

Grace stood over Elsie, performing the best compressions she could. She made sure to keep her arms from bending and a tight grip between her fingers that were interlocked as she drove down her stacked hands, pressing hard with the heel of her bottom hand on the middle of Elsie's sternum. With every drive downwards, she'd allow for recoil. Compressions 30 times before delivering two ventilation breaths with the Ambu bag, as she tilted her head up, pressing the seal of the bag firmly against her face to ensure all the oxygen funnelled into her open mouth. Grace's knuckles were white from the repetitive work of trying to save her patient's life.

Another nurse, Josie, had quickly donned PPE and come in to assist. Grace and Josie worked in synchrony to deliver multiple rounds of chest compressions and oxygen over what felt like hours. All had taken place in a matter of minutes. As Grace was relieved from doing compressions, she stepped back, feeling the adrenaline throughout her body, the angst of potentially losing another patient. Elsie lay lifeless on the bed as the team worked on her for 35 minutes before pronouncing her as expired. Grace stood back leaning against the wall. She felt the smooth, cold surface of the glass stabilise her body that was now shaking. Not another patient. So much death, so much quick acceleration of crisis all around. It had never been easy, but it had never been under the pressure of the current circumstances. Grace could not help but feel like with every death, COVID-19 was winning.

Grace reflected on the fact that even though she and the hundreds of thousands of other healthcare workers had been hailed as *Heroes* for doing their jobs, something felt like it was falling short of the reality that was developing quickly under her. A narrative painted healthcare workers as noble, brave and strong but in doing so inadvertently brushed over acknowledging the sacrifices, the failures, the loss, and the growing degree of emotional and psychological burden carried by so many of them, as they went about the challenging work day in and day out.

The hopelessness that was palpable in Jake's conversation lingered in Grace's thoughts for hours that day. Partially because of her concern for him, but largely because she was realising her own sense of hopelessness was causing her to experience those old, almost hardwired anxious feelings she knew as a child that she had worked to move past. She knew she needed to book a counselling session soon to get ahead of it turning into the panic attacks she had experienced in her late teens and early twenties. There wasn't much time in her life to do it, so she kept putting it off.

# Chapter 6
# All the Lights

All the lights in the house were out after Daddy threw the lamp against the wall. Its ceramic base shattered upon impact right next to Mumma's right shoulder before it fell dark inside. Just as every other time, he had been drinking, and he came home with a litany of grievances that he expressed in violence towards Mumma. With the lights out, the show was over for the evening, as he stumbled over to the couch and fell down beside it in a stupor. He had been yelling and hitting Mumma for what seemed like nearly an hour, tiring himself out.

Mumma, bruised and beaten but still conscious, could be heard gathering herself up from the floor. She made a quiet shuffling sound as she crawled across the floor to the kitchen to reach Lottie and Grace, hiding at their post in the pantry. The girls were frightened and huddled at the back of the floor space. "Girls. You need to listen to me," Mumma whispered with a serious tone, one that she mustered all her remaining strength to convey. "Be very quiet. We are going to leave," she said.

The streetlight streamed in through the window above the sink revealing her messy hair and tearful eyes. The girls nodded silently, unable to speak and shaking from the adrenaline they felt hearing the yelling and screaming that had gone on. In a whisper, Mumma gave them the instructions for what they would need to do next. "Listen, we are going to crawl across the floor behind the couch. Do not make a sound. There is a broken vase, so we must do our best not to get cut." Grace did not know what she feared more; breaking skin on the broken vase shards, or encountering their father's rage, in the dark.

"Will he get us?" Lottie asked in a timid whisper of a voice.

"No Lottie, not if we go quickly. I will protect you from him if he tries to hurt us." "Mumma, should we take the money from the shoebox for Santa

Monica?" Grace had thought about that shoebox and their trip so many times, especially on these nights.

"Good thinking, Grace." Mumma grabbed the money from the shoebox and put it into her pockets. "Okay girls, we need to go now. Very quietly. Are you ready?" They knew how important it was to do exactly as she said in this moment if they were to stand a chance of not waking their father. He could be heard through the wall now, breathing deeply. He often passed out and slept soundly afterwards.

They crawled past the furniture. It looked different from normal, as Mumma usually had fixed the room up before the girls entered. An upside-down coffee table, pictures from the wall either crooked or on the floor with the frames filled with smashed glass, books from the shelf had been thrown all over, splayed out with torn pages and their faces down. The room felt as though an earthquake had shaken it unrecognisable. Grace felt shocked to see how the living room where they would hang stockings and Christmas lights, ate dinner in front of the TV, or lounged with board games on a Sunday afternoon watching football with Daddy, could be so wrecked. Home felt broken.

As she peered around in near darkness, her eyes were adjusting and she saw their game of Monopoly poured out all over the floor and family photos broken by baseboards. As she was looking around, she forgot to look at the floor beneath her as she went. Her hand pressed down on a piece of the broken vase. At this moment, she felt terrified. There was no more room for another bad thing to happen tonight. She wanted to scream out as the small shard pierced the palm of her hand but was able to stop herself. The throbbing in her hand began to emerge and she could feel it bleeding. She quickly grabbed the edge of the glass in her hand and yanked it out and dropped it on the floor, knowing that she would only push it in further as she crawled across the ground on her hands and knees. At this moment, it didn't hurt. Her heart was pounding, and all she could do was listen to the floor boards, Mumma and Lottie in front of her, as they shuffled across the living room, behind the couch where Daddy was passed out.

They made it to the door and stood, as Mumma quietly opened it, praying the regular creak in the lock would not disturb Daddy. It fortunately did not and the three slipped out the door into the cold night. They walked alongside the path on the grass, so as not to make the gravel crunch as they went. "Where are we going?" Lottie asked, holding back tears as she shivered leaning into Mumma's side.

"We have to walk." Mumma looked indecisive as she looked both ways up and down their long, dark road. "We are going to go to Grandma and Grandpa's house."

Grace wondered why Mumma would want to go to their house, since Daddy would be able to find them. "What about Santa Monica?" Grace asked.

"No darling. We need to tell Grandma and Grandpa what's going on with their son." Grace was reminded of the calm that set in when they were around, and wondered if this would mean they could talk some sense into Daddy so he would stop hurting his family. Grandma and Grandpa lived three miles away across town in an unincorporated part of Concord. Mumma didn't have the keys to the car, as they had left in haste with no option to go back and retrieve them.

It was going to be a long walk, along the dark unincorporated roads of Concord. The girls held tight to their mother's hands, walking along the road in their nightgowns and sandals they were able to gather near the front door. Mumma held them tight, rubbing their hands with her thumbs, to soothe them as they walked through the dark night from one bright white and haloed streetlamp to the next. Mumma began to sing a song she would sing to them to soothe them to sleep as they walked. Noting their long shadows cast before them that would fade into the darkness before reaching the next light that was spaced far down the road.

Slowly and softly, she sang, "Amazing Grace how sweet the sound that saved a wretch like me. I once was lost but now I'm found. Was blind but now I see." The girls held onto her hands, hanging onto the tambour of her voice, as a comfort in the cold night. The words hung in the air. Frogs croaked and small animals scurried in the bushes beside their steps. The stars above were all the lights they could see in some parts of their walk.

"Mumma, I don't want to keep going," Lottie finally broke down and protested after walking two miles in her flip flops, feeling the hard gravel on the side of the road dig into her tender feet.

"There is no sense in stopping now, Lottie," Mumma said, encouraging her to muster her strength to get to their destination. The prospect of walking all night was very real to both Grace and Lottie, as they trudged along beside their mother, feeling as though the night would never end. They neared a gas station and Mumma went in to buy some drinks, leaving the girls to wait outside by the firewood pile. They huddled together, wringing their hands to warm them and jogging in spot to keep warm as they watched a young man feed the nozzle into his car and watch the meter go up before sauntering into the store to buy cigarettes.

Mumma returned with a large lemonade and two beanies from the wire stand that hung next to the entry. The girls were happy to cover their heads with hats and drink some lemonade before heading back to the road. The rocks crunched beneath them as they walked along, turning around periodically to make sure Daddy had not chased after them. There was no one coming.

They finally arrived at Grandma and Grandpa's house. It was around 11 PM now and no lights were on in the house. "What should we do?" Grace asked Mumma as they stood outside looking for any sign of movement inside.

"Well. I think we will need to knock on the door."

"But we will wake them up," Lottie replied.

"Yes, I know, but this is very important. We have nowhere else to go." The girls stood back as Mumma walked up the brick stairs and banged on the door. No sound or light or movement could be detected in the pregnant pause they spent in anticipation, suspending their breath to try to hear something. Mumma banged the door again, "It's Barbara," she called in a muted voice.

This time, a light turned on and soon Grandpa emerged in his bathrobe, peering out into the night, at two little heads with red and yellow hats on, and Mumma in her nightgown and house slippers. "Barbara? What are you all doing here?" was the eventual reply at the door.

Mumma shifted her weight, gripping Grace and Lottie's hands a little tighter. "We had nowhere else to go," she said, trying not to make further commotion to wake the neighbours or dogs. The moon was full and cast a silver light on Mumma's face and hair as Grace looked up at her and caught the glisten of her tearful eyes again. The door opened and Grandpa ushered the girls in first. They stood in the entryway awaiting direction for where to go next. In the past, the girls would burst through their grandparents' doors and run wherever they pleased. Tonight, they stood very quietly and still, too nervous to speak or leave their mother's side.

Grandma came down the staircase, holding tightly to the banister so as not to slip in her half-awake state. Grandpa stood by watching her come down, waiting for her to help him navigate this surprise visit. They all watched her descend the stairway, silently and not knowing where else to look. Mumma greeted her with a sceptical tone veiled in hospitality. "We had nowhere else to go. He…He…He…" She had trouble finishing the sentence. This was the first time she would put words to what was happening to anyone other than the apologies she gave to her daughters. Mumma covered her face as she began crying.

"What, dear?" Grandma inquired, wrapping her arm around Mumma. "Come, let's go sit down. Brian, can you please take the girls to the kitchen for some milk? I may have some pound cake left."

Grandpa took his marching orders and the girls disappeared around the corner. Mumma sat for minutes, unable to steady her breath through tears enough to put words together. She also struggled with finding the words to her secret pain and feared, as ever, how others would receive news that her husband had been abusing her. She had kept this secret for nearly three years having seen him slip into alcoholism after long days at work ended at the bar, before he would become violent. Grace would rationalise her husband's small shoves and raised voice as normal, if *Perhaps a little dramatic* she had thought. The shoves and the raised voice turned into hitting hard with his fist or open hand, screaming and throwing furniture before she could really notice the progression had taken place.

It had become customary for him to launch into his rage a couple nights a week. Bruising Mumma's wrists as he would yank her across the room, to throw her into a wall, or grab her hair and drag her along the floorboards, until her scalp bled. The trauma dulled her senses and with that her will to fight back. The fight she had in her had been snuffed out before she realised it needed to be summoned. She created logic in her mind that calculated that her mistakes were the source of his abuse. If she could just do things right, he would not need to become angry. He seemed satiated only when she bled, bruised, or furniture broke and shattered. Barbara lived in the constant space of caution about triggering the violence that she accepted as the inevitable, the inescapable.

The mahogany mantel clock ticked at a steady beat, as Barbara gathered her thoughts. "Marcy, your son has been h-hitting me. He is violent at night when he comes home from the bar." She spoke slowly, taking in her mother-in-law's facial expressions of disbelief as she spoke. The meaning of what Barbara was saying did not seem to elicit a response. To her dismay, she was met with only a plain, unaffected look. It was as if her words did not permeate, they reached out but could not grasp at anything substantial. Her words clawed at a slippery wall, unable to gain traction.

Barbara paused to see if her mother-in-law would in turn react with some sort of empathy. She thought to paint a picture for her. "Do you remember when you came over last time, and you asked why we replaced the two lamps in our living room that you gave us as a wedding gift? And I said that the children had been playing with a ball in the house that knocked them over?"

"Yes."

"Well, it wasn't because they knocked them over. It was because your son threw them against the wall when he was angry and then he threw me against that wall." Marcy sat silently, still displaying the same, unaffected stare, right through Barbara. Barbara began to cry, now in part, mostly frustrated that she had disclosed her deepest secret only to be met with a wall of silence.

Barbara's words hung in the air for what felt like minutes before Marcy spoke. Her same, unsympathetic delivery brought upon a sudden nervous feeling in the pit of Barbara's stomach. "I'm not sure what you are trying to do, Barbara. But coming here in the middle of the night, dragging those poor little girls out of bed with barely any clothing on shows me that your judgment is poor. And here you are in my house, making terrible accusations about my son with no proof whatsoever. Quite honestly, you seem mentally ill."

"How can you be saying this? Aren't you at all curious to know what would compel me to leave in the middle of the night? John has been abusing me for years, and I have been too afraid to say anything to you, to anyone, and I just need you to help—"

Marcy cut her off, raising her voice, "After everything your husband has done for you. He works such long hours at the shop to provide for you and the girls, and this is how you repay him?" It was clear to Barbara that her mother-in-law was committed to denying any counter-point of view. The instinct to protect her son, the fruit of her efforts, caused her to automatically reject any counter notion. She was not curious. She was certain of her perspective, despite contradicting evidence.

They sat in silence, blankly staring at spaces uninhabited by the other. The clock's ticking was the only movement in the room filled with tension. The two were in complete disagreement on what the reality of the situation was. It was a stalemate, and they were unable to progress further in the conversation.

The girls had finished their cookies and milk and talked about school with their grandfather to drown out the sound of their mother's crying in the other room. They did not know what would be happening next, and when it fell silent, both Grace and Lottie thought maybe something positive would come of this late-night journey. Instead, their mother came to the archway leading to the kitchen and asked the girls to clear their dishes and glasses, as they were going to go home. Their mother wiped her eyes with the sleeve of her dressing gown as she waited.

"Brian, could you drive them home?" Brian gathered his coat and keys and without inquiry or contest, led them out to the garage. The car was cold, and the windows fogged, as they got the car running and backed out of the driveway. Mumma sat in the front seat stoically, staring out the window. No words passed between the driver or passengers for the three-mile drive home. Grace listened to the tick of the blinker before every turn. She thought about how so much of life held an unpredictable rhythm. It was the clocks and the turning signals, the metronomes that kept pace while all the rest deviated. Soon enough they arrived, the lights in the house were still out.

Grace noticed her mother linger in her seat, clearly not wanting to get out, but knowing there was no place for her to stay. "Come on, girls," she eventually said. Her voice echoed with a hollow sadness that they had not heard before. The girls undid their seatbelts and thanked their grandfather for the ride. Brian, acted as though it was a regular day and bid them goodnight with a happy tone that felt misplaced for all that had transpired.

Barbara was struck by the intense denial she had been met with. She was perplexed and hurt, and realised at that moment, how separate she was from this family she had married into. She realised that their interests in her wellbeing were only upheld if it aligned with how they wanted to see things. The jarring sound of the car door closing in the night and Grandpa driving away stiffened her back as she called her children to follow her into the dark house. She had left the door unlocked, so as not to make too much sound as they left earlier. They entered. The house felt like a chasm, empty. Mumma turned on the kitchen switch to cast some light into the dark living room. Daddy wasn't in there. Not knowing where he was located was unnerving as they walked hurriedly to their bedroom to pile into bed.

Mumma called for Daddy with a normal tone. "John, are you here dear?" She often spoke to him with a normalcy that was very misplaced for the circumstance, but did so in hope to conjure a normal reply. There was no response. Mumma told the children to wait in their bedrooms. They listened to the floorboards creak as Mumma made her way down the hall and throughout the house, checking each room. He was gone.

# Chapter 7
# Through the Air

Justin held Grace's hand as they walked along the pier at the Berkeley Marina. Emma ran a little ahead, charging at seagulls and laughing as she enjoyed the feeling of her body moving through the air. Justin loved these evening walks with the view of The City, hazy, becoming unshrouded with the evening fog rolling in from the pacific beyond the Golden Gate. Justin looked at Grace. He felt close to Grace. "Do you ever wonder what it would be like if we just packed up and hit the road?" he asked.

"Sounds like someone has serious lock-down cabin fever."

He chuckled. "I suppose so. I just feel like this COVID thing may be just a sign that we need to live our lives a bit more spontaneously. Like seize the day you know? Nothing is certain. Nothing is promised." Grace was silent as they walked. She thought about how people who were not dealing with the pandemic first hand in the trenches of the hospital had the luxury to think about things like spontaneity and what life changes they wanted to make and get out of this situation. As each day wore on, Grace had felt more obligated to the cause of saving lives in this crisis and could in no way see herself at this point abandoning her post. "What's wrong? Do you not like the idea of escaping it all? Starting fresh?" Justin could tell Grace was uneasy with his proposal.

"I just don't see how that's realistic. I mean, of course, I'd love to reimagine my life in which we could do whatever we wanted. But now is not the time. It just isn't and quite frankly, the prospect of running away from this sounds selfish to me."

The word selfish hung in the air between them as they continued to walk. The sound of the water slapping at the pier's legs, rocking back and forth, was all that Grace wanted to focus on after she said her piece. She had called Justin selfish before and knew this to be a discordant theme along the way in their relationship. "Well, I'm sorry Grace. I guess I just thought—"

"You thought what? That I'd drop my job and run away with you and Emma? Like where exactly would you propose we go? I just don't get what you're thinking. Things are different now. We have responsibilities. We are in a pandemic. We can't outrun our discomfort with all this. I don't see any other responsible way than to stay the course."

Justin walked pensively, a little hurt by Grace's strong worded response. "Okay. So maybe I'm just having a hard time. I mean, you get to go to work every day and see your colleagues and do meaningful work. They closed down my school, and I'm just alone all the time and families are struggling and unhappy that we've closed down. I have no set curriculum to teach or even a present group of kids to teach it too. And the world seems to be going to hell in a handbasket. So I just thought, wow maybe it's a sign that we need to do something different."

Grace listened and responded with a more empathetic tone. "Then maybe you just need to work out a way to make this time meaningful, Justin," Grace replied. "Go pick your daughter up from daycare and spend time with her, if you're feeling lonely. Sometimes it's about leaning into what you have, even when it's uncomfortable, so you can grow where you are, and not just search for something different, and float from one fanciful thing to the next."

They walked in awkward silence until Justin turned to her to pull her in for a hug. He whispered against her head, "Thank you for always putting things in perspective for me. I appreciate how dedicated you are to the path you are on. I wish I were as strong as you."

Grace appreciated how well Justin was able to articulate his thoughts and feelings and his flexibility to pivot in his perspective when they had differing opinions. "You help me see things differently too, Just. I mean, maybe we should take a little camping trip or something just to get the thrill of the escape, but not foreclose on our house or forego our careers." Grace laughed at her own humour. "I heard from a colleague at work that privately run campgrounds are still operating."

They had reached the end of the pier that jutted out a great distance from shore. They were surrounded by water that stretched out on the sides and in front. Justin picked up Emma to show her the Golden Gate Bridge poking holes with its rust coloured towers and cables through the top of the fog that rolled low and out over the water before them. They stood, admiring the sunset over the bay now casting rose gold tones in the patches of sky that could be seen above the fog. "Plus you would just miss this place too much," Grace said with certainty.

"I know," Justin replied. They made their way back to the marina parking lot before the sun was completely gone.

That night Justin panned through his photo collection on his phone. Looking at photos he had from years prior. Backpacking in Argentina and Peru. His trip to Italy and Portugal. All the memories he had felt so distant, not replicable anymore. He signed into his travel blog he had made while backpacking through Europe 10 years prior. It had been a few years since he had read his travel notes.

*18 July 2011. What a miraculous place this Venezia is. Last night, we celebrated Redentore. The festival commemorates the end of the plague that had decimated the Venetian population in the 16th century. Wine poured and plates upon plates of seafood and pasta kept arriving as we marvelled at the bursts of light in the sky. The fireworks lit the sky with bright sparks that cascaded over the water. The lights were so bright, you could believe the lagoon and canals were on fire, scorching the surface of the rippling waters.*

Justin sat, remembering that night. How he, his girlfriend at the time Vivi, and their friend Victor had crossed the floating bridge from Venice proper to Giudecca amongst a sea of people, some dressed up in Venetian masks, most all with something to drink in hand. It was a colourful affair. It felt so carefree and ostentatious. Vivi, an art major studying abroad in Florence for that summer, had been the perfect travel companion. She was up for anything. He remembered how her wide eyes absorbed the world without judging it. He had fallen in love with her for the short time they spent together until it was time to part ways.

Now, scanning through the blog and photos of the Grand Canal, Saint Mark's square and the Bridge of Sighs, Justin missed the freedom of being a part of the bigger world. The world was rich in history, culture, and offered a variety of experiences every day, novel and sometimes challenging. He thought about how time had passed, and he had chosen to settle down with Grace in later years. In doing so, he allowed his world to get smaller, more comfortable. And now, he felt a degree of discomfort. He wasn't sure if it was these uncertain times ushered in by the pandemic, and all else that was turbulent in the world, or his own reaction to the conventional path he was on, one that stifled his ability to breathe

the freedoms of his youth. He had not thought about Vivi for many years. They had broken up over his desire to return to the United States, and went their separate ways. She had been a wandering spirit, as he was. Justin typed in a search for *Vivian Burg.*

\*\*\*

The girls lay in their beds, as the moon was peaking around the windowsill. Grace lay awake, looking over at Lottie, her head on her pillow, sleeping with a furrow stuck between her eyebrows. Even in her dreams she could not escape the angst.

It worried Grace to see how her little sister slept with such a concerned look on her face. *She can't even escape this in her dream,* she thought. *Where is he?* She pondered, feeling disconcerted to know that they could not locate their father, while simultaneously dreading what it would be like if they found him. *Could he be in the house hiding? Did he go out after us? Will he return angry and start up another fight?* She could here Mumma downstairs, cleaning up the living room. The familiar sound of furniture being repositioned and glass being swept.

A sinking feeling passed through Grace, thinking about her mother, thinking about how the three of them were trapped in a repetitive violent cycle with their dad and no one seemed to care. Not knowing where Daddy had gone off to was unnerving. She hoped he had left the house and was not lying in wait somewhere in the house, like those horror movies those kids at school would talk about watching with their older siblings. Grace at that moment wished she had an older sibling. Someone to reassure her, to lead them on the way to go. Mumma seemed to have lost more and more resilience and hope with each blow.

Now, with Grandma and Grandpa turning them away, Grace feared Mumma's resolve to break free would diminish even further. Anxiety filled Grace for much of the night in between sleep, with tears rolling silently down her cheeks on the pillow. In his absence now, she felt just as trapped as if he were there and she was waiting it out in the pantry. *Something would need to be done.* Justin and Grace jumped out of their car once at the campsite nestled in the middle of a redwood grove. Justin attended to Emma, unfastening her from her seat and lifting her out onto the ground. The redwood forest floor was filled with soft pine needles, on dry ground, that Emma immediately began picking through inspecting each one. The sounds of the forest rose around them as the three fell to silence, taking in the fresh air, the feeling of the hallowed atmosphere of the woods with a rushing creek running through it. It had been a long drive down, especially the last leg on Highway 1. The enormous cliffs that had risen out of the ocean accommodated a two-lane narrow road along carved out paved rims in the sandstone and granite that led game drivers following the switchbacks down the coastline. Passengers often gasped as they bent around harrowing turns that gave them views of sheer drops for just long enough to lose faith in the driver before bending inwards along the road for a time. Drivers held steady with white knuckles above the wheel, praying the brakes would not give out, or an oncoming car would not overestimate the turn.

It was the rush of the harrowing turns and the rugged California coastline's spread out before her with breathtaking views that felt like an elixir to Grace. The freedom she found driving beyond the reach of cell service and the amenities of the city settled her soul with a sense of escape. Especially these days, Grace's desire to escape the confines of her life, were greater, perhaps not to the extent that Justin had proposed, but she could agree that a break from lockdown was a welcome opportunity. It felt exhilarating to seize it.

As she was when she was a child, she had a great desire to free herself of all that limited her. She looked back at Emma, who had fallen asleep to the rock and sway of the windy highway. Grace thought about courage and what it took now and in the past to face adversity. In that moment, she imparted her hope without a word, willing it as she admired Emma's little sleeping face that she would grow up to be brave. Grace did not see there to be any use in wishing only good things would happen to Emma. She thought it naïve to hang hopes on good fortune. She in her own life had seen enough that fell short of that. She thought the true blessings to impart were the ones that bestowed the resources people would need to face the hardships of life. It was a sobering perspective, but one Grace as a veteran ICU nurse who had stood by the ill and the dead consoling their loved ones, and having experienced her own trauma as a child, knew inner resources were the ingredients people needed to endure when life dealt hardship more likely than comfort or security.

The fog had been receding as they drove down early afternoon, and now, as the late afternoon approached, the chill of its return pierced the air making it cool as water. A nearby campsite began piping out plumes of smoke from their campfire drums, as cooking started and campers returned from their day's adventures on the river or hiking in the forest. Justin and Grace began to set up their tent, making sense of which way the door should face and which was the back or front. Emma stood on the periphery, vying for her mother's attention. Asking Grace to pick her up, or tugging at the pole that Grace was trying to clip onto the tent.

The fog had not yet arrived, and in late afternoon, the dying embers of the sun's rays filtered through the side of the high canopy, in streams that highlighted bright green clover patches, and the amber bark of redwoods that had stood there since the Dark Ages.

Justin gathered kindling from around the base of trees with Emma, who carried three sticks at a time in toe. The fire lit quickly, despite the dampness of the coastal air. The owner of the privately owned campground, Brenda, came by to welcome them and let them know that the showers were closed but they could get firewood from the main house. "I guess we will be sure to count our river swim as our daily shower," Justin joked.

Brenda's face drew stern, like a mother protecting her infant. "There is to be no bathing and no soap products in the river," she instructed. "There's a $200 fine for it," she added pointedly for good measure.

"Oh, not to worry, I was just kidding. We will absolutely not use soap in the river," Justin returned with equalising sincerity before he looked over at Grace, as Brenda moved on to the next campsite satisfied with his answer, signalling that he realised he had struck a nerve.

"I'm sure they get tired of city people coming out here wanting to bathe regularly, especially since they have closed down the shower facilities," Grace added.

"Yeah, I get it," Justin replied, poking at the fire with a large stick he had found. "Look how nice this fire has turned out to be, if I don't say so myself." Justin grinned ear to ear with some primal notion that somehow his manliness had been solidified through the successful construction of this fire. They cooked over the open fire for dinner. Potatoes in foil were placed into the coals, while they roasted premade chicken kebabs later on the slatted grill-top. The fire cracked, tossing embers out of the pit, bright and hot for a moment before they faded into falling ash. The smoke drifted around, causing Emma to cough violently or run away from it. "If you lick your finger and say 'white rabbit, white rabbit', the smoke will move, Em," Justin instructed Emma to scare away the smoke.

"It works!" She laughed and continued to chant, "White Rabbit, White Rabbit!" while dancing through the smoke at a safe distance from the fire drum.

"Be careful, Emma, no dancing around the fire," said Grace as she took her hand and led her to sit down on a camping chair.

As night fell, they sat around the fire enjoying their dinner. The charred flavour of the kebabs cooked over the open flame with baked potatoes stuffed with butter, sour cream, and spring onions. It was Justin's favourite campsite meal to make.

"This is really nice," Grace said, looking up from the flames towards Justin on the other side of the fire. He knew exactly what she meant. Time that could be disconnected from all the distractions of their regular life, connecting them to nature. Where people, man-made spaces, and objects were viewed as potential hazards, nature in its purity and expansiveness, had begun to feel more than ever like a refuge, a respite.

"Being out in nature really feels like one of the few 'safe' places there are left, don't you think?" Justin smiled in agreement. "I wish we would never have to go back," he said, half searching in his mind for a way.

Emma started to fuss, tired of the smoke following her, and with no more food left on her plate. "Mumma, can we have S'mores?" She had learned about S'mores ahead of the trip, reading camping storybooks in preparation with Justin.

"Sure honey," Justin said, as he cleaned up the foil from the baked potatoes and cleared the plates. He returned to the fire with long sticks, a bag of marshmallows, some Hershey's chocolate and graham crackers.

Emma started jumping up and down with excitement 'S'mores! S'mores!' She cried with joy. They skewered the marshmallows and Grace and Justin controlled the sticks as they turned them over in the flames then quickly blew them out, as the flames jumped onto their marshmallows, ravenously consuming the sugar, before the entire thing turned black. "Quick! Grab a graham cracker and chocolate." Justin showed Emma how to pull the oozing marshmallow off the stick by firmly gripping each side with graham crackers and a chocolate piece. Emma jumped at the opportunity to devour the S'more once the marshmallow broke free and sat happily in her camping chair with chocolate and mallow smearing on her cheeks and dripping down her hands. It was so sweet and gooey, a complete mess, and she loved it.

"This is my favourite part of camping," Justin said, licking his fingers.

"I love S'mores, Daddy!" Emma echoed. They sat around enjoying the evening, as owls began to stir and hoot on nearby branches and creatures rustled in the bushes from time to time around the campsite.

Finally, Grace made a motion to put Emma to bed. "Okay, time to brush teeth and head to bed, okay Em?"

"No!" Emma wasn't interested in departing ahead of any opportunities for more S'mores.

"S'mores are all done for tonight, darling," Justin replied. With that, Emma, assured she wouldn't miss out on more S'mores, reluctantly followed Grace over to the faucet to brush her teeth, and then headed to sleep.

"Daddy! Look at the stars!" Emma cried from the dark corner of the campsite, where she had been brushing her teeth by the faucet. Looking up through gaps in the canopy where she was pointing, Justin saw the deepest night sky laying as a backdrop to countless, bright stars.

"Wow Emma!" He pointed out the Milky Way to them and parts of the Big Dipper used to orient to the North Star.

"Where's the moon, Daddy?" Emma asked with a concerned voice, after the initial excitement of tracking all the newfound sights in the starry sky. "Did the birds take him away?" Emma added.

Justin chuckled at her innocent notion. "Maybe so, Em. Don't worry. You'll see him again," Justin replied. Emma took his response and pensively headed with Grace to put away their toothbrushes.

"Say goodnight," Grace whispered.

"Goodnight Daddy," Emma echoed. "I love you."

"I love you too, Emma Bear."

Justin watched the glow of the lantern in the tent outline Grace and Emma's figures as they bent down preparing for bed. Emma got into her pyjamas still chatting about her concern for the missing moon but seemed to find solace in her explanation about the birds. "The birds will take care of him," she could be heard telling Grace. Later, once the lantern had been turned down and Emma was sound asleep, Grace unzipped the tent to return to the fire. Justin sat entranced by the flames before looking up with a welcoming smile, at Grace as she approached.

They sat in silence, listening to occasional wood cracks in the forest and the owls. "You know, you're a great mother, Grace," Justin said, looking at her kindly. "I'm not sure what we would do without you."

Grace took the compliment with a smile and changed the subject. "I think tomorrow we should take a picnic lunch up to the river early in the afternoon when it warms up. We could just hang around the campsite till then or take a little hike up on that ridge trail south of here."

"Sure," Justin agreed. "I'm down for whatever. Big Sur will likely not disappoint no matter what direction we go." They sat silently, enjoying the night, as the flames diminished to glowing embers at the base of the remnants of fire-devoured logs. "Well, looks like the party is over," Justin remarked, as the warmth died down. "I'll pour water over it to make sure it's out," he added, motioning to get the full water bucket he always kept on hand when he lit a fire.

"Okay, do you need any help?" Grace asked.

"No, I'll be fine. Go check on Emma." She went to the tent, kicking off her boots at the door, feeling the shifting Lilo mat beneath her as she used the effort of her tired legs to make it into her sleeping bag, wriggling down and zipping it all the way up. The smell of smoke in her hair and ash on her face. This was Grace's happy place.

The next day, when the weather was warm, they left the campsite to head to the Big Sur River Gorge, which was technically closed to the public. They parked on the roadside a quarter mile from the entrance and snuck into the closed state park on foot to dip down to the river. It was by word of mouth that they knew people were still going there since the closures, few as they were.

The river moved at a lazy pace, shallow with years of drought. They made their way partially on the trail along the edge and partially up the middle of the river, balancing on and tripping over rocks. Emma enjoyed the ride in the hiking pack on Justin's back. It felt good to breathe fresh air, unfiltered from fabric masks. The river, in some spots, was deep, forming small swimming holes in the spaces between some rocks, creating deep aquamarine blue bases in the crystal-clear water. The water was cold and invigorating, as places where fast water plunged pushed past Grace's legs. She felt glad to have her water sandals on, as she gained grip in the crevices formed between large stones under the water. Some of the stones were slippery, covered in moss, but she found the rocks that had the swiftest currents running over them had less slippery moss growing on them and chose to follow that path, even if it meant contending with pushback from the oncoming flow.

The river moved at different speeds throughout, spilling into small gushing waterfalls all around at intervals, then as a bumpy shallow translucency running over rocks, and then a calm turquoise drift. Grace and Justin liked the challenge of carrying all their day's supplies on their backs, and working hard to keep themselves from falling into the water. The redwoods stood by and provided shade most of the way. About a mile up, the treeline opened up and large cliffs surrounding the gorge rose up, with lush plants and wildflowers leaning over to look down upon them. Some hawks circled up high in the gap of clear blue sky and a few people could be seen enjoying a dip and a snooze in the shade further upstream.

"Isn't this magical?" Grace exclaimed, helping Emma out of the pack, once they found a shady section with some enticing waterfalls and swimming holes. They lay their towels on some warm rocks along the river's edge, making a base with their backpack and hiking pack. "Who's up for a dip before lunch?"

Emma was already headed that way and needed to be pulled back to put her floaty and bathing suit on. The water was cold, but warm in patches where the sun had heated it. Clear water bent over rocks and gushed between the granite crevices, creating chaotic flurries of bubbles in the water below. It felt so good to lean against the little waterfalls, like a natural spa with jets kneading out the kinks in tired muscles from a heavy backpack. Leaning against a warm rock, Grace closed her eyes, feeling the beads of water running down her face that had lingered after she had emerged from a startling plunge under the surface to get used to the water temperature quicker. *This is rest.*

Justin managed Emma, as she stayed at the water's edge, throwing pebbles and enjoying the drama of the plonk and splash that they made. Soon, Justin coaxed Emma over to the warm pool to see Grace, and they sat with the gushing water against their backs and swam around searching for an elusive brown fish that Emma had allegedly spotted below the surface. Justin sat and marvelled at Emma as she practiced her kicking and blowing bubbles in the water, as Grace held her on the water's surface and they circled the waterhole. At that moment, he thought about how grateful he was for the simple perfection of this moment with his little family. How all the people he had met and places he had been faded in the light of this bright memory he wanted to capture and never lose.

The next day, they packed up camp mid-morning and headed for home. With an impulsive turn off the main Hwy as they entered Carmel-by-the-Sea, they headed for one last glimpse of the coast from a favourite lookout, behind a large granite rock overlooking a rocky beach with patches of white sand below. They parked in a residential area, near a grove of cypress, and headed onto the trail.

The wind had picked up and blew persistently off the ocean. The chaotic whitecaps had formed out to the distance. They made it to their rock and sat overlooking the beach and Point Lobos to the left. They ate some granola bars and marvelled at a line of dolphins spotted jumping out of the surf.

Grace at that moment thought she should tell Justin what she had seen Elle doing. "Hey Justin. I meant to mention this sooner, but something odd happened the other day at work."

"Yeah, what?" She had piqued his interest, pulling him away from watching the dolphins at length.

"Elle, was with another guy. I couldn't see his face, but I saw her leaning up against a wall with him, looking like they were kissing. He had scrubs on."

"Does Joe know?" Justin quickly replied.

"I doubt it, I'm sure I'd hear about it if he did. I don't think she even knows I saw them."

"Well, maybe best you just stay out of it. It will likely get messy."

"Well, I can't unsee what I saw." Grace's complicated feelings around what she should do with this information gave rise to a nervous feeling.

"All I'm saying is it's really none of your business. I know she's your friend, but if you get involved you may meddle. She's a grown-up and she can make her own decisions with Joe and this guy on her own," Justin replied. Grace felt blocked by his remarks and a little strange that he wasn't immediately siding with a path that would right the situation. She decided not to bring it up any further. On the car ride home, Grace felt nauseous, she mulled over the image of Elle with a man who was not her husband, beginning to half wonder if she had imagined it, hoping she had.

Grace continued to feel unwell for the next few days. She called out from work the morning that she woke up and vomited three times before getting out of bed. This familiar constellation of symptoms, the cramps, the nausea and now vomiting stopped Grace in her tracks, as she was headed home to lay on her couch, after dropping Emma at daycare. *Am I pregnant?* It had been nearly two months since she last had her period. The time had flown with all the distraction at work, she hadn't kept track of her irregular periods so well. Grace decided to turn into the parking lot of a local drugstore to pick up a pregnancy test. The rush of possibility mixed with hesitancy to find out felt complicated. She knew she and Justin had thought about having a sibling for Emma, *But now?* Grace had intentionally been pushing the idea of trying for another baby to the back of her mind over the past months, amid the pandemic.

As she walked into the drugstore, everything seemed to move slowly and she could feel her pulse racing and the push and pull of her breath on the moist fabric of her mask. She wanted to know, but she didn't want to know. Knowing could mean something would change. She forced herself through the motions of walking down the aisle, lining up with the item in hand and purchasing the pregnancy test. The man at the cash register checked the tests through, greeted her in an obligatory manner, not looking up. With a resigned tone, he prompted her through the buttons on the credit card machine and asked her to sign once the purchase went through.

Grace cringed as she picked up the stylus pen to sign. Items that were used publicly, like water fountains, street crossing buttons, play equipment, all felt risky to touch now. *The virus could be anywhere.* In the early weeks of the pandemic, hand sanitiser and cleaning products had vanished off the shelves. She had been carrying some rubbing alcohol in a little bottle that once held the last of her hand sanitiser supply in her purse to carry her over until she could get a real bottle of 70% or greater alcohol hand sanitiser. Grace grabbed the plastic bag quickly and headed through the sliding doors. She made sure to douse her hands with the alcohol outside on the kerb, rubbing it all over the flimsy plastic that encased the pregnancy test. *Everything could be contaminated.*

Grace paused, thinking about how ridiculously compulsive her hygiene practices were now compared to years past. It came with the territory of working in the ICU, to wash, rewash, wipe and wash hands again throughout her day. But now, the attention to what she touched last or how she would next clean her hands was heightened even as she went about her day in her regular life, and she couldn't turn off her vigilance.

Grace got into the car, breathing heavily through her mask and ripped it off. To go into the store was a complicated sequence of steps and considerations to remain safe from the virus. Now, in her car, she breathed deeply, able to let down her guard. She started the engine after a few deep breaths and wiping down the plastic bag that had sat on the counter, as well as her credit card that had slid through the machine. Grace thought about how the news reports had said Coronavirus was living on surfaces for multiple hours, and although its transmission appeared to be through droplets in the air, it wasn't certain if it would transmit on surfaces. Evolving and speculative information that constantly changed had driven Grace into hypervigilance.

Grace drove home and lay on the couch staring at the pregnancy test box on the coffee table for a while. She procrastinated with taking the test, as she mulled over what it would actually mean for her to be pregnant right now.

*It would be a sibling for Emma…Justin wants a boy…I'm nearly 38 and it's now or never…With all that's going on in the world, now may not be the right time…I'd have to be pregnant while working in the ICU during a pandemic. Like the least desirable place perhaps other than in a war to be pregnant…I'll regret it if I don't have a second kid…I want to know…But I don't know if I want to know right now…Can my body handle another pregnancy?…Will it take my focus away from Emma?…Why can't Justin have the babies?…Maybe I can hold off and take the test tomorrow…The result will be the same today as it is tomorrow, so why wait?*

All of Grace's clamouring thoughts left her vacillating between the choice to test or not to test, leaving her stuck on the couch, unable to get up yet anxious about remaining inactive.

A wave of nausea rose up in the form of dry heaving into her empty coffee cup. The contents of her stomach didn't make it up and out through her mouth, there was likely nothing left to heave in the absence of breakfast and multiple bouts of vomiting earlier. Afterwards, Grace sat there, looking out the window at a hummingbird that was zipping around the honeysuckles that hung on the wooden framework of the arbour. *Your life is so simple.* She thought. *The animals just go with the flow and here I am perseverating on testing if I'm even pregnant.* She wished for less thoughts and envied the simplicity of how animals participated in the circle of life, without overthinking it. The challenge of the modern day where so much was controlled, was to relinquish control. The pandemic had been one of those factors that challenged her sense of control, and now this. *Too much to deal with all at once.*

The two solid lines emerged in parallel, affirming what she already knew in her gut. She sat there, on the couch for an hour looking at the test result window. The same thoughts that pushed her around earlier, lingered in a tug of war now. Only, this time, it was definitive, she was pregnant. Grace felt some happiness, but the surprise of today's revelation had knocked the wind out of her sails a little. She felt regret that she had been caught unaware and uncomfortable with yet another area of her life that she felt like she had lost control over.

Grace sat for three more hours on the couch watching back-to-back reruns of her all-time favourite show, *Friends*, and eating microwave popcorn. She intentionally did not look at her phone, fearing Justin may have messaged her and she would need to reply. She was not ready to speak this new situation into existence quite yet. She decided she would book an appointment with her doctor to verify the pregnancy first.

***

Justin's search for Vivi was short and he immediately recognised her, although over a decade later, she was still stunning and looked as though she hadn't aged, wearing her jade bangles and turquoise jewellery. While perusing her public profile on Facebook, he clicked the like icon to one of her posts, a picture of two Venetian Doctor masks, hung side by side on a purple accent wall, with an impulsive click.

Today, having driven all the way home, he was tired but noticed he had received a friend request from Vivi, as she must have noticed his *Like.*

Justin sat looking at the *Accept* button next to her friend request. With curious impulse, he accepted it. Her profile read vaguely but *Current City: San Francisco,* jumped out from the page. She had grown up in the suburbs of Chicago, Illinois, and he had assumed she would have returned home to help her parents run their printing business, when the travel money ran dry. He realised as he entertained that image that he was framing his assumptions quite narrowly. So much could have occurred in 10 years. It had for him. It was often hard for Justin to imagine how people's lives that he did not see take place for many years would have progressed past the places in which he had parted ways with them. He thought of his high school friends as still living in the same town up north, doing the same things they always did, except perhaps with a wife and some kids. He knew that to be true for some.

Justin sat in his study looking at the screen, panning between her photos and the *Message* button, contemplating what to do next. If he was honest, he was intrigued to find out more about who she was now and what she had been doing with her life. *Was she happy?* He wanted to message her and pick up with the ease of old conversation bypassing the formality of having to catch up on the past decade or so with subtle appraisal, where he would have to be sure to cast a positive light on his life, and all that had transpired since they last spoke.

He shut down his computer, figuring he would sleep on it and headed to bed. He was very tired from the long drive back up from camping that day.

# Chapter 8
# Breakfast

Morning came, and Grace woke from a deep sleep filled with twisting dreams that she couldn't quite remember. She could hear Mumma shifting pans over the stove in the kitchen. It smelled like sausages and biscuits, Dad's favourite. Grace looked over at Lottie's empty bed. *What time was it?* The clock showed 9:30 AM. Grace put her slippers and robe on and went downstairs. She could hear her dad ruffling the newspaper as he drank his morning coffee with a civility that betrayed the violence of last night. Mumma looked intent upon perfecting her task of preparing breakfast for the family. She worked with careful precision while cooking eggs and sausages, while setting the freshly baked biscuits onto the cooling rack.

Mumma had often used her domestic skills to smooth over the calamities that took place the night before. It was as if the thick and silky gravy poured over sausage and buttermilk pastry could subdue their traumas with comfort. Cooking was Mumma's language. She communicated her love, her worth, and her forgiveness with the meals she churned out of her kitchen, even when they were made with bruised and cut hands.

Grace stood at that doorway, taking in the enormity of what would otherwise be a typical Saturday morning scene, in any other house where the father had not beaten up his wife and disappeared without a trace the night before. "Good morning Grace," Dad said with an even tone, looking up from his newspaper. The decency with which he carried himself between spells was astounding. It took a great deal of measured denial and perhaps disassociation for a person who had committed atrocities to carry themselves in such an upright manner. His ability to conceal that raw aggression that lay just below the surface was uncanny. It was no wonder Grandma and Grandpa could not imagine their son's transgressions, or perhaps it was because they had the same capacity for denial.

Grace, as a child, could not put words to what she felt and thought that morning sitting down nervously behind the San Francisco chronicle, as he thumbed through its pages. She was glad that the wide-open newspaper pages could be a barrier between them, as to look in his eyes would likely bring her to tears. Nothing was ever said about where Daddy disappeared that night. The girls did not have the nerve to inquire and there was no explanation offered, until it came up a few days later when Daddy entered another rage and began to mock Mumma by saying he had heard every word of her dramatic attempt to undermine him at his parents' house. He mocked her crying and imitated her conversation with his mother almost verbatim. *He had been hiding there and they knew it the whole time.*

"I will always be smarter and quicker than you. Do you think I didn't know you would run off to my parents' house? You are so stupid. They did not and will never believe your lies about me! You are just the lying whore my mother said you were the day we got married." Daddy would often colour his insults with fictitious additives implicating other people's perceptions of his wife to make Barbara feel more isolated. "You will never leave me, Barbara, so you mind as well stop trying and shut your mouth."

Grace covered her ears after she heard that part, as the front room mirror over the mantel shattered with a ferocious scream from her father. Mumma's sobs in between tears in which she sounded to be trying to deescalate her husband, could be heard, muffled by Grace's sweaty palms. Lottie sat huddled over in their pantry doing the same. Blocking out the cruel sounds that would pierce like arrows if they did not put up shields.

Mumma in truth was isolated. Her family and her church were her only community. She had not had the courage to tell her friends at church about what was going on because she feared their judgment and worst of all their pitying looks and half-hearted expressions of sympathy. She never imagined that anyone would be able to help her make the change she desperately needed. With every year that passed, the compounding shame, and fear of judgment or pity in that circle codified her silence. Her natural diffidence made her an easy target. She could easily be made to believe the things her husband said about her. And so she stayed quiet, as her spirit continued to fade.

\*\*\*

A message came through late the next morning. It was Vivi.

"Wow. Justin. I can't believe it. After all these years. How have you been?"

He read her greeting over. *I can't believe it.*

Justin leaned back in his chair for a while, hearing Emma in the other room negotiating the terms of finishing her apple slices.

"Hi Vivi, very nice to hear from you. I am well. How have you been?" he replied and pressed send. Three dots came up showing she was online writing a message back. He waited with anticipation of what she might say next.

"Looks like we are both in the bay. Would love to grab a coffee and sit in a park sometime (seems like all we really can do these days). Are you free this week?"

Justin froze. *She wants to meet me?* He hadn't actually thought his curiosity would actually lead to this. He closed his laptop. *It's a simple invitation to catch up from an old friend...girl...friend...Harmless. Why not meet up?*

He started thinking about how much he really wanted to see her again. How they had left it. Parting their separate ways at Roma Termini for no real reason other than that the currents they were on were leading them to different travel destinations. He was headed to South America to backpack Machu Picchu and she was headed to Australia to work on an organic farm next. It was a time in youth when saying goodbye was not assumed to be a forever goodbye, but rather an *I'll see you later.* More chances to cross paths would arise certainly. Now, 10 years later, that chance had materialised. Justin didn't know how he felt about it. Married now with a kid, this wasn't going to go anywhere beyond some sort of reunion to reminisce then go on their separate ways again, he told himself. It was the excitement of the invitation to live a little out of himself, with someone who knew his past self where more was possible, that drew his reply.

"Sure, I'm free tomorrow. I could meet you at Golden Gate Park."

Just as he hit send, Grace called to him from the other room. The rush of his plans fell flat as he was called in to help her with cleaning up the mess Emma had made in the playroom. As he knelt down and picked up tiny toys, placing them into their sorting bins, he had doubts. *What am I doing? I'm going to have to tell her my life is pretty much about cleaning up and wearing sweats?*

He wished he had been found in a more exotic time of his life. One that he could impress her with his interesting friends and experiences.

She had replied when he returned to the computer.

"Great. 12 PM at the Botanical Gardens and I'll bring coffees. Still like it dark roast with a splash of cream, extra hot? Here's my number, 415-632-5555; text me if you need to."

"Sure. See you then," he replied. *She remembered my coffee order.*

Different households were not supposed to gather, but he figured no harm in meeting her outside for a walk. He'd wear a mask to play it safe. That night Justin lay in bed staring at the ceiling remembering all he could about Vivi. Coconut tanning lotion and peppermint lip gloss. She liked Prosecco, cappuccinos, and sleeping in after late nights out. She had so many friends. Wherever she went, she seemed to make new ones. She was fashionably understated and always looked deeply into people's eyes when they spoke, as if no one else existed. He would have followed her to Australia had she invited him.

Grace leaned over after snapping her book shut. "Do you mind packing Emma's daycare bag in the morning before you drop her? I didn't have a chance to pack it and probably won't before I head out early." It was Grace's work day, she rushed each morning to clock-in on time.

"Sure," Justin replied in a warm tone.

"Thanks," Grace said as she turned off her lamp and turned over on her side facing away.

Justin lay there, struck by the contrast between the freedoms he used to enjoy as a single guy and the daily responsibilities that now surrounded. The shutters cast long angular shadows across the ceiling in the late hours. And try, as he may, he could not count them times over enough to fall asleep. His eyes darted between shadows, all a while thinking of Vivi. If honest with himself, his desire to be free of the limitations of his current life felt great now, and this disturbed his rest.

*** 

Grace pushed through the morning sickness. Feeling faint and nauseous at times with a steady fatigue murmuring beneath every waking hour. She gathered her lunch bag into her backpack to head out the door. Checking for keys and wallet, and her badge. It was hard to leave so early each time. The summer sun rose early and bright. Kids had not been in school for months now, and the traffic patterns of the summer seemed no different. Grace had switched to decaf coffee that sat by her side as she drove to work.

117

The sunlight reflected off the numerous glass windows. Many of which had shades drawn to shelter patients from the brightness of the outside world. She looked up at the hospital. *So much has changed about this place.* She used to think of it as a life raft that she jumped on to do her part. Now it felt more risky to be entering into the hospital. Contagion all around. The mentality of conservation amidst the many months of nationwide PPE shortage had made all the healthcare workers extremely frugal with the way they treated the PPE they got their hands on, and reluctant to throw away a single mask or face shield, as flimsy or as threadbare as they would become. Grace remembered how her grandmother had saved everything, not wanting to part with items, or somehow managing to repurpose items. *We must feel about our pieces of PPE what Grandma felt growing up in the great depression about food and items of worth.*

Entering into the hospital felt different today. Grace was different. The hospital's shuffle and roll continued day and night, working a solution for each patient, to a crisis on repeat. No end to this in sight. Doctors peering intently at telemetry monitors, and typing fastidiously on the rapidly clicking keyboards in the unit, had gravely concerned expressions permanently formed under their masks. As staff became infected, the staffing centre would offer overtime every day. Sometimes nurses stayed and worked a 12- or 16-hour shift. The physicians worked 12- to 24-hour shifts for sometimes 10–14 days straight.

The hospital never slept and for many of the healthcare workers, their lives became a laborious cycle of working long hours at the bedside, leaving to sleep and attend to their families before diving back into the fray. Home life was quiet and isolated whereas the hospital charged continuously with the bustle of a metropolis. The option to travel out of the country had been closed down as borders closed. To Grace, it felt as though the walls were closing out everything frivolous and entertaining in modern life. The hospital halls felt inhabited by the virus. When the doors of rooms with respiratory precautions were left ajar, Grace imagined that the invisible virus was wafting into the hallway. She made sure to wear her N95 and face-shield all shift, even when it clamped on her face tightly leaving red marks and bruises on her skin. The face shields distorted her vision with a glare, so as she moved quickly about her tasks, she had to be sure to account for her altered depth perception and slow her pace to insure she was seeing all she needed to.

As Grace moved through her day, she was thankful to have the protection that seemed to be working so far. The staff who worked in the ICU were instructed to wear respirators throughout their shift, as it was considered a unit with a high concentration of patients with COVID. Even though her headache seemed continuous, and dehydration made her tongue stick to the roof of her mouth, she welcomed the sense of protection she felt under the layers over any of the inconvenience. The work was hard and she would sweat a great deal covered in a plastic isolation gown tied at the waist.

Grace's patients both had COVID. One required regular haemodialysis due to sudden renal failure during the throws of COVID. He had been in the hospital for 25 days, and was 59 years old, a small gym owner, and a father of two. Her other patient, Jean, 40 years old, a paramedic, had recently been extubated. His throat was raw, and his voice was aphonic from the oedema and likely the gap made by bowing vocal cords that had been damaged by the swift passage and longstanding presence of the endotracheal tube placed to connect down into his trachea to deliver oxygen. Intermittent islands of weak sound came through breathy syllables as he attempted to communicate. He whispered a request for ice. It was the first thing he said when the sedation wore off.

He was at high risk for any food or liquid he would be given to aspirate into his lungs, being that they pulled the endotracheal tube just 10-hours ago, releasing him from the ventilator. They had tried to extubate him on day 10, but he decompensated quickly and earned himself another 15 days with the rhythm of the ventilator pushing air in and out of his body, a seemingly hollow cavity, sedated, and dangerously on the brink of death. "We will have speech pathology come and evaluate your swallowing."

"My swallowing? What's a speech pathologist going to do for my swallowing? My swallowing is fine," Jean protested. "That's what they are called, but they specialise in swallowing here at the hospital. Your swallow may be fine but when you've had a tube in your throat for as long as you have probably some damage in your throat or at least swelling that may make it risky for you to swallow."

Jean listened quietly. "Okay, I guess we will do it your way," he said with a conceding smile.

"They like to wait at least 24-hours after long intubations to evaluate you. Right now you are within that 24 hours timeframe and higher risk for aspiration. The last thing we need is more issues with your lungs because you aspirated your first meal." Grace liked to educate her patients on the reasons why things were happening the way they were in the hospital, where many times things didn't make sense to patients, or conflicted with what they thought was supposed to happen.

"Can they come as soon as possible? I can't wait to drink ice water again," he whispered, drawing her close to hear him.

"Yes, we can call tomorrow morning to see when they will come to evaluate. Meanwhile, try to relax, think about other things." Grace knew he, like so many others, would perseverate on this natural desire to satiate his dry mouth and hydrate. He had intravenous fluids running, but something about the cold sensation of ice and water in the parched mouth and running down dry throats was irreplaceable. "I'm sorry. I can give you some mouth swabs or these lemon glycerine swabs if you like to tie you over," Grace offered, knowing her offer was kind of weak.

"Ha. Great consolation."

Grace liked the humorous patients. "I'll take that as a yes," she replied with a smile. To herself, she remarked at how lucid he was, having been so sedated recently. "Jean, you've conquered so much just making it to this point. You should be so proud of yourself. I know Jenny can't wait to take you home. I look forward to toasting with you to your victory over the ventilator and passing your swallowing evaluation, over a glass of ice water."

Jean smiled. His eyes were tiring from their awake state, which had only been about an hour. His body was exhausted from functioning more so on its own now and after weeks in which his muscles had been wasting away with disuse. "Can you turn the lights down?" Jean said again in his whispered voice.

"Sure thing, Jean. Is there anything else I can get you?"

"Yeah, that glass of ice water," he said with a smile.

"Nice try, Jean." Grace chuckled as she closed the door. She loved to finally meet her patients after days and weeks watching closely to monitor their vitals, their lab results, proning and bathing their limp bodies, as they fought the battle of their lives, silently drawing them to the brink. Today, Jean warmed her heart, as she went to the sink to scrub her hands she thought about how fortunate he was to have made it, and how honoured she was to have been able to help him survive this part. She saw how Coronavirus had taken so much from people. Leaving them so often like vapid vessels, debilitated and weak.

The efforts of the physical therapists, occupational therapists, and speech pathologists to come in and rehabilitate these patients was so necessary to continue the recovery of mobility, self-care, swallowing, and often cognition, and even language when stroke complications sometimes took place secondary to Coronavirus. It was not enough to just survive this, the bricks needed to be built back up, to be able to regain a semblance of a normal quality of life and adequate functioning beyond the intensive care unit. Grace was glad they were ordered early in her unit and felt like she saw her patients benefit greatly.

The physical therapist came with an aide later that day to mobilise Jean. They had worked with him to assist in proning and were upping the complexity of mobility tasks with him now that he was awake and motivated to recondition his legs that had become skinny and weak with disuse over the course of the month. He was a tall guy and worked with the physical therapist who wrapped a bright orange gait belt around his abdomen to assist him, once with much effort made it to the edge of bed, while the physical therapist aide helped to stabilise him from behind, to stand-up with a walker placed in front. His legs shook like saplings rattled by the wind, but withstood the task as he was tasked to shift his weight. It took much effort for him to stand, only able to maintain his balance and bare weight through his legs for around 30 seconds, before he was assisted back to the edge of bed, breathing heavily and surprised by how hard such a simple task had become.

"It's alright, mate," the physical therapist said, "We're at the start of the race. No need to sprint just yet."

Jean laughed between laboured breathing. After he recovered, the physical therapist challenged him to do it again. Grace stood outside the door, watching her patient who had all but died two weeks ago, struggle to stand. The physical therapist aide took his vitals at regular intervals between tasks. He maintained the upper end of a normal range for his exertion. His oxygen was trended in the mid-90s with the support of three litres per minute on a nasal cannula. His respiratory rate was driving into the high 20s. He was working hard. All the movement caused him to cough up secretions, helping clear his airway.

The team worked with him on strengthening his limbs against resistance, once he tired of working to stand and sit. *I can't believe just over a month ago, this guy was pulling people out of wrecked cars.* Grace thought to herself as she watched her patient who had been in the prime of his life, working as a paramedic, a first responder, strong and capable, now reduced to a fraction of himself. She could see he was determined, albeit shocked with the loss he had encountered in himself. When no one was in his room, she could see him trying to conceal his tears from the staff who looked on, turning his head, as he would talk on the phone with his wife.

The occupational therapist came with the physical therapists the next day and they worked on performing self-hygiene tasks—brushing teeth and face and putting on pants from a seated position at the edge of bed. His balance would never hold him enough right now to try standing. He cried during his session when trying to perform these once simple activities of daily living. It seemed to become very real to him that he had lost so much strength and ability when he struggled to lift his legs enough to put on his socks and shoes or shorts. The realisation overcame Jean intermittently. In which he would pause in whatever task and tears formed from deep mourning for what he had lost.

The speech-language pathologist, Kiera, arrived late morning for the swallowing evaluation. Jean sat up eagerly in his bed when she arrived with a tray of different food and liquid trials. She completed an oral mechanism exam peering into his mouth and with her flashlight and checking the integrity of his cranial nerves by having him move his eyebrows, tongue and lips and jaw. Grace watched eagerly, hoping today would be the day they could *salud* to a glass of icy water. Kiera administered a single ice-chip via tsp. Jean sputtered, coughing violently in response. The swallowing evaluation was concluded.

She advised they continue with his nasogastric enteral feeding regimen that the registered dietician had been carefully overseeing for the past weeks, with a plan for swallow reassessment tomorrow. She told Grace that for now the typical bedside fibreoptic endoscopic evaluation of swallow option was currently not an option due to the pandemic as that service had been suspended until they worked out the infection prevention workflows needed for the aerosol generating nasal endoscopic procedure.

"He may be able to do a video fluoroscopic swallow study, when he can manage to go down to radiology and show some progress with his swallow that may make us believe he's ready to advance to an oral diet. Right now, his swallow appears weak and healing from the recent intubation." She advised they wait a little time and work on swallow conditioning tasks and allow for some spontaneous healing for the suspected swelling and potential trauma to vocal folds. "Make sure he gets really good oral care with that suction kit, okay?"

Speech pathologists were always nagging Grace about good oral care. *I never would do poor oral care,* she thought, but she gracefully took their incessant reminders. "Make sure you press those pink Toothettes against the side of the cup to squeeze most of the water out. They need to be damp, because otherwise they carry a teaspoon of water. He will likely aspirate that amount of water if he tries to swallow it okay?"

Grace nodded as Kiera left the room. Jean sat, looking upset. "She didn't even give me anything to eat."

"I know, Jean," Grace replied. "She saw that your swallow wasn't up to it today. Rather than give you more things to eat and drink that may go straight to your lungs, she chose to stop the evaluation. She'll be back tomorrow."

Kiera reassessed for a few more days, until it seemed promising that Jean may be able to advance to an oral diet, but she wanted to be sure he wasn't silently aspirating. The pulmonologist agreed Jean would be stable enough to transfer down to the radiology suite where the video fluoroscopic swallow study would be performed. All ICU patients went down with their nurse to monitor them. "It's going to be a good day," Jean said, looking up at Grace, as they wheeled him in the gurney into the elevators. "I haven't had anything to eat in over a month. I've got to pass this test."

"We are all rooting for you," the transporter chimed in. Grace kept an eye on the portable monitor making sure he wasn't becoming tachycardic with all the commotion, as he had recently during physical therapy.

"Am I still alive, Nurse Grace?" Jean chided, as he saw her eyes glued to the monitor. "Yes, very much so, Jean. Let's keep it that way." They both laughed. The humour they had found amidst the complicated and tenuous setting of the ICU was refreshing, making all the intolerable more tolerable and she was thankful to have Jean as her patient.

Kiera met them at the doors of the fluoroscopy suit. She wore a lead apron covering her body and special glasses in addition to all the PPE. "Hi Jean. Looks like you are ready to go. I've got the barium mixed into the food and liquid and we are ready for you." The radiology technologist moved the equipment and assisted the nurse as they transferred the patient into the special chair that moved up and down with a remote and fit in the relatively narrow space of the x-ray machine. The radiologist came in and the Kiera gave a brief report. "This is Jean. He had a 25-day intubation, acute respiratory failure secondary to COVID-19 with pneumonia and tachycardic complications. Pulmonology suspects oedema and potential vocal cord trauma as vocal quality remains severely hoarse. Purpose is to evaluate oropharyngeal swallow and rule-out silent aspiration and determine least restrictive/safest diet level options to inform dysphagia management decisions."

"Sounds good," the radiologist said as he leaned over to adjust the buttons on the fluoroscopy tower. "Hi Jean. I'm Dr Sydney. I'm here to take the pictures."

"I didn't know I was coming for a photo shoot, I would have dressed up," Jean remarked humorously.

Grace positioned the monitor on Jean's lap so she could see it from the anteroom. She wore a spare lead vest in case she would have to jump in. Kiera guided the radiology tech and radiologist as they positioned Jean so there was a full view of his mouth and throat. The team performed a preprocedural time out and lowered the lights.

"Okay Jean. Here is a teaspoon of thin liquid, fluoro please," Kiera said as she passed him the teaspoon carefully, instructing the radiologist to hit the pedal and stepped back to peer intently at the monitor. Watching the black liquid tumble down his throat, the bolus bifurcated at the top of his airway with some liquid spilling like a stream past the vocal cords. He did not overtly respond with a cough or a throat clear as would be expected. Aspiration.

Kiera stayed steady and administered her protocol including cup sips and nectar and honey thickened liquids, pudding, diced peaches, and a cracker. She asked Jean to tuck his chin in and hold the bolus in his mouth before swallowing with great effort as she observed the effect of the strategies. Jean was very motivated and worked hard to follow all of her directions, although multi-step and hard to hear through the layers of Kiera's PPE. "Okay Jean, I got all the images I needed. I'm going to look over the study again with a fine-tooth comb, but it looks preliminarily, you are ready to eat a modified diet texture level. You will be able to have mechanical soft chopped solid textures and nectar thickened liquids safely."

"So I passed?"

"Well, we don't call it 'passing', but you are successfully able to eat and drink without aspiration if we give you some modified textures, and if you do a chin tuck every time you take a cup-sip. Your throat muscles have become quite weak and it's harder for you to protect your airway. I have a plan now for what swallowing exercises we can do to strengthen your swallowing muscles."

"Okay. So does that mean I can eat?"

Kiera smiled. "Yes Jean, you made it. You are cleared to eat. I'll come up to your bedside a little later and review all of the recommendations in depth."

"Wow, thank you, Kiera. Can I order a steak from the kitchen and a glass of merlot to celebrate?"

Kiera laughed as they wheeled Jean out of the radiology suit. Grace returned to the unit and fielded Jean's requests for something to eat and drink graciously, "We just need to wait for that diet order." She watched him from beyond the glass sliding doors at her workstation. She looked up from her monitor where she had been reviewing the most recent lab values. In one swift move, Jean yanked the nasogastric tube out of his nose, pulling the long tube out and throwing it to the ground. Grace rushed into the room after what felt like drawn out minutes as she donned her PPE.

When she entered, Jean was pulling at all of his lines impulsively. "Jean! Why did you do that? You know we were planning to remove that feeding tube properly."

Jean had a different look to him. He seemed to be becoming confused, and rambling incoherently. This witty man was now not able to string together a meaningful sentence. He mumbled about needing to pack his bags. He seemed to have trouble finding words as he assertively explained his plan to Grace, "I'm gonna t-take that bagown with me. You know. The s-screwdriver. No. skeleton has long tripes."

The content of his speech had become nonsensical and slurred. *Is this delirium or a stroke?* Grace thought to air on the side of caution and call a stroke alert, due to this sudden onset of slurred speech, aphasia, impulsivity, and confusion. Grace knew that there was some data starting to come out that indicated a small percentage of COVID-19 patients were having strokes during hospitalisation. Within 30-minutes, he had been diagnosed by the neurologist to have had an ischaemic stroke and was given a Tenecteplase thrombolytic. Grace's shift ended, as she looked through into Jean's room, saddened by the fact that the light she found in such a witty man who had brought humour to his circumstances, was now a vapid body, laying in his bed. She hoped that the clot buster would work and restore his function. He had been through so much. The oncoming nurse took report and felt the same sentiment as Grace, as she too had grown to enjoy Jean, as she had been caring for him for most of his ICU admission during evening shifts.

Grace scrubbed her arms and hands. It was hard to wash the day off, as her patients often lingered with her as she went through the motions of clocking out and grabbing her things out of her locker. She thought about Jean's success in his swallow study earlier that morning and Jean's excitement to finally after over a month be able to eat. His hopes to have a meal tonight had been dashed. *Why does fate deal such cruel hands* Grace thought as she thought about Jean and his wife, Jenny. Jenny had spoken directly to the neurologist before Grace gave report. Jianfei, the PM shift nurse, was going to have to speak with Jenny tonight and comfort the inevitable groans that would take place on the other end of the phone as Jenny would face the prospect of yet another hurdle to Jean's recovery. Her own hopes dashed, as he was starting to show such promise.

Grace drove home, drinking an energy drink. She brought one with her nearly every day of late, to crack open on her way home so she could have a second wind, ready to do what she affectionately referred to as 'night shift'. *It's so senseless.* All that was transpiring all around during this pandemic, seemed to rise up in Grace's stomach, an uncontrollable nervous storm that she couldn't help but feel was beginning to swallow her whole much as she remembered it would do when she was a child, hidden in the pantry. Grace had forgotten entirely she was pregnant, all day. Once she realised, she stopped drinking from the can. *I've got to get a grip. Take care of yourself Grace. You're carrying a baby.*

Grace had not fully come to terms with this reality and had held off making the appointment with her obstetrician. *I'll make the appointment.* She promised herself. Grace pulled into the driveway and pulled up her medical appointment App. She scheduled an appointment, selecting the box. "I'm pregnant." She hesitated before selecting the box, prolonging the limbo.

Pregnancy, a baby, a new mouth to feed and nurture. It was a happy thought, although an inconvenient one. Her life had just started to feel more put together with Emma gaining more independence, sleeping well, nearly potty trained. It made her feel vulnerable to be pregnant. More vulnerable than she was already feeling as a healthcare worker in the hospital at this time. Avoiding the official diagnosis of 'pregnant' meant she could live gripping to what sense of agency she had left.

Grace had been excited when she was pregnant with Emma, but she had no idea what it all entailed. She was floating along a lazy river, fed imagery from friends and family about the bliss of parenthood. She knew now, parenthood was a commitment that had taken every ounce of her. Possessing her heart, her will, her mind, and her physical body more than anyone or thing or place she had ever known. Doing it again frightened her, as she thought about all the challenges, sleepless nights, added responsibility compounded by this strange time. Support systems were fractured, as households had been encouraged to remain separate for most of the year so far.

The days rolled on, and Jean was now aphasic. His language fragmented, his awareness of his errors marginal. He would talk at length, with some real words misplaced and often nonsensical or partial utterances. Jenny, his wife of four years, was given clearance to come into the hospital to be with him. He was considered no longer infectious—the testing showed that the virus was no longer detectable in his body.

Jenny sat with him, showed him pictures and helped him use his right hand which had lost some control since the stroke. The task of getting himself dressed was not just about deconditioned legs, it was now weakness in his hands to grip the clothing and manoeuvre the folds of fabric, oriented correctly over his body. The occupational therapist came to work with him, helping him practice using his dominant right hand to stimulate return of function as well as use his non-dominant hand to perform self-care tasks like brushing his teeth, dressing and feeding himself. He remained in the ICU for a while as his blood pressure was not easily controlled, it would climb higher than what any of the providers were comfortable with, at the drop of a hat.

He was given another Videofluoroscopic Swallow Study for his suspected new baseline. Now, neurological controls of his swallow musculature had become impaired from the stroke. The study showed that although his swallow had become further impaired, he was able to eat pureed foods and still drink nectar thickened liquids from a cup with chin tuck safely. He struggled to feed himself. So Jenny, or Grace, or the licensed vocational nurse would assist him with set up and self-feeding, as able. Grace went down to the cafeteria on her break to grab some hot soup. Chicken dumpling today with saltine crackers. She sat outside, alone, with the other seats at the tables taped off.

Only one person per table allowed, as part of the COVID safety precautions on the hospital's campus. It felt tiresome, all these days, similar to the next, nothing really to look forward to. Like being out to sea, sailing with no land in sight days on end, dubiously holding out for fair weather in waters known to be treacherous. It was clear this disease although was indiscriminate towards who it would infect, lay heavy blows to minority communities.

COVID had revealed so much of the human condition and subjugating systems that lay beneath the surface of the American facade of prosperity and promise. When the surface jolted and tectonic plates moved, how inequitable society had become was brought forth into the limelight. Healthcare access, healthcare literacy, and general health of minority groups was revealed in how a disproportionate number suffered more greatly at the hands of the Coronavirus, in the current system.

So many people were finding themselves without jobs and health insurance and despite federal and local government assistance pausing student loan payments, a temporary moratorium on evictions, stimulus checks, a lot of strain could be felt, as the socioeconomic burdens and pressures remained, if not grew all around. Factors built upon each other indelibly, contributing to a great sense of dis-ease amongst all of Grace's colleagues. Grace was thankful to be employed, although spent every day with the imminent stressor of her fear that she would get COVID and end up like her patient before her in a bed fighting to stay alive. The insecurities of the present global situation, with a pandemic tilting the world on its axis, felt strangely familiar to Grace, who's formative years were spent in distrust of the intentions and actions of her father and the competency of her mother to protect them. The unpredictability of this Coronavirus, which seemed to accelerate and destruct, seemed like a familiar foreboding presence, and it made her feel those anxious sensations rise once again, as she had as a child contending with her father.

The fear of getting COVID with every surface touched, or task performed wore on Grace's nerves and her mind would strain to recall much else. As time went on, she was beginning to feel numb for most of her shift. The light in her eyes that she had held for nursing the sick, selflessly, was beginning to fade.

Grace saw Elle across the courtyard. It made her nervous to see her. She felt secretly hurt that Elle had not disclosed the details of her affair and felt stuck with the information. Thinking of Justin's advice to say nothing, she looked over at Elle and made small talk, hoping she might divulge a clue to what was really going on. Elle did not let on. No plans for Wednesdays at the shady park were made. Grace went about her duties, trying not to let the situation bother her. There was no getting around the fact that they had grown apart. This saddened Grace, but at the time, she knew her plate was full with no room to entertain the drama that surrounded Elle right now.

Grace poked her head into Jean's room. "How are you doing, Jenny? Can I get you a cup of tea, coffee or soda?"

Jenny looked up, still in thought, as she had been gazing at her sleeping husband. "Oh, a coffee would be nice. Thank you."

"Sure thing," Grace replied, heading over to the dietary station to fill a paper cup with hot coffee.

"Thank you, Grace," Jenny welcomed the cup warmly. "The monitor is reading steadily today. Dr August said that he may be ready to transfer to the medical floor tomorrow," Jenny said with a hopeful glimmer in her eyes. The deep lines of grief, trenches dug into her forehead in the past month, lifted with a deep sigh giving way to tears that tumbled uncontrollably down her cheeks.

Grace grabbed for a tissue box, positioning it in her lap and standing by to listen. "Grace, I just thought…" Her emotions pulled the reins, halting her speech as she attempted to explain her shock and dismay in how Jean's medical course had taken them for such a ride with no clear end in sight. "He was so funny, Grace, he had such passion for life. He never worried about the future. And now, he can barely stand, feed himself or string together a single sentence. He cries with me every day, trying to tell me he's sorry."

Grace could see that Jenny's pain was deep, as she was mourning the loss of what was, and what she was realising would be. "I th-thought when he had come off that ventilator, we were on our way past all of this. He was weak but he was going to make it. Why would God let him suffer even more?…he's never going to be the same. I-I don't know how to help make it better. We were going to start a family this year. I don't know if I can do this. I-I don't know if I can care for him. That sounds terrible, I know."

Her tears, uncontrollable, bore the heaviness of a pain Grace had known. Mourning what was and what she thought would be. Grace knew nothing she would say would change the situation, so she sat with her quietly, withholding any other expression but her support. She silently hoped to absorb the load so that maybe Jenny might carry a little less on her own. The burden of grappling with hopes and expectations for the future dashed, was sometimes heavier than coming to terms with the immediate loss itself.

Grace left her shift a little early to attend her doctor's appointment. The medical assistant weighed her and took her blood pressure, making small talk about the hot weather and impending fire season, then handed her a cup with her medical record information stuck to the lid in a brown paper bag. "Now, you know the drill, Grace." Deidre had seen her through her first pregnancy with Emma.

"Thank you, Deidre," she said, taking the bag and heading to the bathroom in the hallway. She had drunk a good deal of water earlier to ensure a good sample. When it was completed, she placed it on a special shelf with a window behind it to be collected for analysis.

"Okay Grace, you will get your results emailed to you within 24 hours okay dear? I'm going to room you now, because Dr Ryder wants to do an ultrasound."

Grace didn't know she might see the baby but realised that given it had been over a month since her period would have been due, perhaps there was reason to take a look at how the baby was developing. The bright lights of the exam room always made Grace feel a bit on edge. Spotlights exposing her, once again, a specimen on a tray to be examined. Dr Ryder, a cheery woman, came in greeting Grace. "So, we have a positive at home pregnancy test and nearly eight weeks since your last period, did you say?"

"Give or take."

"Okay then, I think we should do an ultrasound to see if we can take a peek at the baby." Grace could tell that Dr Ryder was excited to play a role as one of the first to view the babies. She prepared the ultrasound wand and had Grace move her gown, as she smeared cold gel over her abdomen. Grace had noticed her lower abdomen had been hardening, a burgeoning bump. Dr Ryder, focused on the screen, manoeuvring the ultrasound wand around, which pushed down kind of hard until she landed on a small pulsing, dark blob with small appendages. To her, it looked like shadows and shapes.

"There's your baby's heartbeat," she said proudly. Suddenly she could make out the little form inside her. Her baby. "I'm going to take measurements here to see how many weeks along you are." Dr Ryder drew lines and labels on the shadowy images she took that calculated lengths and diameters of the foetal anatomy and other aspects of Grace's uterus. Grace peered at them trying to make sense of what she could see, it was too hard to make out. "Okay, well, Grace. You are definitely pregnant. It looks like you are eight weeks and two days along."

Grace absorbed this news, feeling outside of her body briefly. She marvelled at the fact that the doctor could pinpoint the number of days past a week. "And how many?"

"There is one foetus," Dr Ryder replied. Grace breathed a sigh of relief that she did not identify multiples. It had been a fear of hers that she would have a set of twins or triplets in her second pregnancy. Dr Ryder, amused, remarked with a chuckle, "You aren't the first to exhale deeply with the announcement of one foetus in a second pregnancy." Dr Ryder printed off a series of pictures. "Here's the photo shoot for you to show your husband as proof. It looks like Emma is going to have a brother or sister due on December 9th."

December seemed far away given how long the year had felt so far. "Wow. Okay, well, there it is."

Dr Ryder looked at Grace to see if she wanted to expand more, but Grace did not. She couldn't quite bring words to bear a remark on how she was feeling with this definitive diagnosis of pregnancy, and a real due date, and a real baby with a heartbeat for which she had seven images of on lengthy glossy paper now in her hand. "Well then, my dear, here is a pamphlet on your options for managing this pregnancy if you wish to review. Please see Deidre on your way out, as she will schedule your next appointment."

"Okay, thank you, Dr Ryder," Grace said, as Dr Ryder's white coat disappeared behind the door as she pushed the portable ultrasound machine into the hall. Onto her next patient no doubt. Grace, now left under the bright lights with a bunch of pictures and a diagnosis, sat there for a moment, trying to find something to anchor herself too. There was nothing comforting about the room, except a few thank you cards to Dr Ryder that she had pinned to the bulletin. It was her breath that she found eventually and concentrated on.

She felt nervous energy take over her body, as she tried to combat the spiralling sensation with deep breaths before gaining enough balance to shed her patient gown and put her clothes back on. She felt alone in herself with the physical and emotional journey ahead that she knew was hers and hers alone, no matter how much Justin would support her in this. At the same time, she felt fulfilled with the knowledge that a life, a future, was growing inside her this very minute. It was a treasure she possessed and needed to care for. Yet, she would be lying if she said it did not frighten her.

# Chapter 9
# Beginnings

Across the meadow, flowers about her in rows, Justin could make out Vivi. She wore a pale blue linen dress and a floppy sun hat and a cross body satchel casually hanging from her shoulder. "Justin!" She had recognised him, as he strode across to meet her. It felt as if it had been a lifetime ago that she had left him on the train on the long platform, with only a few emails exchanged in the subsequent weeks, imparting shallow niceties and vague recounts of their experiences, both had been destined to separate adventures.

The same row of sterling bracelets shook on her left hand as she waved. Justin, forgetting the decade, beaming as he approached. "Vivi!" They embraced briefly.

"My God, Justin, you only got more handsome with age!" Vivi laughed as they parted, taking a good look at him. They stood there, taking in each other's presence, ignoring all else outside of where they had left off. Vivi was as beautiful as ever, she had not changed much in her appearance, in the way that happiness preserves a person.

She handed him his coffee and motioned that they start walking the path through the botanical garden. They walked for nearly two hours in total, catching up. She was now a pastry chef, baking high end wedding cakes for chic clientele in San Francisco. Business had slowed during the pandemic. She had never married and had no children. From New York, she had followed a guy out to San Francisco four years prior. The relationship had concluded as a disaster, but she decided to stay and settle. It was the first place she said in the whole world, where she felt at home. He was comforted by how easy it was for him to tell her about Grace, how they met, his job as a teacher, and Emma. Vivi listened with those wide eyes that assured him that her attention was all his, and what he had to say was meaningful to her. They lamented over how the pandemic had ushered in so many restrictions to travel and spoke about how they couldn't wait to get back out there in the world. Justin knew that for him, his obligations to family life had planted him more firmly where he was than Vivi. After the obligatory broad stroked descriptions of their current lives, they dove into reminiscing. Their laughter pierced the otherwise quiet surroundings of the botanical garden, as they recalled the fun they had had when they had set up as street performers briefly, trying their hand at miming in Paris to earn enough cash to pay their way through France on the rail and the time they slept on the beach in Capri, after all the ferries left for the day, with no choice but to take shelter under a colourful row boat turned over on the shore. How the stars had glistened that night to the sonnet of gentle water lapping on the shore, with the boats bobbing and knocking in the harbour.

Justin couldn't help but feel the chemistry they had shared, alive and well, as if not a day had passed. As they walked with measured steps, engaged in conversation, he couldn't help but revel in those old friends, those bright free feelings bursting with possibility that danced around them, even now. As they walked, the afternoon light shifted with the fog returning for the day's end. They both continued now that the roar of their conversation had dwindled down to small talk, both not wanting their walk to end.

As they arrived back at the flower garden, Vivi made a serious turn in conversation. "Listen, Justin," Vivi said, "I know this is a lot here, but I just want you to know that, that, for years, I wished I had asked you to come with me to Australia. I didn't expect after that day when I said goodbye to you, that our paths wouldn't cross, until…" Justin looked at her squarely. "Until it was too late," Vivi said, with an air of sobering finality.

All the promise of her words, words he had hoped she would have said to him a decade prior, dissipated in the misty air. *Too late.* He stood silently with her, holding her, as people walked and jogged by, "I know, me too." They stood there, halting time, willing suspension to somehow recast their fates. And when the moment could not be captured any longer, they stepped back. It was time to go.

"Vivi. Thank you for meeting me here." Vivi smiled. "I hope it won't be another decade until I see you again," she said playfully.

"Vivi, I'm always around." He paused, he needed to tell her this, perhaps the last chance he would have, to complete what he knew he should have said when he had had the chance. He knew that his inability to fully commit to her then, was the reason she had not asked him to come with her to Australia. Perhaps it had been a test, to see if he would follow her, to see if he…"Vivi, you should know that I loved you."

Vivi smiled with sadness in her eyes now. For he knew that what he was telling her, answered a question she had not known the answer to for all of these years because of his selfishness at the time, and absence in her life thereafter. "I'll always love you too, Just." They parted ways amongst the flowers, with no plans to see each other again.

Justin walked away that afternoon perplexed by the intensity of what had transpired, the said, and the unsaid. The closure and the sadness was forged by the chasm between when they left off a decade ago and the present, the *what if*.

She had been so beautiful then and now. His someone that he had lost along the way. Now, no longer lost to him. But, what she was to him now was something different, it had to be. Seeing Vivi unravelled what of him that had been tightly bound, placed out of sight in his present life. Now, he didn't quite know where to place her. As he drove across the lower Bay Bridge, the dark concrete above blocking most of the foggy sky that now enshrouded San Francisco, he recalled the intensity of his and Vivi's meeting.

She did not say that she used to love him, she said that she did, she *does* and she would. He kept mulling over her phrasing, as he sped on the freeway. It felt poetic and dangerous all at once. But he could not stop thinking about her. It was like this new variable transcended the moment; it revealed something in him that had been stirring a long time. He wanted to be as free as he once had. He wanted more.

***

Mumma stopped sewing Grace new dresses in the weeks after that night at Grace's grandparents' house. Her dresses were threadbare and becoming too high above the knee to be suitable for daily wear. Grace would look at the other girls at school and envy their well-fitting skirts, dresses and pinafores. The ribbons looked carefully tied by mothers who took the time to ceremoniously wash and brush their daughter's hair. Grace longed for this sort of attention and care from her mother, silently, while watching the other girls. She never told her mother this.

Mumma spent most of her days in her room, with the blinds drawn. When Daddy left for work and the girls left for school, she would retreat to her room, and go to sleep for most of the day and sometimes into the night. She had stopped attending church, and after weeks and months of her callers from the congregation stopping by to an unanswered door, no one asked after her. Mumma carried out some basic tasks at home, and would do the shopping, but it was up to the girls to draw the water if they were to bathe that day or wash their clothing, if they hoped to have fresh clothing to wear.

Daddy rarely noticed his clothes weren't washed, as he wore tired navy-blue coveralls with oil spots tainted with a thick gasoline odour every day to work. She would wash his clothes occasionally, just to avoid him saying something. Some nights there would be no pot steaming on the stovetop. Their mother would be absent stowing away in her room or sitting in front of the television with a despondent and internally distracted facial expression. Grace would take it upon herself to fix dinner for her and Lottie on these nights. She would boil pasta shells and add a jar of marinara sauce or make peanut butter and jelly sandwiches. Some nights they would mix mayonnaise in tuna from the cans Mumma stored at the back of the pantry and scoop up the creamy tuna salad with saltines.

Mumma never asked after them as she sat in the room watching the television. She had effectively tuned out from the present, numbed herself to her reality, which included her daughters. It was her broad escape to do so. Daddy usually came home so drunk, he didn't notice his wife didn't have a meal waiting for him, nor that he hadn't eaten it.

This particular evening, Grace sat on the front steps, watching the street corner for Daddy to tear around the bend and ride fast over the gravel. She would usually run inside before he arrived at their driveway, and listen to the reckless sound of popping gravel under fast moving wheels coming to a halt. Tonight she stayed on the step. Raw feelings of hatred were simmering inside her. She thought about how she had noticed her mother becoming more and more withdrawn and timid in the months since they had walked to Grandpa and Grandma's house. This had caused her to feel an ill-will towards them, for reasons for which she wasn't certain, only that she knew that whatever her mother had come for they did not give her, they would not give her.

Grace knew that this was her father's fault and every time since that night, her resentment grew, listening through the walls and along the floorboards to the violence he inflicted. Since Mumma rarely left the house or had visitors, she would wander through the house with large bruises on her face and arms and legs, busted lips, and sometimes open wounds on her head, matting her hair with dark red patches of dried blood. Her porcelain skin and movie star facial features had become progressively depleted to the point that she was no longer recognisable. It was as though the weight of living had wiped her beauty clean off her face. Her tired and forlorn features were now what anyone would notice first about her. There were no longer bright eyes and the big smile that Grace had grown up gazing deeply into, memorising every crease and mannerism of her mother over time. She was a stranger, a drifting figure in their home that did not resemble their mother.

Grace often wished her mother would cover up her wounds and bruises and make an effort to look her best. In Grace's mind, Mumma was a lesser target if Daddy could see her beauty and appeal to his softer side. If Mumma looked like her old self, then perhaps things would go back to how they used to be. Normal. Yet, Mumma never seemed to be able to bring herself to follow through with the effort it would take to put herself together again after beatings. As the beatings continued and became more frequent, sometimes two to three times per week, Grace began to side with her mother's logic on the matter. *What was the point?* Despondency would settle into the spaces of their home and Mumma's being that had been carved out by repeated afflictions.

The exception was once per week on Friday evenings, when she would don dark sunglasses and heavy concealer, two shades darker than her natural skin tone, to leave the house to do the grocery shopping. She shopped at night so she wouldn't have to see her old church community housewives who would frequent the market while the children were at school. Grace liked these evenings, even though Mumma would go out, because Mumma would make them bowls of steamy macaroni before she left, and Daddy rarely came home before midnight on Friday nights, too tired to pick a fight at the end of his long work week. The girls would play dress ups in their mother's closet and spend time captivated by the freedom they felt with their parents gone. Free to dictate the mood of their home for a time.

Mumma would return from the grocery store, a little more upbeat than her usual self, putting away groceries and stashing away the excess bills and coins she had received as change. Mumma would intentionally shop the sales and use coupons to maximise her return after buying what would pass as enough food for the week. Grace thought of it as wildly smart that her mother would save for their vacation, their escape through these means, and said nothing when they ate lesser quality of smaller quantity meals.

That evening, she sat on the steps awhile, mulling over the series of nights filled with violent tirades in their house, when Mumma and Lottie were inside. She stared emboldened into the blazing summer sun as it began to relinquish its grasp on the toiling dry earth and dried grasses on the surrounding foothills that simmered with heat. She sat in calculation. Taking inventory of all the things her daddy's actions had affected in their lives. She wanted to tell him to his face that she hated him for what he did to Mumma and for whatever he did to make Grandma turn them away that night. *Maybe he would apologise, maybe he would leave and never come back.* So, she waited, and pushed small stones around with her shoes that had migrated to the steps, watching them tumble off the brick ridges or scatter to the edge of the ledges.

She sat in contemplation, breeding contempt as the memories piled up high and made her feel wild. Time passed, and she awaited Daddy's speeding around the corner. When the time came, Grace lost her nerve, standing up from the front steps as her father slammed the door to his truck and picked up his hat that fell off in the process. As much as her heart burned for the opportunity and enough grit to stand up to her father, she knew she couldn't stand up to him. She feared the possibility. Not knowing if he would fling her as he had her mother at the first sign of insubordination.

Grace went back into the house. Mumma had emerged from her room to prepare dinner, having heard the truck door. She stood over the stove, a vapid shadow of her former self, carrying out common tasks with a hollow expression perpetually fixed upon her. It disquieted Grace to see her mother like this, although as weeks and months had passed, she became accustomed to the gradual decline. Her mother had been the mantle upon which Grace hung her sense of stability, protection and calm as a younger child. Now seeing her mother's spirit and engagement with her family diminish, Grace felt like the underpinning of unadulterated constancy and certainty her mother brought to their home was dissolving and she too was beginning to feel like she was spinning out of control, sucked into the undertow of deep water dragging her far from land.

\*\*\*

Grace took Emma to the playground. Grace sat on the edge of the sandbox, watching Emma run her fingers and spindly twigs through the sand. Tracing shallow lines across the surface of the sand and marvelling at the designs that resulted. She hadn't yet told Justin about the baby. She had stuffed the ultrasound pictures into her purse. Throughout the day her fingers would slide past the glossy surfaces whenever she would rummage through her purse, as a reminder that this information was still very much a secret, waiting to be revealed. Grace pulled the pictures out and panned through the black and white images. All of Grace's withstanding disbelief was thwarted by the grainy figure of a growing baby. A confirmation of the life she was carrying.

Grace felt a surge of despair roll over her shoulders and into her chest, her stomach beginning to fall. *This will be good for Emma. A sibling for Emma.* Grace knew that she felt most motivated about this new pregnancy because of what it meant for Emma to have the sibling that she had always thought to give her. Grace sat quietly, urging her eyes to pull back tears, while trying to push aside her mounting thoughts that made her feel selfish. *Now just isn't the right time. Why did I let this happen? I don't know if I can really do this. How is this going to change my life? I just got settled back at work and now I have to go through this all again. I'm afraid to be pregnant. There are so many things that could go wrong. I don't want to get COVID while I'm pregnant.*

Grace's thoughts darted and when they stuck, they spiralled. She felt fearful, guilty and trapped in this moment. Grace's anxious spells were becoming more regular in the past months. She had dealt with anxiety as a child and in her teens and early twenties until she had sought counselling. She found it unnerving for the sense of dread that something very bad was about to happen to be creeping back into her daily life. She sat, focusing on her breath and the technique she had learned to push the anxious thoughts away. Grace was unable to focus on what Emma was asking her, over and over her little voice with increasing volume requesting confirmation on whether they would get ice cream. "Mummy! Listen to me," Emma said in a direct and angered tone.

Grace snapped out of her distraction, now aiming her focus on Emma's big hazel eyes peering up into hers. She repeated herself, now having gained Grace's undivided attention for a moment. "Mummy, can we go get ice cream?"

Grace smiled. "Yes, Emma girl, I think an ice cream is exactly what this afternoon calls for."

"Yay!" Emma squealed. "We're going to get ice-cream!"

Grace thought, as she got up quickly from the side of the sandbox, shaking the granules from her sandals and skirt, that moving was another technique that could help quell the anxiety. A change of scenery would help distract her from her anxious thoughts. "Come darling, let's go." She walked hand in hand with Emma, feeling her sweaty and grubby hand in her palm. *This little girl. She has no idea how complicated the world really is. What am I doing bringing another child into this screwed up situation?*

Once in the car seat, Grace wiped Emma's hands down and sprayed with hand sanitiser, a regular ritual that Emma was now accustomed to. She knew how to put her hands out for a back and front spray, then how to rub her fingers together to get the sanitiser spread between. Grace was thankful that Emma had now accepted wearing a mask when they went out in public spaces. This had been a fight initially, taking much coaxing and the purchase of masks with special patterns like rainbows and unicorns.

As they drove across town towards the ice cream parlour, Grace drew the connection in her mind between her own childhood and the traumas that had given rise to anxiety. Foreboding shadows originating in her past cast darkness into her present in unexpected places, and as always, she feared into her future.

"Mummy, I want strawberry and mint chips," Emma was ready, as she looked intently out the window hoping to catch a first glimpse of the cheerful shop front painted in candy pink and white. Emma licked her double scoop, begrudgingly letting Grace help her stop the dripping with broad sweeping clean-up licks of the cold and creamy mint chip and strawberry flavours. "Thank you, Mummy, for my ice cream."

"Oh you're very welcome, my darling." *I love being a mum.* Grace thought with a decisive spirit that she knew if she would only commit her mind to would help her along and dissuade her from her trepidation. Emma was growing fast. Three years old in a week's time and had recently begun talking up a storm, with more complex language than she expected for her age. Grace absorbed the moment, watching Emma standing on the sidewalk smiling and waving at the dogs that passed by with an unadulterated enthusiasm that both surprised and endeared the owners. One dog licked the splodges of ice cream that dripped to her feet, eagerly, as Emma giggled with delight.

"Now Emma, we need to eat the ice cream. Please don't waste it on the ground," Grace said with a smile, observing and partially amused by Emma's intent to attract dogs to her ice cream mess.

\*\*\*

Justin sat at home, while Grace and Emma were at the park. He lay in his regular spot, on the couch, watching TV. As he tracked the screen his mind wandered back to the Golden Gate Park Flower Conservatory. To Vivi, standing there, ageless, cool and elegant. He thought about how she had looked at him, and imagined what it would have been like had she asked him to come with her to Australia, or had he fought to be with her. He thought about how a single decision like that could have changed everything. He yearned for an adventure as he looked around at his modest, yet comfortable home. The walls and furniture worn in by the day in and day out of family life.

He began to look at the dishes on the counter and in the sink, the finger paintings taped to the walls, and the stack of bills on the counter. It all seemed so pedestrian. *This predictable and mediocre life* he thought to himself with dissatisfaction as he begrudgingly looked at how the spice rack was alphabetically organised. In this moment, he viewed himself as destined to dullness within the confinement of his home, and the life he had made there. It was suffocating.

After a few minutes, sitting in the muck of his discontent, his disenchantment drove him to his laptop impulsively. He contemplated whether he really should message Vivi, as his fingers entered the password and he pulled up a message box to start chatting. His hesitation was truthfully not with any concern for Grace, rather, he wondered if he would appear too eager if he wrote to her only a day later. He was surprised to see the three dots indicating that she was typing moments later. So he waited to see what she had to say and took it as a sign that she had been thinking about him too.

The door creaked with the familiar jingle of Grace's keys. Emma ran into the hallway as Grace implored her to take off her shoes as she giggled, taking pleasure in her ability to evade her mother. In came Emma from the park with green and pink ice cream smeared along the edges of her mouth and on the neckline and sleeves of her shirt. "Daddy!" She cried as she ran towards him. Justin slammed down the lid of his laptop, feeling the pull of his desire to see what Vivi had written to him and the simultaneous obligation to attend to Emma. "We went to the park, Daddy. We had ice creams," Emma reported gleefully. "The doggy licked it near my shoe."

"Wow Emma, sounds like you had a good time then," Justin said, trying to close down the exchange so he could return to his chat message.

Emma jumped on his lap and began to pretend he was a horse, "Giddy-up, Daddy. Giddy-up!" She said as she rocked back and forth on his lap pretending he was a horse.

"Emma, Daddy has to do some work, okay? Go see Mummy." He could hear Grace, going up the stairs. "Hon, could you take Emma up with you?" He called.

Grace had disappeared into their room most likely and Emma did not appear interested in going anywhere. He was left with Emma pulling on his arm to go show him the hummingbird that was zipping around in the garden outside the nearby window. Justin sauntered over to see the jewel toned creature quickly transitioning in the air with jolts and bursts. Even the tiny hummingbird was free to go and do as he pleased, he thought wistfully. Emma settled down with her collection of pastel ponies with shocks of long brightly coloured manes and tails before Grace came down.

"Hi honey," she said as she entered the room.

*Grace looked brighter than usual, glowing almost,* Justin thought, *watching her go about sorting the mail and tidying the kitchen.* "How was the park?" He asked nonchalantly in an effort to carry on small talk. He and Grace had always had a way of being able to fill their lives with the normalcy of little conversations in the daily comings and goings that shaped the majority of their interactions. They attended to a garden of mutual benefit in the little tasks they carried out to maintain their home and help one another. They often handed off supervising Emma, to gain pockets of reprieve, each one in solitude for short periods. It felt normal, it felt safe to be chatting with Grace, as though nothing had changed within him.

But his interest did not feel genuine, he noticed as he spoke, recognising the duplicity of his attentions. This disquieted him. It was new to feel like the place Grace filled in his mind and his heart was starting to be taken up by his thoughts of and urge to pursue Vivi. A part of nearly every minute during dinner that evening, his mind darted back to the chat window, desperately wanting to check if she had responded. He calculated that there seemed no good time until Emma went to bed, and Grace had headed upstairs for a shower.

As the evening wound down, with common tasks and typical conversations, Justin glanced at his watch multiple times, willing the time forward and the tasks complete, so he could return to the computer. It felt like it took forever to be able to return to his computer.

*Hi Justin. I'm not sure what happened yesterday, but it felt like not a day has passed between us. Do you think we could see each other again? I know you are married and this may not be what you want to do. I just wanted you to know I can't stop thinking about you and what we could have been…xo Vivi.*

Justin sat for a while. Stunned by how transparent her message was, and by how he felt the same way. He recalled Vivi had always known what she wanted and been the type to go after it. He thought about how so many times she had bartered her way along the Seine. Engaging sellers at the arts and crafts stalls with her charm, then telling them exactly what she thought their items were worth and why. She would often be able to secure the best deal on art pieces and trinkets that she would collect. Each with a story about how she got the item at a fraction of the price. For those sellers that would not take her bait, she would take pleasure in making an exit from the dealings with a sharp comment in a disinterested tone.

*I can meet you tomorrow. Coffees and a walk at the Berkeley Marina?*
*Yes. What time?*
*I am free between 830 and 4.*
*Great. How about 9AM?*
*Sure. See you at the Bottom of University near the pier. I'll bring the coffee.*
*J*

Justin reread the message sequence four times, excited about the prospect of seeing Vivi again and checking for any errors in the tone. *Did I seem too eager?* He asked himself. This time, her romantic interest in him was known. He thought about the ways in which he would respond to her advances when they were to meet. He would play it cool, not over commit. Although, he knew that at the bottom of it, he shared the same interest in pursuing something romantic. He didn't feel ready to admit it to himself.

"Hey hon, do you need anything from the store?" Grace popped her head into the study.

Justin jumped a little in his chair, wondering how long she had been standing behind him. It appeared not long, as she was moving past the doorway as she spoke. "Oh yeah, do you mind picking up some of those Australian liquorice? The red ones?" He thought of something, to play off his transgressions, and see how she would respond.

"Sure," Grace said heading to the doorway. "Can you go sit with Emma? She's in the playroom."

Justin closed down his computer. Changing his password, feeling a little paranoid. Emma sat on the rug, playing with her toy ponies, the sun filtered through the partially drawn curtains, illuminating her wispy hair. She hadn't noticed him come in and had she would most likely have asked Justin to join her in her game.

*I can't do this.* Was the first thought that ran through Justin's mind, as a sense of regret for what he was pursuing with Vivi started to confuse the peace of the moment. He sat there for a time. Emma tinkering with her small brushes and accessories to dress her little plastic ponies, redress them and put them to sleep. With that regret, he also felt a pull towards something more. Something more exciting than evenings at home cooking dinner, doing the bath and bedtime routine, and then watching TV until he and Grace fell asleep. *When did life become so...predictable?* He knew the answer to that. It was a gradual descent into formulaic stability paid for with an accumulation of responsibilities and a determination to adhere therein. Two things that had never come too easily to him. The life he had thought he wanted required a great deal of upkeep and self-sacrifice that he had not anticipated prior.

Justin rushed in the morning to drop Emma off at Mrs Corrine's daycare. He passed her into Mrs Corrine's open arms with her backpack, stepping backwards off the step apologetically, as quickly as he had come. He had lost track of time in the bathroom fashioning his hair with putty, while Emma had played around on the bathmat with cue tips.

The morning fog rolled in year-round at intervals. But on this June morning, the sky was clear, as he drove down the narrow hillside roads to the main drag—University Avenue. Traffic moved slowly as it revved and halted to the authoritative whim of several sets of lights. He popped a mint in his mouth to freshen his breath, checking his hair in the rear-view mirror as he idled on his way. He hadn't been preparing himself for a love interest this way for years. It felt foreign and a little nostalgic. He and Grace had been together for so long, it was really only date nights in which they had dressed up occasionally to go out for a nice dinner. Now, though, with the pandemic, there wasn't much in the way of dressing up, or going anywhere for that matter. *It was just coffee.* But knowing she missed him and wanted to see him again and mentioned that she wanted all this knowing he was married, inspired a bundle of nerves to unravel in his stomach. Grace did not cross his mind once as he drove.

He stopped at a local coffee shop. Enduring the short line and lengthy orders ahead of him with eyes on the clock. Vivi stood by her car. She wore high waisted jeans and a white ribbed singlet covered by an olive fishnet cardigan and chunky red earrings, her hair swept back. Justin leaned in to give her a kiss on the cheek, grazing her bosom, before handing her the coffee. The kiss felt different from a regular greeting. *Clandestine.* Vivi appeared very happy to see Justin today—an unspoken agreement to her proposal to reconnect romantically was coming into fruition.

Vivi had been single for over a year. Breaking up with her long-time boyfriend, Jacques, a wine importer who had transplanted from Burgundy to the Napa Valley wine scene, had left her feeling free and adrift all at once. This meeting was exciting to her, albeit she felt the complication of him being married to be a technicality that perhaps did not weigh so heavily against their history. She pushed away any sense of guilt, with a narrative she told herself as she drove across the bay to meet him. *They were always meant to be together, despite time and distance and choices that had separated them.*

"Good morning, Vivi," Justin said with a smile. They headed along a flat trail, joggers and walkers passing them seldomly.

Vivi was visibly nervous. "You know, Justin," Vivi started out, "I was really nervous to invite you here, the way I did."

"I know you were, Vivi," he said her name with the lilt of his old affectionate tone.

"I'm just really glad that you...that you decided to come and meet me." Justin smiled at her, pleased at her honesty and how welcoming she was. They walked generally in silence, speaking very little about sights, all the while feeling that magnetic tension between them. Their skin touched briefly occasionally as they went, sending electric shock waves through Justin's body. When they returned to the car, their coffees spent, Justin could not resist any longer. He found himself leaning up against Vivi against the car door. Like teenagers in a parking lot. He looked around, first to check for onlookers. He put his hands around her waist and leaned in to kiss her, feeling the curve of the small of her back in his palms, pressing her body against his waste. Their bodies still fit. She tasted as she always had.

As they continued kissing, she wrapped her arms around his neck, moving her hands down onto his chest, pushing him back only a little. "Justin," she whispered, "I don't want this to be something if you don't want it...Your wife."

Her hesitancy was disarming and enticed him further. He didn't take pause. He wanted her and only her at this moment and continued to kiss her even more passionately. "I want this," he eventually replied in a whisper as they slowed down. "I want you to come back to my place," he said with an impulsion informed by a brief calculation that it must only be about 11 AM and that Grace would not be home until after 4 PM.

"To your house?" Vivi asked, somewhat surprised. "No, I can't come to your house...but you can come to mine," she said in between kisses.

Justin saw the more careful surreptitious logic in this. "Okay."

***

Mumma was no longer able to leave the house. As leaves seldom drifted towards the crunchy piles that had collected beneath the sycamore trees around Todos Santos, Grace would make her trips to the square alone. Winter's bite was in the wind as pursuant gusts encircled Grace in spirals that lifted her skirt and caused dust and leaf particles to go into her eyes if she wasn't careful.

She would walk to the candy shop for a treat with the leftover change that remained from the money she would be tasked to spend at the grocery store. She thought of her trips to the grocery store in her mother's stead as a chance to go to the candy store with a chore on the way. Only able to carry two bags at a time, her young arms strained under the weight of the staples. A gallon of milk, a carton of eggs, a block of cheese, two loaves of bread, two pounds of turkey lunch meat, a box of cereal, and a block of butter was the bulk of what she would usually carry back.

She didn't mind the extra steps it would take around the block to get to Todos Santos Square to garner a sweet reward. She thought it as her compensation of sorts. Lottie would beg to come with her, but Grace would tell her to stay home. She knew the extra hands of her little sister would be more work than help when navigating the grocery store aisles in search of items, although she contemplated the potential benefit as she carried heavy paper bags home, hoping it would not rain and dampen the paper. The handles would break or the sides split with the moisture. She could handle the feisty wind, alone.

When Grace returned, Lottie would be sitting in the kitchen on these Sunday mornings, waiting to see what Grace brought back for her. Grace would split her gains on candy for them both at Lunardi's and always make sure to get Lottie's favourite—a red sherbet straw at the counter.

Today they sat at the table, savouring their candies. The milk left sweating on the counter. No one in the house except the shadowy presence of their mother who now was largely confined to her room. In an unspoken way, the girls knew not to enter unless it was for something very important. Grace took it upon herself, now at age 10, to pack the lunches, walk with Lottie to school, and make the dinners. The house, although remaining neat under her watch, grew with coats of dust and grime filled edges in the way houses turn without regular attention. Even the rooms were darker in Mumma's absence. Curtains drawn and often too heavy for Grace to tug open and shut with any regularity. It seemed better to keep them closed, in case any prying eyes may pass by. Grace started dinner. She had worked out from years of watching her mother, but with no formal guidance, how to boil the water.

Daddy didn't seem to notice that the meals weren't made by Mumma and carried about his evening routine despite her absence in the tasks that kept the household going. He progressively returned from work later and later. Some days, slumped over on the stoop by the front door or in his truck until day break. When he made it in, he slept out on the couch with the bright light of late-night infomercials flickering on his face. Grace had begun bringing meals to Mumma's room, out of concern that she was not eating, after a few days of not seeing her slip into the kitchen to fix a tea or eat some cheese and crackers before slipping away quietly. Grace would put little meals on a tray, as Mumma had once done on her birthday morning. Grace remembered waking on her seventh birthday to a short stack of pancakes with chocolate syrup oozing down the sides and a scoop of ice-cream balancing on top. Grace had marvelled at the rainbow sprinkles scattered over the pile. She blew out the candle perched on her special breakfast, wishing for many more birthday mornings as special as this.

Now, Grace arranged small turkey and cheese finger sandwiches with the crusts cut off on the plate with sliced apple. She nearly nicked her finger, when wielding the big knife to the task, standing over the kitchen table, instead of the counters which were too tall for Grace to get enough downward force to properly split hard fruits and vegetables.

Grace placed her Mumma's favourite mug with a cup of hot water and an Earl Grey tea bag strung over the lip. Grace placed a napkin and a small chocolate mint from a box she found in the pantry beside the sandwiches. Grace walked down the dark hallway. Grace used these opportunities to deliver the food as a way to negotiate her rightful presence in the room she had once lingered in for many parts of her day. She had sat under the bright windows playing dress up with her mother's necklaces and scarves, while Mumma would fix her make-up and prepare for church or come in from time to time to check on her.

Now, the room, in its dark stillness, closed off from the outside, welcomed her curiosity as well as her sense of sadness. Mumma no longer checked-on her or Lottie. They could come and go as they pleased, had they the nerve. It was up to Grace to do the checking now. An uncertain feeling propelled her to do the caretaking and hindered any sense of joy she may have. The uncertainty grew in the weeks and months that Grace went into Mumma's room to deliver meals. It did not feel likely that Mumma would someday emerge as her prior self. Grace felt anxious as she would approach the tray, hoping her mother had eaten, returning to pick up the tray sometimes untouched and occasionally containing plates containing partially eaten remnants.

She entered the room pushing the door ajar with her elbow as she balanced the tray, careful not to spill. She announced her arrival with a verbal 'knock, knock' as she liked to announce her arrival out of politeness. She stood at the doorway letting her eyes adjust. Mumma, in her regular position, lay as a mound under her covers, sleeping on her side. "Mumma. I brought you a sandwich and some tea," Grace said meekly, contending with the dark silence that appeared to have consumed her mother.

Mumma turned over, surprised by the voice. In a hollow tone asked, "who's that?" forgetting the sound of her daughter's voice.

"It's me, Mumma, Grace."

"Oh Grace dear. Come sit over here." She motioned loosely to a dressing chair by her vanity. Grace was surprised to be invited in and quickly made her way to place the tray down on the vanity and sat on the chair as instructed. Her mother's tone had almost sounded normal with the invitation. The silence between them was suffocating, as she waited to see what next her mother would do or say. Her mother had a tired voice, as though she had not slept in days.

Grace thought it worrisome because all she knew her mother to do was sleep, under a pile of blankets. "How is your sister?"

"Oh. Ah. Lottie is okay. She misses you, Mumma."

"Very good dear." Mumma's voice sounded distant at once, disassociated from the responsibility she should bear for her child, *for her children*. It was as if she was inquiring about an old friend that she hadn't seen in a while. As though time was the culprit.

"Lottie needs some new shoes, Mumma," Grace thought to add, hoping it would bring Mumma back to the reality of the situation.

"Thank you for stopping by," she said coolly, ending their exchange.

Grace stood up, irritated now by her mother's detachment mixed with a feeling of helplessness. She picked up the tray and left without a word. Later that day, Grace had the idea to look under the stairs. She rummaged through her old shoes that were in a box under the stairway and found a pair of pink and white sneakers, now browning at the seams with worn tread and tired laces that looked like they might fit Lottie. *This would have to do for now* Grace thought.

Lottie stepped into the sneakers, easily now through the narrows of the shoes' throats, wiggling her toes, feeling the relief of space now found between her big toe and the end of the toe box. A smile spread across Lottie's face. "Thank you, Grace," she said. Grace smiled, her heart unexpectedly quickened with an anxious feeling. This was luck that she had found shoes, but how would she ever be able to make sure they had all they needed. Grace watched her little sister prance around in the hallway admiring her shoes, as though they were brand new out of a box at the department store. Grace cheered and smiled; glad Lottie was not deterred by their appearance.

It dawned on her that she should ask Daddy the next morning what to do about school shoes and clothes, as her own clothes were getting short at the knee. *Some of the skirts wouldn't look right all that way up above her knee,* she thought. Daddy hopefully could make sure they could buy the things they needed that Mumma used to take care of. She would catch him at breakfast time, likely sober as he prepared for work and would be eating two runny eggs and toast she prepared for him daily. He was usually the most amenable in the morning.

# Chapter 10
# Collided

Justin stood close behind Vivi as she fumbled with the keys. Her nervous hands opened the lock and let them into her nicely appointed San Francisco apartment. They entered the hallway lined with photographs of her travels that lead to a larger room towards the back with vaulted ceilings that let their pale indirect San Francisco light fill the space and illuminate the numerous house plants perched around. Justin noticed the familiarity of the bohemian decor. It had been Vivi's style for decades, and she had managed to splash her style on the walls of spaces wherever she went.

Holding his hand, she guided him into her bedroom, where she began to undress him. No words passed between them as they kissed intensely, undressing each other as they fumbled their way into the bedroom. Her skin pressing against his, felt like home to him. Their bodies collided and fit together as they once had many years ago. He had never forgotten how it felt to be with her. They had missed each other and made love passionately as though they were making up for lost time.

\*\*\*

Grace adjusted her scrub cap, as she peered into the mirror over the sink on the unit. She had washed her hands vigorously between patients for months now and noticed her skin was dry and cracking easily. She used the hospital moisturiser placed next to the sink, waiting a moment for the cool gel cream to absorb into her skin, like a parched desert consuming any moisture that would come its way. She knew she needed to drink more water but had grown weary of the process of taking off her mask for the task. No food or liquids were allowed to be consumed by the staff in the patient care area. It was easier to refrain from drinking anything.

As she worked, the nagging reminder that she needed to be hydrated for the baby lingered until she gave in and took some time on her break to drink as much as she could. Bathroom breaks were sometimes hard to get, but she figured she would have the relief nurse watch over her patients briefly in an hour or so. The familiar sensitivities of pregnancy were returning. Grace felt tired, bloated with faint waves of nausea throughout the day, as she worked hard to keep up with all of the tasks necessary to address the orders rolling in throughout the day. Both of her patients were Coronavirus patients today.

They were husband and wife—Darius Jones and Kendra Jones. They were in their early forties—both had contracted Coronavirus, leaving their four children in the care of Kendra's mother, while they lay limp on their bellies breathing through ventilators. Kendra had been admitted two days after Darius had been rushed to the hospital for acute respiratory failure. Their lungs showed up on the imaging as both filled with bilateral hazy opacities. Cloudy x-rays which had become hallmark images of what damage the Coronavirus was capable of.

Grace watched over them like a hawk. It was heartbreaking to think of their children, ages 10, eight, four, and 18 months waiting at home with their grandmother, Lorna. Grace held back the tears that seemed to come more easily in recent weeks, as she would give updates to Lorna, who called twice a shift each day. She could sense the desperation building in Lorna's voice as she inquired about the lab values she had now learned where meaningful and would send messages from the children to tell their mother and father. "Tell Daddy to be strong. Tell Mummy I will wash the dishes if she comes home." was the latest message she passed on. Grace made sure to say these messages verbatim as she went about working their side-by-side rooms, changing out the catheters, replacing IV bags, taking temperatures, and monitoring the blood pressure. Grace thought about what she would have said to her parents had they been in this situation. She couldn't think of what she would say, try as she may conjure up heartfelt messages. Her memory of them felt defined primarily by the darkest of times and it would be hard to bring words enough. Tragedy was best left relegated to silent images that haunted her some days more than others. Grace sat in the break room, staring into her cup of broccoli and cheese soup from the cafeteria. Stirring the thick contents of the paper cup slowly. A text came through from Jake. "Hey Grace. Big news…I quit."

Grace reread it, puzzled, and responded, "Smoking?" She thought herself humorous.

"Yeah that too. But no, I quit the hospital. I've quit nursing. This ride has been too much. I started drinking and recently checked into rehab."

Grace hadn't known that Jake was ever a drinker. "Oh. I'm sorry to hear what you've been going through, Jake."

"It's okay. All the pain and death every day during this thing really tore me up. I never thought it would, but the next thing I know I'm drinking a bottle of vodka a night after my shift. I just couldn't deal."

Grace thought about her own stress during the pandemic. She had experienced it but dealt little with what it was doing to her. She had largely done with it what she had done with past traumas. Avoided dealing with the pain by diving deeper into caregiving. Instead of attending to her own needs she would make herself purposeful in others' lives.

"Well. Jake, it sounds like you are making the right choice for your mental health," Grace wrote, noting that she herself had been neglecting to reflect on her own well-being in this situation.

"Thanks Grace. I'm going to take some months off and see what's next. I don't know how long I'll be able to stick around in New York. Coronavirus has taken a terrible toll on this city. I want to be free of it."

A surprising sense of resentment crossed her mind. *He's quitting on patients and his teams in this crisis. I thought we would see this through together.* Grace couldn't relate to it, in her own strong sense of duty to keep working hard to save these patients and didn't truly understand how he could quit at a time like this. Discontentment passed over Grace as she thought about how people often just quit when the going got tough. "Wishing you the best!" She texted back a little later. She felt a distinct change in how she viewed her old comrade. Their bond over working in the pandemic's trenches no longer stuck in the same way.

Grace went about her day, paying attention to each surface she touched and washing her hands thoroughly with hot water, scorching her hands. *It seemed like Coronavirus was not impacting children so greatly,* she thought. But what about pregnancy? Grace felt conflicted at her core about having a new baby. The world felt like it was spinning out of control, and the vulnerability of bringing new life into it, felt risky. Her hesitancy to tell Justin about the pregnancy served a key purpose—it kept reality at bay.

"There's a call for room 305 and 306 grandmother, is her name Linda?" The unit assistant passed the phone to Grace. It was Lorna calling in for her daily check in on Kendra and Darius. Today she asked if she could have a Facetime call to hold her screen up to the glass so she could see her daughter. Grace asked her to call her direct cell phone line and she connected Lorna through the glass to see her daughter, 43 years old, proning in the bed, the ventilator working to sustain her. Lorna was alone in her bedroom and cried softly as she looked through her screen. Through broken tears, she thanked Grace for letting her see her daughter and said goodbye quickly as she wiped her tears from her eyes when one of the children came into her room asking for a snack. The prognosis was unclear. It was more of a waiting game to make sure her respiratory support and organs continued to function adequately to get through. The uncertainty in each bed of that ICU reminded Grace each day that she was alive. Something that should not be taken for granted.

***

Grace woke up early, and put on her mother's apron, folding the fabric upwards at the waist's seam so as to make it a little shorter. She had grown nearly two inches in the past year and felt proud to be able to wear her mother's apron fitted with a slight modification. Grace cracked the eggs over the rim of the ceramic bowl and whisked them vigorously. Next she put the toast in the steel toaster, turning it to medium. Grace was now accustomed to making most all the meals she had once observed her mother preparing.

The breakfast today needed to be perfect, so Daddy would be in a good mood. She fried strips of bacon in a small frying pan, jumping back when they sizzled and spurted into her apron, catching her bare arms with a sting. The eggs mixed with a splash of milk were poured into another pan. She made sure never to leave its side, stirring it gently on a lowered heat so the eggs would cook evenly, light and fluffy. Daddy came into the kitchen as Grace served up his plate. Making sure to butter the toast to the edges, as he liked it. She put the jam out in case he wanted to have that too. Grace hadn't tasted coffee but knew how to stir the instant coffee into hot water to the proportions outlined on the jar and placed that in front of him too.

He smiled at her. When he smiled at her, the feeling of approval was electrifying. He sat quietly for a time then remarked, "You make good eggs, Grace."

Grace smiled, "Thanks Daddy." His approval could erase her misgivings instantly. And for a moment it would, but sadly, the misgivings piled faster and higher than these golden moments. Grace dished up Lottie's breakfast and her own before sitting to the right of her father, on an angle that gave him her visibility beyond the flutter of newspaper pages that he kept widespread for most of the meal. She ate quietly, awaiting the right moment to bring up her requests. "Daddy. Lottie has g-grown out of her shoes, and I was wondering if you could buy her some new ones." It took a lot of courage for her to string that sentence together. Hope being what propelled her.

"Did you ask your mother?" was his immediate reply.

"Yes. Well, I asked, but she didn't seem to answer my question."

"Barbara!" He yelled towards the doorway abruptly, making both of the girls jolt in their seats. "Where is your mother?" he asked with an impatient tone, once he had waited a little while with no response. He hadn't seemed to notice her general absence in their day-to-day lives.

"Sh-she's in her bed, Daddy," Lottie offered meekly.

Daddy got up out of his chair and could be heard storming under his breath as he took heavy steps towards the bedroom and flung the door open. They could hear him yelling loudly at their mother in muffled tones, made bearable through the walls. Lottie began to cry over her half-eaten breakfast as Grace sat stoically, wishing she had read the tide more accurately. She had thought the morning hours would be exempt from Daddy's rage but had been terribly wrong. Moreover, she felt badly she had gotten her mother in trouble. She had not foreseen that things would turn out this way. They heard their mother screaming and the bedside lamps crashing with a cracking sound of glass, perhaps the vanity mirror.

Grace gathered Lottie up, and the brown bags of lunch she had packed the night before and ushered her little sister to the door. They couldn't be late for school and couldn't listen to another minute of the destruction. She was at the point that she knew she couldn't save Mumma and did not want to risk her own neck to try. They ran from the house into the bright morning sunlight, inhaling cool air like freedom. As they walked to school, the streams of tears dried down their cheeks and they both tried to mask their pain with wilted smiles as their school friends approached them on the path.

"What's wrong, Lottie?" Her friend Sadie inquired, noticing Lottie had been crying. Lottie looked at Grace, who had composed herself quicker. Grace glanced at her with eyes urging her little sister not to break their silence on the matter with the outside world.

"I just tripped and twisted my ankle on the walk," she lied. To break the silence would risk their necks too, they presumed. If Daddy found out people knew about what was going on, it would for sure not end well for them. So they chose to find the path quietly through the maze of unpredictability that had been woven for them hoping that one day Mumma might wake up, and Daddy might change. Till then, they would scrounge around for fitting clothes and shoes and manage the grocery money that Daddy left on the counter every pay day.

*** 

Spontaneous breathing trials were going well for Darius for 20–30 minutes and his arterial blood gas numbers had reached within normal limits along with the other parameters the pulmonologists and respiratory therapists had been monitoring and working towards for the past 21 days. It would be another day if he continued to trend in the right direction before they would extubate him. Kendra was not doing as well. Grace stood looking through the sliding glass windows into their rooms, feeling the limbo and the loss it would be to lose either of them.

Lorna had called that morning, asking after her daughter. She sounded slightly disappointed that the promising news was coming for her son-in-law and not her daughter. Kendra was her only child. Lorna had raised Kendra alone and the struggle she had had was a fight to give everything she had to her daughter, so that she could have a better life than that from which she came. Kendra had been the first in her family to go to college and earn a Bachelor's of Art in Communications at San Francisco State University, and had a good Public Relations job now for a tech company. Lorna had told Grace how proud she was of Kendra breaking through the expectations society had for her. Every day Lorna wept over the phone with Grace and for her daughter who now was fighting a fight that she could not fight for her. The pain in Lorna's deep grief was palpable through her words. She would pray through the phone over her daughter. "Please Lord, deliver this child from harm's way. I pray Jesus, you will heal your children Darius and Kendra. I pray in the Name of Jesus, Amen." Grace would listen to these prayers, with tears swelling in her eyes for Lorna, Kendra and Darius, and also for herself. The prayers were beautiful. They were faithful. They reminded her of days sitting in church beside her mother and father in a time and space far different from where things ended up. She would hear the choir singing angelic hymns with the light streaming through bright stained-glass windows. Rising from the pews, hard and smooth beneath her, the sounds and the light and the love were harmonious.

She had once known who it was that Lorna was praying to with such confidence. And there, listening to the words tumbling out of Lorna's mouth over her child, Grace felt a chasm between where she was now, and the comfort she once had, as a child leaning earnestly against her bed in prayer. As she looked around the ICU, she could not help but think about how much she wished she could return to that place of peace. The days drew on, each day similar to the last, presenting with new challenges and more of the same. But the day came that Darius was able to be extubated successfully after continued success with the spontaneous breathing trials. Once the endotracheal breathing tube was pulled out of his trachea through his mouth, as the final step in his liberation from the mechanical ventilation he had relied on for the past nearly four weeks. He was weaned from the sedative bridge, dexmedetomidine also.

When Darius was conscious, his first words were aphonic, as the tube had likely carved a gap between his vocal cords, dis-allowing them to approximate fully to make sound. The swelling in his throat was a nine out of ten pain level he communicated as he begged for ice chips. Grace administered intravenous acetaminophen to help with the pain. He asked if Kendra had visited or called. Grace leaned over the side bed rails, as she finished up using the suction brush to clean his teeth and oral cavity.

She paused, realising he was not aware that his wife had been admitted to the ICU a couple days after he had been placed under sedation on the ventilator. Grace wanted to check in with the case manager about whether staff had been given clearance by Kendra's durable power of attorney (named by Kendra as she was rushed through the emergency department doors) to update her husband on her medical status. Eileen, the case manager, replied that Lorna wanted to be the one to communicate any information about her daughter to Darius and would make a point to call in later that day.

Grace returned to Darius' room. "Where is my wife? Does she know I'm here?"

Grace was quiet. She hated these moments when she was bound to keep her patients' privacy when their family members would inquire heavily. It meant she had to keep quiet and endure their frustration with her silence. "Your mother-in-law will be calling you soon to update you."

This visibly unnerved Darius as he drew the inference that the response to the question necessitated formal news to be delivered by Lorna. "Tell me now, where is my wife?" Darius persisted. Frustrated with the vagueness of her reply and the implication that he would have to wait for information he considered himself entitled to. His fear of what her answer would be drove him to ask over and over, tears forming in the creases of his eyes with frustration.

"I'm so sorry, Darius, I don't have clearance to share an update with you regarding your wife at this time. I can call your mother-in-law and see if she would be available to speak with you as soon as possible." Grace backed out of the room, doffing her gown and gloves as she went and washing her hands thoroughly. Grace called Lorna. "Hi Lorna, this is Grace. Eileen, Kendra and Darius' case manager let me know that you will be updating Darius on Kendra's status. He is now conscious and very much interested in knowing where Kendra is. I'm calling to see when you may be available to speak with him, as he is becoming a bit upset with the restrictions on this information."

Silence over the phone met Grace's voice. "Lorna, can you hear me?"

Silence again, followed by, "Yes. I can hear you Grace. I-I'm just reluctant to speak with him right now about Kendra."

"Oh, I see," Grace replied.

"It-it's just that I-I'm not sure I can handle his reaction on top of what I'm going through dealing with this. If he doesn't know, then I won't have to deal with his reaction to the news, and that's about all I can handle right now."

Grace appreciated the honesty with which Lorna articulated her perspective. Grace knew this feeling of reluctance to make information real, as releasing it to another would mean the news would stick to the walls of reality, forever changing its composition and the lives of those who absorb it. *Most news cannot be undone.* "Okay Lorna. I will continue to direct Darius to the conversation you will have with him. *When you are ready.*" Grace hung up the phone feeling tired by the weighty information she carried. Elle's affair, Kendra's status, and her own pregnancy she was keeping from her husband. Everything felt caged within confinement born of secrecy and reluctance.

***

Grace came home from school and went to the pantry to reach some of her favourite chocolate wafer cookies that she hid on the back shelf and shared occasionally with Lottie. Lottie had run outside to the front yard to grab her bike and play with the neighbourhood kids who were swarming the streets on that warm May day.

Grace thought to check on Mumma and bring her a wafer cookie and a glass of milk. Grace and Mumma had sat on the front steps when she was little to eat these wafers, a favourite of Mumma's. They would sip ice cold milk and dip the layered cookies into their glasses, savouring each flaky bite. Grace remembered how the milk would coat the inside of her glass after each sip then slowly run down returning to the pool of milk. Grace wrapped up the wafer in a napkin and poured some milk then carried it down the long hall.

Children in the street could be heard chattering and yelling out to one another through the open window at the end of the hall. In the dark hall, the warm May light glowed and illuminated the textured edges of picture frames stationed along the hallway. The window remained open most of the year, letting in the warm breeze that twisted and lifted the linen curtains on either side. The warmth of the day smelled of jasmine from the bushes that grew along the side of the house.

Grace knocked before she entered. Mumma never replied when Grace announced her arrival at the door. The air in the room did not move. Grace's eyes adjusted along the form of her mother's shape that was no longer an undulating mound. She could see her laying on her back, flattened out. As Grace's eyes adjusted, absorbing the muted light that escaped the closed curtains around the edges and underneath along the floor. She noticed something different. Mumma's breath was not moving through her. Her body, still. "Mumma," Grace said with uncertainty emerging, her heart rate quickening to the silence that met her. "Mumma?" She said again, approaching the bed. She lay still. The breath had escaped her body. In her limp hands and spilled out across the bed sheets were a variety of pills, smooth and various oval sizes. The pill bottle and cap had fallen to the floor. Grace's heart plunged at the sight and she began to shake her mother. "Mumma! Mumma! Mumma! Wake up!" she repeated over and over.

The vigorous shaking increased, feeling through her fingertips for any resumption of movement, any response. It felt like hours standing above Mumma.

Grace's tears blurred her vision and she persisted with pulling the bed covers off and crying out as she took her mother's hand, squeezing it to try to elicit a response all while imploring her mother to waken. The room surroundings faded in the background, as all she could hear was the heavy beating of her own heart, her mother's limp hands, and lifeless body before her.

When Grace finally accepted that her mother was dead, she stood still by the bed, not knowing what to do for a long while. Grace had never had any experience with death before. She stood, paralysed by the anxiety that now swelled within her. The adrenaline pumping through her veins. She did not know what she should do. So, she left the room, to go sit outside on the steps and wait for Daddy's truck to come home. She would find Lottie and tell her not to go into the house. Grace sat on the step watching Lottie play with her teddy bear on an old sun-bleached slide, humming the tune to *Happy Birthday*. Grace marvelled at how her little sister could play, oblivious and unknowing of their mother in the house, now gone. Grace looked on. Seeing a bright innocence in Lottie that had just been stolen from her. One she desperately wanted to capture for herself again. Grace didn't know who to call. She thought about a number she had heard kids at school say when they played emergency rescues. It started with a nine. She was paralysed in her shock. The inaction that she pursued would mean that perhaps nothing had changed for Mumma. *She was still in her room, sleeping the day away.* Grace sat, feeling the press of her bare feet against the sun-warmed steps and the subtle drift of a minor breeze passing across her face and arms. The Concord afternoon heat was typically dense and still. Any little breeze would be noticed. The press of her sweaty hands against the hard surface was her way of centring herself. She otherwise imagined that she may unravel completely like a spool of ribbon down the stairs and out across the path. Grace imagined herself being carried away with the breeze that passed her by, as though her spirit were now as thin as a wafer, adrift, and at the whim of any current that would pick her up and take her somewhere else. Anywhere else. Daddy would be home in an hour or so, that is if he came straight home from work instead of stopping at the bar. Grace shuddered at the thought of Daddy staying late at night and coming home angry at this. As she thought about Daddy, she remembered his work phone number was stuck to the fridge on a little magnet his auto shop had made to hand out to customers the previous year. She got up and went back into the kitchen. It was a small rectangular magnet with a blue, common font on a plain white background with a small Volkswagen beetle in the upper right-hand corner. She took it off and brought it into the hall where the phone sat and dialled.

Patricia, the auto shop receptionist, answered with the same welcoming phrasing she had used for 15 years working the phones. Grace stammered after a long pause in which Patricia inquired if anyone was on the line. "Yes, th-this is Grace."

Patricia recognised Grace's voice. "Oh Grace. How are you doing, my dear? Your daddy is under a car somewhere, shall I fetch him?"

Grace appreciated the smooth, caring voice on the other end of the phone. It was how she thought adults should be. An attentive tone and a forward-thinking level of concern her mother had lacked for years now. "Ah, yes please. Thank you," Grace responded, noting the quiver in her voice. *What would she tell him?* Moments later, Daddy was on the line with a friendly greeting with an air of concern, reserved for the public. "Mumma. Mumma's not feeling well I think," Grace said, knowing very well that she didn't think she was alive, but too afraid to utter such conclusive words.

"Oh. Well, Grace bear, I'll be home in an hour. Ask her if she needs some tea."

Grace paused. "I think she needs to see a doctor now," she said, responding with an urgency she couldn't withhold any longer.

"Oh. Well then, I'll come home right now."

Grace exhaled "Okay" and hung up. Within 15 minutes, the soles of Daddy's work boots were grinding against the gravel path. Grace stood by with weak knees and led him into the house. The smell of absence would be what Grace would forever remember as they entered the bedroom. Grace turned on a light and brought Daddy to the bedside.

Daddy peered past the mound of bedding at her, in disbelief. "Barbara, wake up," is all Grace could remember him saying, as he shook her shoulders vigorously with a growing angst. The tears that she had never seen him cry, the ones they had all shed over his abuse, now poured out that day. He looked as if he were a child, another person entirely, there weeping beside his dead wife, now stripped of the acrid stench of violence.

Grace stood in the doorway watching her distraught father, a revelation of his humanity which had for so long been hidden from them. The ambulance lights flickering in the windows and the sound of metal and wheels of the stretcher taking Mumma out of their home was all that Grace remembered of that evening. It was the last thing she remembered before she and Lottie saw Grandpa at their door and was asked to pack their things.

# Chapter 11
# Endings

Grace returned to Darius' room. "I spoke with Lorna. She will be speaking with you as soon as she can."

Darius was dissatisfied with this answer. "As soon as she can? Where is my wife? I would like to speak with my wife. What happened to her?" Darius became more forceful in his inquisition, as Grace tried to redirect and had only the same deflective phrasing to respond with. Darius became angered, throwing the remote, tethered to the wall, off his bed as Grace left his room as swiftly as she could, to go and check quietly on Kendra.

The dilemma pressed deeply into her chest, where she already had felt the stirring of anxious feelings there. Darius had his cell phone and attempted to call Kendra's best friend, Jasmine, leaving voice messages inquiring about Kendra's whereabouts. Jasmine was aware of Lorna's wishes and instructed to not respond to his calls. In the last hours of Grace's shift, it became apparent that Darius was not going to let this go. He did not understand how procedural exchange of information regarding patients' protected health information was the reason Grace couldn't disclose any information. Instead, he took Grace's inability to respond to his questions about Kendra personally.

Darius began yelling out, screaming at Grace to tell her where his wife was while throwing any items in his reach off his bed, and attempting to climb out. Grace called security. She breathed heavily, watching his every move through the glass, hoping and praying that the security guard would arrive quickly and provide safety. The seconds on the clock mounted high up above the unit ticked by slowly.

Grace watched him thrash around in his room, angrily screaming out for her. She had known this level of rage before. She could not look away and noticed her heart began to race uncontrollably, she needed to sit down. She was hyperventilating behind the nursing station in panic, as the Code Grey was announced over the intercom. Grace waited suspended in time moving slowly in the presence of the danger she perceived for the minutes before security rushed into the unit to take over. Grace had been here before. As Darius in his own angst acted erratically and angrily, it brought her back to the pantry floor, peering through the crack in the door, listening to her father beat her mother in the other room, terrorising the night.

Grace could not stay a minute longer as she saw her patient's anger escalate to physicality the three security officers were working to de-escalate. She suddenly felt extremely claustrophobic, needing to escape. She ran out through the ICU doors, down the stairwell and out the emergency exit doors into the broad daylight. The bright summer day hit her. The towers above bent, and the sounds of passers-by and traffic became muffled. Like moving through water. All the light dimmed and distorted by tears filling her eyes and blurring her vision as they streamed uncontrollably down her cheeks wetting her mask. The moisture seeping through around the bridge and down along the sides of her nose was cold. She ripped it off her face and threw it to the ground, *Not enough air to breath. Never enough.*

The rise of those familiar anxious feelings had grabbed her, making her legs weak. She had to sit down. Grace put her head between her knees as she sat outside by the sidewalk on a low retaining wall, her back brushing loose petals off blooming roses as she sat. She closed her eyes, aiming to calm her rapid breathing and centre herself. It would not slow or gain an even rhythm, as she sat making small gasps between her moans, wishing her body would give back her control. It had become too much. The stress of working through the pandemic, the weight of childhood memories, her angered patient, Jake bailing on the cause, Elle's secret, her own secret from her husband compounded by the dilemma of dealing with her pregnancy, and what kind of future that would be. It all felt to have rushed forward in this moment and closed in on her.

She felt utterly helpless and very alone. Suffocated by the dysfunction everywhere she looked. She noticed she was trembling and placed her hands on the smooth surface of the retaining wall to try to steady herself. Time evaporated from her sweaty palms, as she pressed them down upon the cold cement atop the wall. The grainy surface, cool and solid was all she could grasp a hold of as her body felt as though it was slipping into the abyss of fear that her mind and body had created over and over throughout the years. She felt small in the midst of the downward pressures that spiralled around her. There was too much pain, like water bursting through floodgates and overtaking anything in its way.

An elderly lady, walking by, stopped to ask Grace if she needed any assistance. Grace looked up at her, unable to speak, but shook her head through closed eyes squeezing tears. The lady carried on, looking back at her with a concerned look on her face. Grace's crying was inconsolable, try as she might to draw back, she wept uncontrollably.

A few minutes later, a security guard came out to Grace. The lady had alerted him in the parking garage as she passed.

"Are you alright, Miss?" He inquired with a tender look of concern.

Grace looked up at his large frame, the bright daylight surrounding his dark uniform. "I-I'm sorry," was all she could bring herself to say, as the tears continued to tumble down her cheeks, while she attempted to clean her face up with her bare hands, shaking.

The security guard stood over her and eventually broke the silence with, "I know things are really hard right now in there." He had seen the healthcare workers filing into the hospital day in and out. Their faces fixed with consternation, as they continually returned to work. Trudging in, clutching their lunch bags, with dull eyes for which nothing could surprise. No one had been left unchanged over the many months that had passed with the pandemic touching every aspect of their lives.

The security guard sat beside her for a time as she continued to cry. She began to feel embarrassed that she couldn't regain composure in front of the security guard with kind eyes. She wept without words for a while, as he sat beside her quietly. In that moment, she felt like herself as a child, fragile and fearful, crying on her bed after her mother had committed suicide. The irreversible nature of the situation that had taken a direction apart from what she would have wanted, had brought forth a sense of helplessness. In a different yet similar way, the thought of having her baby, had brought forth a sense of helplessness similarly. As if her fate proceeded forward, regardless of her will for it. For this, Grace wept deeply next to a stranger, beside the busy road, ignoring her responsibilities inside the hospital.

When Lorna arrived and was made aware of how upset Darius had become, she knew she needed to break the news to him. It was no longer only hers to keep alone. She entered the room cautiously, aware of Darius' earlier agitation. "Hi

Darius," she said calmly, "I am so glad to see you are recovering. I understand you have questions about where Kendra is."

"Dang straight I do," he replied, the earlier anger colouring his tone.

"Okay, I'm sorry you have had to wait to hear this, but I thought it best to come from me. Kendra had to come into the hospital too. She was very sick with COVID just like you." Darius paused with wide eyes, taking in the information. He waited quietly, hesitant with fear of gaining the information needed to fill in the blanks that were emerging in his mind. "She had trouble breathing on her own like you did, so we had to put her on a ventilator."

Darius paused, cautious to the acquisition of further information, he presumed none would be good news. "Where is she now?" Darius asked, his voice wavering.

"Well, Darius, she has not been as fortunate as you so far. She is still needing the machine to help her breathe." Darius sat with his thoughts, absorbing yet rejecting what he heard, contemplative and unable to summon any more words. He no longer felt his violent urge, rather, he felt silenced by the weight of what he was hearing. He felt small and helpless in its wake. Lorna added, "My daughter is a fighter, Darius." Tears formed in the creases of her eyes. She felt herself begin to shake. "I have to believe that she will pull through." She bent down placing her face into her cupped hands, her pain swirling inside her stomach, trapped with no release but through the water pouring from her eyes and the air she pushed out through a deep groan.

Both, under the spotlights of the ICU room's lighting, bent over with grief, they sat, overcome by their shared sorrow. "The kids are okay, Darius. Xavier keeps asking to see you. I am so glad he will now be able to."

"When are they going to discharge me, do you think?" Darius asked, sitting up straight, as if ready to spring out of bed.

"I'm sure they gotta run their tests and make sure you are fit to leave first. No one just runs outta the ICU, Darius," Lorna added with a smile.

Darius slouched back down into his bed, agreeing with the sobering fact that medicine and recovery took time. Lorna left Darius with a parting hug. She walked out of the hospital, searching the faces of the staff she passed in the halls. She was struck by how many blank eyes behind masks and face shields met her. Staff walked the halls with purposeful stoicism. Perhaps, just enough to protect their brains from the distress the realities of the pandemic would cause. Lorna exited the sliding doors and found herself pushed out into the dark night. A night in which she had to hurry back to care for her grandchildren, who would likely be waiting for their dinner.

She walked through a hollowed-out existence on these nights, one without her daughter for whom her main life's purpose for the past over 30 years had centred around. Lorna had moved through her days listening for her cell phone to ring with a call from the doctor or nurse for updates, and by remaining busy with the tasks necessary to maintain a sense of normalcy for her grandchildren. She chatted to Kendra in her mind and sometimes out loud, as she moved through the kitchen preparing breakfasts, lunches and dinners, and while cleaning the house and folding laundry. To Lorna, it was as if the upkeep of a continuous dialogue with Kendra about the happenings of the day was keeping her present in the ins and outs of the day's hours, alive and participating in the fullness of her children's lives.

At first, Lorna didn't realise she was talking to Kendra throughout the day, until her youngest grandson, Jason, asked her who she was talking to. Lorna stood in the kitchen, looking into his expectant coffee brown eyes. "Well Jason, I'm talking to your Mumma. You see if I tell her what's going on, then there won't be too much we have to catch up on when she gets home."

Jason smiled at her answer. "But she's not here with us, Gramma," he added quizzically.

"I know, dear. Someone doesn't always have to be nearby to know you are talking to them." Lorna replied pensively.

Jason was disarmed by the sadness in his grandmother's eyes as she spoke. "I hope she comes home soon, Gramma," he added.

Lorna agreed, wrapping his little body in a big hug, "Everything will be alright, ya hear?" She had whispered into his curly hair, feeling surprised by the emptiness she felt in her words.

As the days had worn on, with not much change in Kendra's status, the state of limbo in which Lorna found herself gnawed at her hope. Like a rat chewing through the circuitry of her mind, dimming her senses. Lorna had become singularly task driven, setting her mind to all the details of the days that required attending to in the absence of her daughter. She neglected to care much for her own needs—missing meals and bathing irregularly.

She was on autopilot, as though outside of herself looking at herself executing the tasks of the day with little feeling, and often little recollection of the details of the tasks she completed. Daily, Lorna would ferry between home, her grandchildren's schools, and the hospital. Her path was well travelled along roads by which she would not notice the change in paint on a neighbour's fence, the construction at the elementary school, or the pruning of bushes alongside the road. She found herself in a harrowing story of days upon days of waiting in stagnation, never finding resolution, and not knowing how the story would end.

The only way she could explain it was as though something akin to fog had rolled in and rested upon her, rendering her numb and impeding her visibility, making her surroundings bleak. Occasionally, Lorna would reflect on how the simple pleasures of life that brought her feelings of joy like her grandchildren's laughter, sunsets, blooming flowers, or the smell of fresh coffee no longer triggered a response of appreciation in the same way. She no longer really noticed these things, it was as though the world had become monochromatic and redundant. Her angst now blocked her ability to feel much other than a sense of dread that lingered, lurched and plunged in the depths of her stomach.

Lorna, in her preoccupation with thoughts of Kendra, vacillated between both hope and fear, consumed by audacity and terror at once. The fear grew, as the days went by with little indication of her daughter's progress towards recovery and ability to wean from the ventilator. It was inward travels that consumed Lorna. As she went about her daily routines between the hospital, school and home, she became more prone to forgetfulness, as her attentions always came divided. One side of her mind attended to the task and issues at hand while the other always remained firmly focused on Kendra. It was disorienting to dwell in a place of expectancy for her daughter's recovery yet live in absence of any assurance of it. At times, she felt foolish to hold out hope.

*\*\*\**

When no more tears could come and the salty recesses of her eyes stung, Grace swiftly stood up, and assured the security guard that she felt okay to go back inside. She fixed her hair and placed the scrub cap back on firmly as she walked away from the security guard who watched her go. He had seen many healthcare workers falling apart in their cars, leaving or coming to the hospital, and felt a deep sense of sympathy for the stressors they were enduring inside the hospital, compounded with what they must be enduring in their personal lives.

Wiping her eyes in the restroom by the cafeteria, Grace noticed her eyes looked sunken and her face appeared clearly stressed. *I have to get a grip.* She

166

thought to herself, considering what her emotional state might be doing to the baby. *How will I ever get a grip?* Grace thought back to the days of her early 20s, where everything felt possible, self-determined and free. She looked at herself now in the mirror, inspecting the inroads of the lines between her eyebrows that had become permanent creases.

Grace's mind wandered back to the present need to return to work. She hadn't told someone that she had left. She would tell her manager that she was too distracted to go about finishing her shift as she was having some personal troubles and that she needed a reassignment from the cases in rooms 305 and 306. Elle met her in the hallway leading to the ICU double doors. She stood there, looking at Grace. Grace walked past, hoping she didn't notice she had been crying, feeling the pressure in her face with all it took to contain herself. "Grace, we need to talk."

Grace turned around. "I'm really sorry, Elle. Right now isn't a good time. I need to go see Casey and tell him why I walked off shift."

Grace glanced through the glass pane doors to Kendra's room as she walked through the unit to the far end assistant nurse manager's office. Her heart sank, as she had seen that Kendra's kidneys were failing her, earlier. She thought about her small children waiting for her, and her silent struggle there, kept alive by the force of machinery and medications. Unable to assure them, to comfort them, to hold them, as tenderly as mothers do. She thought about the conversation she needed to have with Justin about the baby and pushed it aside in her mind as she approached the door.

"Knock-knock. Hi Casey. So, I wanted to apologise earlier. I have been struggling personally and when Darius, the patient in 305 was agitated, I think I just got triggered. I sat outside the hospital by the street for the past 45 minutes."

Casey looked up from his computer with a perplexed look. He had managed a number of nurses in the ICU over the course of the pandemic so far who had similar occurrences. "Thank you for letting me know, Grace. But listen, it is terribly unsafe for your patients for you to be abandoning your duties and not telling anyone. We were fortunate that Elle was able to cover you, as she had a patient down in OR. I will need to write you up for this unfortunately."

Grace's heart sank. She knew her sudden and unannounced abandonment of duties was unsafe and irresponsible. At the same time, she felt like her body's reaction to all of the stress was completely out of her control. "I think I need counselling," she blurted out.

Casey looked at her, his eyes changed as he appeared to take in the angst she was noticeably carrying. "Listen Grace. You are an excellent employee and nurse. I will dismiss this issue just this once, but I'm going to send you the resources for employee counselling."

Grace breathed a small sigh of relief, measuring the compassion he had granted her and thanked him profusely for his generosity as she walked back to her shift that was over in 30-minutes, to give her report to the oncoming PM Nurse. Once the handoff was completed, and her final documentation entered, Grace headed out of the ICU doors. Elle followed behind and caught her in the hallway.

"Grace, wait up a minute. I'm really sorry that you had a rough day today. Is there anything you want to talk about?" Grace thought in her mind about how Elle had been secretive and distant with her over the past weeks, and how she didn't feel like she wanted to open up. Elle seemed to read that, as someone who knew Grace well. "Listen, I saw you that day in the courtyard, but didn't know what to say to you."

Grace's interest peaked as she walked. "The courtyard?" Grace said, intentionally inserting an air of naivety in her tone.

"I know you saw me with Blake. He's the guy I'm seeing, from MRI."

Grace stopped in her tracks. "I-I am not sure what to say to you about it. Yes. I did see you. Does Joe know?" Grace tried to sound neutral and not so judgemental that Elle would shut down. Yet, she felt like her disapproval was making her skin crawl standing there in the hall, looking at her friend that she felt she barely knew at all.

"No. He doesn't. It's better this way for him and the kids."

Grace was astounded by her honest logic. "I see. Well, I'm really just going through a lot right now, Elle. I am honestly in a bit of shock about your affair. It makes me feel uneasy. I'm not sure I support it." Grace stood there, feeling a mild sense of relief that she had stated what had been on her mind for weeks.

Elle looked at her, the colour in her face fading a little, as she took in what Grace was saying, causing her to reflect a little. "I understand. It-it just happened and I am not really sure where it is going with Blake, or even what I should do about it. I really didn't want to hurt my husband, but I also have been so unhappy."

Grace nodded acceptingly and stood there with nothing much to say. "Okay, well, I'm just not sure what to say really and I need to go pick up Emma." They parted ways, Grace felt the shadow of Elle behind her as she left, as she made her way through the corridors swiftly. She felt a slight remorse that she could not say something assuring to Elle, demonstrating some support. She rather thought about how cowardly Elle had been first not to say something to her when she had seen her that day and more importantly to be hiding her transgressions from her husband.

Grace struggled to see, now despite things being out in the open about what was happening, how she could relate to Elle when she felt strongly that she didn't agree with her friend's choices. Grace had grown to hate the factors in life that undermined marriages. Be it violence, alcoholism, or infidelity. She had developed abject hatred for these things.

Grace sped home and picked up Emma quickly. She wanted to get home to rest. Grace was feeling extremely tired in the second half of her days. To the point that she sometimes sought to lay on the floor and take a nap while playing with Emma in her playroom.

"We're home, Just," Grace called from the door. "Go say hello to Daddy."

Justin emerged from the shadowy door to his study, the glow of the computer screen illuminating the edges of furniture behind him as he stood in the doorway. "Emma!" He greeted her with excitement and opened his arms as she ran to him then lifted her up above his head in a rocket launch motion.

Emma squealed with delight, requesting the rocket launch: "Again!"

Grace was used to playing second fiddle to Justin's attention when Emma came home and leaned on the banister smiling at them, admiring their bond. In this moment, she felt the feeling sneak up. *We are ready for this baby*. Seeing Justin, as a doting father, made all the apprehensions slip away. After Emma had fallen asleep, Grace went downstairs to sit with Justin in the living room. He was watching reruns of *The Office*, chuckling on the end of the sofa. Grace looked over at him with coy reserve before she decidedly broached the subject. "Hey Justin. Can I talk to you for a minute?"

Justin's face became flushed as he turned to her. She noticed apprehension fill his face briefly as his eyes darted away before looking at her. *What does he think I'm going to say?* Grace waited, while he paused the show. "So Justin, I've been meaning to tell you something. I have a little news."

An expression of relief briefly passed over him as she mentioned news. "What's your news?" He said, searching her eyes for affirmation that it would be something positive.

Grace looked at him. She felt a closeness to him that she had not in a long while. "Well, I-I'm pregnant." Her words hung in the air for moments in which he looked at her in disbelief.

"But we've been so careful. Ah, are you sure?" He responded. His reluctance to accept the plain truth he was presented with irked her. He often denied information that contradicted what he thought should or was to happen, almost reflexively. A stale pause lingered between them. Both not flinching.

This wasn't how Grace had hoped he would receive the news she had been contending with for weeks. Grace turned away from him, staring at the static image on the screen ahead and pulling a couch pillow close to her. "Well, I thought you should just know. Clearly this isn't something that excites you."

"What do you mean, Grace?"

She knew Justin's thought processes by the way he communicated. "You're questioning whether I am pregnant, because you don't particularly like the fact that I am," she said in a terse tone.

"Well, I mean, I'm just surprised that's all. I didn't think we were planning to do this."

"No Justin, we were not planning to do this right now. But sometimes things just happen. I mean, don't you want another child? A sibling for Emma? I thought this was the plan ultimately."

The direct questions stifled Justin as he sat, now turning straight ahead taking his turn to stare at the static screen, unable to conjure a response that he knew would satisfy Grace in the moment while truly reflecting how he felt. He felt queasy. His mind had begun to race with thoughts of Vivi and the passionate and increasingly involved affair he had recently started and how, in truth, the last thing he wanted right now was more responsibility and commitment to his family.

Grace glared at him, a sinking feeling began to emerge, as she looked at him bent downwards now with his face in his hands. *Why is he not happy about this? Why did I think he would be?* She realised that she had been incorrect in her assumption that he wanted a baby and that her own trepidation was the only factor to consider. They sat silently for a time before Justin broke, "Grace, I-I just don't know. I mean, do you want to keep this baby even?"

"Even?" Grace responded swiftly with a raised voice. Although Grace had contemplated this very same question, she was incensed by him asking it and the lack of support she perceived to be behind his question. "Clearly you are not in support of me having this baby, Justin. First you question whether I'm really pregnant after I tell you I am." She slammed the ultrasound pictures she had been carrying onto the sofa cushion in front of him. "Then you ask me if I even want to keep it, like it's a pair of shoes I might return to Macy's. I don't get you. With Emma, you were ecstatic, giddy and all in from the minute you knew I was pregnant. Now, you have nothing supportive to say. This is Justin, a son or a daughter, and a sibling for Emma."

Grace wasn't sure if she was more upset at herself for miscalculating what his perspective on this would be or that he was actually bringing forth her own deep doubts. Her day had been stressful and she had hoped sharing this news would brighten it. "You think you can just come trap me with this news and expect I'm just going to be hunky-dory with it?" Justin now looked at her directly as he spoke.

"Trap you? Is that what you think I'm doing, Justin? I'm sorry, I thought we were in a partnership, a marriage, with a consensual desire to grow our family someday. And now this day has come, you tell me I'm trapping you? Get a grip. You are just being selfish." Grace was raising her voice now, to a level that might wake up Emma. She listened to the baby monitor for a response to the noise.

"I'm selfish? How about you, not telling me for nearly two months about this secret you've been keeping."

"This secret, Justin? I didn't know I was pregnant for a while, and frankly, I've been trying to wrap my head around this and around every other thing that is falling apart in the world right now. And yes, this is my news to share, I'm the one whose body is carrying our baby. I have the right to share this information whenever I choose."

Justin stared at her with an unempathetic look. "Well, you're going to do whatever you want to do, I guess, Grace," he said, shifting his weight forward to get up from the couch. The coldness of his tone sunk to the soles of her feet. "Let's be honest, it doesn't really make a difference what I want anyway." He stood up and began to walk away. "I need to get some air." He walked out the back door and paced beneath the glowing lights.

"Unbelievable," Grace uttered, sensing his detachment to her and to the situation, as she gathered up the cups that had collected on the coffee table.

Justin sat down on the bench. He felt an urge to smoke a cigarette, even though he had quit almost five years prior. The night sky was deep, laced with twinkling stars and a bright moon that he stared into for a time. He felt uneasy, his mind went to Vivi and a desire to be with her now, away from the complicated situation he was now faced with at home. He thought about how her silk sheets felt wrapped around his back as she pulled him towards her. He wanted to feel pleasure that would outpace his discomfort in this moment. His attention then reverted back to the pregnancy. *Why is she trapping me?* He told himself. He had finally felt like the intensity of the early years with Emma were waning and he could taste new freedoms.

Vivi had been an unexpected distraction from the discomfort that had been building in his life where the stressors of the pandemic had closed down his world in nearly every direction he looked. Now, having a new baby meant further compromise, further restrictions. It was like he was being forced to re-up his commitment to his family, to Grace, to a life that was predictable, limiting and conventional. He did feel trapped, not only by Grace, but by circumstance with what this pandemic was doing to close down so many of his options. Justin sat outside, breathing slowly, contemplating what his next steps now would be, as Grace busied herself in the kitchen, trying not to cry.

\*\*\*

Lorna returned to the ICU late evening, as she received a call from the doctor who was allowing her special privileges to come into the hospital to go see her daughter. The entire ICU had been rallying to support Kendra and Darius' cases over the past weeks. As she entered the stark lighting of the ICU, she was surprised to find her daughter sitting in bed without the tube in her throat. Lorna rushed towards Grace. Grace was met with Lorna's incredulous expression. "Is she off?"

Lorna could barely speak, as she looked over her shoulder at her daughter, now untethered to the ventilator, breathing air on her own. It had been 42 days since Kendra had been brought in for an emergent intubation. The Coronavirus had ravaged her body, harming her organs and wasting away her muscles and tissue. Grace met Lorna with a smile, "Yes, we were able to extubate her this morning. She's still drowsy as the sedation wears off, but you can gown-up and go in to see her."

Grace felt a warm feeling as she watched Lorna, who she had never met in person, enter slowly to be by her daughter's side. The virus had swept through Kendra and left behind the wreckage of a high heart rate, blood pressure that spiked and dipped erratically and kidneys that were partially functioning. But she was alive. She was breathing on her own and the Coronavirus had left her body. Lorna held her limp hands, gently lifting her hands to her own masked cheeks, holding them close. Lorna had spent nights fearfully lying awake imagining her daughter laying under sedation, apart from her children and praying for the day she would wake up and breathe easily again.

Through broken tears, Lorna whispered, "You made it. My baby, you made it."

Kendra was in a drowsy state but managed to smile sleepily with her eyes still closed to the soothing words her mother told her. The pain and the trauma of all the weeks she had spent waiting, wondering and fearing pushed through the floodgates as Lorna cried beside her daughter. Tears of relief, tears of gratitude, and a renewed confidence that the God she had prayed to had listened and finally responded. Lorna sat for nearly an hour rocking back and forth on the edge of her seat, holding her daughter's hand and praying through tears of gratitude. When the hour was up, Lorna had to be escorted out of the ICU. Grace noticed that the heavy lines that had run across Lorna's forehead had evened out leaving her face more relaxed. She looked youthful even. It was as though she had shed heartache that had aged her 10 years right there in the room while holding her daughter's hands. The intense moments when loved ones were able to be reunited never ceased to move Grace. Especially now, nearly half a year into the pandemic, the opportunities for loved ones to come into the ICU had been few and far between. Loved ones had been locked out. Only able to reach through phone screens to connect with their loved ones. It had been perhaps more challenging to stand by holding the phone while a patient or loved one grieved than to execute the daily nursing tasks necessary to care for her critically ill patients. Grace had often stood with a stoicism earned through many years witnessing and comforting suffering.

Now, as she stood watching Lorna leave the ICU with a security guard guiding her through the double doors, Grace thought about the argument she had had with Justin. She felt remorse for it. For how she had been unrelenting with him. She knew this about herself. Her ability to say the things that pushed Justin into a corner and didn't seek to make amends. Grace was indeed angry at him for how he reacted. For all the thought and concern she had carried for weeks, contemplating what to do next, only to be met with his self-interested response.

It had caught her off guard to be met with his resistance. His resistance made her waver in her resolve to choose to have the baby.

She stood there, lost in thought. His words, "trap me", lingered in her mind. To Grace, the concept of trapping did not feel like it belonged in the conversation. Yet, it was how he expressed himself to feel. *Trapped.* Grace saw his words to be self-interested and without thought for what she might be going through. She after all was the one carrying a baby during a very strange time. She hated the thought that she would be trapping him into anything, as though she had orchestrated a ploy to limit him. This was a baby, 'our baby'. H*ow could he be so selfish?* His words had pierced through the veneer of her confidence in her choice, leaving her feeling unsteady under the weight of his differing perspective. She hadn't expected him to react this way. *If Justin doesn't want our baby, should I even be trying to go through with this?* Grace thought as she grabbed her bag and headed through the double doors. Her heart raced and stomach turned at the challenging thought.

Once outside, the August night was warm and sweet smelling. People walked through the streets, picking up takeout and some eating outside on the kerbside outdoor dining extensions that had been erected as an alternative to indoor dining. Grace thought about how it seemed that most everything in life had changed. The Coronavirus had tilted the world on its axis, bringing forth a new social landscape, filled with new rules and limitations that she had never imagined would be a part of everyday life. And with months living under the duress of shortages, lockdowns, travel limitations, illness, political upheaval, and civil unrest she expected that there was no end in sight. Reality felt heavy and inescapable.

Grace walked along the sidewalk towards the parking garage. She imagined herself as she was when she was young, jumping over the lines that demarcated the concrete slabs. Balancing and focusing on the fun of jumping from one place to another. The carefree pastimes of her childhood felt so distant. They had ended when her mother had committed suicide. Nothing ever felt the same again then either.

Grace walked, stepping on the lines, her feeling of resentment towards Justin for making her out to be somehow manipulative began to take shape out of a realisation that there was great injustice in him placing blame on her for this. It was a lot to carry, after a long day, with the prospect of a challenging night at home with him. Grace glanced at her watch. It was 4:15 PM and she had been walking aimlessly for 20 extra minutes. She would be late for Emma's usual pick up time. A text came through from Justin, "We need to talk." Grace snapped out of her contemplative state and got to her car, hoisting her bag into the front passenger seat and accelerating along the side roads she took to reach Mrs Corinne's daycare.

***

Vivi texted Justin mid-morning on a Wednesday, careful never to send texts at night or on weekends.

Justin waited for her texts in the morning after seeing Emma off to daycare and with Grace at the hospital. The summer months had been long and filled with leisurely jaunts together. In his mind, he didn't truly recognise his time with Vivi as infidelity. He rationalised it as living out the life he was given but didn't take when he had had the chance the first time around. In that way, it was somehow his for the taking now. He did not want to miss saying yes to Vivi again, not considering that his position to say yes was now different from decades prior when he was single. It was as though his desire to be with Vivi, and to recapture a decision that he let pass him by during his youth, drove him further into her arms, and further into a dissociative state of mind in which he discounted his unfaithful actions. "Hey Just, do you want to get together today? Xx V."

Justin's heart quickened whenever her texts came through. "Let's meet at the Marin Headlands at 10?"

They met at the headlands. Justin loved the bird's-eye view of the bay and the city, looking beyond the golden gate to one side and inwards to the sheltered San Francisco Bay. They circled to find a spot finally in the limited parking lot at the base of the final climb near the Bay Bridge's northern end and climbed up a steep and windy trail. The sun peeked over clouds in passing and the San Francisco Bay sprawled out to the left as they stopped intermittently to take in the pristine views of Angel Island, Alcatraz and San Francisco's shiny skyline beyond. Sailboats rocked and darted at the whim of gusts of wind across the generally calm waters.

Single file, they made their way up the cliff's edge. Coyote brush and sage in the foreground brushed against their legs as the trail was narrow. The day was sunny and partially cloudy, in the high 70s—Warm for San Francisco's standards. When they arrived at the very top, they meandered through the military barracks to the top where the vista of both sides of the bridge lay before them. Today, the regular fog kept itself at bay, and a clear bird's-eye view of the Golden Gate Bridge spread out before them. On one side of the over 100-year-old rust red icon, were the well-travelled, protected waters of the bay and on the other side, the broad and untamed mouth of the Pacific Ocean. Justin and Vivi sat together on a concrete slab overlooking the bridge. They had brough sandwiches to eat.

"Justin." Vivi's voice was now serious. "I don't mean to apply pressure o anything, but I've been thinking about you, and us, and well, Grace and Emma a fair bit lately." Justin looked at her quizzically, willing her in his mind not to broach the perhaps inevitable question. Justin had sought to keep two worlds separate and when uttered in a single sentence, he felt the strain of conflicting interests bearing down on him. "I'm just well, I guess I'm wondering how you think this all will end."

"End?" He looked at her, confronted by the finality of her statement.

"Well, you can't imagine that we can go on pretending that you are single and without a family forever. Or that I will settle for being your other woman. At some point, Justin, you are going to have to choose between us. I am realistic and know these things can take time, so I want you to know I am willing to wait To wait for you, if you tell me it is worth waiting." Her words hung in the air almost foreboding and terribly uncomfortable for Justin to hear.

Justin had not anticipated these questions. In his own delusion, such questions did not exist as both worlds, Grace and Vivi's did not coexist. The had existed in their own rights at different points in time, but now with Vivi's re-emergence in his life, the timelines were now coinciding, and it fel unwelcome. He realised the fallacy in his wishful thinking as he sat there holding his sandwich loosely now in his hand.

"I mean, how do you even feel about Grace now?" Vivi's line of questioning was direct and he could estimate the weight she would place on his response by the build in her line of questioning.

"Well. I mean, I don't know. She's my wife and the mother of Emma. It' complicated, Vivi," he replied, looking into the distance, taking a bite of hi pastrami sandwich. Chewing extensively as if to avoid talking further. He knew that it wasn't that he didn't love Grace. It was that he loved Grace and Emma completely, but for whatever reason, he had grown to find that they did no complete him. He could not bring forth words to explain this. Vivi examined hi face. She saw he was not able to answer her question so directly. And realised in that moment that no question like that could ever be so simple that one may answer it immediately, if ever.

"I have known you a long time, Justin. I know how an adventure excites you. But it's been a couple months now that we've been together. I hate to say it Justin, but I think I can't help it but I think I am falling in love with you, or at least the idea of you. Maybe just the idea of us." Her words trailed off but resonated loudly with Justin. The warmth he felt for her could also be considered love he thought at that moment. "I just need to know where you stand and what you intend to do."

Justin sat with her statement. Never before had she asked for any level of commitment in the few months they had spent together. He felt unsure of how to answer and a longing to have never been asked. He enjoyed the steady life that he could return to, predictable as it were, it was comforting. Vivi was the element of his life that had been missing for so long, as he lived his life reformed to the ways of convention. She represented adventure, spontaneity and passion. *If only both relationships could coexist harmoniously* he thought to himself. Vivi read his hesitancy. She had truthfully expected it. "Tell me about your wife. Tell me about Grace," she probed further gently.

"What's there to say? We've been married five years, we have Emma together. She's a nurse."

"Okay, well, that doesn't exactly answer my question, Justin. You know what I'm asking."

He did. He didn't quite know the answer for himself. Grace had always been a logical choice. She was a committed person, one that stayed the course. In that moment, he thought of her, how hard she worked at the hospital as their family's primary breadwinner, and loving mother to Emma, and now to his unborn child. A wave of guilt passed over him, a feeling he seldom felt, but it was distinct this time, palpable. "Well, she's…" He retreated from the impulsion to tell her that Grace was in fact pregnant with their second child. "She's my wife. She's a good mother, she's a good wife." Justin struggled to find words to describe their relationship to Vivi who by now was sitting there with wide eyes, hanging on every word and waiting for him to give her some indication of what he was thinking about her and if he would leave Grace for her. He left it there, with silence filling the gaps. To be filled with the whim of Vivi's imagination.

The truth was he didn't want to have to choose between Grace and Vivi, and in this moment detected that anything he might say that indicated some level of choice about what he would do next, may jeopardise what he had with Vivi. He liked having a stable home and relationship with Grace and was at the same drawn to Vivi with a chemistry that he did not find with Grace, or anyone else he had ever met for that matter.

"I just want you to know, Justin. That there is no one like you for me and I think you are worth the wait."

Justin smiled at her, feeling like his reticence had paid off, as Vivi had talked herself into drawing her own conclusion to the conversation. *No doubt this will come up again, but for now, I should just kiss her.* Justin leaned in and tenderly kissed Vivi. The tourists that clustered on the cliff edge overlooking the Golden Gate Bridge, remarking, taking pictures, and then walking by Justin and Vivi, were of little consequence to them as they could only see each other. His genuine focus on her and the way he made her feel, made Vivi feel assured that he would be worth the wait.

# Chapter 12
## Silence

Grandma and Grandpa came to collect the girls' belongings the following weekend. The girls went into their room to box and carry out their belongings from their house. They took only the clothes and the one pair of shoes that would still fit them. It was agreed to by their dad and grandparents that it would be best that they stay with their grandparents from then on out. No one from Barbara's family had reached out with a better offer for the girls in the days after she had died.

Daddy would come by for dinner most nights in the week then head to their old home. Grace often wondered if he would find it spooky to live there, knowing Mumma had died in their bed. It was also strange to Grace, that they never spoke about Mumma, it was as if she hadn't ever existed in their world after she died. Grace continued to talk to her mother, in her mind and soft whispers as she played alone or lay awake at night. The ongoing conversation with her mother kept her memory living, and to Grace it was as though she was not missing a single part of Grace's life. This was a comfort. Grace also grew to enjoy the benefit of her grandmother's attention to detail as she ensured the girls had lunch always packed and ready on the kitchen table before school, an after-school snack waiting for them.

Breakfast and dinner would always be hot and ready sharply at 7 AM and 6 PM for Grace and Lottie. It made a difference to feel cared for, and to be able to rely on meals and fitting clothing, haircuts, regular doctor and dentist visits and day trips on the weekends. Grace had known it to be so different when Mumma was alive. The house had fallen to disarray, as they would scrape around the pantry for things to eat after their groceries ran out. Ill-fitting shoes had been the hardest to bear, as blisters formed from their toes pressing against the ends of their shoes, with their heels turning raw with the pressure of squeezing their feet into sizes too small.

As Grace was nearing 5th grade, she became self-conscious of how small her dresses with hiked up hemlines caused ladies in the street walking past her at the square to raise their eyebrows and classmates to snicker behind her back when she had to bend down to pick up a dropped bookbag.

Grandma hired a tutor when the girls first came to live with her as days had passed where both Lottie and Grace had not completed their homework in the months that Mumma had retreated exclusively to her room all hours of the day. Grace sat at the big oak dining table with the glow lighting the pages of her homework packet. The tutor shuffled through the completed papers and had Grace complete another math word problem. The pencil pressed against the paper making a slight squeak as it glided along the forms of numbers and symbols. Grace liked math and felt frustrated that she was no longer as strong in the subject after months of not doing homework and being distracted by the raking pains of hunger for many hours while in school.

The tutor, a college student named Sophia, came weekly for many months and put her through her paces, filling in the gaps, challenging her with repeated problems to solve and ultimately remediated Grace's academics in Math and English back to where she should be. Daddy would come by from time to time, when he was sober and sit down to dinner with them, making small talk as though everything was normal. No mention of their mother or the violence he had once subjected them to.

Grace had sat thinking about how people, from one moment to the next, could be so different. It was as though Daddy had shed his previous self, now domesticated and polite, he would sit at his mother's table and ask Grace and Lottie about school, their friends, and make plans to take them out to the park or for ice-cream at the square on the weekend. Grace liked this side of her father, yet mourned the fact that he did not come to this new way of being in their family sooner. *Mumma would have loved it if he was this kind and interested*, Grace thought one day as Daddy took them for a walk to get ice-cream, all the while asking them about what their favourite candy and ice-cream flavours were. *Why couldn't he just have been kinder to Mumma? She might have stayed.* The question caused her lower lip to press against the top, with a sinking feeling, as she walked a few paces behind him looking up at his neckline bobbing up and down with an ease that betrayed the dark nights he had spent terrorising their home.

It was clear from the first day that Grace and Lottie stepped foot in Grandma's house that Grandma was in charge. She kept the house spotless and delivered delicious meals like clockwork. Whereas Grandpa was a drifting presence in the home. He often busied himself with the tasks she set before him, spending extensive time tinkering in the garage on small projects, and kept up the garden.

From the beginning, Grandma had her hand dutifully and comprehensively in everything of the girls' day, the house and the family. Grace noticed how her Grandma's presence in their lives was steady, commanding and thankfully supportive. It was at first a novelty to receive such direct attention from an adult. Grace had learned to manage in the absence of her mother's presence in their lives for quite some time, often taking small matters in her own hands with no one to show her. It struck Grace to see a female figure command such presence in their lives, but she welcomed it as one does when the sun peeking out from behind the clouds after the rain, warming the earth where plants would lean towards its presence.

Where her mother had retreated and faded, Grace had sought to create her own light for herself and Lottie. As meals were served to her and Grandma took her to the mall to pick out new shoes, she thought back to how she had scratched around for fitting shoes, attempted to alter hemlines of dresses and skirts as she grew, and the arduous trips to the grocery store requiring her to carry heavy bags home. It had felt like survival, in which all sense of safety and security had to be resourced from within. All the self-sufficiency she gained came from a sense of emptiness. She had become a little numb to the luxuries of imaginary play and daydreams. It had been as though her mind could not make the leap from the ever present, ever gnawing concerns of the day, rather concerned with meeting basic needs and the chronic draw of survival mode.

Now, with her mother gone and her grandparents providing for them, she realised she may never have to worry again about feeding or clothing her or her sister. She felt guilty for her gladness in this revelation, realising it had only come to pass that she and Lottie were now cared for and no longer in a situation stained by neglect, because her mother had committed suicide. There was never going to be resolution to the feelings she held towards her mother. The dichotomy of gladness and angst held its dual places in Grace's mind whenever she thought of her.

*\*\*\**

The warming smell of minestrone soup wafted in the hall as Grace came through the entryway. She dropped her scrubs in the hamper and made her way stealthily to the shower. The water eased the muscles in her lower back that had begun to strain under the weight of her growing belly. She had begun to lean back a little to counter the weight as she walked. On her feet all day. Exhausted. As the summer had drawn on, she had noticed her form growing and the flutter and jab of movement inside. She did not want to know the gender of the baby, but figured it was a boy when all her colleagues would remark at how high she was carrying.

The older nurses who now had grandchildren of their own coming, would also remark at how she walked or that what she ate at lunchtime was a sign that she was carrying a boy. Day after day, well intentioned colleagues would approach her in the hall and place their hands on her stomach, waiting for movement. Grace closed her eyes, washing away all the sickness, pain and intensity of her day in the ICU. The hot water's steam surrounded her. The days were hard and there was no other way to transition from them than to wash them away. She thought about all of the bodies lying in the glass door rooms along the perimeter of the ICU. Teachers, doctors, police, mailmen, cooks, mothers, fathers, sisters, and brothers lined the unit, taken from their families, awaiting the day they would be returned.

Sometimes it was a wait for patients to pass away as much as it was for them to recover, given the damage many of their bodies had sustained through the complicated medical courses that had befell them. As one ventilator freed up, more patients would arrive to fill the ICU beds and claim the machines. The work was heavy and task lists unrelenting, as she worked her days being careful not to catch the virus herself. Her manager had tried to assign her non COVID-19 patients when possible, but most often the ICU was packed with COVID-19 patients and no special accommodations could be made. The complexity of her day, the details of her tasks, the baseline fear she operated under all passed through her mind as she stood quietly in the hot water, waiting for it all to unwind. The intensity of her work was binding. It held her together where she was certain she would otherwise fall apart at every turn. But a turn too great for her to hold it together had come. Grace shuddered at the overwhelming feelings she had experienced at work that day. It was as if the intensity of all that was happening was insurmountable. The only way to deal with the now chronic fear and stress was to shed it. The body would take over and release the pain by any means possible. It would undoubtedly continue to build back.

As the course of the pandemic had taken shape as not a temporary challenge, but an arduous journey with no real end in sight, she had begun to recognise the emergence of that numb feeling she had once known as a girl, while her mother was absent, the one that comes when imagination is put to rest in the interest of putting all of one's brain power towards skills of survival. A dulling of her capacity to feel joy and hopeful thoughts had returned. Grace stood under the faucet for a long while thinking about her baby and Emma. How they were the lights she now carried, even in what felt like a very dark world. *I have to be strong for them,* she whispered to herself. As she uttered those words, she realised that early on her mother had tried to be strong for them, but ultimately, she had not been able to carry the weight of adversity she faced.

Grace thought about Justin and his reaction. So callous really. It had surprised her to be met with resistance from him. She had come to realise that he did not meet the hard parts of life with intention to see things through in the same way she did. Perhaps, a baby, during all of this, was another hurdle that he did not feel equipped to handle. Grace exhaled deeply, trying to centre her thoughts back to the baby. She felt a kick and a flutter. *You are safe with me, little one.*

Grace came downstairs after her shower. Emma was sitting up in her highchair, pushing her broccoli around on her plate. Justin looked up from the sink. "Oh. Hi Grace. I didn't hear you come in, love."

Grace smiled and shrugged her shoulders. "Hi Emma darling." She hugged Emma as well as she could while seated in the chair.

"Let me get you a plate. Would you like milk or water?" Justin leaped into action. Grace appreciated how Justin was always eager to feed her. Especially now, in her second trimester where her appetite was growing. After dinner, Grace headed to bring Emma to bed. Justin was in his usual place on the couch. Grace stopped into the study to grab a pair of scissors to cut the tags off Emma's new pink sparkly shoes. As Grace came back out of the study, she was startled by Justin standing right outside of the door. He had seemingly hurried to her. 'Justin! You scared me. I didn't expect you there."

An expression of disregard and preoccupation was on his face. "What were you doing on my computer?" He pressed her with an accusatory tone.

"Your computer? I just came in to get scis—"

Justin cut her off. "Please do not use my computer."

"Okay. I'll keep that in mind." She stepped around him to pass in the hall. As she walked an uneasy feeling passed over her. *What was that all about?* She thought to herself, as she made her way to the kitchen for better light to cut off the tags. Justin followed her, after she heard him closing the study door.

Justin sat on the couch next to Grace. Watching a show and paying no attention to it. *What did she see?* Was all that he could think about. He worried about the rendezvous emails, chat windows filled with affectionate language that Vivi and he had passed back and forth. That may have been left open. His mind darted to his search history for multiple restaurants and locations around the bay that he had clearly not brought Grace to. His preoccupied mind churned, as he attempted to sit still acting as though he was enjoying the show.

Grace looked over at him periodically. "Justin." His heart began to race. *Shit. She saw something.* He looked over to her. "We need to talk." *Shit. Shit. Why is she so calm? Wasn't I the one who told her we need to talk? I'd rather finish that baby conversation.* "We need to talk about the baby. I just need to say this. I-I love you. I love us. I love our family. I know this prospect of a baby may have shocked you and believe me, I questioned if I was ready too. But when you think about it. In all the craziness that is going on in the world right now. A new life, a miracle is well, isn't it a blessing that we should celebrate?"

Justin felt relief as his pounding heart began to slow. *She didn't see anything.* He focused on recovering his composure to answer the actual question she was asking, not what he had imagined she would. In his relief, he welcomed the notion that the baby was something to celebrate, a far better topic than being caught cheating. "Yes Grace. Listen. I'm sorry for how I reacted the other day. The news just surprised me, that's all. This will be good for Emma and yes this is good news that should be celebrated." A bright smile passed across Grace's face. This pleased Justin.

\*\*\*

The word travelled fast, on the news channels, and amongst staff. Vaccine trials had been in the works for months.

Potential vaccines that may be available in November or December were spoken about in hopeful tones throughout the hospital. It would be just a few more months before the world would have access to a vaccine that could pacify the disease that had claimed nearing a million people's lives worldwide over the past months. It was such a desired prospect that it was almost unbelievable. The years and decades of work that had preceded this moment in vaccine development, was now making it possible for SARS-CoV2 mRNA vaccines to be developed in record time, within months of the emergence of the novel Coronavirus in China.

The promising preliminary trial data coming out of the Pfizer BioNTech and Moderna vaccine trials was announced in snippets with a momentum of anticipation now, and served for Grace and her colleagues as a light at the end of the tunnel. Grace sat in the cafeteria skimming through her newsreel to read about the Pfizer and Moderna trials. *A vaccine for this will change the whole world* she thought to herself.

Grace was interested to know how the vaccine would be for pregnant women. Every day, coming to work, more and more aware of her baby inside of her, she had growing reservations about the risk she was taking in doing so. It wasn't clear how much risk, but the few pregnant patients she had seen coming into the ICU over months being placed on life support with emergency C-sections of preterm infants, gave her an idea about how severe the situation could become. Many experienced severe preeclampsia as well as respiratory failure causing risk to the mother's lives and the unborn babies. At the same time, it was her livelihood do so. Many ICU nurses had left for jobs in the outpatient clinics, as they had burned out on the hard and emotionally draining work they had been met with day after day, month after month. Many farewell celebrations took place in their unit. It was hard to see people go, when you were the one staying. They would no doubt move on to different settings, and fill their lives with new concerns, new relationships, new inside jokes. There was something particularly depleting about being the one left behind. The staying, as others moved on, made the sameness of everything look different, holes within the fabric emerged with each departure. When the reaction to adversity is fight or flight, stasis, to Grace, was like entrapment in an unending unfortunate circumstance. Grace couldn't help but feel deserted and with little options to make change. She had responsibilities to her family to maintain her job. She thought about her pregnancy as the timeline she needed to just survive. Then she would have maternity leave, time to regroup, and maybe find something else.

Many of her friends had decided to change their jobs in the course of recent months. Some resigned from working all together, as the pressures of kids transitioning to home-school for the Fall and scarce childcare options, left them with little choice. Grace daydreamed as she went through the motions of her day, of a life where she didn't have to work in the hospital. She thought about Lottie's job, working remotely and the little physical exertion she must have felt. *I picked the wrong career* she often would say to herself, as the days rolled on, filled with suffering and the high stakes of physical risk all around. The strong calling she had once felt towards nursing and healthcare was fading to what she could only describe as chronic duress. Her sense of purpose lessened with every patient that died in her care.

Grace would shudder before picking up the phone to speak with a loved one about collecting a patients' personal effects after they had died. Gathering their belongings into patient bags, so personal, symbolising that person's final imprint in the world, broke her heart. A worn leather band watch, car keys, glasses was ultimately nothing she or any of the doctors could do to save the lives of many people who came through their ICU doors. There was a shared sense of helplessness that the healthcare workers began to feel as case after case proved that the tools they had to combat this virus were not effective enough. The waves of cases filling the hospital floors were a grim sign that the virus was real, it was persistent, and it was consequential to everyone who encountered it. Grace stood in line at the cafeteria, her mind drifted, as she noticed it was beginning to do more so lately, as she disassociated with what was going on around her. Her memory darted to her breakdown out on the street. The unravelling feelings of a loss of control were still palpable. Her stomach would drop as she entertained it. *I have to get a grip,* she said to herself, as she grabbed an egg salad from the fridge case and motioned her preference for a cup of tomato soup. As the man behind the counter stirred the steaming pot with the long-handled ladle, Grace thought more about what was going on with her. How her body's reaction to small adversities was now beginning to be a physiological response of panic, uncontrollable, anxious and, all-consuming thoughts. She realised that truly, the accumulating stress was in fact wearing on her. Like the attrition of sandstone cliffs met repeatedly by waves, gnawing away at their foundations until hollow sea caves remain. Her heart was beginning to race. She thought of her mother, laying lifeless in the bed, the pill bottle spilled, sitting on the step waiting for the truth of what was happening to change, not knowing what to do next.

The undefinable sense of doom spread across her now, without a moment's notice. She imagined the wearing was much like what it had been for her mother in the face of the insurmountable adversity that was her father. Grace used the technique of slow and steady breathing to try to quell her growing sensations of angst, as she stood waiting to pay the cashier. Grace hated that she couldn't stand in line for soup without having emotions that surpassed the situation at hand. It was like compounded memories, traumas, could be re-lived on a physiological basis at anytime, anywhere, often struck unaware. She wanted to escape her skin.

Grace's eyes darted to the exit. *I need to get out of here*, she thought to herself. The heat of the hot cup scorched her palms as she tried to buffer it with a napkin, careful not to drop it as she grabbed a spoon from the nearby dispenser. The cashier was slow to ring up her items, and dallied at the keys when estimating what size soup she should charge Grace for. Grace peered at her, perturbed that the simple dilemma was perhaps all that this person had to worry about in their day, and yet they acted with no haste. Grace slid her card and grabbed her soup, waving off the offer of a receipt. She exited the cafeteria doors into the bright early afternoon light.

The hospital's campus was brand new, with well thought out spaces to sit outside. Grace removed her mask, as she sat down at a table, every other seat taped off to only allow two people to sit at it with adequate social distance. She inhaled deeply and exhaled, focusing on her breath, and blocking encroaching anxious thoughts. She had thwarted the panic with a change of scenery. She realised this, and was glad to have outran the panicked feelings, *for now*. Grace also knew it would not be for long. She knew that on a psychological level and now physiological level it was like she had been changed by all she had seen and experienced in the past months. To her core that was now rendered raw and vulnerable, unsteady to the wind.

\*\*\*

Grace stood over the unit sink. Washing her hands, scrubbing vigorously and lathering up her arms. She went into the med room to get the morning medications to give via IV for her patient in room 321. A middle-aged woman, Darla, mother of five children and hairstylist. The whole family had contracted

COVID, but she was the only one to have been admitted to the hospital's ICU. Grace would neaten her long brown hair that had become tangled and pulled it back when she would be prone, for many hours in the day for a few days shy of a week.

A day ago she had been successfully extubated and was now conscious, yet greatly deconditioned. The trauma of the endotracheal tube had left her throat raw. She could only eat ice-chips and remained on tube-feeding through her nose and an intravenous fluid bag constantly hung beside her. She was deconditioned and tachycardic. She needed oxygen support. Now weaning down to three litres per minute support needed through the nasal cannula that pressed against her nose. Her heart rate would race abnormally from time to time making the alarms chime as the ICU intensivists prescribed beta blocker medication to slow the cardiac arrhythmia, but then her blood pressure would become low. She would struggle to fight the deconditioning effects of not having moved her body very much for so long. As when she moved, she would become hypotensive and dizzy.

The cycle continued for days, under close monitoring, and Grace was diligent about following the doctor's orders for medication adjustments in a timely manner and reporting symptoms astutely and quickly to the attending physician.

Now, 31 weeks along, Grace was feeling like the wind that had been in her sails for her second trimester had now somehow been depleted. Everything was heavier, more tiring. Emma was active and curious about all things. Everything one would want her to be at the age of three, but it was tiring keeping up with her. Work was hard work, she felt she didn't have enough hands to cover all the tasks that had to be completed for the patients.

"Hi Darla. How are you this morning?" Grace chimed as she entered the patient's room.

Darla looked up, her head was weak and she was challenged to hold it up off the pillow as Grace assisted in repositioning her upright in the bed. "I'm doing okay," Darla offered in a slow, weak, hoarse voice.

Grace had a hard time hearing her patients when she wore the CAPR helmet. The air that filtered through blew at a frequency that seemed to block out some of the consonant sounds people would say. She relied on inference and lip reading most of the time. In recent weeks, she had foregone wearing a mask beneath the CAPR, as it was not necessary and her breathing felt more and more challenged through the extra layers as her pregnancy progressed. She also liked the benefit of making a human connection with her alert patients through giving them a warm smile. "Well, I'm glad to hear you are doing okay. I have brought your morning medications. The doctor wants to make sure you get these before physical therapy comes to help you move today."

Darla had lost 15 pounds, and her face was gaunt, much different from the vivacious patient photo Grace glanced at in her chart, as she scanned the medication to pair it with her patient's wristband barcode. Grace administered the medications, after naming and confirming the dosing. Her patient was lucid, but perhaps not able to understand all the medications she was receiving. Grace thought it always good practice to inform her patients of what was going into their bodies. "The physical therapist says she will be here in about 45 minutes. I suggest you rest a bit until then and we will monitor how this new medication is working for your heart."

Darla smiled, her pale face covered in a film of perspiration. "We are going to give you a bed bath today too," Grace followed.

The blinds were down, and now the mid-morning sunlight and beautiful Fall day beyond the panes were blocked. "Would you like for me to open the blinds?" Grace motioned and with Darla's consent edged her way around the bed, careful not to hit her prominent baby bump with the IV pole and bedside table and chair that she navigated her way around to reach the window.

As Grace leaned over to yank on the chain chords to lift the blinds, the monitor alarms above Darla's bed set off. Everything had set off as the blood pressure dropped suddenly and the cardiac monitor flatlined. Her patient was actively dying. Grace ran to the patient to hit the bed controls into a code blue position and hit the code blue alarm above the bed. Darla lay sheet white, lifeless, in cardiac arrest. As her colleagues could be seen rushing around in the hallway to don the appropriate personal protective equipment, Grace engaged in performing chest compressions. The adrenaline coursing through her body and with as much vigour as she could. The faces of Darla's five children and husband she had met over video calls and saw posted on the wall at the end of Darla's bed, passed through her mind with each drive of the heels of her palms into the sternum of her patient as she looked down at her patient's lifeless face.

In the fast pace moment, Grace's respirator helmet, loosely secured to her head tilted forward and tumbled off her head to the bed before falling to the floor, as she was performing the compressions. She noticed a moment later what had happened and panicked as she had been breathing heavily as she worked, and now without the protection of filtration. Horrified by what had happened, Grace stepped back from the patient who lay still on the bed, as her colleagues ran in to take over chest compressions. Grace then scrambled to get out of the room, kicking the CAPR helmet away to the side so no one would trip, while trying to hold her breath.

She broke out of the room gasping for air, as the remaining staff went in to attend to the code. She had been shorter with her breath naturally as her pregnancy had progressed into the third trimester, with less room to expand her lungs. Thankful to have made it out of the room, she breathed heavily through a basic isolation mask that she pulled out of her pocket while standing by watching the measured chaos of a code blue taking place. The exertion of performing chest compressions for only a few minutes had driven up her respiratory rate. She felt adrenaline coursing through her as she stood in the hallway, a bit dazed by the experience, watching them work, hoping it had all been worth it. The Automated External Defibrillator pads had been applied on Darla's bare chest and side and the team stood back as it took its read and advised a shock. Again no cardiac rhythm.

One of the nurses, Joanie, rotated in to relieve Cassey and perform another round of chest compressions. "One, two, three, four..." she could hear them counting off their compressions at a forward pace before delivering oxygen through the Ambu bag. Grace could see the perspiration that was dripping down her forehead, through the glass window and through her respiratory helmet's lens. The lead pulmonologist Dr Rose cued an epinephrine injection to be administered, as Joanie continued with another round of compressions, pounding on Darla's chest enough to break ribs. The defibrillator signalled for the team to stand back to take another reading and then delivered a shock. The team worked for minutes longer until Darla's heart's rhythm resumed on the monitor.

Grace's manager, Janet, was now standing outside with her and asked Grace to step away into her office. "How are you doing, Grace? A bit of excitement here this morning, I see."

Grace nodded with a tense attempt to smile. She knew she had to report what happened, but hesitated to because she feared hearing herself say the words that detailed the risk she had placed herself and her baby at.

"I saw that a helmet had fallen to the floor there. Was that your CAPR, Grace?" Janet inquired calmly, knowingly.

"Yes. It was mine. It fell off my head a few minutes into compressions after I initiated the code." Grace covered her face as she began to cry. "I thought i was secured tightly to my head, but everything happened so quickly and before I knew it, it was on the ground. I'm really worried that I was exposed."

A grave expression passed over Janet's face as she took in Grace's baby bump and the consternation on her face. "Well, it's hard to say if you will get COVID from such a brief exposure, but we will need to complete the paperwork necessary to report this exposure to employee health and the safety team."

Exposure. It was Grace's solemn and worst fear all the months she had been working away in the ICU during the pandemic. They completed the paperwork to report the equipment malfunction and exposure. "If you need to take a breather for the rest of the afternoon, I will have staffing send backup. I understand that this is psychologically weighing."

Grace nodded her head, feeling disappointed in her miscalculation of the helmet's fit as she entered the room, not taking extra time to shake her head to ensure it was secure or even tighten it. Her thoughts turned to her baby and Emma, as she took Janet's offer and headed to her locker in the breakroom. *What sort of mother am I? Why am I even here doing this work?* She couldn't help but let the negative thoughts fill her mind as the undercurrent of her anxiety about the situation caused her to play back every step that occurred leading up to those unprotected breaths and after, as though somehow, she would be able to uncover an answer to her question.

*Was I exposed enough to get COVID?* Grace texted Justin as soon as she got cell reception in the atrium leading to the exit. "Justin. Something bad happened. My respirator fell off when I was doing chest compression on a Code Blue." Grace pressed send after a moment's hesitancy re-reading it and walking through the employee parking garage. She always took pause in the delivery of bad news, wishing it wasn't so and hopeful that keeping it in would somehow diminish the hard truths to something tolerable. She was yet to be successful in doing so.

"Omg. I'm so sorry, Grace. Are you okay?" was Justin's reply.

Grace appreciated his immediate concern. "I'm really hoping I didn't contract the virus." She replied. "I see. Well, what do we do next?"

Grace instructed her phone to call Justin. He picked up immediately. "Hi Justin. I'm not sure what we will do next. Other than that, my manager signed me up for testing tomorrow at a COVID testing site that's a drive-through. I can keep working as long as I don't have symptoms. So, she said I need to monitor my symptoms. I really think it best I isolate myself at home from you and Emma."

Justin listened and slowly responded, "I see. Okay." She heard the hesitancy in his voice. He was weighing the impact of this situation on his own inconvenience. "What exactly happened? I mean, I know there has always been a risk with this. But were you careful?"

Grace hated to admit her lack of judgment with the helmet, as she knew his mutual interest in their baby's welfare further impacted their sense of how high stakes the situation was. "I see. Well, I guess there isn't really much we can do about it now. Don't beat yourself up about this. Accidents happen. And well maybe nothing will happen and you'll be fine."

Grace sensed the paucity in his confidence as he spoke. "Well, I'll go get Emma from daycare then," he said. "I'm running some errands so I won't be able to get her now till around 4:30 PM."

Grace was bothered that he wasn't going to be able to pick her up at 4 PM and the thought of how he wouldn't do things exactly the way she liked them done for Emma in her absence during isolation but would have to live with it. "How long do you need to be in isolation?" He inquired, as if reading her mind.

"14 days." The timespan hung in the air as Justin calculated the burden it would have on his own schedule and plans. "I see. Okay. Well, we will have to just make it work, I guess."

"Okay," Grace replied.

"I'll talk to you soon," Justin responded.

"Okay, I love you." Grace replied, as her mind wandered into the nadir of her dilemma.

Justin sounded uneasy as he replied, "Bye Grace."

Grace hung up and fought back tears. Angry tears. She was deeply frustrated with herself for making a mistake. The fear of getting COVID had haunted her since day one of the pandemic when she began to realise its potential consequences. Now, nearly eight months pregnant, having made it so far. This was terrible. Grace drove along the backstreets of Berkeley, keeping the car in motion so as not to be engulfed by the angst that always seemed to catch up with her when she was not moving. Her ability to outrun this was already predetermined. *There is nothing I can do about this now. What's done is done,* she thought, as her emotions tempered and a ray of clarity began to fill her mind

She reflectively looked out her window at a school playground with lively elementary school children hanging and swinging from the monkey bars and chasing each other. Her mother's voice rang in her mind. *Thou shall not fear*

Her mother had embroidered it on a pillow that sat in the living room. She would remind Grace often, when she saw her child quivering with fear and angst over something that happened that, "the Bible says we should not fear 365 times. Do you know why, Grace?" She would say. "Because it's a reminder for each and every day that we don't have to fear if we trust God."

Grace remembered her mother's knowing smile. Grace smiled in this moment with a chuckle through her tears. Knowing full well that she hadn't trusted God for a long time. *Perhaps she is right.* Grace drove home, slowing at the speed bumps and pulling into their driveway. She got out and put her mask on. Determined to not spread anything in the house. She gathered some of her items and decided she would stay in the bedroom. It had a shower and toilet. Justin would be able to bring her meals to the door.

Grace heard Emma and Justin coming through the door. She wished she could go downstairs and hug Emma's little body. Instead, she sat on the bed and pulled out her tablet to check email and search COVID-19 symptoms. The laundry list of symptoms that could emerge in the first 2–14 days were common, and therefore concerning to experience any one of them. Cough, shortness of breath or difficulty breathing, fatigue, muscle and body aches, headache, sore throat, congestion or runny nose, nausea or vomiting, diarrhoea and new loss of taste or smell were listed. Grace felt the aches in her body, from lifting patients. *I can't assume every little symptom is COVID.* She told herself as she began to pace around in the room. Hearing her family downstairs going about the evening routine.

That night, Justin slept on the couch in the living room, after putting Emma to bed. Justin could hear Emma asking for her over and over as she walked through the hall to go have a bath, brush her teeth and again while walking back to her bedroom to read a story. Justin and Grace had decided it would be better to tell Emma that Grace had to go on a trip, than to tell her she was hiding from her in the other room. They knew if Emma caught a whiff of Grace's presence in the house, she would be camped out at the door calling for her mother with great desperation. Grace moved quietly in the room as she watched TV on her tablet with headphones in and enjoyed a bowl of gnocchi and glass of milk that Justin had snuck up to her around dinner time.

As restful as it was, she felt isolation beginning to wear on her only after a few hours. As the night took over, she tossed and turned, perseverating on a dull ache or a tickle in her throat. *This is it.* Her mind flashed back to the Code Blue, her intent to save her patient, with lack of regard for her own protection. It was a vignette in the bigger picture of what had been going on for Grace and other healthcare workers like her. It was almost with blatant disregard for self and safety that she and others trudged into the hospital day in and out taking risks for their own health in order to save others. Grace marvelled at how this hadn't happened sooner in one moment and kicked herself for not being careful enough the next, as she lay in bed, watching the moonlight grace the far windowsill, unable to sleep. She heard Emma in the other room in a muffled cry for 'Mumma' and her heart lurched.

The next day, Grace came downstairs after Justin took Emma to daycare. The kitchen was in loosely managed disarray—freshly washed dishes and Tupperware stacking on the counter beside the sink, a packet of chips open on the counter. She made herself some toast and wiped down the surfaces she had touched before heading out the door to get her scheduled PCR (short for polymerase chain reaction) test at the drive through testing station along the north side of the main hospital campus. The feeling of fall was crisp and the sky clear outside. Grace appreciated the openness of the sky after breaking free from the confines of her room. The world was still out here, alive, bustling as always with pedestrians, commuting cyclists, pavement construction, and garbage trucks rolling and pausing along the streets of Berkeley.

Grace drove, turning the heat up, as the morning felt a little chilly. Grace placed her hand on her belly. "Here we go," she whispered to the baby as she pulled into the COVID testing drive through. Numerous cars idled along the drive-up area demarcated by orange cones. Ahead, healthcare workers covered in personal protective equipment waved cars through before gathering samples through cracks in the windows and hastily bottling the samples to be sent to the lab. The pace was fast and there were many cars lining up now behind Grace. Signs prompted drivers to have their driver's licence and their medical coverage cards available at the point of service to flash behind glass so they could be registered and accounted for.

Grace had heard about the tests being pretty painful, as the swabs had to be inserted up high in the nose to get the best sample. She braced herself for it. A nurse waved her forward and motioned for her to show her card then a second nurse motioned for her to pull forward to the testing bay. Grace leaned towards the window now partially rolled down. The nurse inserted the thin swab and twirled it around deep in her nose, making her eyes water for 10 seconds and again on the other side. Grace resisted the urge to sneeze, ringing her hands in discomfort, looking up to the ceiling of her car. Soon enough it was over and Grace sat wiping her watering eyes and regaining her composure as the nurse stepped back to the testing bay to process the sample for sending. Grace pulled forward, her eyes blurry still, and followed the signs to get back to the road. She headed into work.

Her manager had arranged coverage for her so she could attend her appointment. She put her N95 on, pressing the seal against the bridge of her nose and around her cheeks and chin. The mask smelled like rubber and chemicals, but it was cleaner air than what else she might be inhaling in the ICU without it. Grace carried on throughout her shift, still feeling the rawness of her nose from the invasive swabbing. Her manager saw her in the hall. "How did the testing go?"

"It was okay. Hurt like hell," she mentioned in passing. Getting back into the groove of work was surprisingly easy for Grace. The task-oriented, autopilot aspects of her job were comforting.

Grace continued with the same isolation at home, and then straight to work for the next few days. The PCR tests were taking a few days to return and she awaited the alert in her inbox that a new test result was ready for her. She ate alone in her car. An option that meant she wouldn't be near others and could stay warm as the fall chill was beginning to take hold throughout the days. Grace glanced down at her phone screen, two days after taking her COVID test. She clicked the link to her new test result that she had been alerted to via text.

Grace held her breath as she peered at her small screen, looking for the message link to select. There, in bold letters, Coronavirus SARS CoV2 Undetected. *Undetected?* Grace sighed with relief as she reread her result. *I don't have COVID. It must have been too brief an exposure. Thank goodness I thought to hold my breath as quickly as I did.*

Grace contacted her manager to give her the good news and went back to work for the rest of her shift. Grace felt the baby moving a lot more these days, with sudden sharp stabs and shifting limbs pressing against her skin. It felt like her stomach was stretching more and more by the day. Grace felt a small ember of joy within her now about the baby that had represented dilemma, unwanted change, and risk. Now, still risk was felt, but the negative Coronavirus test result made Grace feel more confident that things were going to be okay.

To be pregnant during this time was not the same as when she had been with Emma. The general worries about getting listeria from undercooked hamburgers and not taking enough folate in her daily vitamins seemed like minor concerns in a pregnancy taking place during a pandemic. Where unseen germs were all around and it was necessary to make sure she took every precaution as she moved through her days cautious to mitigate the risk. Grace knew a few colleagues who had been pregnant and went out on maternity leave just as the pandemic was beginning. Most of them never returned to work after they had their babies. *That wouldn't be an option for me on Justin's teacher's salary* she thought. But getting out of the ICU and into an outpatient clinic when they reopened more positions for in person visits might be something to aim for.

Grace walked outside for her break. She thought to give Lottie a call to see how she was doing. Grace had not called her enough admittedly over the past months. Stuck in her head with the stressors of work and home, she had felt little resource to spread herself socially, even if for a phone call.

She dialled. "Hello? Grace?" Her sister's voice was comforting. Hearing her voice always reminded Grace of childhood, togetherness, and escape, even when the content of their conversations was now grounded in the present.

"Yes. Hi Lottie. How are you?"

"Oh I'm okay. Just taking a work break and walking outside. It's a beautiful day. Don't you just love all the fall leaves?"

Grace smiled. "Yes, it reminds me of those leaves at Todos Santos Square that we used to romp around in."

"I forgot about those leaves. How's Emma?"

"She's doing good," recognising in the space between her words that she was feeling a little distanced from her little one since having had to be isolated in her room over the past days. "I had a COVID scare. So, I haven't had much time with her because I had to go into isolation."

"Oh no. What happened?" Lottie always showed genuine concern for her sister. She thought of her working in the hospital, the mainstage for the pandemic's imagery that she had watched on TV. She could only imagine.

"Yeah, it was pretty bad. I had a COVID patient who coded. Eh her heart stopped and she stopped breathing. I was in the room when it happened, and when I was doing chest compressions my respirator helmet fell forward off my head. It wasn't secured."

"Oh geez," Lottie imagined the healthcare workers in white zipped up full body jumpsuits with big helmets as she pictured Grace's falling off. "What did you do?"

"Well, I just knew I had to get out of there, the moment I realised it had fallen off. It was hard because I was so in the moment trying to save my patients' life."

"Wow Grace, that must have been really stressful."

"Yeah, I keep replaying it, and while I was waiting for my test results, it was driving me crazy to think about how I should have checked the fit of my helmet, and paid more attention to it while I was doing compressions. I can't believe I didn't get it. I mean she was coughing up a storm in that room all the time. Anyway, I just basically lucked out, I guess," Grace concluded. "Well, I'm glad you are okay, Grace. You know I worry about you in there, working with all those COVID patients. All these months and now with the baby coming."

Grace smiled. "Yeah not all of us can be so lucky to work from home," Grace said wryly. "I guess I picked the wrong career," Grace added with a chuckle, knowing nursing was the only thing she really would ever feel happy to be doing. "There was something else that happened the other week. I think I had a panic attack during work. A patient was yelling about his wife and it triggered me. I had to get out of there. I ran out of the hospital and fell apart essentially on the sidewalk. I was crying, and I couldn't get a grip. A security guard had to help me."

Lottie had drawn quiet, taking it all in. "Geez I'm sorry, Grace. That's horrible. Ha-have you spoken to a therapist about it?"

Grace realised she hadn't considered this option. She had always sought to handle the pain of her situations by struggling through. "No, but do you think I should?"

"Well, it probably couldn't hurt. I mean you are under a great deal of stress with all that's going on at work that I'm sure on some level is traumatising you. Plus you're pregnant, and have a toddler at home. Those are stressors on their own. Is everything going okay with Justin? You have a lot going on, Grace. It might be helpful to talk to someone."

Grace supposed she was right. "I was just thinking I was triggered by my patient's yelling because he sounded like how Dad used to...out of control."

Lottie was quiet. "I'm sure he did. That sound rings in my ears to this day."

Grace chose to move on from the unsettling memory of their dad screaming vitriolically at their cowering mother. "Yeah, Justin and I are doing fine. You know—life is pretty busy with Emma and work, and we really are just trying to survive this whole thing day by day." Grace thought about how Justin had reacted to the news of their baby, a nervous feeling passed over her and she decided not to share how he had shown hesitancy about the baby. *Babies were supposed to be deeply satisfying prospects, not ones that brought angst and hardship in happy relationships.* Grace thought it better not to pile on yet another concern. Grace reflected on that thought as Lottie went on to talk about how she had started doing online therapy to help her during this time and made recommendations for the website to use. Grace glanced at her watch. "Hey, I have to get back to work," she interjected. "I just wanted to check in with you and see how you're doing. I miss seeing you. Maybe we can meet some weekend soon for a walk at Golden Gate Park."

Lottie laughed. "Yeah, that would be fun. I'm free, well, every weekend these days actually. Maybe I can just come to Berkeley if it would be easier for you, ya know being eight months pregnant and all and with Emma." They both laughed knowing that their social calendars had dwindled over the months.

Grace agreed to the offer. "Okay, I better go. Let's plan on seeing each other next Saturday then, I'll text you." Lottie agreed and they hung up. Grace walked back to the unit, feeling more settled to have had the chance to speak to her sister.

She wished she had more time to talk to Lottie.

Lottie was the only person she knew who remembered or cared to talk about their mother. Grace liked to be able to call Lottie at any time to resurrect and examine the artefacts of their childhood memories. It was like piecing together dark and light memories of a puzzle that had felt fragmented with a sort of incongruence that can only be cast by trauma. Lottie was the only one who shared the memories of their mother. Lottie was the only one in the world who knew, and acknowledged all they had been through.

Their father had remarried a woman, Lydia, 15 years his junior who he had met at church when he decided to finally go a few years after their mother died. He had started a second family when Grace was finishing high school and now any talk of their childhood, and his first wife, their mother, inspired stony silence on his part. Both Lottie and Grace did not speak often to their father. They picked up the phone, somewhat begrudgingly when significant matters in the family had taken place. Like Grandma's passing and the decision of where to place Grandpa who was no longer able to care for the family home, or himself. They had spent their later childhood years without incidence of a raised voice much less any acts of violence, and seen him reform his ways drastically.

No matter how he had proven to be as their father, the imprint of his rage that cast shadows in their early life never quite left their bones. Grace felt his rage in Darius' ICU room, and in the persistent grip of the Coronavirus that had taken over her world, and all the people in it. It was something she recognised. It was not something she could shake. That evening Grace enjoyed every minute she had playing with Emma in the playroom. She marvelled at how her little baby was now growing into a little person. With imagination and opinion, and a full set of emotions on display. She was a complete little human, capable of empathy as she soothed her dolls after they got a boo-boo or laughed uncontrollably at the funny faces Justin made. Grace thought about how Emma's life was about to change, drastically. She thought about Lottie and how Emma would love to have a sibling to share in the fun. There was no violence in her world, she was oblivious even to everything that was going on around. No real awareness or stress felt about the ongoing pandemic, politics, climate change. Her concerns were the concerns of the moment. *Grace wished things would stay that simple forever.* Everything that kept Grace up at night, as she was growing up in her young life, oblivious to. Grace cherished the gift of naivety she saw in her daughter.

After Emma had gone to bed, Grace lay in bed with Justin. She felt the warmth of his body lying next to hers. Glad to be able to be out of isolation. "Justin. Do you think this will ever end?"

He knew what she was talking about. "I'm not sure, Grace. This pandemic doesn't really seem reversible. I suppose as time goes on we will just learn to live with it. I heard reports that they are hoping future strains will be less deadly."

Grace appreciated how Justin always gave a straight answer. "I just really wish we could go back to 2019. Our trip to Hawaii with Emma."

Justin smiled. He looked at Grace. "We'll go back someday. I promise."

Grace was comforted by that thought and turned over to turn off her lamp. "Goodnight, Just. I love you."

Justin looked over at her. Lying quietly beside him. He felt a sense of guilt that he knew very well was complicated, as it was outweighed by desire. He didn't think he could give up Vivi. *The best outcome will be if she never knows.* He thought to himself, closing his book and turning to switch the lamp off. He

199

lay in the darkness kept awake by thoughts of Vivi and Grace all muddled up in each other.

The next morning, Grace woke up and stumbled to the bathroom. She had been getting up throughout the night from not being able to get comfortable and feeling hot and sweaty and needing to pee frequently. She looked in the mirror. Her eyes looked tired, her face worn. She noticed how the constant mask wearing had caused her to develop clusters of acne along the outline of where the mask pressed against her face. *Well, I guess this is just the warm up for those sleepless nights again.* Grace thought as she peered at the bags under her eyes. Her youth had definitely faded in the past few years. *Aging accelerated in the past few months,* she thought.

Grace splashed cool water against her face and patted it off with a cloth. She noticed her forehead was feeling warm to touch. With so many pregnancy symptoms, she had not noticed she was running a fever. 100.1 the thermometer read. Grace paused. She knew she wouldn't be able to go into work with a temperature. Grace's heart sank. She was concerned. Justin had bought some very expensive antigen tests a few months prior when they became available. She dug through the bathroom cabinets to find the box. Grace took the test. Two lines. COVID positive.

Grace stood there peering at the two lines. Rereading the instruction sheet to make sure she was interpreting the result accurately. Grace was stunned. All the images she carried out of the hospital with her came flooding back. It scared her to think of Coronavirus patients lying on their stomachs with air being pushed in and out of their bodies. She thought of her baby. *This can't be good.* Grace paced, starting to suddenly feel soreness in her throat and building congestion. She pulled out her phone and searched, "COVID during pregnancy". Her mind became blurry as nervous feelings rose within her while she read snippets of preliminary information that was emerging—*pregnancy complications, preterm, still birth, severe illness, hospitalisation* jumped off the page. Grace put her phone down. She thought to call Justin, as both he and Emma were likely exposed to her and could have caught it. Emma was still sleeping and Justin had left for surfing.

# Chapter 13
# Exposure

Justin had left a note at the bedside. "Gone surfing". Justin had rolled out of bed while it was still dark and overcast and strapped his board to the roof of the car. He drove across the brightly lit Bay Bridge towards the city, whose glassy building walls were beginning to reflect the creamy light of sunrise through patches of fog. He drove to Vivi's apartment and made his way up the narrow stairway with worn maroon carpet in the old Victorian. It was a beautiful building, with an ornate facade, painted off white with eggplant coloured trim and a black glossy door with original brass hardware. The vaulted ceilings and auburn hardwood floors with Celtic knot crown moulding, seeped with old world charm.

Vivi stood in her bathrobe at the door, pleased to see Justin. "Aren't you a sight for sore eyes," she said, welcoming the surprise visit.

"I brought bagels," he said, flashing a bag from Noah's Bagels. "With veggie and strawberry schmear."

"Mmm. Thanks, Just. I'll make some coffee." Justin kissed Vivi, pulling her at the small of her waist towards him with his free hand. It was like old times, when they had been travelling through Europe. He would often get up early and hit the pavement in search of fresh baked pastries and coffee and return with a paper bag full of goodies that they would devour while spending the morning in bed. They set up the bagel tray at the end of the bed in the same way today.

Justin's phone rang a couple times but he silenced it when he saw it was Grace, thinking it would be more believable that he wouldn't answer the phone if he was out surfing.

Justin loved these mornings with Vivi. He felt a freedom with her that he had longed for. Now, in the darkness of a time of stress and uncertainty, she in all her past familiarity, was his escape to a different time, a different story ending.

"Vivi. Do you ever wonder what life would be like if I had followed you that day we parted at the train station?"

Vivi gave a smile, "It would be just like this. Every day."

He smiled, feeling satisfied with the idea. "Who's to say it can't be just like this forever, Justin?" He realised she was circling back to the question she had posed weeks earlier about him needing to make a choice. "You know, Justin, life is about the choices we make. You can choose to be happy."

Justin looked at her with a certain sadness in his eyes. She could see he felt trapped. Trapped in the responsibilities of fatherhood, of work, and his marriage. "Life is too short to be unhappy," she added, kissing his lips and neck.

When the sun had broken through the overcast sky and the light was bright and unfiltered through the large glass bay windows, Justin told Vivi he needed to head back. He noticed three missed calls and a series of texts from Grace had come through, while Vivi was in the bathroom. The first text read. *I need to talk to you. I took a COVID test—It says I'm COVID positive.* Justin froze, rereading the text for some alternate meaning. He began to think about how she had tested negative. *There must be some mistake.* He didn't want to text her back and begin a conversation before he left.

As soon as Vivi returned to the room, Justin jumped up to start getting dressed. "Why don't you stay a bit longer? We could go for a walk at Land's End."

"You know I would, Vivi, it's just that—"

Vivi cut him off with a testy tone, "It's just what?"

Justin didn't want to tell her about this news he had received, as he hadn't quite processed it. At that moment, he thought about how he and Emma had been exposed to Grace the night before when she had stopped isolating and that now Vivi had been exposed to him. "It's just that Emma will be asking for me. It's Saturday and we usually head to the park to watch the sailboats by the marina."

Vivi gave a forced, faint smile. She knew she couldn't maintain his affections if trying to compete with his daughter. Grace maybe. But not Emma. "Okay, well you know I'll miss you," she said, walking to him as he bent down, tying his shoelaces, and kissing his head. "Let's do brunch on Monday, if you're free." Being scheduled struck a chord with Vivi. She had to swallow hard to suppress the urge to show signs of anger. She no longer wanted to be his mistress that he saw at intervals, scheduled and clandestine. She wanted to be with him whenever and out in the open. "Justin. I want you to know that I'm waiting for you. Okay?" she said through the doorway as they embraced and kissed goodbye.

Justin looked at Vivi, her soft curls outlining her face. She was so beautiful to him. At that moment, he wanted to stay in her apartment and never go back. "Hopefully, it won't be too long now," he said, feeling the adrenaline of the notion. Vivi smiled, pleased with his response and watched him as he walked down the long hallway, disappearing down the creaky stairway.

Justin sped across the Bay Bridge, and called Grace. She picked up right away. "Justin. Did you get my texts?"

"Hey babe. Yes, I got the texts. Are you okay?" In his voice, he heard his attempt to smooth over his underlying nerves.

"No Justin. I don't think I'm okay. I've been trying to get a hold of you all morning. You really have to be more responsible with checking your phone. It could be an emergency. It is an emergency."

Justin clenched his jaw, as he felt the weight of responsibility wrap its arms around him once again. *Vivi would never lecture me.* He told himself, thinking of his morning in bed, as Grace described what happened with waking up with a fever and using one of the home tests they had and then now having tested positive again using the remaining test in the box of two. Justin listened, careful to interject little. He could hear that Grace was distressed by the thought of being positive and as she spoke she drew him in with her concern that she had infected him and Emma.

"I just thought I was in the clear, you know? I need to go get another one of those formal PCR tests." Justin followed along. "And there's another thing. I was reading about Coronavirus and pregnancy and I saw it in the hospital. It can put pregnant women at increased risk for complications." He sensed the hesitancy in her voice.

"Like what?" He waited impatiently. "Like. Well I've read that there's potential for pregnant women to have premature babies and complications like severe illness."

Justin's interest was now peaking with concern for his unborn child too. "Grace, I just don't know what we are supposed to do now. I mean, I really just wish you could have been more careful." Grace began to cry on the other end. "Don't you think I regret that fact every minute of every day?" She was angered in her response through the tears. "What was I supposed to do? Quit my career? I'm an intensive care nurse and I made one miscalculation in all the months I've been working bedside. Now I'm paying for it. How helpful do you think you are right now telling me I should have been more careful?!'"

Justin realised he had crossed a line that had pushed Grace into anger. He retreated by maintaining silence on his true feelings about the matter after affirming her perspective. "Just come home already, okay?" She said with an impatience that jolted Justin to realise he had been gone for many hours. That she had noticed with evident strain from the more frequent departures he had made of late. He could hear her coughing and sounding out of breath, more than usual.

He drove home, playing the radio loudly, thinking about the complicated, intertwined feelings and attachments he held to either side of the bifurcated life he now led. He reflected on how he felt entirely more whole by having both relationships going, when things ran smoothly in both camps. But when imbalance struck, the splintering effect of his two intimate relationships left him with not enough internal resources to truly lean into any one situation. Rather, his inclination was to seek an escape from one to the other. As he drove, he thought of Vivi, standing at the door, waiting for him to return and his obligation not to. He thought about how Grace needed him. She was sick. *Am I sick? Is Emma sick? Will Vivi get sick too? What about the baby?*

Justin sat in limbo on the bridge, in a rigid state of consternation, counting the columns before he would get to the Treasure Island tunnel. There was traffic due to a big rig accident blocking two lanes up ahead before the tunnel opening. He tried to call Grace to let her know he would be late, as he slowed to a standstill and inched along the lower deck of the Bay Bridge. Stuck.

Grace wore a mask in the house, as she tried to evade Emma's approaches. She wiped everything she touched, noticing Emma's surprise and mild exasperation as Grace calmly dodged her advances and redirected her to play with a toy across the room. Grace thought to test Emma. If she was positive now, which she may likely be, then they could put all the isolating practices to rest. Grace looked over at the test kit. She thought of the trouble it would take to insert the swab into her toddler's nose, much less run circles around it forcefully ten times on each side. She wouldn't hold still and would likely be traumatised by the experience.

Grace decided to wait until Justin returned home to broach the subject of testing with Emma. Grace looked at the two tests with double lines, dissatisfied with the idea that she had let her worst fears come true. There was no one else she could blame. Grace stood by the windows overlooking the back garden. She closed her eyes. Feeling the mild sting of sleeplessness in the creases of her eyes. The house looked different than it always had. She felt unsettled by how she couldn't put her finger on what had changed about the way the house felt. Home was a refuge and had recently become a cage she was bound to.

Everything looked fragile at this moment, as though it might be lost at any moment if she did not grasp it, while the world turned and with it comfort began to slip away. Grace put on a television show for Emma who sat on the floor with a banana she had grabbed from the counter, half peeled and leaning on its side on the rug. Grace had opened all the windows in the house, and the Fall chill made the house feel crisp and hollowed out. Grace curled up behind Emma, under a throw blanket. She watched Emma's little body sitting cross-legged on the rug, shifting little and entranced by the character on the screen. *Motherhood is harrowing as it is.* She thought. *Why must it be even more complicated?*

She felt guilty for what catching COVID meant for her children, one inside her stomach shifting its weight around and the other before her, innocently sitting in her living room. Not knowing what was happening. What inner turmoil and completely distracted thoughts were running through her mother's mind. *This is not how this is meant to be.* An hour passed, and Justin's keys could be heard jingling at the door, as he jolted the lock that caught often. "Grace? Emma?" There was an urgency in his voice that had built as he had felt so delayed in returning home.

"We're out here," Grace called, listening for his footsteps on the hardwood towards the back of the house.

"How are you doing?" He asked. Looking her up and down expecting to render an assessment of her or some sort of prognosis for her recovery.

"I'm doing okay. I'm just a bit in shock. I can't believe this happened," Grace said, getting up. Justin looked on, without anything to say but nod. "Listen, I think I need to go and isolate myself for now. You should test and also test Emma. If you're positive too, then we can break isolation. But if not, then it's better we try to keep separate and you two keep testing, and staying isolated here at home."

Justin agreed, "Okay, yeah, I'll hang out with Emma here. Will you let us know if you need anything?" Grace nodded and turned her gaze to Emma. She thought not to disrupt her with a big goodbye, although her heart yearned to embrace her little one.

Grace called her doctor's office when she went upstairs. They were closed on the weekend. She left a voicemail to let him know that she had tested positive for COVID and requested a phone call consultation to discuss any precautions she may need to follow considering her pregnancy. The words that had jumped off the page describing all the untoward issues that could arise for women who contracted COVID while pregnant began to emerge in her mind. The worry troubled Grace. It was as though she could not turn off her fearful feelings, they just kept building and closing in on her sensibilities as she sat in her room, on the made bed, staring at the wall.

There was nothing her mind seemed to want to do but perseverate on the pregnancy risk information she had read about and the symptoms that she may or may not be experiencing. Grace decided to email her doctor too, in case he was checking emails over the weekend and felt compelled to reply. Isolation as someone awaiting testing results felt different from the isolation now taking place, as someone with COVID, who was infectious and may develop symptoms.

Grace decided to take a hot shower. The steam and hot water relaxed her shoulder muscles which she realised she had been holding tightly with a clenched jaw for days, if not weeks. The aches of her third trimester had been far worse this time round. She bent down and hung her arms freely, releasing the kink in her lower back that had been working hard to counter the extra weight of her belly. After her shower, Grace watched TV quietly. She listened for all the sounds of Emma and Justin's evening beyond her door. It was a reprieve, she thought admittedly. But the forced nature of living in isolation was something to resent.

As the afternoon faded into night, Grace read some of her latest book and stared at the wall, deeply distracted by the same thoughts that had been swirling around in her head, never abating, and never landing anywhere satisfactory. Her sore throat was becoming sharper and congestion pressed against the bridge of her nose and forehead. She felt a dull headache emerging. Justin spent the afternoon cleaning the kitchen, vacuuming, doing laundry. He found busying his hands helped to settle his nerves that had evidently splintered in various directions over the course of the past days. Now mostly, he was left with the questions of his own COVID status, Emma's safety, and felt grave concern for Grace and their baby upstairs. His mind was now set on his family's well-being causing the concerns he had held onto anywhere outside to appear superficial to him. Justin thought to give Emma a bath to relax her before he gave her a COVID test. There were two tests left in the cabinet. Emma splashed gleefully in the tub, blowing down pillars of bubbles that had accumulated around her. Justin liked to watch Emma play and splash, and grab at bubbles. He looked forward to the day she might hit the surf with him.

After Emma got into her pyjamas, Justin began to tell her about the quick nose test he needed to give her so they could see if she needed to go to the doctor. Emma could sense the nervousness in his explanations as he fumbled to open the test packaging. "No. I don't want it, Daddy," she said decisively, backing away down the hall.

Justin picked her up, as she protested, now very upset. "Listen Emma. We have to tell the doctor if we're sick. The doctor said we have to do this test in our noses so we can know if we are sick. Look see, I'm going to do it too." Justin took the first swab out and through perseverance of resolve to tolerate the swab, he smiled and acted jolly as he swiped the insides of his sensitive nose. He put the swab tip into the solution and made play out of 'stirring' the soup and squeezing drops onto the test window.

Emma liked all the little pieces of the kit that required delicate handling, stirring and squeezing. "Okay Emma, your turn now," he said after setting his test off to the side for a 15-minute timer.

Emma backed away. "No! I don't want it. I'm scared!" She whimpered as he diligently set up the test elements on the counter.

"Listen Emma. It's really important you help Daddy give you this test. It's going to feel tickly and you may want to sneeze, but you need to stay as still as you can so I can stir it in your nose. Okay?"

Emma acquiesced, leaning towards him. He held her clammy hands together with one hand and with the other tried as swiftly as possible to gather the sample. She whimpered and tears ran down her cheeks, as he swabbed both sides 10 times each, as the instructions read. It made him uneasy to inflict pain on Emma, careful not to push the cue tip too high in her nostrils as she moved around a little. "Good job, Emma!" He exclaimed, surprised that she had tolerated the test and that he had been able to complete the task he had anticipated with much apprehension.

He compressed the vial holding the solution stirring in the swab before tipping it upside down to drop three drops into the test window. His test window showed only one line. COVID negative. Emma's was still in process.

"Where's Mummy?"

Justin lied, "Mummy went on a trip." He wanted to avoid the complication of Emma pining at the door for her mother. He successfully ushered her straight to bed without further protest, as he figured he would read her a quick book and return to see her test result in 15 minutes. Justin made noncommittal remarks that placated Emma as she climbed into her bed and listened to him read to her. She fought her heavy eyelids for a time before drifting off to sleep well before the bedtime story was finished.

Justin turned off the lamp and looked over her in the natural evening light. Looking at the outline of her small features and wispy hair against the pillow, he felt that love that draws a father to his children without hesitation. In the clarity of that moment, he was grateful for his little family and wished more than anything that things could be different, simple, as they had been before. Emma's test was also COVID negative. Justin threw the tests into the wastebasket, relieved a little that they both had come up negative. He knew he would need to have them tested in the next few days, just to be sure, as the timeline had been anything but clear with Grace. But for now, for tonight, they were COVID negative.

He thought about what it would be for one of them to have COVID. Not much could change in that she, being so young, would still need close handling and care. It would be inevitable if one of them got COVID that the other would too. The night was quiet, peaceful even. Justin went downstairs and loaded the dishes in the dishwasher and took a shower in the guest bedroom before heading back to Emma's room.

His chat window on the computer was active with messages from Vivi, and follow-up texts. He hadn't messaged her back in a number of hours which was not typical for him, but today he didn't feel like he could spread his attention beyond the immediate needs of his family. He decided not to respond. He wasn't ready to communicate all that was transpiring. He decided he'd stay close to Emma in the night, rather than sleep on the couch downstairs. It felt necessary to be close together in this time of uncertainty. Justin cuddled up to Emma in her small bed. He pressed his face against the back of her head, smelling the sweet smell of apple shampoo mixed with remnants of how she smelled as a baby There, he drifted off to sleep.

Grace lay asleep periodically, and often tossing and turning with aches that now extended beneath her ribs, around her back and shoulders. She had begun to sweat profusely, such that she removed all the covers as the sheets had become wet from under her back. The cold night felt like welcome cooling until suddenly she would feel chills and sought to pull the covers back over herself again. She coughed a deep and dry cough intermittently, blowing her nose also. The symptoms had crept up and now felt like they were solidifying in her body. She lay there with the notion that there was nothing to do but endure the course this virus would take within her body. She didn't want to take any medications to ease the fever or pain as she was pregnant. She had put a pulse oximeter by the bed in case her breathing would change or she had concerns about her oxygen. Laying there in the bed, she realised how good her patients had it, being attended to by nurses. There she lay, reliant on being a nurse for herself. She felt miserable. The baby continued to move and kick at its typical rate and Grace focused on that intently between drifting off into light bouts of sleep.

Grace felt the sweat dripping down her back and soaking into her sheets. She had never sweated like this before. Her headache and her ribs ached when she coughed. Suddenly she noticed that she couldn't quite take a deep enough breath, as though she could not inhale enough oxygen, she started to feel laboured in her breathing, looking down at the rise of her chest working hard. She fumbled over the nightstand to turn on the lamp and grab the oximeter, she knocked it off the nightstand accidentally. It fell to the floor, under the bed. She felt too large and too out of breath to try to get it on her own.

In between laboured breaths, she did the only thing she could think to do— she called out in a weak voice, "Justin. Justin. I need your help."

She heard him waken to her calling. "Grace?" He had jumped out of a deep sleep.

"I-I can't breathe." The onset of laboured breaths had scared Grace and she knew what was happening wasn't good. This was the beginning of the pregnancy complications she had read about. When Justin entered the room, Grace felt a sense of relief to see him. He stood by the door, wearing a mask, peering timidly with one foot still in the hallway.

"Can you check my oxygen?" Grace said between breaths.

Justin's eyes were adjusting, and as he took in his wife, lying in bed, he stared at Grace with a shocked expression. "Your lips are blue."

"Oh no. Can you get the pulse oximeter from under the bed, it fell down." Justin retrieved the pulse oximeter on the floor partially under the bed, as he bent down to look for it, the shock and the adrenaline of the situation was beginning to take hold. *Grace, my baby.* He quickly fixed the device to her right pointer finger and pressed the button to initiate the read. 87% It read in bright white numbers. She knew from years as a nurse that this was not good. She was usually 100% and when patients went lower than 92% it was not a good sign.

She retook her saturation. 87%. *I have to get to the hospital.* Grace calmly asked Justin to call 911, trying not to alarm him. Justin took direction closely and ran to the other room to get his phone. He dialled. He was beginning to panic as he spoke to the steady voice on the other side of the line asking him basic questions, as he glanced back at Grace who was now looking dazed. The focus in her eyes had become distant.

"Please come as quickly as you can. She is pregnant. She has COVID. We need emergency assistance. Please." He hung up, once the operator gathered sufficient information to dispatch an emergency medical response team. Justin stood by, not knowing what to do next but to try to will her into feeling better. *Please don't do this Grace.* He kept thinking. The flashing red lights had approached silently through the sleeping neighbourhood and reflected off the ceiling. A bang at the door came shortly after and Justin rushed down the stairway to answer. A team of three masked paramedics stood on the stoop.

"Hi, please come in, she's up the stairs in the first room on the left." He could tell the paramedics were a little hesitant, knowing that their patient and likely everyone in the house was COVID positive. They stepped around Justin and went upstairs. He could hear them addressing Grace, in calm voices, stating who they were, and asking her questions. He walked back and forth at the bottom of the stairs, not knowing what to do, until the young woman came out of the room.

"Okay sir. She's having some significant respiratory distress and her mental status appears altered. We are going to give her some oxygen and need to transport her to the nearest hospital." *Hospital? This is serious.* With a lack of medical training, he knew she didn't look well, but he knew now that the need for a hospital spelled out that she really wasn't okay. They agreed to take her to Grace's hospital, figuring it would be a good place to go where people knew her and would give her the best care possible. They loaded Grace into a special chair and edged their way down the stairway, step by step careful not to drop her.

Justin looked with distress as his wife and his baby were carried out the door He saw them load her onto a stretcher and into the ambulance. Under the fluorescent cabin lighting, they applied a face mask. Her breaths were short and she did not sound like she could keep focus on anything they were asking them A paramedic ran back to him, standing in the lean of the doorway feeling hi heart in his throat. "You won't be allowed to come into the hospital. There is a no visitor policy due to COVID. I suggest you wait for the phone call. Please fill out this card with your contact information and I'll be sure to deliver it to the nurse."

Justin's hand was shaking as he tried to fill out the card as completely as possible. "Okay sir. Well you have a good night. The hospital staff will be in touch."

Justin stood there, feeling shocked. He noticed he was wringing his hands as he watched them close the ambulance doors and drive away. They turned on their sirens as they reached the main street at the corner. The turning tail lights appeared as a stream of light through his eyes, filling with tears. She was gone.

# Chapter 14
# Doorway

Justin stood at the doorway looking down the street after the taillights. He was paralysed with fear now. Feeling the urge to run after the ambulance, never to leave her side as she was whisked away, at the same time, the urge to succumb to his weak knees, and crumble to the base of the doorway. He did neither ultimately, stepping out onto his driveway, neither able to go or stay. This was a nightmare come true.

Grace and the baby, now with COVID-19, headed into the hospital like all the other people whisked away into isolation, away from their families left empty handed and fearful, to fight this disease. The cold night was all that soothed him. *How can this be really happening?* He asked himself. Balance was predicated on the fact that Grace was always okay. This certainty he had held allowed him to feel free and reckless because he would always have somewhere to return to. She was their family's foundation, the one to stay the course. And now, this comfort and mainstay was in jeopardy. As Justin's mind raced in the uneasy downward spiralling that revolved around how displaced he felt in this situation, a gut-wrenching pain of uncertainty and fear took hold. The vulnerability shocked him.

His pocket buzzed as a message from Vivi came through. "Justin. Are you okay? Why aren't you returning my texts?"

He scrolled through seeing that she had texted him throughout the day with no reply. He wrote back, "Sorry. I'm just dealing with a lot right now." He again wasn't ready to disclose exactly what was going on. "I can't explain much right now, but you probably want to take a COVID test and isolate." He felt like he was doing a service to let her know at least this much. "What?" She replied immediately. He could sense her urgency in knowing more. Five unanswered calls came subsequently. He couldn't bring himself to answer and muted the calls, putting his phone back in his pocket. The shiny newness of their affair appeared tarnished and dull in the face of this real crisis.

He stood a little longer, looking out into the night. The San Francisco Bay fog had now rolled in low, filling his street and passing through with an eerie distortion of the glowing lights in the surrounding houses. He was rendered faint by the angst he felt. "Mummy!" Emma's cry pierced through the night. He heard her crying out for Grace in her room, as she often did when she woke up abruptly in the night. "Mummy!" She had begun to cry loudly, having not heard a soothing voice call back to her in the darkness.

Justin's heart sank, as he thought about having to go back inside to help Emma. Grace had always been the one to console her at night. He walked back inside. As he climbed the stairs, he thought about how he would await that call from the hospital to give him an update. He would then find out what the visiting policy was. He thought of Lottie. *She needs to know what's happening.* It was early morning now. She would likely be sleeping. He paused on a middle step and decided to call her anyway. "Hey Lottie, it's Justin."

"Hi…Justin, is everything okay?" He could hear her refocusing her mind having been drawn out of sleep.

"I wanted to let you know that Grace was taken to the hospital under an hour ago by ambulance. She was having trouble breathing. I'm not sure if she told you but she ended up getting COVID-19 from a patient."

"Oh Justin. I don't understand. I thought she was going to be okay. Do you need me to come over there? Are you going to the hospital?"

Justin was grateful for Lottie's offer. He knew that if he got that call and was allowed to go into the hospital, he would want to immediately. "If it's not too much trouble, Lottie, you can totally not come and we will be fine. But if they call me to be with her, I'll need somewhere for Emma to go. I think Emma would be much happier with you here, and not just me," he said with a half-hearted laugh, knowing that Emma's loud screaming could be heard through the phone.

"I'll pack a bag and be over in about an hour." He could hear the worry in her voice.

"Thanks Lottie." They hung up. Emma was still crying as he entered the room, turning on a hall light that backlit his tall frame. Emma was sitting up in bed, rubbing the tears out of her eyes and now crying so hard that her breathing was upset.

"Daddy!" She cried louder as he came to her doorway. "I want Mummy!" He knew that he was always her second choice. The one who would hold her but be given up at a moment's notice if Grace entered the room. He picked her up out of bed and draped her clinging little body over his shoulder. Her crying slowed as she became soothed by the sway of his walking around the house. Her closeness was a comfort in more ways than it had ever been. He remembered how she had been as an infant. Never falling asleep laying down. She always needed to be upright and carried. "Where's Mummy?"

Emma knew something was different. Justin had rarely been the one to come to her aid in the night. "She-she's a bit sick, Em."

Emma whispered, "Did she go to the horstable?"

*There was no sense in sugarcoating it,* he thought. "Yes, she went to the hospital."

"When is she coming back?" Emma's fearful tone struck Justin.

"Well, hopefully soon, sweetheart." His response was half hearted and shrouded in uncertainty.

"Will she be okay? Will she come back?" Emma began to whimper.

"Yes, Em. Everything will be okay." *Hope must always be sugar-coated.* Emma relaxed into this thought, leaning her head against his neck.

"I feel sleepy, Daddy. Can you sleep in my bed?" Justin lay next to her toddler bed, wrapped in her fuzzy unicorn blanket with a couch pillow under his head, arm raised to hold her hand, as she fell asleep. Justin was awoken by a gentle knock at the door. He had passed out into a murky dream state, exhausted from the shock of the situation.

It was Lottie. She looked so similar to Grace. "Hi Lottie. Are you okay to sleep on the sofa down here?" He ushered her down the hall to the family room. Kicking away toys to make a clear path.

"Did the hospital call?" Lottie inquired.

"Not yet. It's been nearly 3 hours," he replied.

"Maybe we should call them. Did she go to her hospital?"

"Yes, that's where I told them to take her."

"Okay, let me look up the main number." Lottie brought with her more energy to think through the situation. Justin felt numb with fear and fatigue. This idea had not crossed his mind. She dialled the number on her cell and passed him the phone. The operator answered with a sunny and clear voice, fitting of mid-afternoon, not 2AM.

"Hi, I am calling for my wife. She was sent to your hospital by ambulance about three hours ago," Justin said, pressing his head against the phone, not wanting to miss a single message about Grace that he might receive.

"What is your wife's name?"

"Grace N. Anderson."

"Please hold." The pause was lengthy, smooth jazz played and Justin shifted in his seat on the coach as he glanced impatiently over at Lottie looking on intently, the stress reading over his face. The voice returned. "Sir, are you there?"

"Yes."

"Okay, your wife has been admitted to the intensive care unit. Would you like for me to transfer your call to the unit?" The words 'intensive care unit' knocked the air out of Justin for a few seconds. He felt queasy, knowing that it meant her medical condition had become critical. "Sir. Are you there?"

"Yes. Yes. I'm sorry. Yes. I will hold for a transfer."

"Okay thank you, Sir. Transferring you now. Have a good evening." The pleasantries of the operator's script butted up against the crisis of the moment like nails scraping a chalkboard. *Under what circumstances would anyone calling here be having a good evening?* He thought as he listened to the smooth jazz resume. Grace felt beyond his reach, behind phone operators, hallways, double doors, nurses, doctors and glass windows, as he imagined it, and it was disconcerting. He pictured her, pregnant, laying there in the ICU with blue lips and struggling to breathe. He had only been in one once, but felt like he knew the austerity of the setting from how Grace had described.

"ICU, this is Cassey." The nurse sounded bright and wide awake for a near 3 AM phone call.

"Hi, my name is Justin Anderson. I understand my wife is in your ICU. Her name is Grace Anderson."

He could hear a sadness creep into her voice. "Yes, yes, I'm her nurse this evening."

"Okay. Would you be able to give me an update on how she is doing?"

"She has not given permission yet to speak to any family members and I haven't had time to look at her chart to see who we can provide updates to. Please hold on." Justin sat in the pause, hopeful. "Okay Justin," she said, "we can speak to you but I have to go, she is starting to have an emergency and we need to give her a breathing tube right now. Thank you, I will let you know how she progresses."

He heard the angst in her voice that had shifted from only moments earlier. "Ok thank you for what you are doing for her." The phone went dead as he spoke. Justin sat in silence, exhaling his fear, dropping the phone and placing his head into his hands.

Lottie saw his distress and sat by, placing her arm on his shoulder to console him. "What did they say?" She said, eventually.

"They said she is having an emergency and they need to give her a breathing tube. Which means they are going to sedate and intubate her like all the other COVID-19 patients Grace has told me about."

"Like on the news?" Lottie asked, shocked.

"Yeah, like that."

"What about the baby?" Lottie asked, now tearful.

"I didn't ask. She was so rushed and I didn't think." Justin hated that he had forgotten to ask. The rush of the moments to speak passed him like a gust of wind scattering his train of thought like dry leaves. Everything now had fallen to the ground, in disarray. They sat quietly in despair, unable to conjure anything more to say outwardly, but inwardly imagined what was happening over and over and whispered hopefully into the darkness as they leaned into sleep.

The inky sky began to lighten as the morning came, with Justin and Lottie having fallen asleep on either ends of the couch, exhausted and unable to move out of their grief in receiving the news. Emma woke up first and yelled out, "Mummy!" from upstairs.

It was only a quarter past six and Justin and Lottie had finally begun to sleep soundly. Lottie stirred first at the sound and decided to leave Justin, still sleeping. She headed up the stairway, adjusting to the reality of what was happening. She glanced over to the doorway of Justin and Grace's bedroom. *She's not here. This is really happening.* It hadn't been a bad dream. Lottie's heart sank knowing the bedroom was empty, and Grace now filled an ICU bed. "Mummy?" Emma inquired hearing Lottie's footsteps creak on the stairway.

"Hi Emma. It's Auntie Lottie."

"Where's my mummy?" Emma was not fully sold on the exchange "Mummy had to go to the hospital."

"Is she coming back for breakfast?" Emma asked, hopeful that the pull of routine would right the wonky picture.

Lottie opened her arms to Emma, who climbed onto her lap for a hug. She was warm, her now long limbs wrapped around Lottie. "Mummy is going to need to stay in the hospital for now sweetheart." She could feel Emma's back tense.

"But I want her now." Tears began to fill Emma's eyes. "I want Mummy to make pancakes. You can stay for breakfast." The light in Emma's eyes as she wished and hoped for this scenario made Lottie see an additional layer of complication in the situation—Grace was Emma's world, and it was being turned on its axis without any explanation that could satisfy Emma's reasoning.

She would no doubt continue to ask for her mother and her absence would cause distress. Lottie offered to make pancakes for Emma. Heading downstairs, they talked about putting chocolate chips in the batter and slicing bananas on top. Justin slept soundly on the couch as Lottie mixed the pancake batter with Emma sitting on the edge of the counter overseeing the process. Justin's phone rang. It was a blocked number. Lottie woke him. "Your phone is ringing. Looks like the hospital maybe," she said, passing him his cell phone.

Justin stood up quickly and stood at the far end of the living room with the phone pressed against his head. He paced a little, uneasily. Lottie looked on hoping to hear his remarks and piece together what was happening, while Emma dug her fingers into the remaining pancake batter in the bowl. "Yes, I agree. Thank you for the update, doctor," was all he said. He hung up the phone. The air had been sucked out of the room. The colour in his face was now a little paler than before.

"What did they say?" Lottie grew impatient.

"He said she was struggling to breathe a great deal soon after she arrived at the hospital and had to be intubated and sedated. They took an x-ray that showed she has COVID pneumonia in both lungs." Lottie's eyes were trained on his face, unable to blink as she took in the news. "And they don't think her body will be able to heal and grow the baby at the same time." Justin's voice cracked as he became tearful and covered his eyes with his wrist.

"So, what's going to happen?" Lottie was distressed but tried to remain calm in the delivery of her question for Emma's sake. Emma sat preoccupied with the batter in the bowl, now smearing it on the counter, encrusting her hair and face. Neither Justin or Lottie noticed.

"They are going to deliver the baby by C-Section today, a month early."

Lottie stood, speechless. She knew that the situation was serious, and yet not having any ability to have seen Grace in this state, made it hard to picture what was going on. She desperately wanted to have some definitive information about what the outcome would be for her sister and her niece or nephew, yet was forced to remain in limbo within the raw reality that nothing is certain. "I need to go wash up." Justin said, motioning down the hallway. He disappeared down the hall with the sensation of moving through water as he went. Grief and anxious feelings impeded him. He looked in the vanity mirror over the guest room sink, noticing the lines that dug deep in the furrow of his eyebrows from angst and the lines around his mouth etched out from years of laughter and smiles.

*Life is ALL things isn't it?* He thought, remarking at the duality of happiness and sadness evidenced on his face. He washed his face and wiped away his tears. *Why does this have to be so complicated?* He was tired from the long night and the thoughts of what was around the corner for Grace and the baby. This was not how he imagined things would be as they welcomed a new baby. He cringed at the impact of the events that had taken place over the past days. Replaying what Grace had told him about the patient, her negative test, her positive test and now this. Justin pulled out a new COVID-19 test box. He decided to test himself and Emma. Both results were negative. He stood there looking at the result windows, with single lines, wishing Grace could be home with them.

He pictured her outside in the garden picking lemons and folding laundry while watching TV. It was the day to day things. It was the simple things of life that he realised had taken for granted in that moment where he would give anything to have things as they were. Vivi texted again. She had refrained from further calls and now sent one liner texts. "You can't just do this, Justin."

Justin knew he owed Vivi an explanation. "Lottie, do you mind if I step out to go to the store?"

Lottie looked up while still in the kitchen cleaning up with Emma. "Sure! I think you need some milk."

Justin nodded and grabbed his jacket as he went. The morning was chilly. Daylight had transformed last night's street, bringing normalcy to their block of houses that looked as they always did, colourful with fences brimming over with flowers, branches and leaves.

Justin decided to walk to Andronico's a number of blocks away. He needed time to clear his head and a chance to call Vivi. He rang, walking fast to offset his anxious feelings. *She's going to be so upset.* He thought as he listened to the dial tone. She didn't pick up immediately, but when she did her voice sounded hollow and cold. "Justin. Nice of you to finally call me back." Justin fumbled through his explanation of what was happening to Grace and the events of the night before. He told her he was still testing negative and asked if she had had a chance to test. Vivi seemed disinterested in his story, and made little comment. Her empathy was blocked by her dissatisfaction with what she had learned was the reality of the situation. She was not his priority.

"Listen Justin, in the hours you blocked my calls, my texts and my emails, I came to realise something I should have done earlier. You just aren't invested in this thing with me in the way I am with you." Justin listened quietly. She was right. "What we had when we were kids was real. Now, it is as though we have been playing at a re-creation of that despite the reality that you are married, you have a kid, and we both know that once again, we won't end up on the same train together."

She seemed certain in her logic and Justin, although pained at the thought of losing out, could not disagree other than to say, "Vivi. I-I just really am so sorry. What we had was so strong and then unfinished in the way we left it when we were young. You came back into my life and made me feel again like anything was possible. I wanted so badly to believe in it, in us." He paused. He heard her quiet listening. "But, I know I am lying to myself if I believe I can keep you happy and with one foot in our relationship, and one foot in my marriage. I know ultimately, it's just not fair to you and it's not fair to Grace and Emma."

He began to choke up. "I'm an idiot, Vivi. I don't know why I was so foolish to think that I could have both." His honesty flowed from his lips without hesitation, although his candour shocked him a little.

Vivi's voice was warmer in her reply, as she sensed his remorse and confusion, and hearing his perspective gave her clarity. She spoke slowly and directly, "Well Justin, I think us calling it what it is now and not wasting too much more of each other's time is a good thing. Your family clearly needs you now. I can see that what I have to offer just doesn't compare…I think it's time we end this."

Justin's first inclination was to beg her not to leave him and that he would somehow work out a way for them to be together. But as he thought it through, silently soaking in what she had said, he realised this would be an empty promise, also one motivated by his fear of loss more than his real intent to make the changes that would be needed to stay with her. "I want you to know that I was all in this time around. You will always be the great love of my life, Justin. *The one that got away*, as they say. We tried to rewrite it and it was just not the right time, once again." Her melancholic words hung in the balance, as he felt her slipping away. Her words were fragile as snowflakes that would dissolve if he reached out to grab them.

"Vivi. I-I'm…"

Vivi continued, "I want you to know that I will always love you."

Through tears, all Justin could muster through the deep sadness he was feeling, compounded by the consuming brokenness of his current situation coming to bear. "I'm so sorry, Vivi." Tears continued to roll down his cheeks as he held onto the phone call, not wanting to end the phone call. It would mean letting her go. He wasn't ready. She had been a source of comfort and escape from his life. It was her that he wanted to hold on to as much as it was the idea of having her as an option. He knew the finality of the exchange they were having and hated the feeling tearing at his core. They could never remain just friends. He knew this.

"Goodbye Justin." Vivi's voice was composed. The phone went dead. He looked at the screen. The call had ended. She was gone.

Justin felt like he had been hit by a truck. He staggered over to a nearby bench, her goodbye had knocked all the air out of him. He felt light headed and queasy, now, as he crumbled downwards, weak and holding onto the bench, trying to breathe deeply. This abrupt loss mixed with the trauma of what was happening with Grace was almost too much to bear. He sat, dazed with remorse and futility, stuck to a bench and oblivious to anyone who may pass by.

# Chapter 15
# Little Time

"This is Elle, Justin." Justin sat registering the voice, as he had fumbled to answer the phone after many minutes sitting immobilised on the bench. "I'm assigned to care for Grace today. When they brought her in, apparently, she requested that I be her nurse. I wanted to make sure you are also okay with that." "Yes, I'm okay with that. I know you will take good care of her," said Justin, fighting back tears. "I know you are probably sick with worry. I'm calling because I thought you might appreciate a call from someone you know here. The doctor will call you for an update on her medical status. But I thought you should know that she was just sent to the operating room for a C-section. The baby was showing signs of distress on the monitor, and what they thought could wait a little time, needed to be done right away."

Justin took in the news. Evaluating its weight in the spectrum of bad vs very bad. He mustered a few words. "Thank you for letting me know, Elle. Are you able to go with her?"

"No. It's not indicated that I attend. She's fully sedated still and they have a full team in there to attend to her."

"Okay…will you tell her that I love her?"

"I will tell her," Elle replied solemnly.

He hung up. New thoughts about the baby and Grace and the C-section began to replace his thoughts of Vivi. The uncertainty was heavy and outweighed the flimsy and lustful feelings he typically filled his mind with in thinking about Vivi. He had lost track of time. He needed to head back and never made it to the store.

Justin came inside, after deliberating at length on their home's stoop as to whether he should try to get to the store or go back in. He felt nervous to tell Lottie the news he had just received from Elle. Lottie stood up expectantly, watching Emma run to Justin and wrap her arms around his legs. "Where's Mummy?"

"I have to talk to Auntie Lottie right now, sweetheart," Justin said with a grave look on his face. "Go play with your toys, okay?" Emma listened and ran back to her tent to assemble her stuffed animals inside. "So, it seems that they need to deliver the baby." Lottie's face drew still with seriousness, intent on hearing more although fearful about what she would learn. "Elle, her nurse friend, called to tell me that they are concerned that Grace can't do both—grow a baby and fight COVID," he added.

"Did she wake up? How is she going to deliver the baby while she's so sick?"

Justin realised he didn't mention the C-section. "No, she's still sedated. They are going to deliver the baby while she's under. She won't know it's happening while they give her a C-section."

Lottie's eyes widened, reddened, as her eyes became glassy. "Is it safe?"

Justin didn't know much more than what he had been told. "I'm assuming it's safer than leaving the baby inside her," he said with a resigned tone. They stood, contemplating the information.

"So, then if the baby is delivered, as her father I'd think you will be able to get into the hospital to see your kid and maybe even go see Grace right?"

Justin hadn't considered anything past the delivery. Although as Lottie spoke, he came to realise there would be another family member of concern in the hospital, their baby, likely in the neonatal intensive care unit after being delivered early. "I'll have to ask the doctor when they call."

Lottie scrolled through her phone contacts. Thumbing back and forth over her father's name. He was the only family she could think of who may want to know what was going with Grace. Lottie thought about the last day she had seen her dad, when they had spoken out in the street. They had gone to gather things from their rooms in Grandma and Grandpa's house, when Grandma died and Grandpa had agreed to go live in an assisted living facility. She had placed a cardboard box between them at her feet. It was open. Filled with a few stuffed toys, some Saddle Club books and other miscellaneous items.

Packing up her childhood from her old room had brought up a number of memories about her mother. About the days, weeks, months and years that she could remember leading up to her mother's death. Her father had known all of what had happened, yet chose to say nothing more of the matter, of her. Lottie held this fact between them, wishing he would take hold of it. Say something admit his feelings about what had happened. Was he sad? Was he relieved? Nothing had ever been the same for her and Grace afterwards. Yet, it was as though he had moved on past the event of their mother's death without breaking stride, and never looking back.

They had stood there in the stillness of the late afternoon, as bees hummed, dipping and darting amidst the late spring bloom that surrounded the house. The sun was still bright in the sky, and caused Lottie to squint as she looked up into her father's face. He shifted his weight, fumbling to offer to help her carry the last box to her car. "No Dad. I've got it." She had wanted him to say more, to be more, as she sensed the finality of this moment.

Closing the chapter of her grandparents' home, to her, meant his link to them would be severed. She never sensed that she or Grace possessed enough worth to him on their own for him to want to make an effort to be present in their lives, without his parents' influence. She was right. Even as they parted ways and he smiled at her from the open door of his truck, she knew they no longer held onto a common thread.

It had been five years since that day now, as Lottie stared at her phone. Contemplating the ramification of drawing her father back into their story. Especially now. She feared rejection the most. That he may hear the news and expend no remorse or kind words. Grant her only the gaping silence that disoriented her always. She wished to know what he thought more often than she wanted to admit. And so, she pressed the dial button. Listening to the ringtone, with its steady march forward, she contemplated hanging up swiftly. She'd say it was a misdial. "Hello?" His voice came through on the other end, quicker than she could hang up. It sounded quieter, tired.

"Ah. Yes, Dad? It's Lottie."

The pause that drew a chasm between her and he once more sustained only a few seconds before he responded, "Lottie. My, I didn't expect to hear from you."

Lottie knew this was true, as she did not expect to be calling. There wasn't much space left for niceties between them. Their edges had been engraved and hollowed out by painful memories and no longer articulated in the least of ways. 'Dad, Grace is very sick. She has the Coronavirus. Justin had to send her in an ambulance to the hospital last night." His silence on the other end made continuing to speak harder. Lottie couldn't tell whether he cared or was just holding back from hanging up. She quickened her pace to get all the main details out. She would be able to say she had at least let him know. "Anyway, she is pregnant. I'm not sure if you knew that. She's had what they call Severe Acute Respiratory Syndrome because of the COVID-19 disease. Apparently, it's an issue happening with women who get COVID during late term pregnancies. They needed to deliver her baby today. We are waiting to hear how the emergency C-section went. She's expected to stay intubated."

In the pause after she spoke, she could hear her words echoing into a cavernous space. She waited, not having any more facts to share and not at ease enough to insert her own vulnerabilities into the conversation. "Well," he finally offered, "I appreciate the call." He hung up abruptly.

Lottie held the phone, on pause. The doubt in her that had receded when she dialled his number somewhat impulsively, began to emerge again. *Why should I expect anything different from him?* He had stolen away with the message, giving no indication of how it affected him. *He had always been untouchable,* in that way, she thought. Her father was not one to be close or caring enough to become affected by others. His hardened veneer had protected him from being present in his relationships and moreover afflicted by loss.

Lottie felt empty. She wished she could call Grace and tell her how he had made her feel. She was the only one who could understand. Yet, she felt miles away, submerged, beyond reach. She desperately wanted her to come back. The constant presence and what she had thought to be an indelible imprint on her life was now fading. The angst of uncertainty washed over Lottie. It was disorienting and cold. Her older sister, the one who held her trembling body to her on the pantry floor, cooked her dinners and packed her lunches, made sure she had fitting clothes, and always looked out for her, was now incapacitated and far away. Her absence was like a large hole in front of Lottie with no assurances of how it would ever be filled. *What was that prayer Mumma would have us say?* Lottie couldn't remember the words. She thought it odd that the words she had recited nightly had vanished from her memory. Justin saw Lottie, standing with a perplexed and distant look on her face. "Are you alright, Lottie?"

"Yeah, I think I just need to go for a walk and clear my head." She was alarmed by how vulnerable she felt at that moment. Lottie strode out of the front door, grabbing her jacket and squeezing the leather strap of her purse hard to displace her anxious feelings. The overcast sky gave way to the bright sun, a luminous white orb with pale halo rings burned through the veil of drifting fog.

Lottie walked a little down the street. The air was cool and fresh. Her legs felt weak as she went. The gut-wrenching sensation of grief filled her stomach all the way up to her throat. She wouldn't be able to speak if she had to. This had all been so sudden. Nothing looked the same since she received that phone call in the middle of the night. The impermanence of everything stood out to her. *Unpredictability is the only thing we can predict.* She felt like she was floating in the ocean, at the mercy of waves and whatever would happen next.

She thought about Justin. He was dealing with his grief. It was different, he was hurting like someone who's compass was malfunctioning.

He and she were journeying through this in parallel, both too full of grief with the situation to be present as a resource to one another. Neither with enough to give away.

She, if anything, would need to be the one he relied on, to hang in there for Emma, as Grace would. This responsibility unnerved her. She walked, not knowing where her feet would take her and not wanting to go back to the house yet. The smell of bread baking wafted from the house she passed. She stopped, to breathe it in. It smelled sweet and starchy. Comforting like when their mother had baked with the kitchen window open while they played in the front yard. She could tell that her senses had been heightened. She could feel the adrenaline coursing through her. She could not stay still, she couldn't press fast forward, and she could not press rewind. All she could do was walk through the angst and the uncertainty, trying to keep her bearings. The cool air was soothing on her face.

Lottie returned home eventually. Emma greeted her with open arms, excited to see her return. Emma's embrace felt like the only thing holding Lottie together at that moment. She breathed her in, tears welling in her eyes. "Hi sweetheart," she said, "I needed that hug."

"You can have more later," Emma said with sincerity as she darted away to the play area.

Justin was in the kitchen cleaning dishes when Lottie came in. He greeted her with a sad smile. As he waited for word on Grace and the baby, he moved moment to moment feeling the gut-wrenching hurl of every twist and turn of the worst-case scenario he had never imagined. The phone rang. It pierced the thick air that had been hanging coarsely, coloured by the dread he felt towards hearing more bad news. His senses had been trained on the whereabouts of his phone at all times as he had gone through the motions of the day. The calls were the only link he had to what was going on. He reached quickly for the phone and headed out to the back patio. "Hi, this is Dr Bowers. I am taking care of your wife, Grace Anderson."

He stated his intro with a raised querying intonation, to solicit confirmation of Justin's relation to Grace. "Yes, thank you for calling me, doctor."

"I'm calling to let you know that we had to perform an emergency caesarean about an hour ago and were able to deliver your baby girl safely. Your wife is okay, but she remains intubated in the surgical intensive care unit. The baby has been brought to the neonatal intensive care unit for observation and some oxygen support."

*A girl.* Justin smiled thinking of another little girl, as he listened to the doctor speak about Grace's condition and the need to continue to have her breathe with the assistance of a ventilator, and see if the delivery of the baby will help her recover. "The nursing staff will be caring primarily for the baby. But we do have a limited policy for fathers to come in to see the baby for short periods of time. Is that something that will interest you?"

Justin appreciated the invitation. "Yes, I'd very much like to come and meet her." He glanced over at Lottie through the glass sliding door with a brief smile.

"Okay, visiting is for one hour, and between 9 AM and 4 PM daily. They will do temperature checks at the door. Please only come if you are well."

It was around 12 PM, and Justin, getting off the phone, was eager to head to the hospital. He explained the situation and Lottie agreed to watch Emma so he could go right away. "Thanks Lottie," he said at the door, after kissing Emma's forehead. Emma hung her legs on either side of Lottie, sitting comfortably in her arms while mildly protesting his departure. "I'll be back before dinner, Emma, and I'll bring home some orange chicken okay?" Emma loved orange chicken and chow mein dinners and perked up at the thought.

As the door closed behind him, Justin felt a small piece of optimism emerging. *I have a daughter. Another daughter.* Newness amid so much trepidation, brought a largely unexpected sense of promise and hope. Justin's mind shifted to Grace. He wondered what her condition was and wished he had been invited to come and see her also. Maybe her now no longer being pregnant would mean her body would be able to recover. He sat at the red light, with accumulating specks of rain blurring his window view. It wasn't a long drive to the hospital.

Yet, every mistiming in the dense flow of traffic—a red light or slowed car made his skin crawl with impatience. He banged on the steering wheel frustrated with a delivery truck double parking immediately ahead and swerved around honking his horn. He felt a rush of satisfaction by acting upon the indignation that passed through him like lightning. Given all the adversity he had been facing, he felt entitled to behave a little badly on the road.

Justin arrived. Looking up at the hospital towers. They stood glassy and sterile in appearance against the gloomy November sky. *So many lives changed in there…including ours* he thought to himself as he grabbed his messenger bag from the passenger seat and headed to the entrance. He stood in a line of near a dozen people standing on the markers taped to the ground, six feet apart. The greeters awaited incomers watchfully. Masked behind face shields with gazing eyes looking over and through the people in the line. A healthcare worker in bright pink scrubs checked his mask was on properly and waved a thermometer over his forehead before gesturing to him to enter. He walked through, feeling some relief that he was granted admittance given that he had been exposed to COVID.

Justin followed the signage towards a long corridor appointed with bright landscapes to cheer up the walkway towards the elevators. He made his way up to the visitor check-in station for the neonatal intensive care unit. A security guard sat at the station, not noticing that her mask was below her nose. She requested his driver's licence and eyed him intently as though able to compare his masked face to the picture on the card. Justin felt nervous, having to go through all the security check-points felt so procedural, and all to meet his daughter. "Please wait here. I will page the nurse to bring you in."

Justin sat in the waiting room. The room was worn, much as he felt. Sitting, watching the clock above the doorway ticking, 10 minutes behind the time on his watch. He thought about how close he was to being able to meet his daughter for the first time. *What does she look like? Is she healthy?* What would have been a joyous moment he would have shared with Grace in another time, was now procedural and absent of the warmth two parents share seeing their baby.

As he sat, staring distantly a few feet ahead of him on the floor, the thoughts dead ended in longing for what was missing in the situation, and gathered gloom as they morphed into an emerging sense of guilt. It shocked him to be feeling this unnatural feeling. He was ashamed for the first time thinking about his affair with Vivi. *Why was I so stupid? What have I done? Is this what I get for the affair?* He shifted his weight in the cushioned seat and stretched his arm, trying to shake the feelings. Unrest had taken hold with nowhere to escape now contained within the confines of the empty little waiting room. He thought about how he had dove in with a desperate desire for something more than the life he had been given.

In this moment, when all he wished for was to have Grace and his daughter home and healthy, he was faced with a realisation that the hunger he had for novelty and adventure had driven him away from what mattered most to him. He hung his lead low, almost between his legs, feeling poorly. *I took them for granted.* Nearly twenty minutes had passed before the unit assistant came to bring Justin in. They stopped at a scrubbing station where he was asked to wash his hands thoroughly and put on an isolation gown. *So much procedure and process to be able to see my little girl.* He thought as he went through the motions compliantly. The unit assistant handed him off to the nurse by the doorway. Beyond he saw a large isolet with a small bundle laying still on it.

As he approached, he was surprised to see how many tubes and lines were attached to her frail little body. She was sleeping and breathing with increased effort. She was beautiful to him. She looked like Grace. With tiny, perfect features and long thin fingers. His eyes traced over her head covered with a knit beanie. The machine above the isolet displayed measurements with constancy, drawing lined patterns across the screen. It was reassuring to see the lines continue and hear no alarms. Her little life was constrained and preserved at once. There she was. The baby he had been surprised by, considered to be a choice made real. In flesh, binding her to reality.

He was puzzled by how small she was. She looked far too small to be outside of the womb. Yet, there she was, a complete little human, most likely safer now than she had been inside her mother only hours earlier. Justin stood looking over his daughter. Wishing he could hold her, yet deterred by how knowingly afraid he was of how fragile she looked. "Do we have a name for her, Dad?" asked the nurse, as she worked to adjust the oxygen at the wall.

"Not yet. I'm going to wait for my wife to name her."

The nurse quickly concealed an emerging pitying look. "Can I get you anything?" She replied.

"No. Thank you. Is it okay if I sit here?" He smiled warmly in contrast to his sad eyes as he pulled a chair up to the isolet. Justin sat for the remainder of the hour quietly, staring through the isolet at his daughter. It was painful to be alon there in the neonatal intensive care unit. Grace was fighting for her life in another unit and their little baby, now here, not fully ready to be born. The rise and fall of her swaddled chest soothed him. He watched her eyes dart and shift under her closed lids and imagined she was dreaming something beautiful. *Keep dreaming, little one,* he thought. The nurse gently reminded him of the time. It was time to go. His feet headed to the door, but heart felt left behind, beside the isolet.

# Chapter 16
# Breath

The dulling of the afternoon light had set in as he drove home. The bay stretched out alongside the highway, still, spread out steel and glass reflecting the overcast sky. Justin turned on the heat to warm the car. The hospital had been cold inside. He felt it still in his bones. He turned on the radio and listened to a report about the vaccinations that would be available in a matter of weeks. Soon they would be released. The vaccine release was a celebrated light at the end of the nearly year-long tunnel. Something to look forward to. *Something to finally end the global pandemic.*

Justin felt frustration as he thought about how the record speed with which they had been developed relative to previous vaccines was still too slow for their situation, *for Grace.* Justin turned down the radio, unable to keep up with the celebratory sentiment broadcasting across the airwaves and casting a shadow on his own situation. The rain had come and smeared across the windshield distorting the glow of brake lights that now flooded the foreground as hasty drivers navigated the rain.

As he drove on, he thought of Emma. *She has a sister.* All these changes in the past few days felt compressed and disorienting, shaking the ground beneath what had been his footing in the mundane life that had made his skin crawl. He would welcome that unsatisfied feeling over this any day. He breathed deeply, attempting to soothe the rawness. Vulnerability didn't come easy. He thought of his baby girl laying bundled in the isolet. She was breathing in air for the first day of her life, with help. Letting air pass through her, permeating her cells with the outside world. Her lungs had learned to breathe outside of the watery womb and now inhaling and exhaling air in a new environment. *I need to learn to breathe in this new situation.* He sat in the driveway, closing his eyes and focusing on his breath. Insubstantial images of Grace, Emma and the baby swirled around in his mind, unable to take hold. Everything felt so fragile. That night, they made a simple dinner of tomato soup from the cans that Grace had stocked in the pantry and grilled cheese. They sat around the table and lit a candle. "For Grace and for the baby," Justin said as he took a match to the wick. Emma was mesmerised by the flame, watching it flicker and grow. They ate quietly, gazing at the flame reverently as though it was what they could place their hope in to change the course of the situation, as the candle cast a warm glow across the table.

"Our mother took Grace and I walking in the middle of the night once," Lottie began. "I remember she held our hands as we walked along many low-lit streets from one light to the next. We had nothing. Just wearing our nightgowns and the night was so cold. But I remember feeling warm with my hand in hers. I remember she sang to us."

"What did she sing?" Justin asked.

"She sang Amazing Grace." Lottie began to sing softly, *"Amazing Grace how sweet the sound that saved a wretch like me. I once was lost, but now I'm found. Was blind but now I see."* She sang slowly, looking into the flame. Emma and Justin sat quietly, letting her sweet voice wash over them.

In a moment, a feeling of dread passed over Justin. He felt that sense of guilt emerging, as he thought about Vivi. He sat with the feelings, soaking in the muck of his memories of the affair, what he was chasing after. The certainty of his family that he had essentially been willing to sacrifice was now passing through his fingers like granules of sand. He closed his eyes and imagined the Pacific waves beating down on him and his surfboard, being sucked under into salt water turbulence with no promise of emerging in time to take a breath. He listened to Lottie singing softly, feeling sorry for himself. *I deserve this pain.*

Lottie agreed to stay over the next few days to help with Emma and worked on her laptop in the study intermittently. Justin had taken family emergency medical leave and was able to put some rough substitute teacher notes together that morning.

He hadn't received an update since visiting the day before and was beginning to feel a little antsy. "Why don't you call and ask for an update from the doctor?" Lottie suggested. Justin figured it couldn't hurt to call directly. He didn't want to bother Elle. "Hi, this is Dr Richardson." The mildly harried voice said on the other end of the phone.

"Hi, I'm Justin, Grace's husband. I wanted to see if you had any updates on her condition."

"Ah. Yes, Justin. Well. Grace has had persistent low blood pressure throughout her admission. Her oxygen levels keep falling despite what we are able to do for her with the ventilator."

"I see." Justin replied, not fully understanding what was happening. "Can I come to see her?"

"Ah. We currently have a very limited visitor policy during the pandemic. I'll have the case manager call you. I'm sorry I have a pressing matter to attend to." He hung up abruptly, clearly distracted by the next task on his list.

Justin held the phone, working out how he could translate what he heard and barely understood to update Lottie who stood by. "Was there any promising news?" Lottie asked hopefully.

"He said she has low blood pressure and her oxygen is falling, even with her on the breathing machine."

An expression of fear passed over her face. "Well, there has to be some good news. How is the baby?" She pressed.

"He didn't elaborate. He had to go attend to something and just hung up. I don't think he is in charge of the baby's care so I didn't ask."

"I find this very frustrating," Lottie started. "If we weren't in a pandemic, we could be bedside with Grace, asking questions, getting updates, and being there to support her. Now all we get is a few rushed sentences over the phone."

"There's no way to fully know what's going on." Justin nodded his head, agreeing with her disillusionment as he sat on the couch, scrolling through pictures of Grace and Emma at Baker's Beach a year ago on his phone.

"What if they aren't doing all the right things to help her? We will never know." Lottie was becoming clearly vexed as she paced in the kitchen. Justin stared at his phone, with a muted appreciation of Emma moving around on the floor in front of him chatting to her stuffed animals. He was lost in his despair with no real plan emerging.

"How about that nurse friend of Grace's. The one that called you about her first?" Lottie asked. "Do you think she'd let you in?"

"That's a thought," Justin agreed. "If she's working when I get in later today to visit the baby, I'll ask her if she can let me in."

Justin made his way back to the hospital. After passing the check-point, he saw two new parents in the lobby. The father held a baby in the carrier hanging from his forearm as the nurse wheeled the new and tired looking mother in a wheelchair to the exit. Justin watched the little family as they left the hospital. He couldn't help but feel a sense of jealousy. It seemed so unfair to him at that moment that they were able to leave, together.

There he was, empty-handed, having to negotiate his way into the hospital to spend an hour with his newborn and given no apparent option to see his wife. He made his way up to the newborn intensive care unit security check-in. A new guard at the door met him with an impersonal air, driven by procedure, much less than what he hoped for as he awaited seeing his daughter in the doors beyond. Justin shifted his weight with impatience as he eyed the security guard's badge watching her slowly enter in the details of his driver's licence on the computer and print the visitor sticker he needed to wear.

He waited until a nurse buzzed him in and met him in the hall. She made small talk about how busy it was in the unit and whether he knew what the visiting time policy was. Justin entered the room. There she was. The tiny piece of heaven that his heart ached over. He wanted to smell her hair and hold her soft little hands in his. He wanted to whisper to her the certainties he did not have. He wanted her to come home. She remained behind the clear plastic walls of the isolet, quietly breathing and sleeping intently. The monitor pressed on above. He sat watching her little movements, shudders and the curl of the edges of her rosebud lips.

Suddenly, a beeping sound resonated above. Justin's heart dropped as he glanced at the baby and quickly to the nurse who was rushing over. "What's going on?" His nerves were strained beyond return at this point. He could feel his neck muscles tighten and his heart race.

"It's okay. I'm going to have you step outside for a moment, Dad. Respiratory therapy is coming to help work on your baby."

"What do you mean?" He was angered by the lack of answers in the situation as the medical staff filed past him hastily. "She's having difficulty breathing on the cannula," he heard the nurse report to another. The nurse then signalled the security guard who had come to the door to bring him outside. "Sir, I'm going to need to ask you to step into the hallway."

Justin felt a surge of anger rising within him. The injustice of the situation he found himself in everywhere he looked brought about an anger within him that was uncontainable. "Why don't you make me?!" He was fed up with feeling at a loss and being trapped in a situation he did not want to be in.

The security guard stepped closer, now setting his eyes with his. "Sir, this patient is having a medical emergency and you are asked to vacate the room so they can do their job." The security guard had stepped up the intensity in his directive, "If you do not step out, we will need to escort you out of the hospital."

Justin could hear the alarms going off behind him, looking back over his shoulder at the medical team now assembled and working around the isolet. Team members glanced at him and the security guard intermittently to get a read on how safe the situation was turning out to be. Justin didn't have a plan, all he knew was that he had become frozen where he was. He did not want to leave the room for fear. His feet had become planted where he stood. He could hear the staff behind him talking about suction and calling out the monitor's readings that sounded significant and reason for them to continue to work swiftly.

The security guard stepped forward to show Justin the door. He felt threatened by how everything was moving so fast and in the wrong direction. He wanted to rampage through the newborn intensive care unit and throw things. Fight his way out of the squeeze he felt at his core. It took everything in him to take a step towards the door, as he wanted to just stay. To not leave her. To stay and protect her. The security guard recognised the agony he was in and gave him a more compassionate look. "I know, man. I've been here before with my baby son. You just need to step into the hall and they will bring you back in when it's okay to come back."

Justin followed his request now, stepping out into the hallway and pressing against the wall. His body felt like it was numb and unpinned to place or time, as he lingered engulfed with anxiety. *This can't be happening.* His mind did not want to accept that his daughter now too was having a medical emergency. She was so little, so frail and defenceless to the world. The security guard stood by her room's door and kept a side eye on him while looking straight ahead. The situation felt like being trapped in a doorless and windowless room where no certainty of what would happen next, much less the promise of escape could be ascertained.

Ten minutes later, a doctor came out of the room to find him. The security guard came closer to monitor the exchange. "I'm Dr Ambers. Your daughter has suffered what we call acute respiratory distress. Her immature respiratory system has made her very susceptible to difficulty breathing. We are currently able to stabilise her oxygen levels with a high flow nasal cannula and will be monitoring her closely to see if any further intervention is needed."

Justin stood, taking in the information like a sieve, with water briefly filling and passing through it. He could not retain the information largely because of how dreadful it was making him feel to have to entertain the idea that both his wife and his daughter were experiencing significant medical emergencies at once. At the same time, he felt a desperate reliance on the doctor's judgment and skills to fix his daughter's problem. "Please do everything you can for her doctor." Justin held back his tears, standing in the hall watching the doctor return to the room.

The assembled team crowded around and suctioned and placed tubing on his daughter. There was nothing for him to do but wait. After regaining composure, he felt the emptiness of himself, drifting like a vessel without a crew at sea. His fear of loss was a foreboding sort of pain that felt all encompassing, as he stood in the hall, waiting for permission to return to the room.

His visitation hour had ended soon after he was allowed back into the room. His eyes traced the contour of the baby's body, checking over her for signs of damage. She lay breathing deeply and looking more tethered now by lines and tubes. The monitor above pressed on with agreeable readings. His heart rate slowed. She still slept. *I wish this were a dream.* He thought leaning over the isolet to gaze down at her. Justin's phone buzzed in his pocket. He had silenced it as one of the policies required of newborn intensive care and was startled when it buzzed. He was still on edge, feeling the adrenaline course.

It was Elle. "Hi Justin. How are you holding up?"

Justin texted back quickly, "I'm in with the baby and can't text, but can I call you in about 20 minutes?" His time was likely nearly up and he would be escorted again out of the unit. He turned off the vibrate mode so he wouldn't be startled again and knew that he may not be in the good graces of staff once again if he pulled out his phone. Justin sat looking at his baby girl. So fragile with such a tenuous beginning to life. This was not how he had pictured it. It was how no one ever pictured it. Yet here was the situation, separated, fragile, complicated, harrowing.

He paused to remember all the contours of his little one in order to draw comfort in his memory of her when he would leave her again. He walked out of the unit, worn out by his emotions that had run through him so intensively over the past days. He followed the brightly lit corridor towards the elevators and down to the cafeteria to get a coffee. He remembered his phone. "Come see Grace" was in the notification on his locked phone screen.

He wasn't expecting an invitation and hoped he hadn't been too late to reply as it had arrived 20 minutes prior. He quickly texted, "How do I get in?" He watched the text page attentively as he saw Elle typing.

"Come to ICU north side. Text when you are there. I'll let you in. Don't bring any bags."

Justin felt a faint sensation of hope emerge, one that felt foreign and misfitting in the disheartening landscape he was becoming accustomed to. He headed to the north tower, up to the floor he had visited Grace in with flowers on her birthday and occasional donuts for the nurses in previous years before the hospital operated on lockdown. He stood outside of the double doors. Nodding passively as a doctor broke through the doors. It was tempting to wander through the doors before they closed off the unit once more, but he held to the instructions Elle had given him and texted her, "Here."

He waited in the limbo Grace had always spoken about with compassion for her patients' families as they stood quietly outside the unit, awaiting access to see their loved ones, and seeking answers to their many questions about what was happening and what would happen next, with trepidation. "Justin." Elle came out, she was wearing a helmet respirator, looking like she was walking on the moon. "I'm not supposed to bring you into the COVID unit, but I know Grace would want you to be here, and this is important that you have the chance to see her," she said with a solemnity that lingered in the air, evaporating the hope he had mustered at the opportunity to see Grace. "I cannot bring you into the room for obvious reasons since she is COVID positive. But I can let you stand outside. I'll go in and you can call her phone and we will put you on speaker. You can see her at least and talk to her. She is still fully sedated and you shouldn't expect her to reply or anything." He appreciated the opportunity, knowing that Elle was risking getting in trouble bringing him in there. The intensive care unit was visually startling. He walked past numerous rooms with IV poles strung to the outside of the sliding glass doorways, and patients lying on their stomachs, arms hanging limp alongside the beds. It was worse than he had imagined. Room after room was occupied by bodies, seemingly teetering on the edge of life and death as air was mechanically pumped into their bodies. They were young and old men and women lining the intensive care unit hallway in deep induced slumber to await the passing of and hopefully outrun the dreadful disease. It felt like something out of a science fiction movie crossed with a war zone to be walking through.

The nurses around worked dutifully, half noticing his presence, but too busy to say anything. There she was. Room 320. She was lying on her stomach like all the rest. The gown and sheets covering her back. Her head turned facing him, eyes closed and breathing through a large tube feeding into her mouth and down her throat. He didn't recognise his wife. She had been full of life just nearly a week ago. She had been carrying their baby and working hard in the ICU herself. Planning to work all the way up to her delivery date. Now, here she was, still in the ICU, but as a patient. A shadow of herself.

He stood paralysed by his disbelief in what he was seeing colliding with the harsh reality of what he knew to be happening. "I'm so sorry this is happening, Justin," Elle spoke quietly beside him looking on into the room. "The whole team is really upset about what happened to her. We are all doing all we can for her to survive this and make a full recovery."

*Full Recovery.* It felt like something that was so far away from here. The machines, the beeping, the bright fluorescent lights and faceless workers covered in protective equipment moving dutifully around. All the extensive suffering he could see around in the ICU made recovery seem like a pipe dream. "I appreciate that, Elle," Justin managed to muster a response as he held back the urge to let his weakening knees give way. The grief was overwhelming, but he knew he could not make a scene, as an unannounced guest.

"Okay. You can stand out here, just make sure to keep the main part of the hall clear. I'm going to go in there with my cell phone in this plastic bag and I'll call you so you can talk to her on speaker," Elle instructed, as she headed to gel her hands and retrieve her gown from the cabinetry. Justin appreciated the lengths to which Elle was going out of her way to help him see Grace, as painful as it was for him to see her this way and feel even more helpless. The ICU felt like the pinnacle of the drama playing out around the world. Where the rubber meets the road with the path of suffering the Coronavirus had managed to inflict. All he could do was standby quietly, afraid of what he was seeing around.

Once inside, Elle called him from Grace's bedside. "Okay, I have the volume way up."

"Hi Grace." He could not hold back his tears. It was as though being able to see her was a breakthrough to reach her finally and yet a foreboding sense of finality surrounded this conversation. He began crying, speechless and unable to control his breath as he sputtered, repeating, "I'm sorry my love. I'm sorry. I'm sorry. I'm sorry…I'm sorry this is happening" *I'm sorry for what I've done.* Justin's thoughts collided with the enormity of the situation.

"Justin. It may help if you tell her what's waiting for her," Elle interjected, having been there for many conversations like this with her patients before.

"Emma misses you…" Justin managed to say. "She needs you. We need you t-to come back home to us." The deep pain he carried had been ruptured and set forth, rushing out of his core, silently. *You deserved better from me and I failed you.*

All that he wanted to say to her, all that he wanted to confess to her was on the tip of his tongue, but all he could say was that. Elle looked at him with urging eyes, but he didn't know what to say. He paused, frozen. Too afraid to confront the reality of what he had done because it would compound the pain.

He remembered the song Lottie had sung. The one their mother had sung to them when they walked through the night. With nothing more to say, he began to quietly sing to her, "*Amazing Grace. How sweet the sound that saved a wretch like me. I once was lost but now I'm found. Was blind but now I see.*" All the running, all the choices that he had made separate from honouring his commitment to her surfaced within him, like binding pain he could not shake. "What have I done? I-I am so sorry for what I have done, Grace." The guilt and the remorse had been building quietly and now surged, in his helplessness. "I was so selfish. You didn't deserve this. There is nothing I can do to make it better. She wanted me. I felt trapped in the life we made. I can't hardly sleep or breathe knowing that you are here. Our baby is struggling to survive now too. Oh God, what have I done?"

Elle noticed his building distress and the confusing things he was saying and decided to interject. "Justin, I'm going to need to end the call now. Is there anything else you want to tell her before you go?"

Justin recovered a little, remembering Elle was an audience to all he had said. His desperation had clouded his mind. "Yes. Sorry. Grace…I love you. You have always been the one for me. I know that now. I hope you will someday forgive me. Please come home."

Elle was surprised at the window she had gained with Justin's rambling confessions. She quickly hung up and completed her nursing tasks in the room Justin stood by, awaiting Elle's cue for what to do next. He was glad to have his mask on. Feeling somewhat anonymous, as he stood in the hallway trying not to be in anyone's way as they strode past him with purpose. He looked on as Elle attended to Grace before coming out of the room. Once out of the room with her personal protective equipment taken off, she led him outside to the courtyard balcony.

"I have about 10 minutes, Justin. Thought we should get some air." She searched his face to gain eye contact. He looked into her eyes, timidly. "I'm sorry Justin. This is a terrible situation. I can't imagine the kind of stress you are under." She let the acknowledgement hang in the air between them. "What you were saying to Grace made me think that you may have some other things going on. Do you want to talk about it?"

Justin's back tightened and he clenched his jaw. A long silence lingered between them. "I-I cheated on Grace with my old girlfriend," he suddenly blurted out. Feeling the weight lifting in confessing the raw truth. It felt sticky on the outside now. It was the first time he had said it aloud in a straightforward manner. Elle stood there, staring at him with a blank expression. This unnerved him. "What? Aren't you going to yell at me? Tell me how stupid I am?"

Elle thought for a moment about how satisfying it would be to yell at him. But in that moment, she remembered her own infidelity. She shifted her weight, looking out at the cityscape behind him. "Listen Justin. We both know what you did was wrong. But I can't say I haven't done the same thing to my own husband." The pause in her voice caught Justin's attention, bringing him out of his self-loathing stance. "Joe left me because of what I did. I told him the whole story about how I met George here from environmental services. We had chemistry. It was thrilling at first to have a passionate affair here at work. Served as a distraction in many ways. But when I snapped out of the romance and adventure, I realised what I had in my marriage to Joe and what I had been willing to sacrifice was not worth it. So I broke it off, and decided to come clean about it because I thought we could get through it if I was truthful. I needed to regain my trustworthiness through restoring my honesty."

"Did it work?" Justin said, seeing how the formula may apply to his own situation.

An ironic expression crossed her face. "Not in the way I had expected. My marriage ended shortly after." Her sadness lingered in her facial expression. "The pain of what I did, broke him. It then broke us completely. I doubt Grace could even hear you in there, so I suggest you make a clear decision of what you plan to say to her when she recovers. I know from experience that you will need to bear the consequence of whatever you choose. The way I saw it was either live with the guilt of secrecy or face the potential for Joe to forgive me or leave me. The pain of the guilt was too much for me to stand and I chose to gamble with a hope that he would eventually forgive me."

Justin absorbed her advice, recognising that there was no easy path forward and perhaps outcome in his situation. "Do you think she will...recover?"

A compassionate expression passed over Elle's face. "I-I don't know, Justin. All I know is we are doing all we can to reach a positive outcome with her case. You have my word that I will do everything in my power to help her get home to you." He felt feelings of nervousness stir in the pit of his stomach as she spoke with uncertainty, solidifying his own. *Nothing is certain.* "Understood. Thank you, Elle. For everything today. I appreciate you sticking your neck out to help me see her and the advice you are giving me."

"Any time," she replied wryly. Their newfound comradery at the bottom of the pit they had found themselves in brought humour to them both. Justin headed to the cafeteria for a warm cup of coffee. Standing in line, he thought back to their baby in the isolet, bundled, nameless, and so fragile. Grace, sedated, lifeless to see with the monitor's steady lines serving as the only proof that she was not dead. It was traumatic for him. He had never imagined such a collision of misfortunes, within his family. He thought about Lottie, at home with Emma. Thankful that she had come to help him manage through this.

# Chapter 17
# Released Leaves

Justin pulled up the driveway. The driveway was covered in dry leaves that had fallen piece by piece by the large maple that grew contently along the fence line next to the driveway. Large maple leaves drifted silently into the hood of his car in the few minutes he sat pensively. He found himself drifting into thought, often muddled and troubled in his thoughts that couldn't quite connect with the knowledge of what he should do next, more often in these days. He looked up to the stoop ahead of the small landing he had before the door.

Lost in thought, he hadn't paid attention enough to recall his drive home, nor notice the old man in navy coveralls sitting on his steps. The man stood when he was seen and sauntered over to Justin's car. His eyes were familiar. Justin rolled down the window with a quizzical look. The man approached. "Hi there. I'm sorry to show up unannounced. It's just I didn't have a way to reach you. I'm Grace's father. You must be Justin." He greeted him with a hesitancy in his eyes. Unsure of how he would be received. Grace had mentioned very little about her father over the years. Only that when their mother died, his parents had raised her and he had somewhat been uninvolved with their lives. She had been reluctant to say much about him or her mother.

Justin paused, still in his seat, feeling the discomfort of this surprise meeting, and left only with the option to engage. His emotions were dulled at this point, after the overload of the morning and he felt as though he had very little to give to the situation. "Oh. Yes, I'm Justin. Does Lottie know you are here?" He shook his hand. Feeling the weakness of old age had changed what once must have been a strong handshake.

"No, she doesn't know I am here." Justin thought it strange that he had arrived out of essentially nowhere, unannounced. "Oh," Justin replied, surprised.

"I have been thinking a lot about Grace. I realised I handled the situation poorly over the phone when Lottie called me with the news. The way I've always seemed to handle things with my daughters." He looked over to the maple. "I was watching the leaves falling from a maple tree just like this one outside of my house yesterday and realised what those leaves do. Being released from the branches is a lesson in letting go. I couldn't stop thinking about how much I have done and not done for Grace and Lottie in the seasons of life when I had a chance to be the father they needed me to be and the husband their mother needed me to be. Those seasons just passed me by…I was too stubborn to change."

Justin stood now by the car listening. "I appreciate you sharing this with me, but this is probably something you should be sharing with Lottie instead of me. She's inside with Emma right now."

He smiled, "I know I am probably more than you bargained for with all that you must be going through. I'm not sure how Lottie will react so I hesitate going inside and surprising her with the little one there. Do you think you could do me a favour and tell her I'm outside. See if she is willing to speak with me out here?"

Justin saw the wisdom in his approach and agreed.

The house was warm and he could smell baking in the kitchen at the far end of the house. "Daddy!" Emma came running down the hall at the jingle of his keys. Justin held her longer than usual, appreciating how full of life she was. He was glad she didn't fully comprehend the intensity of what was going on for Grace and her little sister. She didn't know that the baby was born yet. With the chaos of everything, he had thought it best to announce her little sister's arrival when things were less tenuous.

Lottie looked up from the oven. "Justin, how did it go?" She once again searched his face for answers.

"I got to see Grace. Her friend, Elle, another ICU nurse, snuck me in."

"Oh wow. Were you able to talk to her?" Lottie hung on his every word.

He whispered now, making sure Emma was busying herself with some figurines at her table. "She is still sedated and on the ventilator. She appears stable. It was very hard for me to see her. I think she's in good hands though. Her friend Elle is on top of her care." Lottie smiled. Justin remembered her father was standing outside. "Lottie, it seems that your father has paid a surprise visit and is asking to speak with you. He was on the steps when I pulled up."

Lottie looked strained by this news. "Did he say why he is here?"

"He said something about wanting to make things right with you." Lottie gave an incredulous look, as she headed to the front door, grabbing her jacket.

She opened the door to see him. His stature at the bottom of the steps was diminutive. He was elderly now, coming from the auto shop no doubt judging from the grease-stained coveralls, carrying a large satchel over his shoulder. He looked up at her, a glint of relief in his eyes that she had decided to come out to meet him.

"Dad. What are you doing here?" She inquired, knowing their last exchange over the phone had been strained.

He stood there trying to gauge how angered she may be. "I-I felt like I should come." He didn't really have any other reason than the compelling sense to connect with her and apologise. "I wanted to tell you that I am here. I am here for you. For Grace and for Emma."

Lottie gave him an annoyed look. "So you've now decided it's a good idea to appear out of thin air to be here for us. What about every other time? What about when I called you the other day?" Lottie was angered more so now. Thinking about how this visit was on his terms. "You can't just come here and expect us to welcome you now that you are ready to have a relationship with us. To gloss over everything and somehow act like what happened was okay. Nothing can change what you did to her and what you did to us. I honestly don't think I have anything left to say to you."

"Please Lottie." His weakness was new for her. "I'm just asking that you let me be here, in your life."

"Have you ever considered what hell you gave us? You abused our mother until she became unrecognisable to us and to herself. You are the reason she killed herself. We will never recover from what you took from us with what you did over and over to her, mercilessly. You even lied about it to make your parents believe that she wasn't mentally stable and she had no way to defend herself or seek help." Lottie had begun to raise her voice, noticing its crack in the places of emphasis that mirrored her heartbreak as she spoke. "Grace is very sick right now Dad. I am trying to wrap my head around why you would think it's a good idea to come here and drag up the past. Make us deal with your guilt and need to be forgiven while Grace is suffering in the hospital and we are worried sick about her."

"I just thought, I should let you know that I am here for you. That's all I wanted to do. I can't change what I've done or not done. I just hoped you might be ready to forgive and forget, and deal with the present circumstances together, as a family."

"Dad, stop. Why must everything be about what you want? Did you come here thinking we would see what a great benefit it would be to forgive you and let you be our rock in this?" Lottie interjected, tears falling. "You are not what we need now. You stopped being what we needed you to be so long ago. Just please go. I really can't do this right now."

Lottie turned away, heading to the door, squeezing the door handle as she turned it. The steadying of her determined grip around the smooth brass handle kept her from tearing up anymore. She pushed the door forward decisively, then stopped at his voice. "Lottie. I'll go. But please take this. She would have wanted you to have it." Lottie looked down at the worn shoebox that he had retrieved from his satchel. She recognised it immediately. It had been the box Mumma stored up high in the pantry and would stash all her leftover grocery money inside.

She remembered it distinctly—it contained a means to escape. Promises to hope for. Ultimately, it had become nothing more than a box that collected spare change with a postcard picture of the Santa Monica Pier. But she wanted to have it. To hold it again, even though its contents never became that trip to Santa Monica, to her, it symbolised the kind of hope for the future that she desperately needed. It was a connection to her sister and her mother. She walked over to her father and took the box. "Thank you. Grace will want to have this too."

He stood and watched her go as she stowed away back into the house with the box. She closed the door swiftly behind her, finding the pain of seeing him again, her mother's memory in her arms and Grace's illness all surging within her. She felt the immense heartache course through her body, rendering her helpless against an overwhelming sense of hopelessness. *Nothing will ever be like Santa Monica was supposed to be.* The sobering thought of life's reality—stark, painful, raw when it had been imagined as bright, carefree and light once. She went upstairs to take a hot shower and wash away the grit of the whole weighty experience with her dad.

That night, Justin and Lottie sat by the fireplace after Emma was asleep. It felt comforting to be together under the same roof, awaiting news of Grace. The glow of the flickering firelight warmed Lottie's face as she looked pensively into the flames. "Do you think she will be okay?" She finally broke the silence with her question.

"I don't think anyone knows the answer right now." Justin said, regretting the fact he could not give a definitive answer to the very same question he longed to be able to have answered.

"It's just that she is in the prime of her life and at any other time, we would be celebrating. I would have thrown her a baby shower and we could have eaten petit fort cakes and drank sparkling lemonade. It just breaks my heart that we never got any of that. This whole thing. This whole pandemic has stolen everything from us." Justin sat listening to Lottie unravelling her thoughts. "When my dad came by today, I just felt so much anger and helplessness all at once. It was like dealing with him was just one more burden. I don't know if Grace ever told you what our childhood with him was like. You know, before our mother died…"

"No, all she really mentioned was you went to live with your grandparents."

"Yeah, we did. But a lot happened before that. I don't think she really likes to talk about it, but our dad had a drinking problem and he would come home and beat our mother up. Like most nights. I remember Grace and I would huddle in the pantry listening to our mother plead and scream as things would be thrown and we would hear her get hit or be thrown against the wall. I will never be able to unhear those sounds. I wasn't very old, but I remember Grace would hold her hands over my ears, jolting a little at every loud crack and sound from the living room."

"Anyway, this went on for a long time. Eventually, our mother gave up on being a mother and wife. She sank into what we would call depression I think. She slowly stopped taking care of us. To the point that she eventually did nothing more than stay all day in her room, with the lights off and blinds shut. Looking back now, I realise she didn't have the means to help herself. Grace looked over at the box she had placed on the side table. All she had was hopes that she stowed away in that shoe box. It was her leftover grocery money. She told us one day we would go to Santa Monica with what she had saved. We believed it. Could even taste the cotton candy and the funnel cakes she said they sold on that pier.

"We dreamed of that place as though it would be the answer to all of our troubles if we could get there. When she stopped dreaming, and stopped praying, she just faded away. When it was all happening, I think Grace knew that she would have to step up to make sure I was taken care of. Grace made sure I had meals and clothes for the months that she locked herself away in the room. Grace tried to help her. She would bring her food and urge her to come out. But nothing helped. I think Grace fundamentally learned how to be a nurse in those days when she would attend to me and our mother both needing her to care for us. Grace never complained. She rose to the occasion of whatever was called of her. She has always been that way.

"Then, one day our mother killed herself with a pill overdose. I remember thinking how glad I was that she didn't have to suffer anymore. But I know Grace blamed herself. Grace saw Mumma's death as a result of her not being able to do enough to keep her alive. As time went on she became determined to become a nurse. To save people's lives because she couldn't save her own mother's is what she told me once. That stuck with me."

Justin had sat listening quietly, absorbing the sad story. "I am…I am so sorry. I had no idea."

"It is what it is, I guess. Seeing my father brought up all those memories." There wasn't much to say other than that, as the two sat on either end of the couch staring into the fire.

The two fell asleep on either armrest and awoke in the darkness that still held down the early morning. "Elle just texted. She said Grace has been improving with her spontaneous breathing trials and they are hopeful they will be able to extubate her." This good news came unexpectedly and delighted both Justin and Lottie. Extubation meant Grace would be one step further in her recovery and one step closer to coming home. They made breakfast with a renewed sense of hope and satisfaction in living that comes with confidence in positive things ahead.

Justin looked across the table at Lottie and Emma. He had thought it strangely comforting to have Lottie staying with them over the weeks. Having another adult, someone invested in both Emma and Grace had made a world of a difference to him. She resembled her sister in many ways. Her mannerisms, like Grace's, brought forth the facade of normalcy, in fleeting moments, as though Grace was home.

Justin appreciated how Lottie upheld her role as a doting aunt to Emma, even though her own grief in the situation had to have been piercing. Her strength was something he knew he did not have. He felt like the feelings of uncertainty and anxiety in the situation had been swallowing him whole, day after day regurgitating him and throwing him into the next day. Until today. The light in the kitchen looked different, as it cast a brightness over the counters and glossy fruit in the bowl. Justin made an omelette and dished its pieces up onto plate awkwardly as Lottie and Emma sat at the table, smirking at the effort with which he wielded the cast iron pan.

Justin's phone rang. It was Elle. He fumbled to place the hot pan on a nearby surface before answering. "Hi Elle."

She spoke in a hushed voice. "I'm on my break so only have a minute but wanted to let you know that in rounds this morning Dr Crew said Grace is ready to be extubated."

Justin smiled at the news. "Thank you. Thank you so much, Elle, for letting me know."

"Alright, I've got to go." She hung up the phone quicker than he had a chance to reply.

He put the phone down. His face beaming. "She's coming off the ventilator today," he said to Lottie with an excited tone.

"What's a ventitater, Daddy?" Emma asked.

Justin had forgotten that Emma was listening. He hadn't explained to Emma what was happening to her mother, much less that she had been kept alive over the past weeks by a ventilator. Now that they were coming through the woods, he figured it would be okay to tell her the truth about it. "It's a machine that has been helping Mummy to breathe. Now, they think Mummy can breathe on her own and she won't need the machine anymore."

Emma's wide eyes widened at the thought of a machine helping someone breathe. "Thank goodness," Lottie said with a sigh of relief. "It's been about four weeks now." Lottie's eyes glistened as she thought with marvelling relief that finally, Grace was making it through. It had been a very hard month watching and waiting for news on her progress every day. As though every exhale came with a smothering hesitancy for what would come next. Grace had been able to breathe on her own in the spontaneous breathing trials and the anaesthesia was being weaned down. She lay quietly, looking up at the bright lights and sensing her breath, as a team gathered around her preparing for the extubation. The sensation of her body in space, achy and sore pressed against the creases in the sheets and bed beneath her became in focus. She heard the masked faces murmuring in an upbeat fashion, as they moved around the bed adjusting lines and pressing buttons all around. *I am alive.*

Suddenly, the ceiling tipped and she began to feel her body moving towards upright like in a capsule taking her somewhere else, as the nurse elevated the head of the hospital bed. The movement felt fast and made her feel faint nausea, the weight of her bones could be felt pushing through in her back, hips and tailbone as she acclimated to her new positioning. It felt strange to be seated upright. The suction came, loud and aggressively as the respiratory therapist worked quickly to suction mucus out through Grace's mouth as well as the endotracheal tube still lodged in her throat.

*What is this?* she thought, soaking in the familiarity of the scene, from a vantage point she had only imagined in the past. She knew where she was. She had been the nurse in the room while the extubation procedure was happening more times than she could count. She recalled that she had tested positive for COVID and laying in her bed had been having trouble breathing. She remembered Justin at the door as she was loaded into the ambulance. She remembered arriving at the hospital and being rushed down a corridor and greeted by the team of her colleagues who must have swiftly intubated her when they saw she was pregnant and experiencing acute respiratory failure. Hurried images of rushing to the hospital under a face mask flashed before her eyes, as she sat recalling what had happened by piecing together nervous sensations, bright lights, beeping and people talking to her with muted sound, as images of her trip from home to the hospital.

The nurse then began to undo all the tape and straps that had been in place to secure the tube. Grace's heart quickened. She remembered being pregnant. *My baby? Where is my baby?* The feeling of loss and disorientation in the moment ran through her like a charge of electricity. She could see that her stomach was no longer as rounded under the sheets. Panic began to surge within her as she realised she was no longer pregnant. *Did the baby die?* "Stay still, my dear," the respiratory therapist said as he disconnected the tube that linked between her mouth and the ventilator. She knew she couldn't yet talk or try to as the extubation procedure was underway. But all she wanted to do was scream for help, *Where is my baby?* It was as though Grace's high alert was wearing the anaesthesia off faster than it would typically.

Dr Crew could see the growing distress in Grace's eyes as he asked her to take a deep breath and exhale through the final steps of the extubation. As she exhaled they deflated the small holder that held the endotracheal tube in place in the trachea and mouth. He then urged Grace to take another deep breath and cough hard to cough out any mucus she still had in her lungs. She coughed hard over and over, trying to cough out the sensation of mucus but with little return. Her cough was weak, and her throat felt raw and swollen.

"Welcome back, Grace," Dr Crew said with a smile. Her voice was a whisper, extremely hoarse. He looked at her, with a sigh of relief as she breathed with a mask he placed over her nose. "You know the drill, Grace. Make sure you take deep breaths now and cough ever so often to clear any of the remaining mucus."

Grace was compliant, although she felt like she was dying inside. "James. Where is my baby?" She mouthed the words with weak phonation carrying the sound of what she asked.

Dr Crew could not hear over the suctioning and behind the hum of his respirator helmet, but he read her lips. He smiled. "She's okay, Grace. We were able to deliver her shortly after you were intubated by C-section. She's in the neonatal ICU."

Quiet tears of relief mixed with fear rolled down Grace's cheeks, as she sat up looking out into the hallway. "I want to see her." Grace felt as though she was waking up from a deep sleep yet felt physical pain all over, as though she had undergone a strenuous journey that had worn down her body. She felt disoriented in her new body—fatigued, weak and empty. "When can I see her?" Seeing her baby was to her the only relief she would find in her condition at present.

"I will call up to see what can be arranged." This was not easy for Grace to hear. She, even though weak and still with the sedation wearing off, wanted no less of an answer than *Yes, you can go see your baby*. It was unbearable to her to know she was so close to her baby and yet had not met her.

Grace lay in bed, the press of time felt non-existent in the place she now found herself, trapped. Stuck in bed—the rhythm of the day's events could only be told by the changing of the nursing shifts, as the blinds remained drawn and artificial light filled her room. Her throat was dry and immensely sore. Every swallow and attempt to speak was taxing. She felt exhausted by just the smallest amount of activity. The nurses would help to reposition her in the bed. Her physical therapist would help her to the edge of her bed, having her press her feet to the floor and pump her legs. Grace felt like she had been hit by a truck. It surprised her to see how much her body had deteriorated. Her blood pressure was unstable and dropped drastically when she tried to stand, causing a rush of faintness to take over her body. She was unable to stand and felt surprised as her knees buckled beneath her. Her heart rate would race when she tried.

Each day, she felt a little stronger, yet every little task her body tried to do was taxing. If she made progress with her mobility, she paid with more fatigue.

Her mind was foggy. She felt like her thoughts were slowed and it was extremely hard to maintain focus on an idea, while trying to think through her problems, or even to listen to anyone speak to her. It was as though she moved through water, suspended with very little to grasp hold of. Grace didn't know herself in the way she had before, but the mental strain it took her to articulate the ways deterred her from thinking about it too much. All she knew was that she needed to work as hard as she could to regain her strength and abilities knowing she had two little girls waiting for her.

A few days after Grace was extubated, Elle came to visit while on her break. "Knock-knock. Hi Grace. How are you feeling?" Grace was pleased to see Elle. "It's good to see you up and breathing on your own."

Grace smiled. "Yeah. Should never take that for granted. Did you see me while I was under?"

Elle came to sit by the bed. "I actually was assigned as your nurse for about three weeks of your intubation."

Grace gave a thoughtful look and smiled. "I remember asking them to assign you to me when they rushed me in here. Since you're the second-best nurse here and all." Grace laughed weakly. "So did you see them deliver my baby?"

Elle's brows furrowed. "No, it was a bit of an emergency as they saw your blood pressure climbing. They whisked you away to the operating room for a c-section quite quickly. I cared for you when you returned though."

Grace nodded with an appreciative smile. "It's a terrible feeling to be pregnant one moment and then wake up weeks later like this. The doctor said they are waiting for me to test negative before I can go to see my baby. Hope it will be any day because it's been so long. I don't even know if they will discharge her home with Justin before I can get out of this room. The testing takes forever to get back too. So here I am." Grace fiddled lightly with her cover sheet. "Just waiting for that. I think they will hover-lift me into a wheelchair or at this rate I'll be able to march to the newborn unit myself."

She laughed faintly, feeling how tiring it had been to string sentences together. She hadn't spoken much in the days since extubation, but noticed her voice, although hoarse, was improving and the pain had subsided a great deal. Elle smiled looking deeply into Grace's eyes. Knowing that their last interaction had been strained. "I've missed you, friend," Elle said.

Grace smiled. "Yes, me too. I appreciate all you have done for me. I mean I know you were just doing your job, but I'm really glad I was in your care throughout all of that."

Elle reached over and squeezed Grace's cold hand resting on the sheets. "I was honoured to be your nurse, friend. And you have no idea how happy we all are that you made it through." They smiled. Knowing the details of what had driven them apart no longer mattered, as they had been humbled by the gravity of what they had just been through together. "Well, I better go clock in. I wanted to just see you and say hey. I know Justin hopes to come see you soon. I've been keeping him somewhat updated. He has been allowed to go see the baby."

Grace smiled at the thought. "Thanks Elle. Come by any time."

Elle nodded. "I will." as she dashed out the sliding doors. As Elle walked down the hall, she felt glad that she had withheld any mention of what Justin had told her as she knew it wasn't her place or the time to share.

The next day, Grace's Coronavirus test result returned as undetected. The virus had finally left her system. It felt good to be past it. Despite the fact that it had left her body in debility and with a constellation of strange symptoms. Grace continued to feel fatigued and weak in her muscles. Her hands ached and her head ached intermittently. Standing took the wind out of her and her heart would race and blood pressure jumped around as if on a whim. Everything felt out of balance. Her chest x-rays showed her lungs were still filled with ground glass opacities and she felt it heavier to breathe from time to time. The nurse added litres of oxygen to her via the nasal cannula when her oxygen would drop to the low 90s. Dr Crew came into her room on his morning rounds. "Hi," Grace said, noticing her voice was getting closer to normal.

"Hi Grace. I wanted to stop in and chat with you. We are still having a hard time stabilising your heart rate, your blood pressure and your respiratory rate. So, I know you've had your heart set on going to the NICU, but I don't think you are quite ready yet." Dr Crew took in the disappointed look on Grace's face.

"I was just hoping I could see her. Can they bring her to me?"

Dr Crew looked up. "No, unfortunately, all neonatal babies must stay in their unit. It would be especially risky to bring her here into the ICU."

Grace nodded, knowing that this would have to be his answer. "I understand."

"We will keep working on your medications and monitoring. As soon as you are able to tolerate going down there, we will bring you." Dr Crew left.

Grace put her head in her hands, pressing her fingertips into her forehead, searching for relief. The whole unexpected experience had filled her with a sense of angst.

# Chapter 18
# The Road Takes Us

Grace sat looking out her window at the narrow slice of the outside world. The view was framed with maple leaves that had been weathered dry by the California sun and still held fast to brittle branches. Some flying off with a gust of wind. December's chill had arrived and the sky was overcast and misting now. There was news on the television about the Pfizer and Moderna vaccinations being available to the public. People signing up to get vaccinated. The war on COVID would finally end with the advent of vaccinations that were developed in record time and came with promise to change the course of the pandemic.

Grace watched on TV with her eyes tearing up as the first person in the United States, a critical care nurse, got the novel COVID vaccine. She felt the relief of a future she could see made brighter and more hopeful because of what the vaccinations would be able to do for people in the face of the Coronavirus. She smiled as tears ran down her cheeks, not wishing to stop crying, but thankful to feel, again.

The emotions shifted to a sense of melancholy. She was unable to pinpoint initially what the source of her despair might be in this moment that was clearly celebration heard around the world. She thought longer, pensive as she watched the news headline of the novel vaccination dissolve into a traffic report. *Had I only been able to be vaccinated before that Code Blue, perhaps none of this would have happened.* She could see her blurred reflection in the glass door. looked up to tubes, monitors persisting above her, and her body now worn and debilitated beyond her years. The thought troubled Grace. How the sequence of things had happened to her directly created the outcome she now experienced. Her mind wandered suddenly to her mother. Grace had witnessed the sequence of the events that had accumulated to a painful end before her eyes in her mother's life. Had her mother had different circumstances, perhaps she would not have sought to escape it. So much of what happened to her felt out of control, dictated by a force greater than herself. *Are we just all subject to forces beyond our control?* She thought about how she had often thought that the road one travelled on in life was more a result of one's choosing, directed by one's will. It seemed now like a naive notion to disregard the impact of the complicated, the messy, the hard, the unpredictable challenges that most predictably befall those travelling along. *The road takes us where it will.*

Grace felt frustrated that she had not had the advantage of access to this vaccine, she told herself there was no use in contemplating a different story. *What has happened has happened.* The day had been long, and Grace felt disappointed still that she was not deemed ready to leave the unit and go to meet her baby. The emptiness she experienced in not being able to meet her baby was immense. Between spurts of sleep, her mind would perseverate on what was missing. She longed to hold her baby bundled in her arms. She wanted to hold her close and to truly know she was safe. The emptiness was real. Her baby born and now alive in the world had not yet been made fully real without having been able to see her.

Grace sat, watching the rain stream down the glass. She closed her eyes and pictured Emma. Sitting in the living room under the big window. Her wispy hair framing her face. Grace's heart sank further as she realised how absent she had been during her hospitalisation. Time had felt irrelevant, yet much of it had passed. She had been in the ICU for over a month now. And now, that the fog in her mind was beginning to recede, she was beginning to think more deeply about what had happened to her. To process the trauma of her own journey with this illness. A trauma she had witnessed in her patients over and over in the past year. She had compartmentalised her thoughts and worries, not really considering how this may all be affecting Emma.

Her immediate worries had been about the new baby. These glimpses into the complexity of her situation scared her, and she would only be able to entertain such thoughts for a while before the fog would take hold again in her mind, blurring her concerns and numbing her pain. Elle walked past the glass door Grace called her in. "I'd like to write something. A letter to Emma. I don't want to scare her with my voice over a video call, but I want her to know I'm okay and how much I miss her. Can you get me some paper and a pen?"

Elle nodded with a smile, "I'll be right back." She brought Grace some printer paper and a pen. "That's a good idea, Grace. I know this must be so hard being apart from her. I can try to get the letter to Justin when he's next in the hospital to visit the baby."

Grace was thankful for this and began to write. The feeling of the pen in her hand felt foreign. Putting words to the page was harder than it had ever been. Her mind felt unfocused, yet she was determined to write.

\*\*\*

Lottie leaned over her elbows, as she wrapped both hands around the ceramic mug, feeling its warmth in her palms. "Do you think it would be okay if I tried to go see Grace too?" She said, having been quietly lost in thought.

Justin looked up at her from his phone. "It would have to be through Elle, since the hospital visitor policy is still so restrictive. I'm not sure if she will be able to let us both in."

A ray of hope lit Lottie's face. "Yeah. I understand. If it's at all possible, I would really like to see her. I need to show her something our dad brought by. Do you mind asking Elle?"

"Sure." Justin replied, not looking up. He texted Elle who replied shortly after, "Yes. you can both come at 12 PM today." Lottie was pleased.

After the interaction with her dad, Lottie felt a strong need to see Grace. Lottie had felt conflicted about how she had treated her father. After all that had happened. A small voice inside her made her unsure of whether turning him away was the right thing to do.

The plan would be to drop Emma off at daycare then head over. They piled into the car, turning the heat on blast. Justin took advantage of the asynchronous schedule and recorded his lessons ahead of time for his students to watch during the day, after they had completed their morning session with him, so he could be freed up in his schedule. His principle had supported the format, in this new virtual age that had shifted the primary responsibility onto children and families to access their virtual education. They dropped Emma at daycare and headed to the hospital. Pulling into the hospital parking lot, they managed to get a front row parking spot as a car was leaving. "It must be our lucky day," Lottie exclaimed.

"I'll need to go first to see the baby and then see what Elle says we should do to get you in through the check-in." The short line and screening table outside of the hospital entrance made it all the more guarded.

"I think I'll have a better chance of getting in if we say we are coming together to see the baby." Justin nodded, not really sure if there was any sure bet strategy. A sharp wind cycled through the parking lot, lifting leaves to dance in spirals above the asphalt, as they made their way walking quickly to stay warm. They soon stood in line. Lottie carried the box from her father in a large tote bag. They filed in line, agreeing to approach the scanners together and state they were each here to visit the baby. The masked screeners checked their temperatures by scanning their foreheads with a thermometer. The green lights flashed and they were directed to the check-in desk by a large sign telling visitors to have their ID available.

The check-in clerk paid little interest in who they were, entering both names into the system and directing them to the elevators beyond. "When you get up there, one of you can go in at a time." They felt the thrill of making it through as they headed down the corridor, past the gift shop to the elevators. The hospital felt cold and stark under unapologetically bright lights that stretched the length of the white walled corridors that split off in different directions. The double doors released them outside of the newborn intensive care unit, bringing a hush to their chatter as they exited the elevator, as they approached the security check-in desk.

To their quiet surprise, the security guard allowed them both in to see the baby at once. They put on their gowns, gloves and new masks under the supervision of the nurse who ushered them towards the isolet. Lottie looked around the room, wide-eyed. She had not spent much time in a hospital before and felt a little uneasy looking around at all the equipment. But there she was, a tiny baby swaddled, sleeping soundly in the isolet at the centre of the room.

"Here she is," Justin said, his eyes smiling.

"Oh Justin. Look at her." Lottie said with, as someone who's breath is taken away. "She's beautiful, Justin." They stood and stared in at her, watching her breathing and grimacing from time to time. Her eyebrows raised occasionally The nurse, who had been hovering by the monitor, asked Justin if he would like to hold her hand and adjusted her swaddle to release her small, skinny arm with fine little fingers out from within the fabric.

Justin reached his gloved hand through the isolet panes and gently took hold of his daughter's small hand. He felt her fragile, soft fingers grip his finger, and in that moment tears swelled in his eyes. He had never in his life been so taken with the fragility and perfection of life itself. "My little one. Daddy is here. It's going to be okay." He said, through tears. Lottie stood by, silently.

"She has been started on feeds from the bottle," the nurse said, coming by Justin. "If she keeps it up, it won't be long until she can go home. I understand her discharge is a little more complicated given her mother is still now also in the hospital. We will plan to give you all the training you need. As I presume, even if her mother is released she may need a great deal of help from you as she continues to recover. Have you decided on a name for your little girl?"

Justin had not considered a name. "I am waiting to speak to my wife. She was just extubated."

The nurse gave a respectful smile and nod as Justin let go of the baby's hand, and she closed the hatch on the isolet. Justin and Lottie remained still, watching the baby through the isolet, as though holding vigil, as the nurse headed back to the nurse's station. "Grace will be so happy to meet her," Lottie said quietly, still looking into the isolet.

"Her life will be complete with our two girls," Justin replied. Thinking about how Grace had looked when they brought her Emma immediately after delivery. She had glowed with a radiance that is only captured when the throes of determination and effort give way to the bliss of accomplishment against the odds, wrapped in overwhelming love.

"She is a great mother. This little one will be so fortunate to have her," Lottie said, feeling the sadness she felt about her own mother slip in. Her memories of her mother were fragmented. She remembered warm days, laughter and picnics behind her most imprinted memories. The ones in which her mother was being abused in the other room and when her mother seemed to give up by taking up a reclusive existence in her bedroom for months before she died. How Grace had stepped up to be that mother figure, and then her grandmother had done the same. Both in the shadow of their mother. One that had seemingly dissolved by forces that felt out of control, unstoppable. "Shall we try to see if we can go see Grace?" Lottie asked Justin, taking in the time. Their hour-long visit was nearly up.

"Sure," Justin said. He texted Elle in the hall once they left the unit.

Elle responded a few minutes later. "One of you can come now."

Lottie knew it had to be Justin. She would take her chances to be able to see her afterwards. This would be the first time he would see Grace since coming off the breathing tube. Justin gowned up again to go into her room. He stood outside, looking in at Grace. She was now sitting up, looking expectantly towards the door. He stood at the doorway with a small wave then slid the door behind him as he stepped in. Grace sat there, her face gaunt and her body beneath the covers looked slight. She was weak and the glimmer in her eyes that she had carried with her since the day he met her, had dulled.

"Justin," she said, her voice weak and raspy. Justin's pain and angst had been pent up waiting for this day in which he would see Grace awake again. He drew to her and sat by her, taking her hand in both of his, holding tightly. Tears rolled down his cheeks, as the relief of seeing her alive set in.

"You made it, Grace. You survived it," he said over and over, staring into her eyes.

Grace's eyes were moist with tears, yet she had little strength for crying. She held his hand, taking in the gravity of the pain he was clearly going through, still somewhat numb to her own. "How is Emma?"

"She's good, darling. She's good. She can't wait for you to come home." It had been so many weeks of uncertainty in which he had been separated from her. Unable to see and hear what she was going through or whether the doctors and nurses were making the right calls. "It is so good to see you, my darling." Justin said, tearfully, holding his forehead to his hands that clasped hers.

"Did you see the baby?" She said with a weak whisper.

"Yes. Oh Grace. She's beautiful."

More tears began to stream down Grace's cheeks at the thought of her little one, whose existence was somehow made real through his account. None of the staff had given her any insight into how her baby was doing, as she resided in a different unit under the care of a different team. She was too tired to make much movement, yet deep feelings began to emerge. "I need to see her."

Justin had been given the update by the doctor that morning that this would be in the plan when Grace's medical stability improved. "I know. The doctors are concerned you aren't stable enough right now." Grace gave little protest knowing he was right, and not having enough energy to exert. Justin could feel Grace's disappointment. "I will video chat the next time I can go in there. Okay? Elle and I can coordinate, so you can see her."

Grace smiled at the thought. "That would make me so happy."

Justin remembered Lottie sitting outside. "Listen, I brought Lottie and I think Elle can bring her in. I'll have to step out, but would you like to see your sister?"

Grace's eyes lit up. "She's here?" she said in a mildly astonished tone. "Yes I do."

"Okay, my dear. I am so glad to see you are recovering. I will come back to visit tomorrow and will call you over video chat, when I am in the baby's room. Speaking of baby, what should we name her? The nurse was pressing me about it today."

"Phoebe," Grace responded quickly with no hesitation. "It means pure, radiant and bright. I think of her as the light at the end of this long tunnel I have been in."

Justin smiled. "That sounds like a good name to me." He kissed her hand and pressed it against his cheek, looking into her eyes intently. Behind them he hid the remorse he had for letting his eyes and his heart wander from her over the past months. When standing in something real, like his wife winning her battle with the Coronavirus, he realised he had been running on falsehoods. He had told himself lies about what he needed and where he should be. He felt ashamed. "Phoebe. That's a beautiful name. Okay I'll go and get Lottie," he said quietly.

Lottie, who had waited patiently outside the unit, felt a jolt of nervousness as Elle ushered her into the big ICU. It looked like the set of a TV show or the nightly news that spotlighted the plight of healthcare workers tirelessly contending with the pandemic. But this was all real. The reality of the still bodies she saw lying prone beyond the glass doorways scared her. The smell of the space, bodily fluids, barrier cream and hand sanitiser mixed in the chilled circulating air, turned her stomach. She began to look downwards as she walked. Afraid to take in the suffering all around.

"She's in there," Elle pointed through the doors and handed Lottie a gown. Elle looked through the glass, the bright lights behind her cast her darkened reflection in the foreground. Beyond, Grace lay. Eyes closed and breathing shallowly. *My God. What happened to her?* She was shocked by how gaunt Grace's face looked. As though all the life and exuberance had been drained out. Lottie had not imagined that Grace's physical condition would have deteriorated so greatly. She had imagined her preserved as she was, taking a break from the battle under sedation, to re-emerge, as healthy and full of life as she had been. She looked as though she had aged a decade.

"I brought something important to show her. Do you mind?"

Elle looked down at the box in Lottie's hands. "Sure." She opened the door for her and they entered quietly. Lottie, hesitant to disturb Grace's sleep, sat quietly in the chair beside her bed, while Elle worked around them. "Grace. Your sister Lottie is here," Elle announced after a few minutes. "She's been quite tired."

"I can imagine," Lottie said quietly. Still taking in the change she saw in her sister.

Elle elevated her head of bed. "She was awake for Justin," she explained to Lottie. "He must have tired you out, Grace," she said.

Lottie drew closer. "Grace. I brought you something I think you would like to see."

Grace opened her eyes drowsily. "Lottie," she said, smiling and loosely holding her gaze. "You're here."

"Yes. I'm here and I am so happy to see you."

"I never thought this would happen," Grace said slowly, conserving her energy.

"I know, Grace. I'm so sorry you've had to go through this." Lottie wished she could take Grace's pain from her. Seeing her big sister appear so small, frail, and vulnerable didn't make sense. Grace had been anything but, all this time. Nearly a year of working on the frontlines day in and out. She was a healthcare hero who had joined the effort to save others, no questions asked. Yet, had not been able to save herself from the disease. Grace woke up, alert enough to keep her attention on Lottie. "Grace. Dad came around the other day. He gave me this box." Lottie placed the worn shoebox on Grace's lap.

Grace recognised it instantly. "Is this...?"

"Yes." Lottie's eyes met Grace's. They remembered looking at the box on an upper shelf in the pantry and how much hope it had contained for them.

Grace opened it slowly. Inside, paper bills and coins shifted around. "This was all for Santa Monica," she said, rustling through the coins and paper bills

"Yes," Lottie said. "I want you to keep this with you, as a reminder that we still have a trip to Santa Monica to take, okay? When you're recovered, we will go and walk those crooked planks and feed day old sourdough to the seagulls that Mumma always promised we would. The memory of imagining cotton candy and a Ferris wheel of lights over the dark ocean on that pier at night took shape in Grace's mind."

"We still owe it to Mumma to take that trip," said Grace, smiling. "There's something under here." She had dug her fingers in, sifting through the slippery coins and flimsy bills to retrieve a piece of paper with their mother's handwriting on it. It was a letter. "Can you read it, Lottie?" Grace handed it to Lottie, too tired to read.

Lottie began.

*Dear Grace and Lottie,*

*By the time you read this, I will be gone. There will be little to say about how I left you, and I know that it has already been a long time since I was truly able to be the mother you have needed me to be. I don't recognise myself anymore and do not see any way back. But for all my shortcomings, I want you to know that being your mother has been the greatest honour of my life.*

*Remember me with the grace and courage with which you will live your lives. The courage to go on that I did not possess. I hope you will always have Santa Monica.*

*Love always. Your mumma,*
*Barbara*

Lottie could not hold back her tears as she closed in reading the letter aloud. Grace too, overcome by her emotions. They had not heard their mother's voice for decades and to read her words and see the still glossy ink of her penmanship stretching across the page brought them back to the encouraging and wise things she would say to them. The comfort of her voice they deeply missed, and wished to hear so often.

"I am sorry, Lottie," Grace said through tears. "I am so sorry I couldn't save her." Grace's tears tumbled down her cheeks now. Her guilt poured from her with a furry that couldn't be contained any longer. "I am so sorry, Lottie. I couldn't save her. I tried. I didn't know how." Grace's breath was halting, as she spoke in spurts above her gasps anchored in angst.

Lottie reached over the hospital bed and drew Grace towards her, holding Grace's head in her arms. Lottie breathed in Grace's hair, whispering calmly with a steadiness she had learned from Grace as a child. "It is not your fault, Grace," Lottie whispered over and over. "There is nothing we could do."

Grace wept in the pause of Lottie's embrace for a long time. Their closeness brought back the familiarity of the many nights they had huddled together at the floor of the pantry, waiting for the commotion in the next room to fall silent. Grace had carried for many years the sense of responsibility for her mother's death. Believing she had not done enough. She had gone to her room day after day to bring her food, but never thought to remove the pills in the cabinet or beside her bed, or let anyone know what was going on. She had followed along, in a sort of tacit compliance with the steady march down the road her mother had taken to the end.

"We were just children. You cannot blame yourself," Lottie said, trying to reason with the grave sense of responsibility Grace bore in her eyes, as she looked pensively towards the floor. "It was her choice to leave in the end," she sat quietly, holding Grace's head as they both now dwelt in their loss, and for all that had transpired.

***

A few days passed and Grace's blood pressure continued to dip when she stood up. She worked in therapy. Standing with a gait belt wrapped around her, to steady her if she fell, as the physical therapist helped her to work to regain her balance. As she stood up from the edge of the bed, she felt a little dizzy. Weeks lying in bed, with the weight of gravity off her legs and feet, she felt unsure of where her feet would land. As she gripped the sheets, pressing down onto the cold slick floor with her feet covered in socks with grippy soles, she felt the discomfort of the challenge. The unnerving ritual of pressing down and pushing forward as the physical therapist encouraged her to come to her feet, scared her every time. And with every successful rise to her feet, standing on solid ground, she felt more confident, little by little. Grace thought of Emma, and Phoebe now. Lying in her bed, wishing she could be home with them. Elle came in with her phone. Justin had called over video from the newborn intensive care unit. He peered into the small screen to make sure Grace was watching before guiding her view towards the isolet. Not being able to leave the ICU had gnawed at Grace, as days had pressed on without being able to see her new baby daughter Today was the next best thing. There she was. Phoebe. The precious life, making its way through despite all the madness of the world around. Perfect and fragile she lay on her side, sleeping to the hush of oxygen through a cannula. Too drowsy to protest or quarrel over all the lines she had attached to her at this moment.

"There's our girl," Justin said, beaming with fatherly pride. "Grace, she is the most beautiful little thing. I can't wait until we can all be together."

Grace smiled, quietly beholding her little one. Her eyes traced the contours of her small features, for which she sought to engrain in her memory. "Can I talk to her? I'm not sure if she can hear me." Justin nodded, bringing the phone closer to her head. "Phoebe…Mummy is here. I want you to know that I love you so much my darling. I'm coming to get you soon. We made it." Her voice cracked with the emotion of the victory and her despair worn in through the distance she felt from her children. It was almost too much to bear.

The strain caused her to motion to Elle that she was ready to cease the video chat soon after. "Justin, I need to go. Thank you for showing her to me. I miss you too."

Justin swung the camera around to capture his face, as he walked towards the door. "I miss you so much, Grace. Emma is asking about you every day."

Afterwards, Grace placed her hands over her face. The warm pads of her fingers, soothing her eyes that felt dry and sore in the bright lights in the ICU. *Do you think I'll make it home soon Elle?* She said quietly. Elle never welcomed such questions from her patients, who's presence in the ICU was predicated on the fact that their health was tenuous. She met Grace's question with her hope. "Yes. I'm hopeful you will soon. Your vitals and labs are looking stronger each day."

Time had passed slowly in the ICU. Marked by the change of shifts and repetitive motion of clattering food trays and swift lab draws, and vital checks. Grace, was moved and prodded regularly as she lay in her bed. Through the haze of each day, Grace dozed for much of it. The doctors rounded and stood at her door, looking in, often with perplexed looks as they read the monitors and cast exchanges in a murmur beyond her reach. Nights became day which then seamlessly became night.

Emma's face beamed through the small screen. "Mummy!" she exclaimed as her bright eyes and smiling face came into focus.

"Emma!" Grace smiled tenderly as she admired Emma through the screen.

"When are you coming home Mummy?" was Emma's first question.

"I don't know, Em. It will be soon."

"Okay Mummy," she said, as her tone wilted.

"What are you doing today, Emma?" Grace changed the subject.

Emma's eyes brightened. "I go'ed to the park." She smiled. "Daddy pushed me big on the swing!"

"Up in the sky so high?" Grace asked. Grace could imagine her little girl, flinging her feet out and holding onto the swing's chains as she mimicked the soaring of birds. All of a sudden, Grace started to feel nauseous. "Emma. Can you give a big hug to Daddy and Auntie Lottie for me?"

Emma smiled at the thought. "Yes Mummy."

"I have to go now, okay?" She felt too unwell to continue with the conversation, "I love you, sweetheart." She had begun to feel herself perspire a little—the warping feeling of nausea took hold of her. It felt as though it radiated from her throat. She wanted to vomit but couldn't as she heaved. Elle quickly grabbed an emesis bag and placed it under her chin. Grace continued to heave, but very little came up. Only the slight taste of acidity arose, as she spat out clear frothy saliva.

"I feel cold, Elle." Grace's face had become sheet white. Her breathing had become heavy. "I-I can't breathe" A look of shock on Grace's face shocked Elle into action. "What's happening?" In a matter of moments Grace's oxygen and heart rate were actively plummeting on the monitor and her face drew blank, eyes and head rolled back.

"Grace! N-no, no, no!" Elle lunged to hit the code blue behind her bed. "Stay with me!" She cried with desperation. She banged on her shoulders with her hands and dropped the bed into position before she began the delivery of compressions with all her might on Grace's chest. "You can't do this," she said, as tears and perspiration mixed, stinging in the corners of her eyes. "Not now. Stay, Grace. Emma and Phoebe need you!" She spoke as if to command Grace back as she worked hard to get her heart pumping again.

The grit of the task was nothing in comparison to the level of adrenaline Elle felt, as she pushed hard to try to resuscitate Grace. She didn't notice the team assembled, as she cried and pleaded with Grace to respond. In sudden fury, she was gone. Her mind felt cloudy, and all she could sense was her breath and her throbbing hands that had failed her, that had failed Grace. All of the oxygen in the room seemed to disappear. As she stood there, by Grace's bed, she was paralyzed by complete disbelief with sweat and tears pouring down beneath the seal of her mask. Thoughts began to stream in her mind, cutting through the dense fog that was accumulating. *She's gone. This can't be happening. This isn't how this was supposed to end.* Elle eventually stepped back, collapsing against the wall as she looked upon her friend, her colleague, a mother and a wife, now dead, despite everything they had brought her through with the disease, it still had the final say.

The physician pronounced Grace to have expired at 3:03PM. Other nurses came to turn off the monitor, disconnect her lines and draw a sheet over her body that lay still under the bright lights. Instantaneously, the unit was made hollow by sombre repose that comes after desperate commotion. Everyone in that place who had worked the months and years with Grace in the trenches, felt the aching sorrow of the loss. Her death was palpable in the halls and inlets nurses retreated so their patients would not see them crying.

Elle knelt in the corner of the hall outside her room, overcome. It was nearly an hour before a social worker was sent to help her to a quiet waiting room. Elle sat silently, still perspiring, and feeling lightheaded with grief. She felt as though every fibre in her body was going haywire, and the excess energy had nowhere to go. She felt the dissonance of the denial that her mind was attempting to grasp onto as it sought to reject the reality of what had just happened. She pictured Grace alive moments before, persevering and holding her there in her mind, as if it would preserve her.

*What did I miss?* She asked herself, over and over, as she searched her memory for any indications prior to Grace's swift decline that would have been opportunities to change the course of what happened. Yet her mind was dulled, held hostage by shock. She could hear her heartbeat in her ears. Numbness coated her arms and legs as she sat trying to come to terms with what was happening. As the cold wind blew brittle leaves that rattled down the street, Justin sat on the front steps of their house. "Hi Justin. This is Dr Crew, Grace's physician here in the hospital." Justin braced himself for the update as he always did with bated breath and bundled nerves. "There is no easy way to say this. We lost Grace about an hour ago." The words hung heavy in the cold air as Justin tried to make sense of a sentence that his mind could not accept. The line fell silent as he sat with Dr Crew's news, feeling as though he was falling.

Justin felt an immediate loss of control in his body, almost dropping the phone. "What do you mean?" He managed to say, his voice quivering, hoping he had interpreted the doctor incorrectly.

"What I mean to say is that your wife unfortunately passed away about an hour ago. Her body just gave up, Justin, and we could not resuscitate her despite all our efforts."

Justin was overcome with the onset of grief that slammed into him, leaving him weak and unable to catch his breath. "What do you mean? She was getting better." His voice cracked. "She just spoke to our daughter about coming home. I'm sorry, doctor. I don't understand." His mind wanted to reject the facts as he paced his driveway, trying to grasp any redemptive piece of information that may have passed through the phone.

The doctor described the turn of events in a sober tone, pausing for Justin to remark. Justin could not find his voice. As the doctor's explanation drew to a close, he expressed his condolences. "I am very sorry, Justin. We all loved your wife. She was a truly talented and wonderful nurse. I know she loved you and Emma more than anything in this world."

Justin's heart broke as he suddenly pictured her smiling face, dressed in her black scrubs, headed to work, kissing Emma, and grabbing her lunch as she went. *This could not be happening.* What Dr Crew was saying felt unconscionable, like a misfitting jigsaw piece being jammed into articulation with the receiving edges of a puzzle. *This is not how this was supposed to go.* "Listen, I will have some of our team members contact you soon to arrange the resources you will need moving forward." He paused. "Again Justin, I am very sorry for your loss."

Justin murmured gratitude for the call as he hung up the phone. He could see his breath wafting into the cold air, but could not feel his hands or his feet. *Moving forward?* He could not see a single way to move forward from this moment. His feet planted firmly on his driveway and his will paralysed by the grip of despair that was now tearing through him, unchecked, and unremorseful in its destructive pursuit. He stood, unable to move, looking into the street as cars traipsed by, eclipsing the wintery daylight. A dog walker passed by with a jogging dog pausing to investigate his leg, before being gently pulled by his owner to press on. The world around, continuing on its usual schedule.

Justin felt queasy. *What will I do without you Grace?* He felt sick and let the sudden nausea give way to vomiting remnants of his breakfast into a nearby bush lining the driveway. He knelt in silence, feeling the acidic burn of his stomach contents coating his throat. He had nothing left to vomit. Yet his queasiness persisted. He could not know whether to commit to a posture of stoicism or unravel in a pool of tears. Neither mattered, he figured now, as the fact remained *she was gone.* There was nothing anyone could do about it now.

His mind turned to the house. Inside, Lottie would be playing with Emma. Another layer of angst drew upon him as he thought about what he would say to them when he returned. He decided to wait outside a little longer. The shock was like a thick film coating his skin that he was unable to shake. *There will be no going back from the moment they hear this news.* Standing there in his driveway meant that the dreadful news somehow was not fully made real if no one knew. The shock turned his stomach violently, causing him to bend over. His heart ached for Emma. *Her mother is gone.* He squatted, putting his head between his hands and lowering it between his knees. Being low to the ground helped him breathe and feel less lightheaded. *Breathe Justin.*

He closed his eyes and pictured the sea behind him, as he faced the shore at Montara beach with rambling waves breaking upon his back, the force of water pummelling him. The sea would crash to the shore around him and reach as far as it could, spreading across the sand, grabbing anything it could to take back with it. *Grace has been taken.* He felt akin to the impermanence of the shoreline, battered and stolen from by a greater force. There he was, carrying the worst news of his life and grappling with it.

His heart was breaking not only for what was happening, but for what had happened. What he had not been able to tell his wife. What he had done. He never thought that he would be robbed of the time it would take to make amends. Yet in the stark, clear grey day, hearing the news from the doctor, it was abundantly clear to him that he had miscalculated fate. He had taken for granted the gift of time he had been given, just as he did many things in his life. The cold, bone chilling reality hit him. *I am too late.*

***

The quiet of the night surrounded, as windows in the neighbourhood glowed, with the flicker of dinner time and small stoked fireplaces. The lights were dim to his thoughts, as early evening gave way to a deeply dark and cold night. Justin paced in the front room, unsure of how he would carry out the responsibility of sharing this news. His grief was cavernous. Each thought about Grace echoed and amplified in his mind with seemingly nowhere to escape. He had not had the nerve to tell Emma, and planned to wait until she was asleep to let Lottie know.

He heard Emma's door creak, as Lottie emerged on the landing. She had put Emma to bed in his absence. She came down the stairs, seeing his face, pale and motionless. "What's wrong, Justin? Is it Grace?" she spoke directly in a hushed voice. Her intuition told her so, as she took in Justin's tall stature that looked in this moment fragile enough to blow away in the wind. He nodded, breaking into unabated sobs. Lottie drew to him to hug him. "Tell me," she whispered, holding his head bowed, as she would comfort a child.

"She's gone, Lottie. She died today." His words gave way to more tears.

Lottie could not believe what she was hearing. "No Justin, there must be some mistake. How do you know? She was doing so well." Lottie's brief denial gave way to deep sorrow as the news claimed her. She could not escape it. It stuck to her. Time and everything in the shadowy room in which they stood appeared changed. Now faded into an abstract background, flimsy and dulled. The rigorous force of heartache held its grip on them as they stood together, tethered by the agony of incompletion. Nothing made sense. The rise of their emotions fell after a time, and they pulled away stumbling to the comfort of each end of the sofa.

There they sat. Both exhausted by grief. Unable to speak. Though Lottie had many questions about the sequence of events that had taken place, she thought it better to wait. The moon had reached through the front window and cast silver rims on the furniture with a sombre blue hue throughout the room. Her eyes traced the windowsill, looking out into the window. Remembering how she had helped Grace hang those sheer curtains and had sat with her on this sofa drying her tears and listening to her complain about work over a glass of wine. Nothing now looked the same. It was distorted by astonishment in what had happened, what had been lost. They remained stationary on each end of the sofa till sunrise, and had passed through the night vacillating from deep sleep to agitated wakefulness under the murky grip of their newfound sorrow.

The pale morning shrouded in fog slowly lit the room. In the last couple hours, they had both fallen into deep sleep. That which is forced upon those who have nothing left in them. Lottie woke first, hearing Emma upstairs, grumbling as she woke, calling out for Grace as she always did, and moving around in her bed. For the first moments, Lottie was disoriented, expecting to hear Grace answer Emma. But soon reality descended upon her, pushing on her shoulders first, forcing her to lay back against the hard armrest, uninspired to get up. *I miss you Grace.* Her thoughts of her sister, vivid memories and bright lights drifted past her mind's eye as she stared blankly into space. *You were taken too soon.*

Tears quietly rolled down Lottie's cheeks as she thought about their childhood. About walks to Todos Santos Square, holding each other closely on their pantry floor, playing make believe outside for hours in the hot Concord sun as Mumma cooked in the kitchen. Grace's childhood had been Lottie's childhood. Grace had been the reliable one who had watched over her as they crossed from their past life before their mother died, and into their later childhood life when they had gone to live with their grandparents.

She was a comfort and a relic from her earliest memories of Mumma, when she had been vivacious, caring, accessible, and enraptured with the joys of having her children. Their memories shared together had kept Mumma alive in that way. *Now, there is no one else to remember.*

Lottie pulled herself up off the couch eventually and staggered up the stairway to Emma's room. She stood in the doorway, smiling. "Auntie Lottie. I want Mummy," she said with mild protest to her arrival.

"I know, sweetheart." Lottie did not know what to say. Justin would need to be the one to break the news to Emma. Lottie would till then maintain the limbo of speaking in indefinites when Emma would ask about Grace.

"Where's Daddy?"

Relieved to have Justin to offer, Lottie replied, "He's downstairs sleeping on the couch."

"On the couch? We don't sleep on the couch." She laughed at the thought. "We sleep in bed."

"You're right, Emma." Lottie laughed too. It felt strange to laugh. Letting any sign of joy break through the cracks of a veneer that had calcified around her overnight. It was as though the weak laughter that awkwardly jolted and tumbled out of her was tethered by melancholy and perhaps would never soar again. Deep and gnawing sadness over her sister's death had moved into her being and would likely take up residence long term. She felt changed with little closure about how Grace had died, and still with the persistence of uncertainty for what would happen in the days, weeks, even hours to come.

She sat with a distracted line of thought as Emma kept trying to draw her into the immediate moment. Talks about her tea party that she was assembling on the bedroom floor with her invitation to sit and eat. Lottie wanted to curl up into a ball on that floor. Feel it press against the length of her body. There she would stay, immovable and impermeable. Instead, she attempted to react with marvel as Emma poured her a cup of 'strawberry tea', passing her a saucer and teacup. "Would you like some cake?"

Lottie played along mindlessly, "What cake do you have?"

"Chocolate." Her mind compartmentalised from the immediate demands of Emma's engagement and conversation to her inner thoughts, processing her inner turmoil. Loud squeals of delight that burst out of Emma's mouth caused Lottie to jump. The stimulation would usually be pleasant, but in this moment, in her state, she couldn't bear it much longer. It was agony to feel so sad while trying to play along with the joy of a child.

"Emma darling. Let's go downstairs and make breakfast. See if your daddy is ready to wake up." Lottie felt relief when Emma obliged easily. Movement helped soothe Lottie's frayed nerves. Coming down the stairs, Emma spotted Justin and quickened her steps. "Be careful on the stairs," Lottie said, taking one of her hands to slow her.

Once at the bottom, Emma ran and leaped onto Justin's sleeping body. "Daddy! Wake up! It's morning!" She spoke loudly and boisterously without the impedance to boldness that the measure of fear or sorrow brings. Justin stirred and turned away, continuing in his pursuance of sleep, despite Emma. "Daddy! Please wake up." He didn't stir any further. "Let's go to the kitchen, Em," Lottie offered, wishing she had the resolve and luxury to sleep as Justin seemed to. She figured her thoughts had become too agitated now to be able to fall into any sort of peaceful sleep for the rest of the day, even if she didn't have Emma to look after.

The medical social worker was the one to meet Justin at the door to the hospital. He stood in the lobby, looking around, remembering how he would come to the hospital to pick Grace up when she had started working at the hospital. She had taken a PM shift, letting her out in the middle of the night and he hadn't wanted her to leave work alone. He would hand her a warm tea and escort her to the parking garage, where they would drive home in the first months before she was able to transfer to a day shift position.

He imagined how she had walked through the foyer. Cup in hand, smiling at him through tired yet relieved eyes. He held back tears by biting his tongue as the medical social worker, Brenda, approached him. *Those same tired eyes.* Her greeting was imbued with the caution of one approaching someone who has suffered great loss—bracing for how they may react. Justin took a calm approach, although he felt like he was combusting inside. He made sure to look her square in the eyes when she spoke and smile as though interested in her small talk that had commenced once she had become confident that he was not going to fall apart.

She ushered him into one of the nearby small conference rooms used to consult families, in times like these. There were two chairs placed on either end of the room to allow for social distancing. Listening to her and looking around was like moving in slow motion. *This can't be happening.* Justin was told he couldn't see Grace's body as there were strict rules and she was a COVID patient. He felt at ease with not having the option, as he wanted to remember her as she had been. Not as another body in the morgue that was a casualty of the pandemic.

He signed the paperwork, not noticing much other than his pen dragging on the paper as he went. Brenda spoke slowly, pointing out the highlights of what he signed. The body would be sent to a local morgue he had driven past many times. He shuddered at the thought of becoming its patron. *We are too young for this.* His heart dipped, as it had been all of a sudden intermittently throughout the day. When the numbness that enshrouded him would clear for a moment and he was pierced by the gravity of what had occurred and what was happening. "I'm sorry. I can't really breathe right now with this mask," Justin interrupted. "I need to get outside for some air." He hastily exited the small room, leaving Brenda, understanding and patient while sitting by. He strode through the lobby, bypassing nurses chatting as their day shift was ending. He burst through the double doors, as though crossing a finish line and tore off the mask. He heaved in deep breaths trying to slow his rate. His heart was pounding. The tears he had been able to conceal by inflicting pain on his tongue, poured from his eyes as he bent over along a retaining wall, unable to stand. *Grace, I need you.* He was unable to go back inside and Brenda had assumed as such soon, and headed out after him through the double doors.

Seeing how distraught he had become, she stood quietly for a while, her large compassionate eyes fixed on him, waiting for him to gather himself. That time came eventually. "I'm so sorry, Brenda. I'm not sure what came over me. I'm just so sad. I-I can't believe this is really happening."

"It's okay, Justin. No need to apologise. It's expected that you are going to grieve. With sudden loss, many loved ones say they feel like they can't get hold of their emotions from one minute to the next. This is completely normal." Justin held on to the term normal as a source of lukewarm comfort. Before all this, Justin hadn't been nearly so fragile. The waves of emotion that now consumed him in his grief surprised him. "There are going to be many bumps in the road,

Justin. I happened to know Grace too. She was a bright light that will be sorely missed here."

Brenda paused, struck by her own emotion but quickly able to regain her composure. "I have some resources here, and some support groups you may be interested in. Feel free to look them over when you are ready."

Justin nodded, taking the stack of loosely bound papers into his hands. The afternoon's chill surged as a gust of wind that pushed its way through the courtyard where they stood, riling up stray trash and dry leaves as it went. "I'll reach out in a couple days to see how you're doing." She handed him her card before she turned and left to attend to her next case.

Justin sat on the retaining wall, preparing himself to get up and walk to the car. *One step in front of the other.* He told himself, now queasy. He decided against going up to the NICU to see the baby, as it would only remind him further of how Grace was now gone. He needed to get away from the hospital. He wanted to drive to the ocean, dive head first into the waves and bob ahead of the white caps waiting for a wave to ride. The rocking ocean would soothe him.

He drove home on autopilot, stopping at the lights in a daze. Partial thoughts concerning what to do next, formed and dissipated in his mind. All he could picture was Grace, sitting in the hospital bed. Him holding her hands for the last time, and not knowing it. He did not know how he would be able to tell Emma. The thought frightened him. He could hardly manage the grief he held, filling yet depleting him. How could he ever have enough capacity to hold Emma's too?

That night he sat around the table with Lottie and Emma, the candlelight flickered as the flame on the dining table busily consumed the wick. Dinner was a nice time at the end of the day. It always had been with Grace. Justin spoke in abstractions to update Lottie on his time with the medical social worker and the forms he had to sign, so Emma wouldn't notice as she chomped on her buttered noodles. They both sat quietly, pushing their forks around on their plates. Chewing slowly at their thoughts of the finality of the situation. There was no rewind button to be pushed, no way back to before she died. No way back to any opportunity to change what happened.

Lottie had offered to stay for a couple weeks to help Justin with Emma and soon the baby was expected to be discharged from the hospital in about a week' time which would bring a whole host of adjustments. Emma had continued to go to daycare during Grace's hospitalisation and still now.

Lottie worked remotely so set up in the living room with her laptop for most of the day while she was there and would pick up Emma early most days so they could go to the park. Lottie was happy enough to stay. They had entered into their own isolation bubble. She knew she was a help to Justin who looked as if he had depended greatly on Grace for cues to care for Emma. She preferred the hustle and bustle of the evenings attending to Emma and the routine. Thinking of returning now to her quiet, well-manicured apartment, in San Jose, made her a little nervous. She would have to face her grief alone there. She knew that being of help to Justin at this time was what Grace would have wanted her to do. *It's what Grace would do.*

After dinner, and kitchen clean-up, Justin played at a tea party on the floor with Emma. Lottie looked on with a smile. Watching the curves in Emma's mouth as she smiled and smirked at her father's humorous advances in the game. She could not remember a single time her father would have played with her like that. Nor could she remember any humour about him. He had been distant at the best of times. Yet, watching the two play, Lottie began to feel a disquieting pull to reach out to him. Despite all her misgivings, she knew he had the right to know Grace had passed away.

Saturday morning, Lottie rose early and headed out leaving a note for Justin and Emma who were still sleeping soundly. She drove through the Caldecott tunnel, deep into the hill, away from the fog that had been brushed up against it. He still lived in Concord, in their old house. It was Saturday. He would be home, watching sports on TV, and eating chex mix. She imagined him there now, just as she had remembered him in their home as a child. The maple trees that bent graciously around on the wide road were now brittle with age, working at their duty of forming new buds so they would be dressed in the spring. Their branches were bare now, rattling in the winter wind that accelerated in spurts, the sky overcast above.

Lottie pulled up the gravel driveway. Pausing as she turned off the engine. *Perhaps I can just leave him a note.* She pushed through her discomfort, opening the car door, bracing for the harsh crack of cold metal as it closed behind her. She walked up to the door, remembering listening for her father's shoes shuffling along the fine rocks when he returned home, then hiding. The door had been repainted, a cheery red. Something different about the house all around struck her. Flowerboxes lined the front.

273

"Hon, someone's at the door." A woman's voice called out over the undulating sportscast that could be heard through the open kitchen window.

"See who it is," was the reply. The door opened wide, as a middle-aged woman, smoothed her apron. She was covered in flour. "Lottie," she said, attempting to mask her surprise. "I'm Allison, your dad's wife."

Lottie stood on the step unsure of how to respond. She hadn't calculated any other variables than the news she had come to deliver, it was too much to process, let alone form a reaction to. "Oh." she managed to speak. "I'm happy to meet you. I'm sorry. I had no idea that Dad had remarried." The awkwardness of their meeting like this washed over both their faces.

"Well, I suppose there is much to catch up on." She welcomed Lottie into the kitchen, taking her coat. "Can I make you some coffee or tea?"

Lottie sat at the same table she had sat at as a child. It was surreal to her now to be sitting at it, as a grown adult. She pictured her homework in front of her. A glass of milk, the peanut butter and jelly sandwich Grace had fixed. "Um, water is fine," Lottie said, turning to look towards the living room where she could hear her father still seated.

"The quarter is nearly over. I'm sure your father will be along as soon as it goes to the commercial break." Allison smiled invitingly. Her smile appeared a little desperate to hold things together in the moment, where words could not bridge the divide between what needed to be explained, and what had never been said. When Lottie sat silently, not assisting with any efforts to alleviate the awkwardness of their meeting, Allison excused herself to the other room. She could hear Allison whispering to her father that he needed to come into the kitchen immediately.

He surprisingly took direction and emerged through the arched entrance, looking pleasant and welcoming. "Lottie. It's so nice to see you. I didn't hear you come in."

*That was a lie.* Lottie gave an obligatory smile. "Nice to see you too."

"You met Allison. She's my, er…my wife actually. I know we have a lot to catch up on." He glanced between them sheepishly.

"Dad. I've come with some bad news."

His face changed in response to the seriousness in her voice. "Oh."

"It's Grace."

"Yes?"

"Well, Dad, she died a few days ago in the hospital."

A stony silence filled the warm kitchen. He looked away, perplexed by the news, mulling it over, eventually to return with a question. "Did they say what happened to her?"

"Not sure really. All we know is they tried to resuscitate her and it didn't work."

"How is the baby?"

"She's okay. She's in the NICU for another week before we bring her home. I'm staying at Grace's house to help Justin and Emma."

Her father pinched the bridge of his nose with his fingers, closing his eyes and scrunching his face. "I think I need to sit down." His face was pale as he stared at the floor beyond Lottie.

She felt a fullness form in her throat. Trying to swallow it down was impossible. He began to cry. It was unexpected in Lottie's estimation of how he might react to the news. Allison drew to him and patted him on his back. She had not been so affected, not knowing Grace, but clearly concerned for her husband. Lottie shifted in her seat, her own vulnerability still folded and hidden beneath the layers of contempt she held for her father. She watched him, unable to summon up the empathy and compassion she knew to be fitting of the situation. She was hurting too. She had nothing left in her for others. After what seemed like a long while, Lottie stood and pardoned herself. "I better be going. I just wanted to make sure you heard the news from me." Her father looked up at her with an expression of gratitude as he nodded quietly. He followed her to the door, wiping his eyes with a handkerchief and straitening his belt. "Thank you for coming to let me know in person. You have no idea what it means to me. I want you to know that I heard everything you said to me the other day and I respect that. I just want you to know that despite that, I am still here for you if you ever change your mind. We are all capable of change," he said with a weak smile before giving her a light embrace at the door. It felt forced to hug him back.

Lottie walked away from the house, unable to fully process or imagine what his story had been since she had been a part of it. Her pain felt as though it crawled over her skin, as she walked. She traced over where he had held her in a hug. She remembered what his hands had done to her mother and a nervous feeling lifted in her stomach. She looked over at the old oaks and remembered the tree swing that used to hang there. Grace would lift her up when she was too small to climb and push her high and fast. Grace had always been there. Through the hard years after Mumma, college, new jobs, new apartments, boyfriends. She was a constant for all of it.

*What now?* Lottie did not like the feeling of being in a world where her big sister was no longer there to guide the way. It felt senseless to think that she would no longer be there to pick up the phone or check in on her. This realisation was jagged and sharp, raw and bottomless. Grace had been so much to all of them. Having her inextricably linked to her own childhood made her absence feel deeply close to her core, touching the bottom of the ocean of despair that now engulfed her. She was surprised by the terse intrusive thoughts of anger she felt about Grace that now emerged in her mind. She quickly strode to the car and fumbled with the keys before she dove in, trying to get off the street as she cried tears she had not known she had left in her. Lottie slammed her fists on the steering wheel, pressing her head against it releasing a rageful scream, to no one and nowhere in particular. She needed to release the pent-up anger she was feeling. *God! Why did you let her die? Why did you both have to leave me?* Lottie thought about Mumma and Grace, now both gone. She wailed with warm angry tears pouring from her uncontrollably. Banging her fists over and over until they hurt. When her wailing diminished to a whimper, she curled up against the cold window. The cool glass pressed against her forehead and cheek felt calming. *This isn't fair.* She remained there, motionless, staring quietly out at the street. Her nose was running and a build-up of mucus ran down her throat. She had been so concerned with Justin and Emma that she had not been in touch with her own grief that was now bursting through her weakly sewn seams. *Nothing will ever be the same again.*

Lottie stayed away all day. She needed space to think and feel. She needed to be alone. Lottie turned on the ignition and drove to the Oakland Redwood Regional Park. It was a special place she had liked to go and think. Driving down into the messy woods, through to park near a clearing before heading along the trail to the grove. The air was cold, and filled her lungs like drinking water. As she passed through into the grove, the height of the redwoods opened up like a cathedral. She loved how, without fail, she felt transported away from it all whenever she was here.

In the filtered light beneath the canopy, she found the space where prayer lifted and stuck to the treetops, rivalling the concave ceilings in which Renaissance painters recreated the heavens. The stillness inspired silence. Only the stirring of small animals scurrying between landings could be heard. Lotti walked, looking up as the sunlight peaked through the amber trunks lining the hillside, fanning out into broad streams that made gold of the ferns and flanks of countless trees. A gully and stream to the right, trickled lightly, as not much water had come in a long while.

Lottie walked, padding along through soft forest flooring that absorbed her footing and grounded her. Fallen logs, moist with dew and covered in delicate moss were inhabited by thousands of ladybugs during the winter. This was the time of year where the trail here was made ruby. Red, shiny backs that waddled and bumped, sometimes inspired to take short flight, could be seen along the trail, coating logs and bramble at the base of ferns. Lottie sat in a clearing surrounded by the coastal redwood trees, giants frozen in space and time. She rested at a picnic table, and pulled out her journal. *What should I do next?* She wrote on a blank page. She stared at her words.

This was the first thing that came to mind when she put the pen to the paper. She curved her fingertips around the edges of the soft leather-bound journal, open and awaiting her reply. It was hard to find an answer now, without Grace to help her work it out. The path ahead seemed dim and foggy without Grace. She sat in silence, listening to the crack of a nearby tree, the flutter of wings transitioning to another branch and gentle tapping of a woodpecker above the ridge. *Live.* was the answer that she heard, echoing in her ears. She jumped a little. Not sure if it was her own subconscious that rendered the word like a whisper. She wrote it down. *What does it mean to live?* Was the next question she posed on the page. The blank space below stared back at her expectantly.

Lottie sat pensively. She thought about her mother and her sister and how they had daydreamed about the prospect of making it to Santa Monica. They had dreamed of escaping their life all those years ago. Mumma never made it. She and Grace never went. The idea at the time was palpable, imagined to be as good as real. Lottie thought about her memory of imagining what it would be like to ride the Ferris wheel way up high, arms spread out breathing in a sunset. Lottie closed her eyes. She imagined Grace sitting by her.

***

The doctor called to let Justin know that Phoebe was ready to come home. She had shown to be stable for days and gaining weight. She was a healthy and strong newborn that did not need an acute level of care. Justin took the call with trepidation. He had imagined that this day was coming, but had in many ways felt relieved that Phoebe remained in the hospital being cared for by the nursing staff around the clock. It had bought him time to deal with the shock of what had happened. To focus on getting through the days without the added stress that a new baby brings.

Justin admittedly knew that Grace had done all the work when Emma was first born. She had carried the load quietly and dutifully and he had stood by letting her do all the night feeds, diaper changes, walks, and baths. He had not felt he had a place in the process and as a result had not gained the experience he now wished he had. He didn't feel prepared. He would have to receive this fragile baby and nurture and care for her without her mother. It felt as though it may be impossible to do. He packed a diaper bag in preparation to head to the hospital the next day.

Folding her little clothes, he remembered how Grace had so carefully folded and put away Emma's clothing. *I wish you were here.* He thought quietly. The nursery was ready enough, and Justin pulled the baby items they had collected for Emma, out of the garage. He had bought some diapers and a new sheet for the crib. "Will Mummy come home with my sister?" Emma's naive questions pierced Justin's heart whenever she would inquire about her mother's whereabouts and schedule for return. He would exhale slowly before replying, so as not to let her detect the waver in his voice.

He realised he needed to tell Emma. It had been nearly a week. As time went on, the more strange it felt to have Emma anticipating her mother's return.

"Emma darling," Justin said, putting a hot chocolate in front of her as she sat at the table. "I need to talk to you about something." Emma looked up wide-eyed, as if expecting a good surprise. "It's about Mummy."

"When is Mummy coming back?"

Justin shuddered, his stomach lurched forward. "Mummy is not going to be able to come back, darling." The words felt like lead on his tongue and pierced like daggers in his stomach.

Emma sat, looking incredulous. "Why?"

Justin had not thought through how he would explain what happened, as much as he had committed to the plain notion that he needed Emma to know. He realised he was a little out of his depth at this point. "Mummy wanted to come back from the hospital because she loves us very much. But Mummy had to g to Heaven instead." He realised his diluted version must have sounded reductionist to even a three-year-old.

"What's Heaven, Daddy?"

"It's a place where we go when we die." He couldn't believe he was having this conversation, as it happened. It felt surreal, it felt too much.

Emma's lower lip quivered. "I don't want Mummy to die. She needs to come home."

"I know, sweetheart. I really wish she could, honey."

Emma cried in his arms, burying her face into his chest. There wasn't anything more to be said. Nothing could change the fact that Grace, his wife, her mother, was gone. He held his little girl in his arms rocking her, and with no certainty repeating, "It's okay. It's going to be okay" as his tears fell.

# Chapter 19
# Runaway Train

They drove up to the special parking spots right outside of the hospital that were reserved for parents bringing their newborns home. Justin bit the inner side of his cheek as he pulled up to a man wheeling a new mother in a wheelchair towards their car, the baby in a carrier on her lap. *That would have been us.* The thoughts of what could have been crowded his mind most days, in a haze that felt endless.

He unsecured the carrier and brought it through the automatic doors into the lobby. Up to the NICU, on his regularly trodden path, he now made his way for the last time. Everything felt as if it were moving in slow motion. He could hear his nerves echoing in his ears to the beat of his heart. The prospect of taking Phoebe home without Grace was something he had not had enough energy to entertain in great detail, as his grief as it were drew him into the past and gave him little view of the future.

He had been living day to day, trying to get by. Now, the adrenaline was clearing a little and the reality of what was happening was setting in, as he approached the security guard's desk to check in. He felt his palm sweating around the handle of the carrier. He was scared. He felt unprepared, unfit even to be bringing this baby home right now. Brenda, the social worker, had made a special point to connect with him during this transition. He read her face as concerned as she looked him over, as he approached the NICU doors. He hadn' bathed in days, nor shaved in weeks. He carried the beleaguered air of someone trapped in grief.

"Hi Justin. Before we go inside, I wanted to connect with you to see how you are doing." Justin realised that she had detected that he had not been coping very well and this was of some concern to her, given that he was coming to pick u the baby. "Some days are easier than others," he said reticently. "I have Lottie staying with us to help me with Emma," he added quickly, as reassurance.

A slight expression of relief passed over Brenda's face, behind her mask. Her eyes widened, "So do you feel ready to bring your daughter home?"

"As ready as I'll ever be," he lied. Not feeling like he could be vulnerable with her, standing in the hospital hall.

"We have temporary foster programs available for families who are facing challenging circumstances at the time when newborns are ready to leave the hospital. This may be something you would want to consider."

Justin paused, to make sure he was hearing correctly. "Are you kidding me? I've lost my wife, not my mind. You expect me to hand over our newborn baby to strangers?" He was raising his voice to the point that people walking by stared at the commotion.

"I'm sorry if this upset you. I was just wanting to make sure you are aware of the options you have. Your circumstances are very challenging right now, and no doubt what challenges you are facing emotionally and psychologically by the loss of your wife will be exacerbated by bringing a newborn home."

"I'm sorry, but what do you know about the challenges I am facing?" He felt his blood boiling, tipping him over into rage. "You walk around here telling people what their 'options' are. Like I'm supposed to pick an ice cream flavour. But all I can process right now is that my wife is dead. Grace died two floors above where we are standing nearly a week ago. She's gone Brenda. And now, I have two little girls who I have to raise on my own. What options do I really have?" Justin had become unhinged, standing in the hallway. The anger and grief had taken off like a runaway train. "You wanna talk to me about my options? What option do I have at this point but to scrape myself up off the ground, and drag myself through another day for our kids? I'm it, Brenda. I'm all they have."

He couldn't hold back his tears now. Gritty tears born of anger. He covered his eyes with his hand, turning away briefly. The injustice of his situation had grabbed hold of him, strangling him. "I know I'm the second option. What I could give for it to be Grace here with them and me six feet under. She should be here. Here with her daughters. Not me." His heart was racing, as he spoke, dulling his hearing. "I have no interest in farming out my daughter to a foster family right now. It would break my heart even more. You can take that option off the table. Am I clear?!" Yelling at Brenda gave Justin a strange and recently unfamiliar sense of control. It felt exhilarating to capture some power in the situation.

Brenda appeared unstifled by his display, as though she expected this from him. "Okay Justin. I understand that you're very upset about how I approached this. I respect your wishes, but it's my duty to make sure that the baby is discharged to a safe home environment." She read his body language, closed off, perturbed. "How about I check in with you in a few days to see how it's going? There are no big red flags here that would stop us from discharging Phoebe home with you, but just want to make sure you have access to the resources that can support you and your family in this difficult time."

Justin realised Brenda was just doing her job. He was a little annoyed with himself for taking such offence. He could see how he was losing control of his emotional responses under all the stress. "Thank you for your help, Brenda. I know you are just doing your job. I'm sorry I snapped."

Brenda's compassionate eyes fixed on his. She could see Justin was hurting under the duress of the situation with his children, weighed down by his lingering grief. Justin went into the room where Phoebe had been for weeks now. Her colouring was flush pink and she met up with the nurse who was dressing her in a newborn onesie Grace had picked out for her to go home in, the second week into her pregnancy. A shock of pride mixed with sorrow framed Justin as he stood beholding his little girl, getting ready with the nurse who attended to her with swift and capable hands, to load into the carrier, free of all the lines and tubes that had once sustained her. He smiled, as she yawned, bringing her hands up to her mouth and arching her neck and back to inhale deeply. She had Grace's nose and eyes. Justin grinned, under his paper mask. He felt excited to be able to hold Phoebe, and bring her home finally.

The nurse accompanied them out to the car. Carrying patient bags filled with diapers, wipes, formula and bottles. Justin locked the carrier handle into his bent arm and carried Phoebe through the hospital corridors making their way to the exit. The carrier was covered with a hospital issued swaddling blanket to block the light. Justin was comforted to be leaving with so many supplies. He had the basics of the nursery ready at home, but not much past what Grace was able to put together before she got sick. He hadn't thought of all the wipes and diaper he would need.

The nurse waved them off, as he leaned forward in his seat, twisting his torso to get a glimpse of the back of Phoebe's head bundled in a blue and pink stripe hat. She sat rear facing in her car seat, silent. He hopped out of the car to check to check one more time to make sure her belt was secured and that she was breathing. Standing by the door, he felt relief to see her little chest rising and falling. He felt himself hanging on that rhythm. Double checking that it was not abating in any way. He felt on edge with the weight of the precious cargo now in his care as he drove through the backstreets of Berkeley, too reluctant to take the shorter freeway route. *Grace, I wish you were here.*

***

Months passed and the pandemic wore on. Vaccinations became available and the promise of normalcy rested on the horizon with still the ominous news of new variants threatening all the progress made. Buds broke forth with light pink blooms on the cherry trees early. Little rain had come and the Northern California sun had once again tricked the blossoms to think it was spring early. It was now truly spring and the grasses on the hillsides encircling the bay were becoming golden. The days had slowly become longer and their life stretched from nights to days with the ease of summer to come. A knock came at the door. Justin answered it with Phoebe in his arms. It was Elle, she looked as if she was coming from a shift at the hospital in her purple scrubs. "Hey Justin."

"Come in." Elle looked around the open foyer. The house was the same as it had always been, but the light seemed to hit differently. "Can I get you something to drink?"

"Sure thanks." Elle was glad to have something to drink. Her shifts were regimented with breaks and wearing the PPE limited her ability to drink water readily. It had been about four hours since she'd had something to drink.

They sat at the counter in the kitchen. Elle remembered sitting at the island where Grace would serve her up with charcuterie and wine and they would laugh in hushed voices knowing the penalty would be that Emma would wake up and their fun would be halted. "I've been meaning to bring this to you for a while now." She put a folded piece of paper out in front of Justin. "It's a letter from Grace. To Emma and Phoebe." A pit in Justin's stomach rose as he looked at the paper, folded neatly. "She wanted to write it just before she…" A grave expression took over Elle's face, as she thought back to the helpless moments leading up to Grace's death.

*Dear Emma and Phoebe,*

*This year has been like no other. When the pandemic hit, I knew that being an ICU nurse would put me in the front lines. I spent many nights worrying about what this meant and had to come to terms with the risk I put myself and you in every day. I felt like I had no choice but to answer the call to help people affected by this disease. I have been there to witness so many people's suffering through this dreadful time. So much so that I didn't realise I would so easily become one of them.*

*Now, sitting here in this hospital bed, I don't recognise myself from before this ordeal. I am a shell of who I was. You may never know me again as who I was before this all began. I want you to know I am sorry that I let this happen. I am sorry that I couldn't keep us safe. I don't know where this path leads here, and I am trying very hard to see through the forest now. I want you to know you are the light on the other side of the dark woods and I will try my hardest to get back to you. I want you to know how deeply I love you and how I hope for a better world for you both. Know everything I do is for you.*

*Be brave, my darlings.*
*Your loving mother,*
*Grace.*

Tears blurred his vision as he read her poignant words. To him, it was if she knew that she wouldn't be coming back. He wept at the table with Elle sitting by quietly, rocking Phoebe. After a time, Justin wiped his tears with his sleeves. "I'm sorry, Elle. It's just been so hard without her. I never imagined this would happen to us." Elle sat with him, listening quietly. "I should have never taken her for granted, lied, and cheated on her. She didn't deserve that…and now she's…" As he said it, his guilt flooded to the foreground.

"I know, Justin," Elle said quietly. "You had your reasons for what you did as did I in my marriage. I'm sorry you weren't given the time to make things right. I guess what we can learn is that the reality is that time isn't promised to any of us." The impermanence hung in the air. "I just feel so angry with myself. What am I even doing? I am a single dad with two daughters and their mother is dead."

Elle saw the desperation in his eyes. "You're doing what you can."

This affirmation caused Justin to shift his weight. "I'm just not what these girls deserve. They deserve Grace." Elle took a deep breath. He felt an inclination to run away. The thought of dropping the kids off at Lottie's house and telling her that he would send money and visit on weekends had crossed his mind many times. The sleepless nights, the ear infections, the crying and the labours of living had worn him down greatly. He felt like he was stuck in a deeper rut than ever before and desperately wanted to escape.

Elle looked at him. Knowing his nature, because she knew her own. "I'm sure you've been thinking of what the alternatives could be. But maybe you should consider this challenge as your call to be brave. To be there for your girls and to lean into the difficulty of raising them without Grace."

He looked up with dubious eyes. "Honour Grace by not bailing on the lives she gave you." Her words sat him down right where he was. She had seen him for what he was. A man driven to seek fair weather in life. He was not good like Grace. He was cowardly and selfish at his core. And he knew it. He always had.

"I don't know if I can," he said timidly. He was struck by the thought of the numerous times he had bailed. The same patterns of escape inscribed on the epitaph of every challenging scenario he had faced. This would be another in the long line of discomforts that he would seek to escape. He looked at Elle and clenched his teeth. "I guess, I just don't know what it is to commit to something that is hard…"

"It means doing the one step in front of the other work." Justin contemplated it. "It's not going to be easy. But nothing worth anything ever is. When you think about how they deserve Grace, think about doing what Grace would have done."

Justin nodded, knowing he was betraying his nature to do so.

# Chapter 20
# Santa Monica

Lottie arrived at Santa Monica, after a long unplanned drive. She had been cleaning her closet in the morning, when she came across Mumma's old box of money she had left with Grace in the ICU. Justin had returned it to her, knowing it meant more to her than he, in the weeks after Grace passed. Tracing her fingers along the old world red and black font, "Santa Monica Pier", she thought of her mother and of Grace. Feeling suffocated by her grief and driven by formidable feelings that linger in the spaces of loss, she took the box and got in her car to drive down the coast with no real destination in mind at first. She sped past Pacifica and Half Moon Bay, then followed Hwy 1 along its sky-bound route overlooking the ocean. Before she knew it, she had made it to the Central Coast. She decided to keep going until she reached Santa Monica.

How she, Grace and Mumma had imagined coming to Santa Monica, together—an escape from the darkest of their days. It had felt tangible, tastable, touchable, attainable from a distance, as a small child listening to the promises of her mother describing how their trip would be. Arriving in the trendy Santa Monica District, and driving through the streets lined with large stores, felt different from how she imagined it. But as the sky opened up at the foot of Colorado Avenue, and the ocean lay out before her, she saw the pier. It jutted out with the whimsical old-world appeal that her mother had described. She smiled when she saw the Santa Monica sign mounted on the entrance archway. It felt almost like revisiting a childhood memory. But it had never been.

As she got out of her car, in the sandy lot to the side of the pier, she gazed up at the tall palms. *They are as tall as you said they were, Mumma.* Walking through the pier's entrance was like stepping into the hopes and dreams cast by Mumma and shared with Grace before they left. In being here, she felt connected to them again.

She carried the box, in a canvas bag slung over her shoulder. The metal coins slid and rattled around inside, but she didn't mind. The noise was overshadowed by the busyness all around. The sun floated over drifting clouds that cast billowy reflections on the calm Pacific. The gulls swirled above and dove sharply, gathering aggressively amidst fallen French fries and pieces of sourdough bread strewn on the long-weathered planks that made up the pier. The swell washed back and forth at the base of its legs—worn and soggy, encrusted with barnacles. Lottie walked, taking in all the sights and smells-cherishing the uncanny descriptions her mother had foretold of this place.

Santa Monica Pier was long and people filed past the lamp posts towards the outcropping of souvenir shop fronts, restaurants and cafes that leaned around the edges. Stopping to take pictures or gaze out at the salty vistas on either side. The air was lively and swirled all around. The yellow and red Ferris wheel buckets rotated with a predictable turning on the far end, with a roller coaster that boasted screams as it roared cantankerously along its rickety tracks with its trademark dips, twists and turns. Below the white hatched framing, Pacific Park nestled as clusters of concession stands and gaming booths with brightly coloured stuffed toys luring in lines of people to try their hand.

Lottie walked quietly along the pier. She felt its history under foot as the worn-down wood shifted and shook with each step, revealing the tide playing beneath through small gaps between planks. It had now been over a year since the pandemic began. Now with vaccines available, she noticed people wore masks variably while crowded in spaces with little regard for the lack of social distancing. She hadn't spent time amongst so many people in years. Her skin crawled a little, as she adjusted her mask, paying attention to any cough she heard in the crowd. Lottie thought about how the world was choosing to move on from 2020, and vaccinations had become the ticket to ride whether you chose to be vaccinated or not. The ticket to opening up society—the restaurants and entertainment now back in full swing. The carrying on of living full steam ahead was evident all around, and embraced by the masses jubilantly.

It was surreal to her to see how the world had reassembled itself. Picked itself up and put itself back together with the appearance of barely missing a beat. The reality was that COVID still circulated, with new strains evolving in South Africa and Europe. It seemed there really was no end in sight, but it seemed in spaces everywhere, the decision had been made to press on and reopen for the sake of recapturing social connections, freedom, and a sense of normalcy. *Perhaps there is wisdom to dancing in the flames,* Lottie thought, as she admired with a sense of irony as to how happy people seemed and how normal everything appeared.

It became evident to Lottie that perhaps she had been naive to have thought that society could suppress its way of life at length. Lottie had rested for months in the stasis of stringent COVID restrictions, not leaving her house, feeling a sense of cause within it. Adhering with the pandemic restrictions, in her mind, beyond promoting safety, had been tantamount to paying respect to those lost, those who had sacrificed—to Grace. The reopening of society was a signal that the world was moving on. Those who had been lost to the Coronavirus, would be left behind in the dark past, forgotten to a time of pause and limitation. Resuming life again was the choice made no matter what it had cost or would cost many more people.

She stopped to watch a street performer. A man dressed in a suit, painted in gold from head to toe. He stood on a plastic crate, still as can be, and only breaking his pose intermittently to steal a glance from a passer-by, or remove a flower from his pocket. *Life never stays still*, she thought as she watched for a time as the street performer morphed with charisma. Lottie's heart had been heavy in the many months since Grace's death. She had vacillated between anger at the patient Grace had caught COVID-19 from to Grace's PPE malfunctioning to the fact she had never dissuaded Grace from working in the ICU during the pandemic that claimed millions of lives. In her anger, her assumptions were that if only these things could have been different, Grace would be here. *If only.* Intermixed with her anger was a loneliness she had never experienced before.

Lottie had spent weeks and months finding herself falling apart daily, thinking of Grace. She steered away from spending much time with Emma, Phoebe and Justin, as Emma reminded her so greatly of Grace when they were children. She couldn't yet stand to see her, to remember. And so she sent little letters, toys and things in the mail to Emma and Phoebe instead of driving up to Berkeley to visit. She told herself it was better this way. It would be too hard to see them.

Grace had been her best friend, perhaps her only true friend. Lottie knew she herself retreated in the years after their mother died, fearful to take chances, to move forward with a life of her own, as though she somehow wasn't worthy of her own story. As a result, she spent her years focusing on her career and avoiding letting boyfriends and friends in for fear of being disappointed in their ability to hurt her, to abandon her. She was still defined by the story of the scared little girl huddled on the pantry floor. She walked to the end of the pier, past men fishing. She leaned out over the far end, gazing down to catch a glimpse of the pier's ruffly underskirts splashing playfully against her legs.

It had been March the previous year when Grace had told her about how the Coronavirus patients were coming to the hospitals in the Bay Area. She had been dubious, just as Californian's doubted consequential rain. "Grace, it's under control. It's going to be okay." She remembered saying with such certainty. The notion of anything being under control seemed laughable now. It did indeed rain, in the most unpredictable, uncontrollable ways—the Coronavirus soaked everything in sight, causing erosion in weak places, exposing the roots of large trees finding themselves clinging to the side of a ridge or falling. And as the rain continued over time, it rendered the landscape unrecognisable.

At this moment, thinking of the enormity of the past year and a half, she shed some tears that fell on the railing as she looked out to the wide blue ocean. *There is no way to control how life unfolds. I suppose the only choice is to live it,* she thought. She took the box out of her bag and rested it on the railing. Opening it, she looked at the money and the picture of the Santa Monica Pier. She remembered the light in her mother's eyes as she had marvelled at all the fun they would have here and the hope in Grace's eyes when they had promised to take a trip here once she got better. She slowly lifted it and tied one of Emma's ribbons she had kept around it to secure the lid. She then held it out over the water, letting it slip from her hands from the edge of the pier. She gazed down as it landed upright with a splash, submerged before regaining its buoyancy to float gracefully on the water's dips and ridges.

"We made it," she whispered to the Pacific.

## ~The End~

Made in United States
North Haven, CT
27 April 2024

51846076R00159